HEART

OF THE

EMPIRE

Book One
The Broken Lands

CARRIE SUMMERS

To:

Rascal, Spot, Thunder, Snuggles, Ashes, Muffin, and Stripe,

Seven kittens who delayed this book but made up for it in purrs and love.

Chapter One

Savra
A tide-swept beach in Cosmal Province

A shovelful of wet gravel sloshed into the sluice box. The frigid splash slapped my belly, drenching my tunic.

"Hey!" I screeched.

A laugh burst from my sister's lips. Shovel in hand, Avill flinched as I flicked seawater at her face. On the beach behind her, a man picking over the tide line glanced up and smirked.

"It was an accident!" she protested.

"And I'm the Empress of Atal."

Instantly, Avill's face stilled. She turned, splashing through knee-deep water that tugged at the rolled cuffs of her pants, and stabbed her shovel into the mud. The shovel came up streaming sand and water. In a smooth motion, she slid the load of sediment into the wooden trough between us. Not a single drop splashed.

I pressed fingernails into my palm. I shouldn't have mentioned anything about the Empire. Not today.

"It will be okay, Avill," I said. "I swear."

The sea's chill sank into my muscles as I plunged hands into the trough. As I sifted the gravel, the current carried away smaller particles, leaving heavier pebbles rolling beneath my palms.

"I didn't say anything," Avill said.

"But you were thinking it."

"Okay, so maybe I was," she snapped. "Because what if you're wrong, Savra? What if they give you a Function somewhere far away and I never see you again?" Planting the shovel, she stuck her hands into the sluice box. Her brow furrowed as she plucked a stone from the muddy water. A plain, slate-colored pebble. She sighed and tossed it into the rip current that frothed a few paces behind me.

I glanced at the foaming sea where the pebble had landed. The waters of the Stornisk Maelstrom were restless today—we needed to watch our footing. "Everyone from Numintown gets assigned to the sluices."

"I bet that's what the girl from Agartown said, too."

Morning air filled my nose, pungent with the resiny scent of the brush that tangled Cosmal Peninsula's hills. A surge in the shore current tugged harder at my cuffs, grains of sand pelting my calves. I shifted my feet wider, working my toes into the muck for stability. If the pull grew stronger, we'd have to stop working for the day. A few months ago, my friend's mother had been swept into the Maelstrom. Lost forever. Now the family had to work double shifts until their quota got adjusted.

"The thing in Agartown was years ago."

Avill stared at me, eyes wide. "But she vanished, Savra. Right after she got her Function writ. She didn't even get to say goodbye."

I pressed my lips together. Avill collected stories of disappearances like a crow hoarding shiny objects. She turned them over and over, inspecting every facet in hopes of finally understanding why our father had left us.

"You think I'm being stupid," Avill said. "Fine. I'll stop worrying if you'll make me a promise."

I sighed. This conversation was starting to make me nervous, and I'd already spent the morning banishing my worries. "I don't think you're being stupid."

"Just promise me you'll run away if they try to take you. Go fugitive. It will be easy to hide in the brush. I'll bring you food and things."

As if I'd get farther than the road out of town. "I wouldn't make a very good fugitive, you know."

"You could find Stormshard. They'd take you I bet."

I had to look away to hide my skeptical expression. Even if the rebel group was real, I couldn't imagine what use they'd have for a seventeen-year-old sluice miner. I knew Avill secretly hoped that's what had happened to our father. She wanted to believe that he'd joined the Sharders to protect our home. So I straightened my face and turned back to her.

"All right, Avill," I said. "If they give me a different Function, I'll hide. I promise."

She swallowed as relief softened her expression. "I'll try to stop talking about it then."

The water in the trough began to clear as the current washed away the cloudy sediment. I closed my eyes while running hands over the gravel. Beneath the ring finger of my right hand, I felt the telltale smoothness of a nugget. With a grin, I plucked it from the trough and held it up for Avill's inspection. Black iron, globular and as dark as squid's ink.

"Nice find, girl," said a woman working a sluice a few paces down the beach. Around ten Numintowners were mining the troughs this morning. Our settlement operated five boxes on this beach, plus another half-dozen closer to the peninsula's tip. "That should fill your quota for a week."

Avill smiled, strands of honey-colored hair falling across her face. As usual, the expression was more desolate than genuine. Just twelve and still thin as a broomstick, Avill seemed older. It was as if her worries roosted on her shoulders, plucking the last breaths of childhood from her body.

As I dropped the nugget into my collection pouch, the sand beneath my feet shifted. Voids opened beneath my heels as the slope suddenly dropped away. I squeaked and bent my knees, throwing my arms wide for balance.

The ground heaved.

"Get ashore," a man yelled from the beach. "Quake!"

Storms. The land jolted back and forth while the shore current muscled into my legs. Behind me, the heavy rip current of the Maelstrom sucked at the shore. With knuckles white and fingertips clawing into splintery wood, I pulled myself around the upstream end of the sluice box.

"Avill!" I yelled as I reached for her. She was too light to fight the quake and the sea together. "Take my hand!"

Between me and the beach, my sister shuffled with knees bent, leaning into the shore current. As she glanced back, a surge in the flow sent her staggering.

Waves sloshed over the top of the wooden trough as the land tilted and juddered. I stumbled and went down, water pouring over my shoulders and pinning me against the sluice box.

"No," I shouted as Avill turned against the gushing current and started back for me. Another lurch yanked two of the sluice box's legs from the muck. The box overturned, mud flying. Seawater tunneled up my nose. I blinked and sputtered.

Avill toppled beside me. Pawing the water, I found her warm back with my palm.

I shoved. "Go," I coughed as the ocean poured into my mouth. On hands and knees, I struggled for the shore. Saltwater blurred my vision. The bluff fringing the narrow strip of beach was a dark shadow that tilted like a seesaw. As I tried to orient on it, another thrust of the earth knocked me over. The sea closed over my head.

Strong hands grabbed me under the armpits, dragging me like a sack of onions. Coughing, I paddled my feet. The freezing water retreated from my body, waves slapping as the sea released me.

Finally, my toes dug into dry sand. My rescuer lowered me to the beach. As I rolled and blinked away the stinging water, the rocking of the earth slowed. The man who'd dragged me ashore dropped to a seat, breath rasping.

"Avill! Save her!"

A light hand fell on my shoulder. "Save yourself next time," Avill said softly. "You worry too much about me."

I shoved myself upright. "Thank the skies," I said, wrapping her in a hug. Her thin body shivered in my grasp, and I rubbed her back and arms to warm her. She pushed me aside, rolling her eyes in embarrassment.

"Your sister's right, you know," my rescuer said. I met his eyes. Denill was a neighbor. He usually worked alone, picking the tide line for Maelstrom-metals and relics rather than mining the sluices. "Avill was nearly ashore when you fell."

I sighed. Fair enough.

Wet hair clung to my face. I swiped it away and looked out to sea. Three of the sluice boxes had overturned, but it looked like everyone had made it onto the beach. No damage done, but the earthquakes had been getting worse lately. Every time the ground shook, Cosmal Peninsula tilted farther into the sea. The Sinking

Province, as some called it, slid down the Maelstrom's throat year by year. Denill's home already slanted too steeply—soon we'd have to help him prop up the downhill corners.

As I climbed to my feet, a shout came from the path leading to town. I leaned around Avill and squinted. Someone was running along the trail, jumping over branches where low brush leaned onto the path.

When the newcomer, a boy of about ten, burst onto the beach, he planted hands on his hips. I recognized him now. He'd come with the registrar's party, the group sent to assign official Functions to Numintowners who'd come of age.

"Savra Panmi?" he called.

My heart thudded hard against my ribs. "Yes? That's me."

Despite his small size, he managed to look down his nose at me. Atal-born, no doubt. To him, my provincial—Prov—birth made me either a pest or a slave depending on his needs.

"There's been a change of schedule. You're summoned to the town hall to receive your Function assignment."

I stood, blinking. No matter how brave I'd acted for Avill, I couldn't stop my fears from rushing back. I was about to learn what I'd be doing for the rest of my life. Even if I already worked the sluices most days, my Function assignment would make it official.

"Now?" I said stupidly. "Why?"

"As if a Prov has the right to ask questions." He rolled his eyes. "Yes, now. And I suggest you hurry."

Chapter Two

Kostan
Steelhold, high above the imperial capital, Jaliss

When the bottom of the door rasped over the thick wool carpet, I continued to stare out the window. Beyond the iron bars protecting my receiving chamber from would-be thieves or assassins—or were the bars to keep me in?—the palace courtyard bustled. Servants hurried through the morning sunshine, carrying baskets and stacks of laundry, and in the center of the open square, liquid black-iron sand flowed over the spouts and cornices of the fountain. The same view as always. But I still enjoyed the fresh air and the taste of sun on my cheekbones.

In the hallway outside my receiving chamber, one of my guardians cleared his throat. Sighing, I gave a last glance at the jagged cliffs beyond the chasm, and farther, the snowy crest of the Icethorns. Young men like me were not granted the leisure of enjoying the morning. I turned to face my duty.

The girl shuffled in as I crossed the room to my polished cherrywood chair. She hunched as if she could hide in plain sight, become as invisible to me as I was to her. As soon as the door shut behind her, hiding my expression from the guardians, I grimaced.

"Your binding, sire," she said.

I nodded then went red with shame over the lapse. The girl couldn't see the gesture; her eyes had been removed before she was admitted into service of the imperial Scions. That I could forget her suffering, even for an instant, spoke to the person I'd become. Hardly better than the elite-class parents who'd spawned me.

I wished I could ask her not to call me "sire," but I knew it was hopeless. And as for getting her to use Kostan, impossible. The only people who used my given name were the other Scions. Regardless, I reached for her forearm as she approached, touched her gently to help her find my chair. She winced at the contact, her cheek twitching under the silk mask that covered the upper half of her face. I didn't blame her.

"I'm sorry to startle you," I said softly.

She didn't reply, only pressed her lips together in a tight line.

As the girl lowered herself to her knees, hands groping for my lower left leg and foot, I shifted on the cushioned chair to make it easier for her. She laid a hand on the gold cuff that encircled my ankle and fished out a small key from within the folds of her wrap. My guardians would have given her the key just before she entered my receiving chamber, and they'd demand its return the moment she passed from the room. For now, she crabbed sensitive fingers along the rim of the cuff until she found the keyhole.

I noticed that her hands trembled. I clenched my fists, wishing I could convince her I meant her no harm. She was new to the palace—I was sure of it. Though the girls who changed my dressings wore identical silk wraps and masks over their eyes and noses, I did my best to learn their faces. By recognizing them as individuals, I did nothing to return their sight. But I had no other way to honor them.

The cuff fell away, clanking to the floor and releasing the top edge of the linen bandage that covered my foot. Despite myself, I breathed a sigh of pleasure as the girl unwound the strips of cloth, allowing the cool air onto my skin. I wore the cuff and dressing at all times. To sleep. When walking through the palace courtyards. While bathing. Though fresh dressings were soaked in light perfume and the servant girls dusted my skin with talcum powder before rewrapping my foot, after the three days between changes, the strips of fabric always stank. And where they covered the mark on the sole of my foot, a wound which wouldn't heal for two more years, blood crusted the cloth.

The girl's lip twitched at the smell, but she kept her composure. I didn't apologize; if the guardians overheard, they would punish her for prompting the act. Instead, I fought the rush of shame. I should have become used to this by now, having worn the cuff and dressing since the occasion of my branding on my second birthday. But the older I got, the more humiliating the situation.

It was nothing compared to what the girls endured, of course. Sometimes, I fantasized that if I ascended the throne, blindfolds would replace the cruel custom of removing the servants' eyes. But for that to happen, I'd have to be declared worthier than the other Scions. Unlikely, at best. Among other things, my secret wish to abolish the custom of blinding the girls surely made me unsuitable.

"The basin is here," I said as the girl patted the air, searching for the low table and the rosewater-filled bowl atop it. I nudged her hand toward the bronze basin, ignoring her renewed shock at my touch. Bowing her head, she placed the bowl on the floor then groped for my leg and lowered my foot into the lukewarm water.

Her fingers were gentle on my skin, and I hated myself for the shiver that traveled my spine. I'd had passing attractions to young women, especially Vaness, one of the other Scions. With Vaness, it had gone farther, a few kisses that had ended when we finally wised up to the danger. At nineteen, I couldn't control my body's desires. But I would never take advantage of a servant, especially one of the poor girls blinded by the guardians. In any case, I had no plans for a lasting relationship. At least not until Ascension. If taking the throne were—somehow, impossibly—my fate, I refused to doom anyone to a life as the Emperor's wife-consort.

After washing my foot, the girl cupped the back of my heel and lifted it from the basin. With a cloth of the softest linen, she patted my skin dry. Where the fibers brushed my wound, tingles spread up my leg—the brand no longer hurt unless it became infected, a rare occurrence due to these regular cleansings. I closed my eyes, imagining I could sense the shape of the wound. Due to the spell worked into my flesh by the gold iron used for my branding, the lines burned into my foot should have changed shape in the years since. On the occasion of the Ascension—the morning of our twenty-first birthday—all thirteen Scions would have our cuffs removed and our feet examined. Our scars would determine who rose to the throne, leaving the remaining twelve to serve as imperial ministers during the new Emperor's reign.

Or rather, outwardly, it would be the shape of the scar which marked the new Emperor or Empress. In truth, the scars simply reflected our inner worthiness. Or so said the aurum mages, those metalogists who worked with Maelstrom-gold and altered bodies with their enchantments.

The girl kept her head bowed while she worked, dipping a wad of cotton into a pot of salve. She spread the ointment over the sole of my foot. Next, she used a patch of sheepskin to dust the talcum powder onto my skin.

"I appreciate your gentleness," I said, keeping my voice low and expressionless so as not to endanger her by showing too much emotion. At the age of thirteen, I'd moved to a private chamber from the Scions' dormitory. Shortly after, I'd made the mistake of asking a kitchen servant for her name. She'd been beaten for daring to answer. I no longer attempted to make conversation with those who served me.

As the girl wrapped fresh dressings around my foot, low voices penetrated the heavy wood of the door. Footsteps clicked over the stone floor in the hallway. Moments later a sharp rapping came at the door.

The girl emitted a terrified squeak. If someone were to open the door and see my uncovered foot, she'd be flogged—or worse. Her hands shook as she hurried with the dressing, and she fumbled the roll of linen. It unspooled across the floor. Frantic, she clawed the stone tiles in search of the lost bandage.

"Shh," I said. "I'll get it."

"No," she whispered. "It's my failure."

The knock came again, the heavy thud of a fist that set the door shivering.

"A moment," I yelled, putting stern tones of command into my voice.

The girl whimpered as she gathered the bandage in a wad and attempted to continue the binding. As the door swung open, her shoulders rose as she ducked her head, tensing for a blow.

A man backed into the room, and my eyes widened at the sight of his burgundy robes trimmed in scarlet. The garb belonged to a ferro mage of the master rank. Skilled in working Maelstrom-blessed black iron, ferros possessed strange powers that few people outside the order understood. And a master, at that. I couldn't remember my branding, but as far as I knew, that was the last time I'd been near such a high-ranking mage. The instructor who trained me to use the silver ring which had been attuned to my spirit was just a first-year argent mage and wore an azure tunic to mark his lowly station.

"What's going on?" I asked." The girl has been more than efficient. She simply wasn't given enough time to finish."

If she was grateful for my attempt at her defense, the servant didn't risk showing it. Instead, she patted the ground near her knees in search of the gold cuff. Checking that no guardians were watching, I slid the metal shackle into her hand. Quickly, she replaced it around my ankle. The key clicked as she struggled to slip it into the lock.

"Well?" I asked.

"Kostan, Scion of the Atal Empire, you are summoned to an audience with the Emperor," the ferromaster said. "Prepare yourself with the greatest haste."

Finally, the servant managed to secure the cuff. She slipped the key back into her wraps and backed away, crawling with her forehead nearly touching the floor.

I stared at the mage's back. The Emperor? Despite being an official candidate to replace the man, I'd never seen him at a distance closer than a couple hundred paces. Only his ministers, high-ranking mages, and the Prime Protector were granted audiences. And, I supposed, his wife-consort.

No wonder, really. Given his cruelty and the brutal rule of his protectors, I suspected that half the Empire's citizens wanted him dead. *I* wanted him dead.

"What's the purpose of the audience?" I asked, keeping my voice level.

"That is not for me to discuss," he responded.

The tension in the mage's frame set my nerves on edge. I didn't wish to anger the man. Of the three orders of metalogists, the ferro mages were the most secretive—and some whispered, dangerous.

I stood from my chair, carefully settling my branded foot into the deep carpet. Fortunately for the servant's sake, the bandage remained in place.

Upon seeing the retreating girl at the edge of his vision, a confirmation that my brand was once again covered, the mage turned to face me. My pulse sped when I recognized him by the deep lines bracketing his mouth. He wasn't just a master. He was the head of the order. Ferromaster Ilishian's portrait hung in the entrance foyer of the Hall of Mages. I forced my expression to remain flat as I ducked a bow in a show of respect.

"If you're ready?" he asked, hands folded in front of his body.

I lifted my bound foot and rotated it at the ankle, then slipped it into a leather boot matching, but of a larger size, that on my other foot. The bandage was lumpy and wrinkled due to the girl's panicked work. It would be a long three days walking with ridges pressing into the sole of my foot, but I wouldn't let my discomfort show and doom her to punishment. Besides, a little pain might be just the distraction I needed to keep my feelings for the Emperor from showing.

Gritting my teeth, I nodded and followed the Ilishian into the hallway. It was time to face the man I'd hated for as long as I could remember. The man I was being groomed to become

Chapter Three

Savra
Numintown, Cosmal Province

M y sandaled feet, still sopping wet, crunched on the crushed
seashells covering Numintown's narrow streets. The stiff cuffs
of my pants chafed at my calves. When I stopped to roll them back
down, the boy who'd fetched me rolled his eyes and paced.

"I don't want to disrespect the registrar by dripping all over the
floor while she signs my writ," I said.

"As if the registrar cares about your respect," he returned,
curling his lip. He stomped on a scallop shell, smashing it to bits.
"But here's some advice. Don't give them the same sort of trouble
you're giving me."

Trouble? Other than unrolling my pants cuffs, all I'd done was
stop at the edge of the beach to strap on sandals. "I don't mean to
cause problems for anyone," I said.

"Somehow I'm not convinced. You Provs are all the same.
Complaining about your Functions even though the Empire is just
trying to take care of you."

A trickle of anger entered my blood, but I took a deep breath. He
was just a child. Of course he wouldn't understand how it felt to
have a stranger in a faraway capital decide your life's purpose—elite-
class Atal rarely worked, and when they did, it was in an occupation
they'd chosen.

"I'm not complaining. I just want to receive my writ."

He shrugged. "If you say so. Anyway, I'm just trying to help you
out. The registrar is already threatening to impose rationing on your

town to spite the geognost for interfering today. You really don't want to make her angrier."

Geognost? A twinge of excitement warmed my chest. I hadn't heard anything about an earth mage in town. They were the rarest of the mages, with less than a hundred spread across the entire Empire. If true, the story of the geognost's visit would be retold for years.

As I kicked the wrinkles from my unrolled trouser legs, I remembered someone on the beach muttering about the arrival of a second party of strangers. Maybe the earth mage had been among them.

The boy stomped another shell. "Ready?"

I nodded, wringing a few drops from my auburn braid before flicking it over my shoulder. Starting toward Numintown's center where the streets met like spokes on a wheel, I glanced over my shoulder. Avill had hurried off to fetch Mother—she'd want to see me receive my writ. I hoped she'd arrive in time.

The town hall stood two floors high, overshadowing the neighboring stable and sheds. It had been a few years since the building had been leveled, and the upper story leaned sharply over the street. I couldn't be sure, but it seemed the quake had shifted the building, tilting it farther than yesterday. Despite myself, I felt embarrassed that people as important as the registrar and a geognost were seeing our community's central building in such a state.

With my damp clothes, I shivered as I stepped into the shade of the porch. The boy kicked one of the awning posts as he climbed the stairs, setting the decking shivering.

He snorted. "I don't see how you Provs even survived without the Empire's guidance."

We survived just fine, according to what the town grandparents said, stories handed down from *their* grandparents who'd lived before the Decree of Functions. That had happened a century ago. A century before that, Cosmal Province had been an independent nation. Then the Atal Empire had come.

I took a deep breath before stepping into the stuffy confines of the building. A bench stood against one wall of the entrance hall. Upon it, a boy and girl my age waited their turn with the registrar. Wilona, one of our nearest neighbors, bounced her knee and chewed a hangnail, her dark hair a curtain before her face. The boy, Enno, sat with his knees splayed and eyes flitting. His father, a burly man with deep creases on his face, had come as well. The man crouched on the floor beside the bench, elbows propped on his knees.

I shuffled to a corner as the Atal boy opened a door and poked his head in. "Found her," he said before shutting the door.

"Is Ikirni inside?" I asked the others. Four of us had turned seventeen in the last few months, a large group for Numintown.

Wilona shrugged. "The waiting area was empty when I arrived," she said, speaking around the fingertip she was gnawing. For once, she didn't sneer at me. Wilona often accused me of sucking up to the Empire by working so hard at the sluices. But really, I just wanted to help Mother. Our quota had been smaller since my father disappeared, but not *that* much smaller. Not without some proof of his death. For all the Empire knew, he'd simply deserted his duty.

For all we knew, they were right.

Anyway, Wilona was just trying to find fault because everyone in town knew her mother was an imperial snitch. In the Provinces, the Empire couldn't keep watch on everyone—there were hundreds of Provs for every Atal. When an argent mage came to ask questions about illegal activities and pluck the answers directly out of a suspect's mind, it was almost always because a snitch sent a message.

Enno yawned and tapped his toe on the wooden planks of the floor. A pebble had been trapped against one of the bench's legs. Freed by the vibration, it rolled and skittered across the floor before bouncing off the far wall.

If the town hall wasn't leveled soon, the building would topple.

Moments later, the door squealed open. Ikirni shuffled out, white-faced and with her writ pinched between thumb and forefinger. My breath caught. Why did she look so rattled?

"Well?" Enno asked.

"Sluices," she muttered.

Before we could ask more questions, she ducked her head and bolted for the door. When it slammed shut over her retreat, I flinched. Wilona's arms pressed closer to her body, and her hair fell farther over her face. Enno didn't move, but his knuckles blanched white where he gripped the flesh of his upper arm. No one spoke.

A footfall clicked against the wood planks of the floor. The registrar stood in the doorway, her deep blue uniform decorated with polished wood beads. Upon her shoulder, the Registry crest was embroidered in gray thread.

"Savra," the woman said. A command, not an invitation.

I swallowed, glancing at the door that led outside. Already? Mother would be so disappointed.

"Must we suffer a delay while you find your wits?" the registrar asked.

"Sorry," I said, ducking my head as I hurried to the door leading into the chamber.

A single table dominated the center of the room, chest high with no chair. On it, an ink pot rested beside a stack of parchments. The writs, I assumed. The shades were drawn, and a handful of candles burned in holders along the walls. The registrar shut the door over Wilona's and Enno's whispers. She crossed the room with long strides and rounded the table to face me as I approached. A pair of armored protectors—the Empire's soldiers and guardsmen—and a notary wearing the sash of office stood against the back wall. Swallowing, I nodded at them.

Motion from the side wall caught my attention. There, a robed figure shifted. A man. Wearing such strange robes, he had to be the geognost. Henchmen stood on either side of the mage. The fighters wore soft leather and penetrating stares, a stark contrast to the expressionless imperial protectors.

"If you're done gawking..." the registrar said. "We have a few formalities to cover before issuing your writ."

I swallowed and faced her.

She produced a small vial from the pocket of her uniform. The glass clicked against the wood of the table as she set it before me. "Drink this."

I stared at the little bottle. "What is it?"

"Assurance that you will answer our questions faithfully," she said.

"But I—"

"Drink it."

No one had told me to expect this. To be fair, I'd never asked. But I'd assumed my official assignment would be a simple signing of the Function writ. Biting off protests, I lifted the little bottle and sniffed the rim. The contents had no smell, but through the yellow-green glass, I spotted flecks of something suspended in the liquid. Grimacing, I set the rim against my lip and tilted it back. The serum burned as it flowed down my throat.

"What's more desirable, pewter or black iron?" a woman asked.

I jerked, shocked. Where was I? What had happened?

"Savra." She snapped her fingers in front of my face. "Pewter or black iron? Which would the Empire rather have?"

I was standing in a dim room. My knees were locked, thighs and calves clenched. Finally, I realized where I was. The town hall. This was my Function assignment.

I coughed. "Excuse me. I was..."

"Disoriented, I know. It's normal when the elixir first hits."

"How long since I drank it?"

"Answer the question."

"Black—black iron, of course. Any Maelstrom-metal has a use, but the quotas only specify gold, silver, and black iron."

The registrar nodded. "What is the ancient Atal word for vengeance?"

"What? How should I know?"

The woman rolled her eyes. "Seems the elixir diminished your manners. 'I don't know' is a sufficient answer."

"Sorry," I said, swallowing. "I don't know."

"What provides the most value for the Empire? Picking the tide line or placer mining the sluices?"

I shrugged. "The best relics wash up at the tide line, but it could be months between finds. So, sluices, I guess."

"Describe the nature of the living soul."

I stared at her. How did this relate to my Function? I felt a strange tension in the room while I considered my answer. Even the mage's henchmen, who had been shifting as if to keep limber, froze.

"It's—I suppose it depends on the person."

The registrar cocked her head. "All right. What do you see in *my* soul?"

"I..." If my aura-sight had come over me, I could give her an answer. But how would she know about my fits? "I can't see your soul," I said, then added, "right now."

I sucked my lower lip between my teeth. Where had those last words come from?

The mage detached from the wall and approached the table. He had a wan face, pale and somehow sad. A peaked hat covered his hair. I thought he might be around sixty years old.

The registrar's gaze flicked to the man, and her eyes narrowed. Her expression brought to mind the boy's comment about the geognost interfering with Registry work.

The mage brushed his hand through the air as if shooing away her glare. "By all means, continue," he said.

A small muscle beneath the registrar's eye twitched as she returned her attention to me. "Is it better to till the land after the harvest, or should you wait until just before planting?"

I sighed. The order and purpose of these questions made little sense. Was the Registry trying to determine whether Numintowners were shirking their Function duties to spend time farming? Didn't they have Wilona's mother and the other snitches to keep watch on that?

"I don't know."

"What's the best way to temper steel intended for a broadsword?"

"I don't know."

"Does the night know how to whisper?"

My words caught in my throat as images of my nightmares roared to life. "Unfortunately, yes," I said, the words bursting from my mouth before I could even think to stop them. I didn't understand. Usually, I was so careful with what I said—years of caution with Avill's delicate feelings had taught me that.

I expected a follow-up question, but the registrar simply tapped her index finger on the table and continued.

"What sort of ink is best for committing words to vellum?"

"I don't know. My mother taught me to write with squid's ink. It's all we have."

"Can you read?"

"Only the common tongue. Peninsular dialect."

"What happens when we die?"

"In Numintown, the grandparents say we'll be reborn."

"I didn't ask what Numintowners claim. If you don't know say, 'I don't know.'"

Before I could stop myself, my mouth opened. "We remain," I said, though I couldn't understand where I'd gotten the answer.

The geognost stepped closer. Rotating a silver ring on his finger, he ran his tongue over thin lips. "Stand still," he commanded.

I couldn't have moved if a rogue wave had risen before me. Just the thought of defying him made me feel as if I would retch. Inwardly, I shuddered when he laid a hand on my shoulder, his gray eyes searching my face. A tiny wrinkle formed between his brows.

"Scribe," he said. "That's your Function. You'll travel to Jaliss with me. There, you'll be trained in writing the capital dialect. After, you'll be placed into service at the geognosts' monastery."

I stared, still unable to move. Scribing? I didn't even know where this geognosts' monastery *was*. Avill's words from the morning sprang to my thoughts. Don't let them take you, she'd said.

"Master Havialo," the registrar said. "I appreciate your interest, but the Registry has already assigned her a Function. Her expertise at the sluices will serve the Empcror's glory."

The mage—Master Havialo—turned an expressionless face on the woman. Moments later, the floor trembled, the beginning of a shake. A gust of wind struck the building as the earth rocked beneath us. My heart raced, but I still couldn't move. Only storm winds blew that hard, but the sky had been clear when I'd entered the building. I knew almost nothing about geognosty. Was the gust the earth mage's doing? And what about the paralysis? I couldn't make myself want to move, no matter that my instincts screamed at me to flee.

"Her Function is scribing," Master Havialo said, still fiddling with the silver band on his finger. "You'll record the results in your ledger after we leave. I will see she presents herself to training after I escort her to Jaliss. She'll obtain her writ there."

As he spoke, the registrar's eyes grew distant. She nodded blankly then jerked when another burst of wind slammed the building, setting the framing shivering.

My thoughts felt sluggish, my muscles filled with ice. During a quake, the safest place was outside. Still, I couldn't make myself move.

After a moment, the registrar shook her head, a confused look in her eyes. "The Prime Registrar will not appreciate you threatening our authority."

"Perhaps your prime will take it up with me directly, then," the geognost said. Following his words, the earth beneath us heaved again and then quieted.

"I'll see to it," the woman said through gritted teeth.

"Now," the mage said, turning to me. "I assume you know how to ride."

Ride? Now? How could this be happening? "Master Havialo," I said. "...Sire. I'm supposed to become a sluicer. Everyone from Numintown does."

"Apparently not," he said. But something in his face, a certain stiffness, suggested his casual shrug was anything but.

"W—When?" I asked. I'd promised Avill I'd turn fugitive if they tried to take me away. I'd have to run tonight. Today. As soon as I was out of sight of the mage and registrar.

"Saddle two horses," Master Havialo said, glancing at one of his henchmen.

The man assented with a curt nod and strode for the door. He rolled a shoulder as he passed before the stony gaze of a protector.

Master Havialo turned to me. "You have until the mounts are ready. We leave immediately after."

"Wait. What about my things? And I need to see my family—" My throat closed down over my next words.

He scanned my clothing. "You'll receive a uniform when we reach the capital. If your other garments are like these, they're unsuitable for travel anyway. I'll see to your provisioning at Dukket Waystation. If your family is waiting outside, you may say your farewells. Otherwise, perhaps you can pen a letter. In the common tongue. Peninsular dialect."

Was he mocking me? I balled my hands into fists. Why scribing? Had something in my comment about reading brought this on?

"Of course, if you just stand there chewing your lip, I'm afraid you'll forfeit what little time you have." He nodded at the door.

Stumbling, I hurried to the exit and fumbled at the latch until I managed to open it. Wilona, Enno, and his father were just reentering the hall, having abandoned it during the quake. Their eyes widened when they saw me.

"Well?" Enno asked.

"My mother and sister. Are they outside?"

Enno shrugged. "I wasn't paying attention."

As I shoved out the door into the bright glare of midday, Wilona called out. "Wait, Savra. Where's your writ?"

"Oh, just let her go," Enno said.

Wilona said something in a low tone lost beneath the rush of blood in my ears. As the door clicked shut, I scanned the trampled area in the center of Numintown. I needed an escape route. Inland would be best. The tangled brush between the shore and the peninsula's spine would hide me until I could find somewhere more permanent.

Moments later, hoof beats sounded as a pair of freshly saddled horses trotted from the stable. The henchman sat astride one and tugged the other's halter by its lead.

I bolted just as the door opened behind me. Down the stairs and along the front edge of the porch. From the doorway, a man muttered a curse.

The earth reached up and slammed me. Except that wasn't right. I'd fallen. Caught a toe. How? I rolled, scrambled, tried to gain my feet. The street lurched, sending me toppling and the horses snorting.

When I tried again, the geognost—Havialo—was abruptly beside me, lifting me by the arm with fingers strong as iron cuffs. "Listen to me, Savra," he said near my ear. "You are in more danger than you can imagine. Do what I say, and you and your family may live. Fail to listen, and you—and they—are most certainly dead."

"I don't—"

"I know you don't understand. But you will have to trust me. Everything depends on this."

The horses drew up beside us. Somehow, my foot found the stirrup, and my other leg swung over the animal's hindquarters as I heaved myself up. Some part of my mind was responding to his warning while the other parts still scrambled for ideas. Me? In danger? How could this be happening? I'd made Avill a promise. But if the man spoke true, I had to go in order to protect her.

With a forced calm like an eggshell ready to crack, the geognost circled the mounts and took the reins from his henchman.

"Proceed as we agreed," Havialo said before mounting up.

The henchman nodded as Havialo clucked to his mount. Just like that, we were trotting away from Numintown. Away from Avill and my broken vow to always stay near her.

Chapter Four

Ilishian walked through the palace corridors with quick, birdlike steps. His expression discouraged—no, forbade—questions. Like cold clay waiting for a potter's hands, his flesh lay unmoving over the bones of his face.

While pacing down the final corridor leading to the Emperor's chambers, my scattered thoughts coalesced into twin daggers of hatred and fear. Soon, I would look evil in the eyes. But what if I saw my own reflection there?

I swallowed, took a deep breath and forced my fists to relax. I even glanced at the walls, noticing the ornate onyx carvings mortared between the granite blocks. Emperor Tovmeil had something to say to me. Perhaps I'd take this opportunity to say something back.

On either side of the double doorway into the Emperor's chambers, candlewicks sent flames as long as my forearm toward the ceiling. In the fires' hearts, teardrops of deep purple danced. As Ilishian approached, the tongues of flame leaned toward him. I stopped a few paces back while he tapped on the door. A muffled invitation penetrated the heavy mahogany.

"Armor your spirit," the mage commanded.

I nodded and pinched the silver ring I wore on the middle finger of my left hand. Like the other Scions, I'd been given the band on my tenth birthday. I'd worn it for a year before my argent-mage trainer allowed me to sip Maelstrom-blessed seawater from the Tempest Goblet, attuning the band to my spirit. After the Ascension, if I were to become a minister rather than Emperor, I would receive a single gold ring blessed with aurum magic to strengthen and speed my body. As Emperor, there would be many, many more blessings. A black iron ring and accompanying ferro rank, to start.

As I focused my mind on the silver encircling my finger, hard and smooth against my skin, I groped for an awareness of my spirit's boundaries. It had been over ten days since my last session in the Hall of Mages, and as always, my control over my spirit-self wavered. To concentrate, I pressed my tongue against the back of my front teeth. My first, flailing attempt to harness my internal power grazed Ilishian's spirit instead. He curled his lip in disgust. It took three more tries before I sank a hook of my awareness into my personal well of power. With a relieved sigh, I expanded my thoughts to encompass my spirit, commanding it to ward against attack.

"I'd heard you struggled with simple spirit control," Ilishian said, his voice tinged with disdain. "I hadn't realized how hard your instructor had worked to gentle that news. It's a wonder the Goblet didn't reject your attempt at attunement."

My eyes flicked to Ilishian's hands—like many high-ranking mages, he wore both a silver and a gold band along with the black-iron rings on his fingers and in his earlobes. A good metalogist could master any of the three disciplines, argent, aurum, and ferro, but usually focused most of their energy on one. He noticed the direction of my gaze and smirked.

I raised my chin. It wasn't as if I hadn't heard the criticisms before. Even the other Scions could sense my fumbling attempts at manipulating my spirit-self. And as for controlling the minds of others, not even ten attuned rings would grant me that ability.

My failure to wilt under his disappointment sparked something in Ilishian's eyes. "I was beginning to think you had no spine at all," he said. "I thought we might all be doomed."

"What's that supposed to mean?"

"You'll find out soon enough," he said, squeezing the latch and pulling open the door to the Emperor's private chambers.

As I passed the candles, heat brushed my cheeks. The flames were testing me. My spirit armor crackled in response, feeling as if sparks traveled over my skin. Moments later, the sensation vanished. I stepped into the Emperor's rooms.

I wasn't sure what I'd expected. The public hall where elite subjects could pay tribute—at the distance of hundreds of paces from their ruler—dripped with Maelstrom-relics and gems. Candles burned in holders forged from Maelstrom-blessed black iron, no doubt enchanted to immolate any attackers. As for the Emperor himself, Tovmeil never appeared without at least a dozen protectors ringing him.

But now Emperor Tovmeil stood before me in a simple chamber furnished with straight-backed chairs that appeared fashioned by journeymen woodworkers. He wore a simple tunic and trousers, the fine weave of the linen the only concession to his station. If rough-spun, the clothing would have been more suited to a Prov labor than the ruler of the entire Atal Empire.

I was so shocked I lost my grasp on my spirit armor. Behind me, Ilishian snorted in disgust as he shut the door with a click.

"Would you like to sit?" The Emperor asked me, gesturing to one of the simple chairs.

My tongue lay dead on the floor of my mouth, a useless corpse. All my hatred stood behind it, clamoring for justice.

Emperor Tovmeil clasped his hands behind his back as he paced two steps one way, two steps the other. A thoughtful look consumed his features. After a moment, he raised his eyebrows.

"Perhaps this will be easier if I simply command you. Sit, Scion Kostan."

Still, I stood frozen by anger and shock. The Emperor rolled his eyes, strode to a chair, and sat.

"There," he said showing his palms. When he did, a heavy bronze bracer peeked out from beneath his tunic sleeve. Bronze was an uncommon metal to be worn beneath clothing. Unless one of the Maelstrom-metals had been melted into the alloy, it wouldn't grant him special abilities. But it wasn't ornamental either. Otherwise, why hide it under his sleeve?

Finally, I stepped stiffly to the chair and sat, keeping my face even. Surely, my feelings for the man swam in my eyes, but I wouldn't speak them aloud. Not yet.

The Emperor cast his gaze toward the door. "Ilishian? Would you sit, my friend?"

The mage shook his head and remained beside the door. "Better I stay here in case we have need of defense."

A flash of regret crossed the Emperor's face. "You're right, of course." He turned his eyes to me. "You wonder why you're here, I assume."

"I was under the impression we wouldn't meet in person unless I Ascended," I said, only remembering after a moment's pause to add, "your eminence."

The corner of his mouth twisted in a bittersweet smile. "Please forgo the ridiculous title. In any case, the selfish part of me still yearns for the day when I pass on the throne. It's contemptible, isn't it? Wishing to lay this burden on someone else? Though to counter that, I will say I've never relished having to choose between exile and execution following the ceremony."

"I imagine not," I said, off-balanced by his words. I wanted to tell him the real abhorrence wasn't his thoughts on the Ascension. It was his treatment of the Provs and even the merchant-class Atal. Yet somehow, I couldn't reconcile my image of a savage tyrant with the man sitting three paces from me, elbows on his knees and fingers laced loosely together. Emperor Tovmeil seemed almost... gentle.

He sighed. "I wanted to kiss the Prime Astrologer when she brought news of your birth omens so early into my rule," he said. "Not that an emperor may lower himself to such acts of affection. In any case, I pity the rulers who sit the throne into their seventh or eighth decade."

I found myself nodding in agreement. The Emperor was only fifty years old. He'd Ascended just ten years before the astrologers proclaimed that thirteen Elite-class children—no more, no less— would be born during the new moon at the midpoint of Deepwinter. And true to their prediction, the other Scions and I were born within minutes of one another during the darkest night in the eight-year seasonal cycle.

In two years, one of us would Ascend. Most elderly emperors chose execution following their abdication—after fifty years ruling an Empire, beginning a life somewhere beyond the Stornisk

Maelstrom seemed impossible. But Emperor Tovmeil was young still, in relative terms. I wondered if his choice would be different.

"You hate what the Empire does, don't you?" he asked, interrupting my thoughts.

My stomach clenched, forcing breath out of my lungs. I'd prepared to tell him how I felt, but now that the question was forced, my courage fled.

"The girls who clean our brands," I said after a moment's fumbling. "Blindfolds would work as well as removing their eyes."

The following silence pressed down on me like the blade of the headman's axe. From behind, I heard Ilishian shift.

"Look at me," the Emperor said after a moment.

I met his blue-gray eyes, determined to recover my bravery. The Emperor didn't blink as he pulled back his sleeve to show the bracer I'd glimpsed when he sat. He raised it before me. Forged with ornate designs, the metal fastened with three clasps on the inside of his forearm. It stretched from his wrist nearly to his elbow.

After giving me a moment to inspect it, he dropped his arm to his lap. "You were meant to learn these things upon your Ascension, but circumstances have forced me to act. I deeply regret burdening you with this knowledge early."

"My Ascension?" My head ached as I drew my brows together in confusion.

He brushed away my question with a wave of his hand. "In a moment. Have you learned of the Ascension Relics?"

I looked more closely at the bracer. Now I understood why he wore it. Judging by the burnishing at the edges, it was a Maelstrom relic, softened by the kiss of the waves. But I'd never heard of relics associated with the Ascension specifically, unless you counted the Tempest Goblet.

"I haven't."

He nodded. "Neither had I when my time came. But some Scions are more... cunning when it comes to learning things that should be hidden from them."

At the implied criticism of my abilities, I tamped down a flare of pride. Instead of speaking, I simply nodded.

"In any case," he went on, "when an Emperor or Empress Ascends the throne, two relics are attuned to the new ruler. This—"

He pointed at the bracer. "—and this." He pulled back the collar of his shirt, revealing chiseled muscles and a pendant on a heavy silver chain. The pendant itself was a polished banded agate, lines of red and purple crossing the stone.

"The Heart of the Empire and the Bracer of Sight," he said. "No one but Ilishian, me, and those present at my attunement knows of these relics. Not even my wife-consort—I remove them before visiting her. If you've become accustomed to having servants help you bathe and dress, perhaps it's time to send them away. Because if these become yours in two years, you will have a need for privacy you've never known."

"Yes, your eminence."

"As I said, I have no need for titles."

"And you still haven't answered my question about the servant girls. There is no need to blind them."

"I was like you," he responded. "Though you won't believe it now. The servant girls you are so concerned about... I helped one escape. I was about your age when I crept outside my room in the middle of the night. I hurried to the servants' quarters and grabbed the nearest blind girl from her bed. She protested, of course, out of fear of punishment. But I carried her away out to the wall anyway."

"And?" I asked. If he'd been successful, perhaps I follow his plan. But if I helped some escape, wouldn't more girls be blinded in their places?

Emperor Tovmeil swallowed, then continued. "When the guard at the gate looked away, I slipped onto the path overlooking Jaliss. I guided the girl to the inside edge of the path and told her to hurry. But I'd been wrong about the guard. He hadn't looked away. My guardians felt I'd been too soft with the servants lately. They wanted to teach me a ruler's hardness. As the girl fumbled her way down the steep descent, a protector grabbed me. He got a hand over my mouth before I could yell, but the girl's ears were sensitive. She turned long enough for me to see the panic on her face before the second guard slammed into her. He'd been waiting on the path the whole time. He knocked her over the edge. She screamed until she landed in the city below."

Though shame colored his cheeks, he met my gaze. "Much of the relics' history is lost," he said. "None of the diviners can find a purpose for the pendant. One old tome calls the Emperor the 'Heart of the Empire.' The same name as the relic. Maybe it's a coincidence. But without a heart, a body dies. I wear the pendant because I'd rather not find out what happens if I cast it aside."

"And the bracer?" I asked.

Against the wall, Ilishian cleared his throat. The Emperor glanced at him. "He needs to know," he said.

I looked over my shoulder to see Ilishian shrug. "As you say, *your eminence.*" The sarcasm in the final words made me wince, but a glance at Emperor Tovmeil showed no reaction.

"Put simply, this bracer gives me knowledge I never wished for. While I wear it, I see, in my mind, the many ways the Empire falls. Scene after scene of fire and flood and war and death. Scholars, historians in particular, often debate why the Atal Kingdom—now the Atal Empire—has lasted so long. They talk of astrological portents and geography, ruthlessness and resources." The man shook his head. He raised his forearm between us. "The Empire stands because the Emperor sees its end every day and does what he must to prevent that fall."

"If you asked most Provs, they'd say it would be a good thing if the Empire fell," I said.

Behind, Ilishian gave a huff of disappointment. "I told you this would have no effect."

Ignoring the mage, Emperor Tovmeil kept his eyes on me. "I've wished to end Atal rule more times than I could count. But it's not so simple. In every case, when the Empire falls, the people die. I've watched my subjects burned alive, drowned when the sea swallows the lowlands, starved in a blight that lasts a century. Without the Empire binding Atal and the Provinces, we simply don't survive."

A somber silence flowed from the corners of the room. I wanted to argue the points—how could he know these visions were true?—but the absolute conviction on his face stilled my tongue.

"When I Ascended," the Emperor said softly, "one of my first wishes was to stop blinding the Scions' servants. But the moment I called for a scribe to draft the order, knowledge of the consequences hit me like a rockslide. Is it better to take the eyes from a handful of girls or to take the lives from hundreds?"

The Emperor's hands were once again laced together, and as he spoke his knuckles went white.

"Not every law comes from my lips," he said. "In fact, though I am ashamed of this, I often leave the rules and their enforcement to my ministers and advisers. I'm weak in that way. When some poor Prov is dragged to the gallows and hung for the sin of wanting food for his children, my conscience allows me to blame my ministers for their ruthlessness. Maybe you will be stronger. Maybe you will find small mercies for your subjects. I hope so."

"So the bracer told you I'll be Emperor?" I asked.

He shook his head. "Nothing so certain. But my sight tells me that if you aren't declared Emperor, the Empire does not survive. If you don't Ascend, Atal falls. What do you know of the Breaking?"

"The rifts, you mean?"

He nodded. "We do what we can to hide the situation from the Empire's citizens, but the land is tearing apart already. New chasms open every day. Quakes rattle the Provinces. In my visions, the rifts get worse until the continent shatters, gorges splitting the Empire from end to end. Cosmal Province is swallowed by the Maelstrom." He shook his head. "Only a strong heart at the Empire's core can hold our land together. You."

As his words sank in, I felt as if chains wrapped my chest, forcing the air from my lungs. My words were lost, drowned in the sea of my thoughts.

"Difficult times are coming," the Emperor said." I've spent days in this room looking for an answer, and I've come to believe there's nothing I can do to prevent it. The Ascension itself is threatened. Enemies surround the throne. I cannot see them clearly, or I would identify the traitors and have them killed. I only know that Ilishian is loyal. You must trust him. But beware: some of your future enemies will begin as friends. If you fail, it will be due to betrayal. Most likely, by a young woman. Her hair. There's something about it that stands out."

My brow knit again. Friends? At best, I had a few acquaintances. And the only women I knew were Scions and instructors, plus the emotionless protectors guarding the walls. My gaze flicked to Ilishian who continued to stand, expressionless. "I—okay. I'll be careful."

The Emperor stood, extending a hand to help me from my chair." I kept you longer than I intended. When you leave this chamber, wait in the hallway beyond until you're sure there are no nearby footsteps. Ilishian will follow behind to make sure you're not spotted. Return to your chambers and resume your daily schedule as if we've never spoken."

I'd come into the room hating the Emperor and everything he stood for. Now I had no idea what to think. Had he been honest with me? I couldn't conceive a reason for him to lie. Still, it was so much to take in. So hard to believe.

Clenching my jaw, I faced him and bowed.

"You must live, Scion Kostan," he said. "You must Ascend and do what it takes to hold the Empire together. Without you, everything is lost. I'm sorry." With that, the Emperor turned away from me. I stood frozen for a moment then stepped toward the door, my head whirling with doubts.

Chapter Five

Parveld
Somewhere on the vast Atalan Plateau

Though the fire crackled and snapped, a cheery glow in the high plateau's darkness, its heat scarcely cut the chill. The man who called himself Parveld—a good, Atalan name—pulled the thick blanket tighter around his shoulders. Above the dancing flames, a sharp ridgeline sliced into the sky, jagged teeth sharp against the stars.

He sucked a strip of jerky, softening the meat before sawing at it with teeth worn by age. Parveld's bite hadn't fared nearly as well as the rest of him. An old mind and teeth trapped in the body of a young man. A strange prison, indeed.

He chuckled at the thought. What sort of person could find reasons to complain about eternal youth?

Then again, when people yearned for long lives, they rarely thought about the loneliness the years might bring. And they rarely considered the march of decades spent watching humans war and scheme, conquer and oppress.

Parveld jabbed a stick into the fire and stirred the coals, sending embers swirling toward the heavens. In his younger years, he might have let the stillness of the night and the darkness beyond the firelight set his nerves tingling. But now, despite the cold, the emptiness brought him peace. There were many dangers in this world and even greater threats in realms beyond, but if evil were to strike him tonight, he'd rather have spent his last hours relaxing than fearing the end.

Besides, he had work to do still—the visions had told him that much. His death would come, but not yet. For the last two centuries, he'd followed a trail that led here. Never had he envisioned stepping off that path before the final destination. Parveld had traveled far and wide, seen distant lands and people that were nothing but whispered rumors in these parts. He'd loved and lost and loved and lost again. But more than anything, he'd prepared for the coming events.

And now, as inexorably as the stars marched across the heavens, the time of reckoning approached.

The Emperor's enemies closed in. Swords might already be at palace throats. Soon, the girl would be found if she hadn't been discovered already. Parveld slipped his hand into his pocket and ran a finger over a bracelet, gold and silver strands twined around and around each other.

Soon, he whispered into the aether.

Emotions flowed from the piece of jewelry, warmth edged with both gratitude and readiness.

With a nod, Parveld withdrew his hand from the pocket and laced his fingers around his bent knee while he watched the sparks dance. He'd been camped on this high Atalan plateau for two weeks, sheltering in a canvas tent when the frosty nights grew intolerable, wandering the nearby ridges when the weather allowed.

But tomorrow, he'd break camp and set out for Jaliss.

Tomorrow, the final test of his life's work would begin.

Chapter Six

Savra
On the road north from Numintown

My head wobbled on my neck as my horse trotted behind Havialo's mount. We were traveling north along the peninsula's coast, toward the distant border with the mainland. I didn't know how long we'd been riding. A couple of hours? More? Already, the sun glared down as it sank through mid-afternoon. The constant drumming of hooves made my head ache. But even without the pain in my skull, my thoughts were muddy. Was I in shock? Everything had happened so fast. Why had I abandoned my family on just one man's words?

Each time I blinked, the scene blurred. I struggled to focus, only gaining a sharp view of the road moments before I felt the need to blink again. In the back of my mind, I knew none of this was normal. The elixir? Had it done something to me?

The road bent to the right, and my horse faltered. I snatched the saddle's polished metal pommel and groaned as the break in my mount's gait sent me reeling.

Looking over his shoulder, Havialo pressed his lips together. He tugged on his reins and brought his horse to a walk. Blowing in relief, my mount slowed, head low as he plodded forward and drew even with the mage.

On either side of us, dense brush pressed close to the road. To the left, a gentle slope dropped to the churning waters of the Maelstrom. Opposite, the land climbed through rolling, brush-choked hills to the peninsula's spine where a few rounded humps of granite pushed up through scraggly pine forest. The afternoon sunlight gave the air a golden tone.

"That concoction they force on you is nothing but hedge witchery," Havialo said. "Someone high in the Registry organization believes it engenders honesty. In truth, it's not so different than tossing back a mug of ale. You'll feel better soon."

Like a stone attached to my shoulders, my head rolled to look at him. "I need to go home."

The geognost leaned back and rummaged through the saddlebags he'd hastily lashed over his mount's hindquarters. Producing a water skin, he handed it over.

"Impossible. We can only hope my men succeeded in their tasks. Otherwise, we likely won't make it off the peninsula."

I took a swig of water and handed the container back. "What tasks? I still don't understand what danger I'm in."

"It's complicated."

I flopped forward over my horse's neck and tried to reach the lead attaching the halter to the mage's saddle. If I could just get my mount turned around, I might be able to outrun Havialo. I wasn't a particularly good rider, but I was light and less likely to tire a horse.

Unfortunately, the motion caused my head to swim. I nearly toppled from the saddle.

"Listen, Savra," Havialo said. "You are to be a scribe. It's a good Function. You'll be much more comfortable in Jaliss and the monastery than you were here."

"But I don't want to be a scribe. I want to be with my family."

His eyes narrowed. "That's no longer possible. Forget Numintown. It's for your own good."

"What could be good about forgetting my home?"

His cheek twitched. "You are your father's daughter, that's for certain."

I stiffened in shock at the mention of my father. The sudden shift in balance made my stomach churn, and bile rose in my throat.

"I think I'm going to be sick," I whispered.

Havialo surprised me by yanking his mount to a stop and climbing down. He offered a hand. I hesitated, but then my stomach clenched again. Accepting the help, I climbed down and took a seat at the edge of the road, my head between my knees.

Havialo led both horses to the inland edge of the road and examined the brush. After a moment, he plunged into the tangle of foliage, tugging at our mounts to follow. I looked back toward Numintown. What were my chances of escape if I took one of the game trails too narrow for the horses to follow?

"You wouldn't get far," he called. "Ordinarily, you'd just feel tired, maybe a little dizzy, after drinking that awful Registry potion. Almost everyone blames the excitement or disappointment of finally receiving their Function. But our quick ride aggravated the concoction's effects."

Okay, maybe he was right about my escape chances. I pinched the bridge of my nose—even sitting I could scarcely keep my head up.

Havialo continued crashing through the scrub. "Aha," he called over the tangle of branches, "This will do."

Do for what? I wondered to myself.

The geognost returned to the road, having left the horses behind. Eyelids heavy, I accepted help to get upright then plodded behind him toward the gap in the brush. Before stepping into the thicket, Havialo glanced back to the south. His face fell in disappointment.

"I'm sorry," he said quietly.

Even with my wits dulled by the elixir, my pulse suddenly roared in my ears. I staggered as I turned to follow his gaze.

A black plume of smoke towered over the landscape.

Numintown was burning.

Chapter Seven

Kostan
Steelhold grounds

The Emperor's words swirled in my thoughts as I hurried away from his chambers. When I neared the palace's conservatory, the click of Ilishian's footsteps trailed off. I glanced back to verify that he no longer followed me. I was alone.

A few paces into the bright light of the glass-domed conservatory, I stopped and took a deep breath of the humid air. I needed time to think about the Emperor's words, but a glance at the sundial in the center of the room told me that wouldn't be now. It was almost midday, and if I didn't run, I'd be late for patrol.

I hurried past trees and potted plants, transplants from the coastal provinces, and shoved out the door onto Steelhold's grounds. The glare of mountain sunlight sent daggers to the backs of my eyes. I squinted, blinked, and turned for the armory. Gravel crunched under my feet as I rounded the far corner of the palace, but I was relieved to see Donevin, one of my fellow Scions, disappearing through the armory's front door.

A few paces before reaching the building, I slowed and focused on my breath. No Scion should arrive at a patrol panting.

Only a few high windows admitted light into the building. Even though Steelhold was considered impregnable, the Order of Protectors took no chances with their weapons' security. At night, the armory's iron doors were shut and chained. By day, a detail of three protectors stood watch over the entrance. I greeted the guards with a somber nod then stepped forward to join my fellow Scions.

"Cutting it close," Vaness muttered.

I shrugged. "I didn't feel the need to hurry."

She arched an eyebrow, the smirk on her face showing she didn't quite believe me. I glanced at her sideways, hiding my smile. She might pretend to be the hardened candidate for Empress that our birth and customs demanded, but I'd seen her softer side. When we'd kissed, she'd been just as soft as I imagined any woman might be. Vulnerable, even. I remembered how her breath had quickened when I'd touched her coal-black hair. It hadn't worked out; neither of us was so stupid as to think we could actually have a relationship with one another, but I still thought about her sometimes. If we'd been born on a different night, we wouldn't have the throne looming over us. I wondered what that would be like.

In any case, she was the closest thing I had to a friend. I'd learned to avoid bonds early on—when our nursemaids were exiled to teach us this lesson, I'd cried for three nights. After that, the guardians had rapped my knuckles with a stick if I dared show that kind of weakness. As Emperor or a minister, I'd choose a wife-consort from among the elite-class Atalans. My consort and I might even find some sort of affection for one another. But I couldn't expect more than that.

Sometimes, I still ached for someone to care about. Maybe the other Scions felt the same. But we'd never admit such a glaring flaw to each other.

When a guardian entered the armory, we stood at rigid attention. The guardian paired us off without speaking, simply pointing then waving each designated couple out the door. After years of daily patrols, we needed no further instructions. Vaness and I were selected together, and we wordlessly grabbed scimitars from racks along the wall then headed toward the Chasm Gate to begin our patrol.

Hundreds of years ago, Steelhold had been carved from the sheared-off top of a hard granite peak, creating the fortress that now perched like a waiting raptor above the city below. It had been a massive undertaking by earth mages and slave labor. Centuries later, the bare stone floor of the Hold still showed the marks of the pickaxes, though polished by centuries of foot traffic. Most of the buildings had been shaped from the mountain at the same time the Hold was cut, their granite walls rising seamlessly from the stone floor. Others, like the palace with its massive conservatory, were built later, their walls a mix of stone blocks, mortar, hardwoods, and glass.

Vaness and I crossed the Hold's grounds at a comfortable pace, shoulder to shoulder in companionable silence. Above, a pair of ravens circled, their feathers shining when they banked and caught the sun. The day's heat brought a prickle of sweat to my brow.

Just three gates broke the seamless defense walls surrounding Steelhold. The Sun Gate looked over Jaliss. It was the most traveled because its access path, painstakingly carved from the cliff itself, was wide enough to accommodate a steady-nerved mule. The Shadow Gate opened onto a much more treacherous descent which combined narrow paths with ladders of iron spikes jutting from the sheer stone.

The Chasm Gate didn't lead to Jaliss at all, but rather the Atal strongholds wedged deep in the Icethorn Mountains. Near the gate's massive iron portcullis, we stopped and inspected the guards. By custom, neither of the gate sentries met our eyes. Fists to chests they stomped their feet to acknowledge our arrival.

Beside the gate, a narrow staircase climbed to the wall's top. I felt the effort in my thighs as I tramped up the steps. Behind me, Vaness didn't even get winded. She'd always been the fittest among us, probably because she worked the hardest at it.

From the top of the wall, the view never failed to fill me with longing. From the Chasm Gate, an impossibly high bridge connected Steelhold to a narrow road that wound into the craggy peaks at its back. Vaness joined me at the rail overlooking the gorge between Steelhold's perch and the mountains beyond. With a smirk, she hawked and spat.

"Charming," I said, knowing she'd only done it to get a reaction.

She laughed, a rare sound. Something had put her in a good mood. Maybe it was the resounding defeat she'd handed Donevin while practicing with staves yesterday. I resisted the sudden urge to drop an affectionate arm over her shoulders. Most likely, she'd be horrified if I tried.

"Shall we?" she asked, blue eyes squinted against the sun.

"Duty calls."

In truth, the patrol was ridiculous. Three dozen guards stood atop the wall, each pressing fists to chests as we passed. If an attack happened while we were up here, no doubt we'd be herded into the safety of the palace. And after Ascension, none of us would dare expose themselves up here. But seeing as I'd spent my whole life inside Steelhold, leaving only for an occasional tour of the city, these walks were the closest I came to freedom. I had no plans to mention how purposeless they were.

Along the front wall, we looked over the capital. Tens of thousands of people, Atal and Prov, lived in Jaliss. From our vantage, people and horses were nothing but insects. Pressed close to Steelhold's cliffs, the massive homes of the elite-class families looked like toy blocks. At this height, it was easy to ignore the misery that most of the citizens of the Empire endured. Well, easier anyway.

From behind, I heard shouts and whirled to see two men shoving each other on the grounds below. Delivery carts stood abandoned, one with root vegetables and the other holding pottery. One of the men cocked a fist and slammed the other in the gut.

Moments later, metal clanged as a protector ran to the scene. Without hesitation, he backhanded the man who'd thrown the punch, iron-studded glove slicing the man's face as his head snapped back. The Prov crumpled, boneless and bleeding, to the ground.

My gaze flicked to Vaness in time to see her wince. Pity? Or was she simply imagining the feeling of a metal glove smacking her face? Almost instantly, a snarl of disdain replaced her grimace.

"Even with the Decree of Functions to guide them, Provs still lack the self-control of a civilized race," she said.

I flinched inwardly. She didn't really think that, did she?

When I looked down on the scene again, I straightened in surprise. Twelve ministers served Emperor Tovmeil, dividing the work of implementing the Emperor's edicts. The members of the Ministry were reclusive, but when they emerged from their hall, it often meant difficult times for the Scions. Perhaps because they'd endured twenty-one years as Scions themselves, they wished to pass on the misery. I'd been beaten as punishment more than once when I'd said something which displeased a minister.

The man standing below was the worst. According to rumors, even the other ministers found Brevt sadistic. As the fallen man bled on Steelhold's granite, Minister Brevt stood over him, a feral smile contorting his face.

After a moment, he looked up and locked eyes with me, his grin widening. I contained a shudder and turned away.

"Let's go," I said, holding down the sickness that rose from my stomach. The Prov who'd been struck still hadn't risen. Quite possibly, they'd have to wheel him out of the Hold in his own delivery cart, abandoning both at the bottom of the ascent trail for his widow to discover. Or maybe Minister Brevt would have the body dropped from the top of the walls. Of all the ministers, he chose such demonstrations most frequently, claiming they kept the Provs in line.

Vaness had already turned and continued on, indifferent to the scene or at least appearing that way. I hurried to catch up.

As we rounded the final corner of our walk, I slowed, reluctant to leave the wall and its fresh breezes. Plus, once I returned to my chambers, I'd have no choice but to contemplate my audience with the Emperor.

"Hey Vaness," I said, knowing my tone was less casual than I hoped, "do you ever wonder who will Ascend?"

Her lips twisted in amusement. "What kind of question is that? Of course I wonder. Shouldn't it be on all our minds?"

"I mean—of course we all want to be chosen. But you ever think about our differences? What kind of rulers we'd make?"

Her brows drew together as she peered at me, suspicious. "Why?"

I gritted my teeth. I shouldn't have asked. "Nevermind. I guess I am just in a philosophical mood."

Vaness snorted. "You? The man who demolished a training dummy in four slashes last week? I never figured you for a philosopher. But to answer your question, yes, I have thought about the kind of emperors we'd be. I'll say this: if you Ascend, I feel sorry for any Provincials who dare defy your rule."

Despite myself, I raised my eyebrows in shock. "Me? Why?"

"Do you really need to ask? Because you're the most ruthless among us, of course. If anyone is capable of putting Provs and rebels in their place, it's you."

I felt as if ice water filled my chest. Me, ruthless? Sure, I strove to appear hard. We all did. But I thought that Vaness, at least, could see through me. After all, she *had* kissed me. But if she thought I was this merciless Scion yet had still found me attractive, what did that say about her? I'd always thought we had similar secrets regarding our views on the Empire.

Apparently not.

She nudged me in the shoulder. "I just gave you the biggest compliment a Scion can receive, and you're standing there like a mule that's been knocked in the head. Get over yourself, Kostan. Everyone knows you're the best among us. We're just hoping the brands don't figure it out."

I steeled my face into an expressionless mask. "Then I'll have to hope our scars will agree with your assessment."

Chapter Eight

Savra
Beside the coastal road, Cosmal Peninsula

"I have to get back!" I shoved Havialo as he tried to grab my shoulders.

"You can't," he said. "And you can't help them now."

Swaying on my feet, I stumbled across dusty ruts toward Numintown and the smoke plume. "My family is back there."

"Savra... My men went to find your mother and sister. They'll guide your family to a sanctuary."

When I whirled to look at him, my heel caught. I fell hard, jarring my spine as I landed on my rear. Havialo looked down at me with a strange mix of frustration and pity. In the late afternoon light, I noticed that his eyes weren't the gray color they'd appeared under candlelight, but rather a light sea green.

My chest ached with the helplessness. "A sanctuary where? What about everyone else?" I thought of the other townsfolk, families like mine who spent long days bent over the sluice boxes or pacing the tide lines in hopes of earning another month's food. Careworn faces, bodies reduced to sinew and leathery skin. Not everyone in Numintown had been my friend, but they were still my community.

Stiffly, Havialo extended a hand. He grasped my wrist and lifted me from the road. "I'm sure most of them fled. There weren't many protectors with the party. Their point made, the Registry delegation will move on quickly. But I must be honest. The survivors may wish they'd been killed outright. Once a town falls under rationing, starvation often follows."

It was too much to take in. I closed my eyes as my head spun.

"Why burn the town?" I asked. This had something to do with me, I knew it. Otherwise, why would the geognost send people to lead my family away?

"It's pointless to try to understand the Empire's motives." The mage's hand was surprisingly gentle on my shoulder as he nudged me forward.

Dust puffed from my feet as I shuffled. Edging through the break in the thicket, I pulled my clothing close to keep it from snagging. About thirty paces from the road, the horses snorted in a small clearing.

"I need a better answer," I said, pulling together the remnants of my wits. "You know why they burned Numintown. You thought it might happen. I can't just follow you without understanding why."

Havialo exhaled. "What would you like me to say? Yes, I was concerned. The registrar was inexperienced. She'd likely never encountered... she'd likely never faced the situation you put her in."

I balled my fists. "What situation? Why? I don't understand."

"And with good fortune, you won't until the proper time. Listen to me, Savra. It's difficult to accept, but you must simply move forward. Returning home will only endanger you and everyone you care about. Someday, you will have answers. But it won't be today."

"Then please take me to my family and this sanctuary."

"Impossible. I'm sorry. These events are the very reason your father left. He worried this would happen someday. He never wanted to abandon you, Savra. Or your family."

The mage's words from earlier crashed back into my mind. "You know my father?"

Havialo nodded. "We can discuss this later. But yes, I know Evrain."

The words were a cold breeze whipping me back to alertness. "Where is he? What's happened to him? Please tell me!"

Master Havialo laid a hand on my shoulder before stepping to the horses. "As I said, later." He ran his hand down my gelding's neck. "For now, there are things I must prepare. The fires are evidence that the registrar's inexperience didn't mean she was completely inept. If Numintown is to avoid starvation—and if you are to avoid the gallows—I must take more drastic steps."

Once in the clearing Havialo broke sticks from the brush behind the horses and hurried to weave them into the thicket separating us from the road. He paused briefly to judge his work before trotting back to gather more branches.

"Are we making camp?" I asked. I had little experience in the wilderness, even the hills near Numintown. But that was only because I'd had a warm bed in our small house. I could help the mage if he explained what I needed to do.

"Depends," he responded as he grunted and twisted another of the tough branches. Finally, the green wood fibers parted with a pop.

"Depends on what? Is this part of your drastic plan?"

He brushed past me, dragging the branch behind him. The leaves rustled against dry grass. It had been a few weeks since the last big rain. "If you want to help, the horses could use care. After they're brushed down, replace the saddles. We may need to leave quickly."

"All right. But I wish you'd explain."

He stabbed the severed branch into the thicket then fluffed the leaves to make it look natural. "The registrar's party will come this way soon. We need to be ready."

Maybe he meant for us to hide and let the registrar pass. Better that than fight. No one tangled with protectors, at least not if they wanted to wake up the next day.

The haze was finally evaporating from my thoughts. My fingers and toes began to tingle; I hadn't realized they'd been numb. As my mind cleared, I fought despair. I'd left my home and I still didn't know what the danger had been. But judging by Havialo's rushed movements, this wasn't the time to ask. With a wary glance at the road, I trotted to the horses and started working leather straps free from their buckles.

Havialo shaded his eyes and looked toward the descending sun. Licking a finger, he held it up as if sensing the breeze. "Are there usually thunderstorms in the afternoon?" he asked.

I glanced toward the coast. "During Chilltide. But not very often now. Why?"

"I noticed the clouds over the sea," he said, pointing to the horizon line over the Maelstrom. "I hoped to use them. This close to the coast, the tidal force would usually be plenty for me to work with. But the currents here are tainted. I might as well eat rotten meat."

As far as I understood, a geognost could gather energy from the natural world and channel it elsewhere, but only if the land had power to give. Back at the town hall, it seemed he'd found a pent-up fault in the earth and released it, channeling the power into the wind that had gusted against the building. Maybe he could gather energy from a storm, too, but as for this mention of a taint, I had no idea what he was talking about.

"Well, it hasn't rained in weeks," I said, "but we might get lucky." Lucky. The word sounded hollow. If fortune had had a role in today's events, I would rather not trust anything else to fate.

Havialo glared at the sky before stomping back across the clearing and tearing another stick free. "Well, we'll have to hope. I don't see another alternative."

I tugged on a hunk of hair that had escaped my braid. "I'd be more help to you if I understood what's going on. And..." I swallowed. "If you want my cooperation, I need to know why you rescued me. Even a short explanation."

He raised a brow at me. "I seem to recall a large fire starting shortly after our departure. Would you have preferred to remain for that?"

"Of course not. But look at this from my perspective," I said as I pulled the saddle from my mount and leaned back to balance its weight. "How do I know you weren't involved with the fire?"

He sighed, then stuffed a hand into his pants pocket and produced a letter.

"From your father," he said. "If you could move a few paces out of the way, it would help."

The saddle thumped to the ground. Hands trembling, I grabbed the sheet of paper and unfolded it. I recognized my father's shaky letters immediately. He'd never been strong with reading or writing, and I could only imagine what it must've taken him to pen this. When I was young, his face had reddened in embarrassment whenever he tried to read in front of us.

Havialo,

I understand that you no longer believe in our cause. But I did you a favor many years ago. You know of what I speak. After this, you'll never need to hear from me again. But I need you to make one last trip. Numintown. My family. My daughter turned seventeen this year.

Signed,

Evrain Panmi

A tear slid down my cheek as I read my father's words over again. It had been seven years since he left, and we'd heard nothing in all that time.

"May I keep it?" I said.

The mage waved his hand as if to dismiss the question as not worth asking. With extreme care not to further tatter the edges, I folded the note and tucked it into the inner pocket of my jacket. I could feel it crinkling there, pressing against my ribs through the light fabric of my tunic. My father was still alive, and more, he still cared about us. I pressed my forearm against the paper, holding it against my body while I searched the saddlebags for the curry comb.

With a last glance at the work he'd done on the brush, the mage shoved through the narrow passage leading to the road. I followed in time to see him scan the horizon back and forth. The clouds had built, surprising me after so many weeks. Still, I doubted they'd actually produce rain.

When the mage turned, he gestured at the sky. "Almost near enough to harness. I suspect it will be enough."

I glanced to the south, thinking of Avill and Mother. Smoke still rose from Numintown, shearing toward the Maelstrom's heart when it hit winds up high. Had the mage's henchmen really led my family away? Would they find shelter if it stormed?

"Enough for what?" I asked. "I need to know."

Havialo glanced at me, his lips making a hard line. "I can't let the registrar pass. Clearly, she wasn't swayed by my... demands that she change the ledger and mark you as a scribe. It would have been easier that way." As he spoke, he twisted a silver band that encircled his middle finger. After a moment, he pulled it off, curling his lip in disgust. "Argent magic is a foul art anyway. I only used it because I worried my powers alone wouldn't intimidate her into obeying."

I nodded slowly as he tucked the ring into his pocket. I knew the basics of metalogy. Argent mages, those who wore silver to channel their power, manipulated spirits. An argent could command someone, mind to mind. But I hadn't known that earth mages could gain argent ranks.

"Savra," he said, "if you are to successfully enter training in the capital, we'll need to alter the ledger ourselves and bring it to the Hall of Registry in Jaliss."

Staring at his grim face, my fingertips went cold as I realized what he planned. Still, there was a chance I was wrong. "You mean to steal the ledger," I said, hoping that was the explanation despite what I suspected. "That's why we're waiting here."

The mage sighed. "No one from their party can return to the capital to dispute your Function assignment. Plain enough for you?"

"You're going to kill them."

"Unless you have a better idea."

More auburn-red strands escaped my dissolving braid as I yanked. "There must be another option."

"Unfortunately, I don't think so."

"Why do I need to go to the capital, anyway? I was planning to turn fugitive if I had to leave Numintown. If I do, no one has to die, right?"

"Wouldn't work."

"Why?"

"It's complicated. Your father has specifically asked for the right to explain this stuff to you. I gave him my vow."

"Well, I don't care what my father says. The registrar was just doing her job."

He shook his head as if disappointed in my innocence. "Do you know what else happens if we let them pass? I've seen it a dozen times when Prov settlements displease the Empire. Rationing is not pleasant, Savra. And for something like this, Numintown may well be dissolved. You don't want to know what happens in that case."

"Then I'll—"

He cut me off, slicing his hand through the air, then pointed to his ear. I cocked my head to listen.

Hoofbeats.

Chapter Nine

Kostan
Scion's bedchamber, Steelhold

Flipping the pillow to expose the cool side and punching it to fluff the goose down within, I rolled over. Again. Judging by the slant of moonlight through my bedroom's barred window, midnight had come and gone. Maybe I'd get an hour or two of real sleep before the dawn bells sent the pigeons flapping past my window.

I doubted I'd be so lucky.

I hadn't had a good night's sleep in the tenday since the Emperor summoned me. Every time I'd lain down, his words had echoed in my mind. The Empire would fall unless I Ascended. I must do whatever was necessary to keep the throne strong. The Bracer of Sight would show me the consequences of failure.

Why would Emperor Tovmeil tell me these things? Only the shape of the scar on my foot could declare me Emperor, and that wouldn't happen for two years. Was he hoping I'd gain the brutality necessary to Ascend? No matter the man I wished to become, I couldn't change my soft heart.

The nights after a girl came to change my bandage were the worst. For years, I'd told myself I'd forbid any more blindings if I rose to the throne. Now I couldn't even be sure of that. After all, I'd never been bold enough to try to help one of the girls escape. Emperor Tovmeil had, but once he Ascended, he chose to continue sacrificing their sight for the greater good.

A cloud skidded across the moon, plunging my bedroom into darkness. I rolled over again, jerking the covers to pull the wrinkles from them. My brand ached, which made me wonder if the lack of sleep was making my body weak, allowing an infection to take root. In a way, I wished for it. If my fate was to follow Emperor Tovmeil's example and continue his brutal rule, maybe I deserved to suffer, too.

When the door cracked open, admitting a vertical beam of lantern light, I jerked, heart racing. The guardians allowed no one to enter my bedroom at night.

So stupid, I cursed myself. The Emperor had warned me the throne's enemies were closing in. Yet here I lay wearing nothing but my underclothes, no weapon within reach.

As a shadow slipped through the door on silent feet, shutting it without a sound, I held perfectly still. I kept my breath as even as I could manage. If the intruder believed me asleep, at least I kept an element of surprise. Martial training, including both bare-handed and weapons fighting, had been part of my daily schedule since I was five. Unlike my fumbling attempts at spirit armoring, I was a good fighter. Quick more than strong, but effective. My practice scimitar leaned against the far wall of the room, about four long strides away. The cutting edge was purposefully dulled, but it would be better than nothing.

"You're a fool to think I don't know you're awake. Get dressed," the shadow hissed.

I blinked. "What?" I whispered.

Moments later, the moon escaped the cloud's veil and once again lit the room, showing the intruder. He wore a dark cloak, the hood casting deep shadows over his face.

After a moment, he snorted in disgust and tossed back the hood. Ilishian glared at me. "As I said, get dressed. Now."

I pushed aside the covers. "It would have been wiser to knock. I was preparing to slit your throat."

He huffed in annoyance. "A true assassin would've been upon you faster than you took to realize I'd opened your door. And that dull knife you call a scimitar might as well be in another province given where you stored it. From now on you'll keep a weapon within reach."

I sighed, rubbing my eyes. "Are you going to explain what's going on?"

"Emperor Tovmeil is dead. We must get you to safety. Tonight."

I jerked upright, blinking away the haze. Occasionally over the last days, I'd imagined blades aimed at my back, eyes peering from the shadows. But I'd been focused on the notion that Emperor Tovmeil believed I must Ascend. Apparently, I hadn't listened to him carefully enough. Tovmeil? Dead?

"How? What happens now?" As far as I knew, an Emperor had never died before his successor's Ascension. We'd never been taught who would rule until the chosen Scion would take the throne.

"Assassins aided by magic. That's all I know. We can discuss it at length later. We must go. Emperor Tovmeil extracted a promise from me. If there were ever a threat, I would get you out of Steelhold. Nothing mattered to him more than that—in fact, he commanded me to choose your life over his if I were ever in the position."

I swung my legs off the bed. The stone floor was frigid against the bottom of my unbandaged foot. I ran my hand through my hair. "What about the other Scions?"

"They don't matter. Once you Ascend, ministers can be appointed from among the elite class if necessary. The Scions were expendable in the Emperor's view."

Expendable. Vaness's face sprang to my thoughts. I remembered the feel of her lips. Her laugh. Regardless of her words that day on patrol, I still believed we shared something the other Scions lacked.

"Vaness is not expendable to me." I hardened my jaw. "I won't leave her to the assassins."

Ilishian narrowed his eyes. I could almost hear his thoughts, his disgust at my inability to put the Empire first. A few days ago, I might have regretted showing the weakness of emotion. But now I was too tired to care about this ferro mage's opinion. Ilishian could judge me how he chose. He wouldn't deny the Emperor's last wish by abandoning me.

"I'll make you a bargain," the mage said. "As soon as we are out of Steelhold, I'll send my apprentice, Azar, to rescue Vaness. Just as the Emperor trusted my loyalty, I trust Azar."

I threw aside the covers and stood. "Fair. What do I need?"

"Enough clothes to be comfortable in the night's chill. We will work out further necessities once we have a clear picture of the situation. Now hurry, please."

I snatched my trousers from their puddle on the floor and yanked them over my underclothes, fastening them with a leather belt. With a quick glance at the practice scimitar, I discarded the idea of bringing it. As the ferro had said, I needed a real weapon close at hand, not some dull knife. From my trunk, I grabbed a simple linen tunic, lined leather jacket, and a wool hat. Finally, I pulled on my mismatched boots.

With a nod, Ilishian scurried to the door. He cracked it and peered outside before motioning me forward. When I stepped into the hallway, I gasped. The guardian who'd been posted outside my door lay dead on the floor, tongue protruding, his face blue-black and mottled. I grimaced.

"Was he part of the plot?" I whispered.

The ferro mage shrugged, face blank. "I don't know. The enemies' faces were hidden from the Emperor. But I couldn't take the chance."

"So you killed him... just to be safe?"

Not even a flicker of regret crossed his face as he set off down the hall. "I suppose that's one way to put it. Guardians are replaceable. The future Emperor is not."

The horror of his words pecked at me like a flock of crows. This man had died simply because Emperor Tovmeil had believed I must take the throne.

I swallowed back my disgust and sidestepped around the corpse. No matter what the Emperor had claimed, I'd never become the kind of man he'd been.

Chapter Ten

Savra
A thicket near the coastal road, Cosmal

"Stay with the horses," Havialo hissed from the edge of the clearing. We'd dashed into hiding, and now he was edging toward the road again. The sun was near the horizon, the red light of evening spilling like blood over the peninsula.

I knew I should protest. But what about Numintown? Could I live with my choice if I let the registrar dissolve the settlement? Somehow, this was my fault. I just didn't understand why.

"Are you sure?" I asked. "What if I talk to them? Convince them I'm not what they believe?"

"If you expose yourself, you'll be dead before they draw within thirty paces. The protectors carry poison-tipped crossbow bolts. They don't take chances."

"My father wouldn't want this," I said. "He would find another way." And if I was wrong about that, maybe I no longer wanted a reunion.

Havialo's jaw hardened. "We didn't always agree on methods. But he would recognize our lack of options here."

The plume of dust from the approaching riders was now visible over the tops of the brush that surrounded us. Havialo glanced at the sky, raised a finger to feel the breeze again, and nodded. "I can bring the storm the rest of the way." He paused and stared at me. "Savra, you can run if you won't be part of this. But it won't change what I have to do. If the registrars are not stopped, Numintown *will* suffer the consequences. The Empire doesn't take chances. Even if you can't stomach what must be done, I won't have the death of every Numintowner on my head."

The words stunned me into silence.

With a nod, he shoved into the thicket. "I'd appreciate it if you attempted to calm the horses, but I suppose you'll make your own decisions."

As he disappeared into the foliage, the sun dropped behind the hill at our backs. Out to sea, the storm clouds billowed, gray and black with sheets of rain pouring out the undersides. A downdraft gusted up from the shore, rattling the brush and smelling of rain.

Feeling helpless, I stepped to the horses and buried my face in my mount's mane. The storm crept closer, thunder rumbling in its belly. With the wind howling, I couldn't hear the hoofbeats of the approaching riders. But I knew they'd arrived when I heard a shout of panic.

"Quicksand!"

I cocked my head. Had I heard that right? After so long without rain, the road was an inch deep in dust. Beneath was nothing but hard packed earth and stone.

"In the brush!"

"... saddlebags!"

The storm churned overhead now, blackening the sky and flattening the tops of the bushes with its violent breath. All desire to run fled me as I crouched down, the horses' reins wrapped around my fist. Abruptly, the air felt too warm. The hairs on my forearms stood as tickling fingers brushed my forehead. I looked up and screamed—the horses' manes were standing on end.

With a flash and an earsplitting crack, a bolt of lightning lanced from the clouds, exploding in the road. The horses shrieked and reared, wrenching my shoulder as I frantically tried to unwind the lead from my hands.

Another strike split the air, cracking as if inside my skull. I clapped my hands over my head, squeezed my ears with my forearms. Like a nerve struck with a hammer, jolts sped from my shoes up my body. Sparks leaped from the ground to the horses stomping feet. With a crash, the beasts were gone, tearing through the brush. From the road, I smelled cooking meat. A tense silence ballooned as sparks leaped across the spaces between my legs, from my chin to my knees, and across my eyelashes. I made myself smaller, whimpering, certain I had moments to live.

Over the course of heartbeats, the sparks crackled and died. With a quiet soughing of wind through the brush, a final gust bore down on the area and faded away.

Rain began to patter on bushes and leaves, frigid drops splattering on my head and hands.

The moon had risen, the clouds long fled. I huddled in a ball, shivering in my wet clothing. The geognost hadn't returned—I didn't have to think hard to know what that meant. I knew I should move. I should verify that Havialo was dead, try to hunt down the horses. But I feared what I'd see on the road, and I was just so cold.

So instead, I curled on my side, hugged my knees to my chest, and waited for dawn.

Sometime later, a thump jerked me from my doze. My legs shot out and connected with a stand of brush, setting the leaves rattling. I made a fist, ready to defend myself.

"I apologize," Havialo said. "I lost consciousness. It occasionally happens when the source of power is difficult to control."

"I—" My jaw worked slowly, stiff from cold and confusion. "I thought you were dead."

"As I said, I apologize."

I rubbed a clammy hand over my face. "The registrar's party?"

"Do you really want the details?"

I shook my head as I pushed up, planting a hand in the sodden grass. When the night air hit the newly-exposed side of my body, another shiver rattled my bones.

Havialo plucked at my clothing before drying his hand on his cloak. "Ordinarily, I would've sent the rain away. But as I said..."

"You were unconscious."

He pointed to a pile of saddlebags, no doubt the source of the thump which had wakened me. "The scroll tube will contain the ledger. It's sealed with wax, so we'll wait to check it until we near Jaliss. No need to expose it to the elements before then. I have contacts who can alter your entry before we present it to the Hall of Registry."

"What will you say when we do?"

He cocked his head. "I don't understand."

"Doesn't a registrar usually deliver the ledger?"

The corner of his mouth twitched. A smile? "You're thinking ahead," he said. "Good. Despite what the Empire would have you believe, lawlessness continues to plague the Provinces. It wouldn't be surprising for a party from Jaliss to be set upon. We'll tell them you escaped the bandits. I found you in the nearest town where you were waiting in hopes someone else survived."

I shivered, partly from cold, but mostly at the reminder of what the mage had done. No one in Cosmal Province loved the Empire. But killing an official representative of the regime along with her notary and protectors? No one would consider it. If I returned to Numintown now, I'd have to lie to people who'd known me since birth. They'd spot the dishonesty sooner or later. I dropped my head to my knees, wishing I'd fled before the storm began.

"If I'd run while you..." I swallowed, searching for words. "While you stopped the registrar, what would you have done?"

"I would've tried to track you once I regained consciousness. I promised your father, remember?"

Havialo unfastened one of the saddlebag's leather straps and opened the lid. Rummaging, he pulled out a coarse wool sweater and tossed it to me.

"Exposure is dangerous, even this far south. Worse once we get on the mainland. If there were any dry wood about, I'd risk a fire despite our need to move quickly. You must let me know if you start to feel unnaturally warm. It's the first sign your body has grown too cold and is sliding toward death."

The words set me shivering again—I'd never heard of someone dying from the cold. I opened and closed my hands, working the stiffness from my fingers before sliding the sweater over my head and arms. The woolen garment smelled of a man's sweat. Immediately, my shivering slowed.

"There's little point in trying to recover the horses," Havialo said.

"I tried to keep a grasp on the reins. Sorry."

"And I tried to strike with a greater measure of control. We both did our best. In any case, we'll need to make more progress tonight,"

Havialo said. "I apologize for that—I realize you've been through a lot today."

"I don't want to be here anymore, anyway." Now that I was sitting upright, the smell of roasted meat once again reached my nose. I couldn't bear to think about what lay on the road.

"We'll hurry for the Cosmal Crease. Two nights of hard marching by my guess. We'll take what we need from the saddlebags, and once we reach Dukket Waystation, I have a friend who can help us resupply."

"Master Havialo?" I asked. "Would they really have killed me?"

"Call me Havialo," he said. "And yes. From this day forward, if anyone loyal to the Empire figures out who and what you are, they won't think twice about putting an arrow through your heart."

Chapter Eleven

Kostan
Steelhold grounds

Ilishian led the way across the fortress grounds, a shadow slipping along the edge of buildings. Overhead, the stars were faint presences behind the silvery moon. Chill air cut through my trousers and stung my cheeks. By midday, Steelhold's open grounds would be as uncomfortably hot as the night was cold—it often felt as if the very air hated the presence of the Hold, trying day and night to force us from our perch.

As I crept along behind the ferro mage, I imagined assassins' eyes on me, their blades blackened so as not to reflect the moonlight. An arrow could take me at any moment. I jumped, startled, when a rat scurried out from under my feet.

Near the rear wall of the Hall of Mages where a narrow aisle separated the building from the outer walls, Ilishian stopped.

"You're sure he's dead?" I asked, realizing I should have asked sooner.

"Certain." The man looked over my shoulder and nodded at someone. I turned to see another mage approaching, her light-colored robes marking her as a recent apprentice to the ferro order.

"Good," Ilishian said. "I appreciate your haste, Azar."

Azar was winded from her swift approach. "It's happened then?"

Her mentor nodded. "The wards were tripped. His stone went dark. Tovmeil is dead."

Azar gestured toward me. "We proceed then? Out the Chasm Gate?"

Under other circumstances, I might have been more distracted by the young mage's attractive features. She had high cheekbones and curves that not even an apprentice robe and a moonlit night could hide. As I pulled my eyes from her, she handed a pair of nondescript cloaks to Ilishian and me before donning her own.

Ilishian sucked his teeth as he pulled on the disguising garment. "It will have to do."

"And then what?" I asked, planting my feet in a wider stance.

"We'll get you somewhere safe and wait for news."

"When will we return to the Hold?"

Ilishian's cheek twitched. "When the traitors have been exposed and no sooner."

"We'll remain in the mountains?"

He shook his head. "There's a difficult path that leaves the road not far beyond the gorge. It exits the mountains about half a day's walk from the city. We'll circle around that way."

I didn't mention that I'd never ventured into the mountains, that my only experience beyond the walls was my handful of trips through Jaliss. Ilishian probably knew that already, and if he didn't, it would just give him more excuses to avoid consulting me.

"The three of us will easily find a safe spot within the city," Ilishian continued. "I'll contact the Hold afterward and begin sorting friend from foe. We must preserve the Ascension."

"The four of us, you mean," I said as I shrugged into the cloak.

Ilishian looked at me quizzically.

"Vaness. You promised to send Azar back for her."

He pursed his lips, then nodded, frustration on his face. "You're right, I did. Fair enough." His gaze turned to Azar. "Once we're across the bridge, you'll attempt to get Scion Vaness out safely. We'll wait for you at Graybranch Inn in the Splits."

Azar nodded, her face set. "As you say."

With a nod, Ilishian set out again, leading us on. Near the Chasm Gate, only scattered lanterns flickered. But atop the wall, fires burned every few paces. I remembered the view from the city, glimpsed on a long-ago trip to the astrologers' high tower. Seen from Jaliss, Steelhold was the burning crown on a pedestal so high it seemed to scratch the clouds. Forbidding and utterly dominating.

My toe hit a pebble and sent it skittering across the stone. On the wall, a guard turned and quickly doused his torch to better see into the darkness. I froze, only to suppress a cry of horror when the man's hands went to his throat, tugging at a dart that now bristled from his neck.

He crumpled as Ilishian tucked away the black-iron tube he'd blown the dart through.

Guilt spread through me like oil. That man had died because I was clumsy. I wanted to stop this, refuse to go further, but I remembered the Emperor's words. If I didn't Ascend, hundreds of thousands would die. Our civilization would be ruined.

Ahead, a span of bare stone separated us from the Chasm Gate, the moon glaring down on the approach. I swallowed and paused behind Ilishian. Azar's quiet breath warmed my ear as she pressed close. My thoughts once again flitted to what I could see of her body beneath the shapeless robe and cloak. I pushed them away. Now was not the time.

With a nod, Ilishian started across the empty space. I followed, pulse rushing in my ears. When we neared the gate, the sentry whirled.

"We have business in the strongholds," Ilishian said, brushing back his hood. "I'm taking these apprentices for training."

The sentry on the right stomped twice to acknowledge the mage's high rank. But he didn't move to turn the winch that would raise the iron gate. "I have orders from the Emperor, conveyed through Minister Brevt. No one is to leave tonight. There have been rumors of Stormshard movements in the city and surrounds."

A renegade group, Stormshard had been hassling the Empire for years. But they were an annoyance more than anything. Hardly reason to close down the Hold. Unless... had all the raids on caravans and interference with couriers been a cover while they moved on the ultimate target? Emperor Tovmeil had made it sound as if his enemies were close. Inside the palace walls, even. But maybe he'd been wrong. If so, how had a ragtag group of renegades managed to get assassins into the Hold? Then again, if Brevt had given the order to lock down the Hold, did that mean he, not Stormshard, was behind the murder?

"I appreciate your loyalty, Protector. But Minister Brevt is mistaken. I spoke with the Emperor late this evening. He'd heard of these resistance operatives, and much of what we will do in the strongholds will directly oppose their work."

In any case, the guard's face hardened. He wasn't falling for Ilishian's story. My shoulders tightened as the ferro mage reached for his robes and the blowtube and poisoned darts within. The act came so easy to him. This just wasn't right.

And yet you're just standing here letting it happen, I thought.

Without stopping to consider my actions, I stepped forward and threw back my hood. The guards immediately dropped their eyes, the habit ingrained after years of averting their eyes when a Scion drew near.

"There is little time," I said. "We must be well away from Steelhold before dawn if we are to disrupt this plan."

"It's irregular," muttered the guard who'd first confronted us. "A Scion leaving the hold."

"I'm sure irregular things happened in the years before the Anisel Uprising, too. If I'm forced to summon the Prime Protector from her bed, I doubt you'll wish to explain our delay."

"No, sire. And I don't wish to argue with one chosen by the stars. But the Minister—"

"Is ignorant. Or perhaps he's a Stormshard ally. Open the portcullis, Protector, or I'll do it myself."

At my side, I felt Ilishian's simmering rage. In his mind, it had been foolish to expose myself when he could have dealt with the problem quietly. When news got out of the Emperor's murder, the fact that I'd left the compound within hours would cast suspicion on me and the mages escorting me. Better to be a suspect than stand by while more men were murdered for my sake, though.

Eyes still fixed on the ground at my feet, the guard clenched and unclenched his leather-clad fists. After a long, tense silence, he stomped twice then nodded at his partner. Together, they grabbed the wooden pegs on the portcullis winch and started raising the gate.

I kept my face even, fixing a faint look of disdain over my features as I stalked to the opening gate. At least my years of training as a Scion taught me to control my emotions. From the outside, I was the ruthless candidate Vaness believed me to be.

Just as the pointed spikes on the bottom edge of the portcullis cleared chest height, a shout went up on the far side of the Hold. The alarm gong clanged. Beside me, Ilishian stiffened.

"Go. Now," he said under his breath.

Ducking our heads, we slipped beneath the spikes. When I glanced back, Azar had vanished, likely melting into the shadows now that we'd passed beyond Steelhold's walls.

Ilishian strode onto the bridge as if unconcerned by the rising clamor from within the fortress. Hand falling on my hip where I usually belted my training scimitar, I swallowed and hurried my steps to draw even with him.

"Will Azar be okay?" I asked.

"She was wise enough not to show her face. Unlike you."

"Those men didn't need to die." I wouldn't apologize. Besides, we'd made it, right?

"Yet you've complicated our task. As you recall, we must find a way for you to Ascend. Difficult when you left Steelhold under suspicious circumstances."

"I'm sure we'll find a way to persuade any who might accuse me. Or would that require too much creativity from someone who would rather kill those who dared hesitate to obey?"

I knew this wasn't the time to confront the man, but the night's events were finally breaking through my carefully constructed control.

"The politics of the situation are clearly beyond your young mind," the mage said as we neared the center of the high span.

I ignored the barb as I glanced back at the Hold. Along the wall, more torches now burned as patrollers ran to and fro, securing the perimeter. A cloaked figure stood motionless at the stone rail, silhouetted in the moonlight. Judging by the height, I guessed it was Azar. I hoped she was faithful to her promise to retrieve Vaness as soon as we'd disappeared from sight.

"Master Ilishian! Scion Kostan! In the name of the Ministry and the Empire it serves, I command you to halt!" When the man's shout rang out in the cold night, the ferro mage jerked.

"Minister Brevt," he called. "The Ministry's handiwork this evening is a blow to the throne, no doubt. But know that the Ascension will still happen. No plots can upset the stars' will."

I clenched my jaw. So Brevt and his cohort *were* behind the plan, or at least that was Ilishian's conclusion. I thought back to the minister's cruel grin that day when I'd patrolled the walls with Vaness. He must have been planning my murder even then.

"Don't stand there like a fool," Ilishian said under his breath. "Keep walking."

I shook clear of my thoughts and carried on. Vibration from my stomping footsteps traveled up my legs, jarring my knees. With every step, it seemed to grow.

After a moment, I realized it wasn't just my footsteps vibrating my body. Beneath me, the bridge had started to shake. After another few paces, a deep rumble rose from the heavy stone blocks of the span.

A fist of fear clutched my heart. We had no shortage of earthquakes in Jaliss and Steelhold, and they'd only been worsening lately. The Chasm Span had withstood hundreds of years of shakes. Yet this felt different.

"Potential energy in the suspended arch. Enough of it from the natural buttressing of the stone," Ilishian said behind me, his voice tight. "Go. Run."

He dashed forward and shoved something into my hand. Clutching the metal chain and hard lump of stone, I nodded. He didn't need to explain any more than he had. Geognosty. My eyes widened as my legs pumped.

Where had Brevt found a geognost willing to do someone else's bidding? The earth mages were stingy with their magic, putting it only to purposes of their choosing. Earth magic wasn't something that could be given through Maelstrom-blessed metals or countless hours of instruction—a geognost was born with the ability. Moreover, one master earth mage likely commanded more power than an entire order of metalogists. Their power lay in harnessing the natural energy in the earth and heavens. A boulder teetering on a cliff's edge represented enormous potential. With just a mental nudge, an earth mage could send it plummeting or she could allow it to drift to earth, channeling the immense destructive power into the earth mage's grasp. Stories told of geognosts who had siphoned the energy of an earthquake, turning it back on the shaking clay and raising a fully formed citadel from the earth. Others had gathered the force of the tide and lifted moisture from the sea, the resulting rain ending a years-long drought.

The Chasm Span arched over a drop almost too deep to fathom. Supported on either side by natural ramparts in the cliff, it represented enormous potential. Easy to nudge into action.

The light of the moon seemed to dim as panic closed on my vision. I sprinted over the shuddering stone pavement. Beneath me, the bridge trembled and shook. Somewhere behind, a loud crack split the air. I heard Ilishian yell but couldn't understand the words. I risked a glance over my shoulder, saw him standing with blowgun raised, his head swiveling as he searched for the geognost.

And then, the ground gave way beneath him, crumbling with a grating roar that beat against my eardrums and rattled my teeth. Ilishian screamed as he fell, his voice fading into the chasm below.

My toe caught an uneven edge. I stumbled, careened toward the edge where the crumbling bridge gave way to open air, only caught my balance a step before the brink. Behind me, more stones fell, whistling as they plummeted to earth. Thirty paces separated me from the end of the bridge where a narrow track rose through the gash in the mountains.

My breath hissed and wheezed as fear choked down my windpipe. I shook my head. I wouldn't give in. Not while my feet still pounded solid stone.

One long stride after another, my boots slammed the bridge beneath me. Twenty paces left. A distant part of my mind noticed the shouts, a woman among them.

"Run far and fast, Kostan," she yelled. "You are the Empire's last hope!"

Azar. She must still be atop the wall, must have seen her mentor's fall. Ilishian was gone. The Emperor was dead. Countless enemies moved on the throne, ready to destroy the Atal Empire.

Ten paces separated me from the end of the bridge. To my right, one of the squared-off stones that edged the bridge groaned as the mortar holding it gave way. The massive block rotated and fell away, somehow graceful despite its ungainly shape. I gagged and leaped over a widening gap in the pavement ahead.

And suddenly, my feet skidded on packed earth and embedded rocks that had been smoothed and rounded after centuries of traffic on the road.

Behind me, the bridge fell away. After a thousand years, the Chasm Gate now protected nothing but open air. I stopped and turned, staring at Steelhold. It was the only home I'd ever known. A home and a prison. But at least within its walls, I'd known what each morning would bring. I'd understood my future. Now, the only way forward was through treacherous mountains. I had no food, no water. Just a leather coat, a roughspun cloak, and the strength of my body.

The cool metal in my hand caught my attention as something heavy slipped off my palm. I caught the chain in a tight fist and lifted the object Ilishian had given me into the moonlight. The banded agate pendant of the Heart of the Empire swung slowly in the air.

Slipping the necklace over my head, I gave the burning torches of Steelhold one last look and turned, trotting into the unknown.

Chapter Twelve

"See it?" Havialo asked, pointing. "The Cosmal Crease."

At first, I'd thought the shadowy hump on the horizon was a band of fog or a forested hill. But now, I spotted the dark cracks splitting the rise. Haze from the sea hid most other details.

"Not much farther then?" I said, trying not to sound too relieved. After all, he was carrying all the weight. We'd packed the useful items from the registrar's party into a single pair of saddlebags which Havialo kept slung over his shoulders.

He shook his head. "No, not much farther."

As we drew closer, the slant of the ground steepened. Now and again, little tremors rattled the earth. I'd underestimated the size of the Crease. Badly. What had looked like low bluffs and cliffs were jagged precipices, freshly heaved from the ground. The broken terrain reminded me of what happened when I buried my feet in wet sand. As I wiggled and pulled them free, the sand would mound up, breaking and cracking, folding and crumbling. But here, the upper end of the peninsula was being bent and twisted the Maelstrom sucked the lower end down.

Around what looked like a quarter hour's walk from the Crease, Havialo ducked off the road into the tangle of brush and boulders. After a moment's confusion, I noticed the trail, a faint track overgrown with rattling foliage. We followed this for a few hundred paces before turning to parallel the road. Havialo shoved aside brambles and branches, grunting as he forced his way forward.

"Was there something wrong with the road?" I asked, brushing aside hair that stuck to my sweating forehead. A few paces on, I stopped and stripped off the cloak and wool sweater—it stank even worse when warm. Rolling them together, I wrapped them around my waist and secured them with a knot.

"Better if my friend doesn't know we're coming."

"Why?"

"Well, we didn't exactly part on good terms. If we surprise him, he won't have as much time to remember our little quarrel."

Great. "But he'll help, right?"

He didn't face me when he responded. "I hope so. Just don't get too comfortable once we arrive."

Waystation Dukket sprawled at the base of the Crease, a low-slung collection of buildings surrounded by packed earth and hitching rails. None of the buildings were taller than the height of a man—in fact, I suspected that many travelers would have to hunch while inside—and the roofs were thatched with straw. I understood why when my gaze passed over the far side of the waystation. There, a pair of buildings had fallen inward, the straw piled above the timbers. Earthquakes—better to have a low roof of straw fall upon the occupants than an arching ceiling of heavy timber and slate tile.

We stood near the edge of the cleared area, covered in scratches and leaves from our venture through the brush. After inspecting the layout of the waystation, Havialo led us on a path that skirted the grounds until we were near the stables. There, he straightened his shoulders, coughed, and strolled from the brush as if this were the most ordinary approach in the world.

After a moment, I swallowed and followed him.

The geognost stopped at the stable entrance, a wide door split in half so the top and bottom could be opened separately. The bottom half was closed and latched, while the top had been swung aside, exposing a dim interior, dust floating in sunbeams that pressed through the thatched roof.

Havialo kicked the lower door a few times, setting the wood and the framing shivering. "Hello!" he called.

A pale face emerged from the darkness, hair stacked in a crooked pile atop his head. The man squinted into the light that fell through the door. "Who is it?"

"Ho, Teppo."

The man's face darkened. "I'm not sure if you're brave or stupid to come here, Havialo."

At the acid in his tone, I took a step back. The motion caught the man's attention, and he turned his glare on me. "And don't think bringing an innocent girl with you will make your treatment any kinder. I heard what you did to Evrain."

I jerked at my father's name. Havialo nudged me with his knuckles. A warning?

"Evrain was angry that I had no more heart for our cause, that's all," the mage said. "And we've since made amends."

"You know my father?" I blurted, unable to keep quiet.

I hadn't thought the man could look paler, but in response to my question, the remaining blood drained from his cheeks. He slammed the latch bolt open and threw aside the door. Grabbing me by the arm, he yanked me into the dark of the stable. Havialo followed, glancing outside before pulling both halves of the door shut. I blinked as my eyes adjusted.

"Teppo. Listen to me. Evrain asked me to retrieve her. It's a favor owed. Whatever else passed between us, I mean to keep my word. He wants to bring her into the cause. I don't agree. But she is not my daughter."

A strange look crossed Teppo's face. Pity? Regret? "No," he said somberly. "She's not."

"We need supplies," Havialo said. "My visit to Numintown didn't go as well as I might have hoped."

"Then perhaps you should have left the situation alone. Let her live out her life sifting gravel and fueling the Empire's dominance."

Deeper into the stable, a horse snorted and stamped. The hoof strikes kicked up clouds of pulverized straw that danced in the bars of light. The air smelled of animals and oats.

"He told you about her, right?" Havialo said. "You know she wouldn't have been safe."

"Maybe he said something," Teppo said, hefting a pitchfork and stabbing into a stack of hay along a wall. He lifted free a forkful and stepped across the central aisle to pitch it into a manger where a mule waited, snuffing.

I'd been standing near the wall, watching the men go back and forth. Sick of them talking about me as if I weren't there, I pushed off the wall and stepped between the two men.

"How do you know my father? Please. All Havialo tells me is he wants to leave the explanation to him. But it will take weeks to get to Jaliss."

"Well, there's one thing I'll say, considering the mage all but blurted it out already," Teppo said. "We are part of a movement. A shared philosophy. Well, your father and I are. He—" He jabbed his thumb at Havialo. "—was once part of our cause. But then he betrayed your father's band, which resulted in half the men and women locked in a Jaliss prison. Which makes me want to call the protectors over to deal with a rogue geognost while I take you back to Numintown. It might be boring, but at least there you'll be safe."

"Numintown isn't safe. Not anymore," Havialo said. "And about your father's band, there are always two sides to a story. You saw the note, Savra. Evrain asked me to bring you to him, and that's what I'll do. With or without Teppo's help."

After a moment, Teppo heaved a deep sigh. "Why don't we sit? I have to finish feeding the animals. Won't take long." He gestured toward the far end of the stable where four stools surrounded a low table. A single lantern cast dim light over the area.

At the thought of sitting, my feet immediately began to ache. I didn't wait for Havialo's response before shuffling to the table. There, I slumped onto a stool and pillowed my head on my arms.

"Bread and cheese would be good if you have some," Havialo said on his way to join me. "The girl isn't yet two days from being dosed with that foul registrar's potion."

The stableman stopped his work and laid the pitchfork aside while he stared at me. "And she walked all the way here?" he asked.

Havialo shrugged. "As tough as her father, I guess."

"Indeed," Teppo said, following his words with a low whistle. "Havialo, did Evrain really send you? It's been a long time since I had word from him. I'm concerned about his Shard."

Havialo turned, showing empty palms to the stableman. "I swear to you, Teppo. Yes, he sent me. I understand why many of you disagreed with my methods for dealing with the Empire. But I never lied to you, and I'm not lying about this either. Evrain long suspected she had the talent. He knew she'd be in great danger when she came of age. And I was the best choice to collect her."

Stormshard. So the group *was* more than a rumor after all. And my father was part of it.

"So he was right about her talent..." With a sideways glance at me, Teppo picked up a metal pry rod and started working the lid off a barrel. When the wooden disk flapped up and toppled to the stable floor, he grabbed a hand-held scoop and shoveled a mound of rolled oats from the barrel.

"Wild?" he asked as he crossed the stable and leaned over a stall railing to dump the oats in a horse's bucket.

Master Havialo shook his head. "Dormant. She can be grateful for that."

I rolled my head to look at them. "The talent is another thing he says my father has to explain."

Teppo froze. "She doesn't know?"

Master Havialo sighed and sank to a seat. "If it were up to me, she'd be in the sanctuary with her mother and sister. Maybe she'd never learn what she is. But you know Evrain. Anything for the cause. I'm leaving it to him to tell her. Train her if he's determined."

Scooping another measure of grain, Teppo marched to a stall and poured it into a mule's bucket. After, he dusted his hands on his pants, hung the scoop on its hook and settled the barrel's lid into place. With a wooden mallet, he tapped the lid tight in defense against mice and weevils.

I yawned and closed my eyes.

"Wine, Havialo?" Teppo asked.

"Just food and water, thank you. We'll need provisions for the sea crossing, but for now, shelter and a chance to recover will do."

I cracked my eyes as Teppo moved past the table, heading for a small side door. "Stay here," the stableman said. "There are a few around here who wouldn't take so kindly to seeing your face. It's one of the few things I've heard Sharders agree on."

Havialo inclined his head. "Evrain used to call us the hydra. Hundreds of heads and opinions joined only by our hunger to rescue

Provs from imperial tyranny. I suppose I should be honored to be so notable that I've unified Stormshard against me."

"Don't flatter yourself, Havialo."

The door opened, a bright flare of late afternoon sun pouring into the stable. Teppo stepped outside, shading his eyes against the light. Once the latch snicked shut, Havialo jumped to his feet.

"Up! Hurry! I know you're exhausted, Savra. And I'm terribly, terribly sorry. But we have to go. Now."

My cheek had welded itself to the skin of my forearm. Dazed, I peeled it away, leaving a red mark on my arm.

"Wait. Why?" I asked, trying to summon the energy to stand. "He just went to get food."

Havialo shook his head. "I give us five minutes before the protectors are on us. I didn't want to believe it at first, but Teppo has gone snitch. He belongs to the Empire now."

I rubbed my face as I staggered to my feet and stumbled for the split door. Havialo dashed past me, saddlebags bouncing against his ribs.

"How do you know?" I asked as Havialo fumbled at the latch bolt. Once he'd slid it aside, he snatched a broom that was leaning against the wall.

"I'll explain later." He lifted the saddlebags off his shoulder and held them out. "Just until we're away from the grounds." Hefting the broom, he seemed to be testing its balance. Did he mean to use it as a makeshift fighting staff?

The saddlebags threw me off balance, but I hitched them high onto my shoulder and limped out the door. Behind me, Havialo backed out of the stable, sweeping the ground as he went. "Run," he hissed. "Get into the brush."

Watching over my shoulder as I stumbled and ran, I realized he was sweeping away our tracks. Once he'd finished clearing the area around the door, he sprinted behind me, trailing the broom's straw across the ground. When my thighs crashed into the thicket at the edge of the station's yard, he plowed up behind me, breathless.

From the other side of the stable, I heard the first shouts.

Chapter Thirteen

Kostan
Somewhere in the Icethorn Mountains

T*here's a steep track, treacherous, that empties onto the plateau a half day's walk from Jaliss. We can circle around.* I remembered Ilishian's words. He'd said the trail left after the gorge. But which gorge was that? The chasm between Steelhold and the Icethorns? The narrow valley I was currently following?

I'd walked without stop through the rest of the night and into the new day, yet I'd seen no hint of a trail leaving the road. The rutted track cut through the mountains, following the edge of a ravine and shaded by tall cliffs. Though the sky was a deep blue overhead, I still shivered, warmed only by the effort of walking.

Ravens circled overhead, reminding me of days on patrol with Vaness. Stone clattered as heat on the upper faces of the cliffs warmed the rock and sent pebbles spilling from the heights. At least there hadn't been any earthquakes, though I'd crossed many rubble fields where a shake had sent stone raining down on the road.

My hand fell on the pendant hanging beneath my shirt. The Heart of the Empire, worn by rulers of Atal for centuries. As I trudged on, I wondered if I could have made a better decision. Waited for help, maybe. My stomach was an empty pit, my tongue a strip of leather. Even if I found this trail, Jaliss lay two days distant. A difficult prospect without food or water. But I'd never survive in the high mountains alone. My only hope lay in returning to the capital. Once there, I could find a place to hide. Head to the Graybranch Inn and ask for word of Azar.

Ahead, a large boulder hulked along the edge of the track. Sunlight kissed the top of the stone, promising the first warmth since Ilishian had pulled me from my bed in the middle of the night. When I reached the massive stone, I laid a hand on the rough granite. The rock's grain was as harsh as the mountains and the Atal Empire they bounded.

I didn't want to go on. Even if I survived this, what next? Should I hide for two years then present myself at the palace and demand to Ascend?

Maybe I should just walk away. In Anisel Province, a handful of ports traded with lands beyond the Maelstrom. It would be a long journey to reach the sea, but maybe it was the best choice. Why should I be loyal to Atal? If the Empire fell, could I really be blamed?

I scoffed at the thought. As if I could ever outrun my guilt if I left. Besides, I wasn't sure I could make it to Anisel alive, much less earn myself passage away from this land.

Around the backside of the boulder, a series of rounded ledges provided a ladder to reach the top. I sighed in relief as the golden rays of the sun warmed my face. Yawning, I stretched out on the boulder's top. Granite crystals pressed into my back as I watched the ravens soar.

I closed my eyes, and for the first time since my audience with Emperor Tovmeil, fell asleep within moments.

My feet were wooden blocks, numb and clumsy. My brand was a burning hot poker shoved from my heel to my knee.

After sleeping atop the boulder, I'd woken with a savage thirst. In the Icethorns, the streams only ran during certain seasons, such as when Deepwinter gave way to Warmingtide. It was nearing Chilltide now. Stream beds held nothing but dry, silt-crusted stones.

I'd found Ilishian's trail, at least. Or so I'd thought—the track had split off the main road not long after the narrow ravine widened out into a rubble-strewn vale. But that had been hours ago. Since turning off the road, I'd staggered through a frigid night and under a merciless sun. Another night had fallen, and I felt no closer to finding my way clear of the mountains.

In the recesses of my mind, I knew my thirst was a severe problem. During the early morning hours, I'd stumbled from shadow to shadow, licking hoarfrost from the undersides of rocks. A few, gnarled pines dipped roots deep into the mountains' skin. I'd picked a handful of needles and chewed them, hoping to bring moisture to my mouth. Now, as I staggered through the pressing darkness, awaiting moonrise if only for the illusion of warmth in the silvery rays, I no longer had the energy to lower myself and search for moisture with my tongue.

Besides, the strange heat spreading up my leg from my brand could only mean one thing. My wound was infected.

If I didn't find somewhere to clean it, someone to cut the bandages free and apply salve to the marks, it wouldn't be thirst that killed me. Two generations past, a Scion had died when his servant failed—perhaps by mistake, maybe on purpose—to properly tend his wound.

Somewhere on the slopes above, rocks clattered down. Most likely, they'd been loosed by an animal. Hunting cats stalked these crags. I couldn't bring myself to worry about that. Instead, I took another shaky step, waiting for my death or the moon or whatever lay ahead.

Vaness's voice flowed, ghostly, from the stones and the air, echoing off cliffs and into my ears. "What are you doing out here?" she asked.

She appeared beside me, falling into step with my slow progress. As I turned to look at her, dizziness sent my head spinning. I stumbled, stomping down hard on my infected foot, and cried out.

"That's not like you," she said with a laugh. "That's not the boy who fought on after the swordmaster had sliced to the bone on your weapon hand."

"Why are *you* here?" I asked. My eyes felt hot, drawing vivid colors and details from the moonlit landscape. Beside me, Vaness scampered over jumbled stone. She wasn't here... I knew that. I was delirious. But she felt real.

"Plus, you fled Steelhold at the first hint of a threat. That's not your style either."

"My style... You think you know me so well, but you're wrong." I glared at her, my head stuffed with wool. "What you said on patrol... it's not true."

"Am I? Or are you deceiving yourself? I've spent every day with you since we were pulled from our mother's breasts. Perhaps your self-image is just a fantasy." She bounded onto a boulder and smiled down at me, so sure of herself.

"I'm not wrong. When I Ascend, things will be different."

"When you Ascend..." She sneered. "You won't even survive the night."

"Says the girl who's not here."

"Look up ahead," she said. "What are you going to do now?"

I dragged my eyes from the trail before my feet and scanned further along the valley I was descending. In perhaps two hundred paces, the moonlight shone on a cairn, a stack of rocks the marked the point where the trail split into three.

I shook my head in despair, causing a sudden headache to beat against the inside of my skull. My toe caught, and I fell, rocks cutting into my hands. Blood welled from the gashes, but there was no pain. Only the stabbing agony in my heel and the throbbing in my head registered. I tried to rise and fell backward, landing hard on my tailbone. Vaness laughed.

"Here," she said, extending a hand.

I looked up at her face, the pert nose and twinkling eyes. A hint of mischief plucked at her features. I shook my head. I would not embarrass myself by reaching for a hallucination. With a groan, I climbed to my feet and staggered on. Time moved in fits and starts, and when I blinked, I was standing before the cairn.

"Which way?" I asked, mostly to myself.

"Originally, you left the main track by a right turn. That means the plateau is down and to your right. Then again, the trail to the right might be nothing but a sidetrack. You have no way to know."

As Vaness spoke, she dug her toe into the trail and kicked a rock free.

"Did Azar get you out of Steelhold?" I asked while I stared at the cairn. "She promised."

But she hadn't, really. Ilishian had extracted no vow from her. And besides, after the catastrophe at the Chasm Gate, escape would have been very difficult. I wanted to ask Vaness whether she still lived, but I couldn't make the words come.

"Go right, Kostan," she urged. "You can't know it's the proper way. But the longer you stand here, the sooner your infection will reach your heart and mind."

She had a good point. I took a shaky breath and stepped onto the rightmost fork in the trail. Swaying on my feet, I continued on. A few hundred paces along the path, I started to shiver and sweat at the same time.

Vaness was gone. I didn't know where. I could scarcely lift my head; most of the time my chin rested on my chest. The trail seemed fainter now, but maybe that was my imagination. The route was ascending, winding between outcroppings toward a high ridge. In the recesses of my mind, I knew these were bad signs. Jaliss was downhill. But I'd come too far to turn around. I'd collapse before I made it back to the fork. And so I pushed on.

Through what seemed like cotton shoved into my ears, I heard more rocks clattering. Distantly, I wondered if the stories about bandits were true. Right now, even thieves would be a welcome sight. I might convince them I'd have value if ransomed. Or maybe they'd just end this quickly.

My shin hit a rock. I threw my arms forward to stop my fall, but not fast enough. My elbow cracked the ground, followed by my head.

More sounds filled the narrow valley, pebbles clicking as they fell, gravel crunching. Footsteps.

I couldn't bring myself to care. It had to be thieves; a hunting cat would never raise such a racket. When a shadow blocked the moon, I rolled my head, skull loose on my spine. As I squinted up, I wished I'd thought to bring something worth stealing. I didn't like the thought of the bandits being angry at me for failing them.

I blinked, attempting to see the thief's face.

When I spotted the insignia of an imperial protector on the man's uniform, I simply closed my eyes again. They'd found me. At least I might learn what had happened to Vaness before they killed me.

Chapter Fourteen

Savra
Crashing through brush outside Dukket Waystation

Ahundred paces into the brush, Havialo shoved the broom beneath a thick tangle of undergrowth. He snatched the saddlebags off my shoulder and pushed into the lead. Back at the waystation, men and women shouted. Branches broke as someone crashed into the thicket, but the sound was distant.

"Bunch of fools! Split up and search the area. There are only two of them!" Moments later, grunts tumbled through the brush as multiple people shoved into the foliage.

With a nervous glance over his shoulder, Havialo pressed aside a branch thick with leaves and plunged deeper into the brush. I followed, as quietly as I could, but exhaustion made my limbs clumsy. Each step was getting harder.

Ahead, the mage crouched even lower, peering into a tunnel in the brush that looked like animals had made it. Dropping onto hands and knees, he crawled inside, mage's robes snagging and leaving strings behind. As I half-crouched, half-fell to follow, I plucked off the most obvious strands and balled them in my hands.

Behind, much closer than before, a branch crackled then snapped. I dove into the tunnel, twigs clawing at my scalp and snagging strands of hair still trapped in my braid. I shook my head to free them. Dizziness rose from the leaf-strewn ground, grabbing hold and sending me sprawling.

My arms were like limp seaweed while I tried to push my chest off the ground. I blinked specks of crushed leaves from my eyes, squinted down the passage, held in a cough brought on by the musty earth.

A few body lengths onward, the tunnel split. I couldn't see Havialo but I wormed forward on elbows and knees. Somewhere deeper into the brush, a twig snapped.

Or was that behind me?

I froze, cocking my ear.

Another crack of a stick, creak of leather, and a steely grip closed around my ankle. I screamed as my attacker hauled me free of the tunnel, dragging my shirt up to my ribs and exposing my belly to the twigs and pebbles that covered the ground. As my shoulders cleared the tunnel, I rolled. My captor wore a protector's uniform. His face was set in determination, and even his jaw muscles bulged.

On instinct, I kicked. A lucky shot—my foot slammed into the man's groin. The air left his lungs in a gust as he bent double, releasing my ankle. I scrambled away, diving into the brush. Sturdy branches resisted me every step. Havialo must have been following faint trails—either animal or human—this whole time. Unable to push my way through, I flopped on top of the brush and tried to squirm forward as if I were swimming.

No use.

Within moments, the hand latched me again. The protector snared the other ankle, too, and dragged me back to the path. I grabbed at handfuls of brush which bent then broke. Handfuls of twigs clutched in my fists, I slammed down to the ground, elbows first.

I groaned as the man twisted my legs, forcing me to roll over. Transferring his grip so he pinned both ankles with one hand, he dropped his shin over my waist, shoving the breath from my body. The man weighed as much as a mule. I thrashed, punching with my fistfuls of sticks, but his meaty arm and shoulder were all I could reach.

"Here!" he yelled toward the waystation.

I beat on his shoulder again, for all the good it would do. His disinterested expression sent a shock of cold through me. I'd heard stories of the protectors' cruelty. People who fled the law had their legs broken and splinted to heal crookedly. Or sometimes the protectors removed a foot. Thieves had fingers chopped off and their cheeks branded. And so on.

"I didn't do anything," I protested between shallow breaths.

The protector didn't acknowledge my words. His expression remained unchanged. Had he been born emotionless, or had his training stripped his humanity?

Shifting more weight onto the leg pinning me down, he yanked a wooden whistle from his pocket. The shrill tone sent ice down my spine. From the direction of the waystation, more branches snapped and rustled. Where was Havialo? Teppo's words flashed to mind. The mage had betrayed my father, leading to the capture of Father's men. For all his talk of keeping a vow, Havialo was a traitor. He'd probably abandoned me here.

At once, rage roared through me. I bucked my hips, dug my heels into the ground, twisted and aimed a punch at the man's neck. If I could just get the right angle...

His fist came from nowhere. Sparks exploded across my vision as my jaw lurched to the side, joint cracking. My ears rang.

"Wait!" someone yelled. Maybe Teppo, maybe someone else. "We need the girl!"

The man ignored the order. I blinked away tears as he cocked his arm for another punch. His knuckles were white where the blood had been squeezed from the skin.

Somehow, I knew that if he got another blow in, I was done. Either dead when the hit snapped my neck or wishing I was when the protectors punished me for resisting.

A familiar tugging pulled at my senses, a plucking originating deep in my spirit. *No*, I thought. *Not now.* The protector's weight shifted as he moved to put force behind his punch. Feebly, I tried to move my head aside, but I'd already lost control to my aura-sight. A colorless veil fell across the scene, dimming my vision.

The man's spirit hovered above me, moving in languid time to the slow descent of his fist. I shoved the vision away, desperate to regain control. But I only fell farther into the sight's grasp.

It often happened like this. During times of stress, or when the nightmares threw me from sleep and into the arms of my mother. When I woke her with my screams, Mother's aura flared red with fear, slashed with steel-gray concern.

But I sensed nothing from the man attacking me. His spirit was dull. Lifeless. An empty, sucking void. My very soul shied away from the pit in the center of his body.

And somehow, I shoved.

Recoiling from the experience, as if my mind had been bowed like a twig that bent and bent until it finally snapped, I slammed back into my body.

The protector's gaze had gone vacant. His fist thudded against the ground a finger's width from my ear. Elbow buckling, he toppled sideways.

As I pushed against his legs, now pinning me with the sheer weight of his bulk, brush crackled nearby. A head and shoulders appeared above the leaves, backlit by the setting sun. Another protector—I recognized the uniform by the hard lines of the leather spaulders covering his shoulders. I squirmed away, finally slipping my legs from beneath my unconscious captor.

As I wiggled backward to the far side of the clearing, the wind started. The gentle breeze swelled within heartbeats to a full gale battering the thicket. The protector who'd just arrived squinted against the sudden storm, holding his forearm before his eyes to defend against the razor edges of leaves slicing through the air. He shuffled forward, blinded by the fierce wind.

A whirlwind, the gale only increased, seizing sticks and twigs and small pebbles and hurling them at the advancing protector. The wind howled in my ears, but I soon realized it didn't touch the ground. The protector's feet were just a few paces away, untouched by so much as a breeze. But in the tempest above, I could no longer see the man's waist, much less his head and shoulders.

Havialo stuck his head out of the animals' tunnel. As the mage motioned for me to follow, a loud crack penetrated the howl, and a fist-sized stone dropped to the ground. The protector toppled into the clear air beneath the tornado, an area of his skull caved from the blow.

My gorge rising, I crawled after Havialo. Branches tore at me while the howling wind fell behind us. We didn't stop moving until we reached the base of the Crease.

Chapter Fifteen

Kostan
Lost in fever dreams

"I don't sense loyalty to the Empire. But he's conflicted... I can't really understand it."

A man grunted in response to the woman's words. "What do you think, Falla?"

She responded, voice sharp enough to cut. "Too risky. I don't know why we haven't sliced his throat. But I'll respect your choice."

I tried to open my eyes, but the lids were glued together. A small moan rose from deep in my throat. Something—fingers?—brushed my forehead. I drifted.

When I woke again, I was shivering, sweat coating my body and soaking the blanket beneath me. My swollen tongue filled my mouth, choking me. A fistful of fabric was clutched in my hand. I tried to unclench my fingers to release it, but a full-body shudder wracked me. The sole of my branded foot brushed the bed, and I screamed when the agony filled my leg bones all the way to my hip.

"Shh," another woman said. She draped a cool rag over my forehead. "Drink this. It will ease the pain." She set the rim of something frigid against my lip.

I wanted to obey because my leg was liquid pain, waves of searing hurt sloshing up and down the limb. But I couldn't make my lips respond. I tried to open my eyes then realized my lids were already cracked. Nothing but black surrounded me.

A strangled cry leaked past my swollen tongue.

Cool fingertips pinched my chin and pulled my mouth open. Stinging liquid poured across my tongue and down my throat. I gagged then swallowed.

A gray mist seeped across my blind vision then fell over my body like numbing fog.

Chapter Sixteen

Savra
Traversing the Cosmal Crease

I'd heard stories about the Crease, but none had captured the reality. Travelers claimed it had grown more impassable by the year as Cosmal Province had tilted farther and farther into the sea. But to me, the tales had been mildly interesting at best. Now I understood. Where the peninsula met the mainland, the narrow neck of land was folded and cleft, the earth's bones exposed to the moonlight. Deep fractures plunged through raw dirt while cliffs the height of twenty people soared in menacing overhangs.

"I thought there was a road," I said, eying the shattered landscape. From one of the high cliffs, a sheet of stone cleaved free and crashed down, raising a cloud of dust that hid the impact zone. The falling rocks reminded me of the stone which had crushed the protector's skull. I forced away the thought—nothing I could do would change what had happened.

"There are two. The Imperial Crossing and this."

"This?" I squinted.

"The smugglers' track. The location shifts as the Crease changes and when the protectors get too near to finding the route. You can see the first cairn if you look closely."

I squinted and then nodded when I spotted the small stack of stones marking the entrance. "Who built it?"

"There are black marketeers and Sharders who specialize in finding a safe path between Cosmal and the mainland. Good for us, because I'm sure you've heard the tales of travelers swallowed by crevasses."

"What about Teppo?" I asked. "If he used to be with Stormshard, wouldn't he follow us here?"

"I mentioned using the sea crossing for a reason. His ignorance about what had recently passed between your father and me had already made me suspicious—his excuse for leaving the stable only confirmed his guilt. He had no reason to leave the stable to fetch food. There was a full cabinet right beside us."

"What's the sea crossing? I thought the only way off the peninsula was through the Crease."

"Most people believe the same. But there's a channel off the eastern coast where the Maelstrom is *almost* predictable. It only works if you're traveling north, and even then, you're more likely to be shipwrecked than survive."

I grimaced at the idea of people desperate enough to take such a chance, but then realized I was in a similar predicament. "You think Teppo believed you?"

"He never was very bright—he's probably waiting for us on the beach now. In any case, once someone goes snitch, the smugglers sniff them out within weeks. He won't know the location of this track."

"I hope you're right," I said.

"Being forced to choose between poor options is never a good situation, but I wouldn't suggest this if I didn't believe we'd be safe. I couldn't bear to fail my vow to your father."

Swallowing, I nodded.

At sunrise, we set foot in the Crease. We'd finished the last swallows from our waterskin when I'd awakened, and my throat already burned with thirst. But Havialo assured me we'd find water on the other side.

Above, the sky was an even, steely gray. The overcast made my nerves prick, bringing back memories of ear-splitting cracks, flashes of lightning, the screams of horses. The trail passed beneath towering cliffs of crumbling dirt and across slopes so steep that every footfall released an avalanche of dirt. Sometimes, we stepped over cracks in the earth so deep their bottoms were lost in blackness.

Cairns marked the trail about every hundred paces, scraps of colorful fabric stuffed between the stones.

"So much power waiting here," Havialo muttered as he paused at one of the rock stacks.

"I've never met a geognost," I said.

He glanced over his shoulder. "As you can see, we're rather ordinary, despite our reputation."

Was he just being modest? Earth magic—at least as far as we'd been taught—was by far the most powerful force in the Empire. I'd hardly have called that ordinary.

"You can harness the power of an earthquake, right? Does that mean you can tell whether the ground under the trail is stable?"

He cast me an ironic smile. "I'm not sure you really want to know what's going on under this particular trail. Especially since it's our only way forward. But as to harnessing a quake, it's more like I can sense where I might nudge the land to breaking—which in the Crease is just about anywhere. If I did, I could gather the sudden release of energy and use it. But I can't predict how one shift might cascade across the area. For all I know, a wave of earth might bury Dukket Waystation."

"But sometimes you can predict what will happen. Even redirect the energy, right?"

He nodded. "When I... stopped the registrar, I focused the energy of the storm. All the lightning that might have struck came down at once. But it was a close thing. I barely kept control."

Stepping around a switchback, he began ascending the slope in the opposite direction. Dirt loosed from his steps poured into the tops of my shoes. I hurried out from beneath him. After another couple of turns, we reached something of a plateau. Atop this flat stretch of land, a few plants had dared to take root. Footprints crossed the block of earth to the far side where another cairn marked the descent from the tabletop of land.

I hurried forward to walk next to him. "Will you tell me about Stormshard? If my father is part of it, I should be prepared."

His steps faltered. "A description of Stormshard depends on who you ask. I'd tell you it's a failed resistance movement. A flame that guttered out for lack of air and fuel. Your father disagrees, I'm sure."

"Teppo made it sound like you were kicked out."

He walked faster, almost as if he could outrun my question. "That's open to interpretation."

"He said you betrayed my father."

Havialo froze in his tracks and whirled to face me. "Teppo had no right to accuse. Your father is like a brother to me."

The anger on his face stole the words from my mouth. Swallowing, I nodded. Still, I noticed he hadn't explained the situation, either.

"If you feel Stormshard is misguided, do you think I should be worried about reuniting with my father? And how does that fit in with making me a scribe."

He pressed his lips together. "Your father's heart is in the right place. Everyone associated with his... movement cares deeply about the cause. And he cares for you. Because of our history, I am committed to bringing you to him. As for receiving your scribe's writ, it's not part of my promise. But what if you don't care to live a Sharder's outlaw life? Consider it a gift from me if you like. A legitimate Function and the chance at a normal life. If you want it, anyway."

I wasn't sure what to say. He was giving me a choice between following my father's path and starting a new life far from my family and everyone I'd known. I wouldn't be ready to choose until I saw my father again. But I appreciated what the mage was offering.

After another hundred paces, we reached the edge of the plateau and stopped. I stared over the brink, spine tingling at the drop and the trail's next segment.

From the edge, a rope bridge stretched across a hundred paces of open air. Wooden pegs had been pounded into the earth to secure the bridge on both sides.

"Care to go first?" Havialo asked.

"Didn't you have some promise you wanted to keep? Something about delivering me to my father safely?"

He rolled his eyes before setting foot on the bridge. "Never trust a flame-haired woman," he muttered.

We descended from the Cosmal Crease, haggard and parched, hours after we'd started across the smuggler's track. A small stream trickled along the base of the slope. I fell to my knees and drank so fast my head ached from the cold.

"You'll need to stay here," the geognost said after he'd taken his own drink. "It may be tomorrow before I'm back."

I looked around. The ground at the base of the Crease was broken and boulder-strewn, providing plenty of shelter. Scattered pine trees broke the rubble, the forest growing thicker toward the north. We'd be traveling that direction, I assumed, though my knowledge of mainland geography was sparse.

"Where are you going?"

"Supplies. Scorlit Post sits near the exit of the Imperial Crossing. An hour's walk from here."

A boulder stood between me and the forest. As I stepped around it, a strange roar seemed to rise from the trees.

"Do you hear that?" I asked.

"The famous winds of Guralan Province. You'll have the pleasure soon."

I grimaced and slipped back into the shadow of the boulder, blocking most of the sound. "I'm tired, but I can walk another hour. I'll go with you so you won't have to come all the way back for me."

He'd been reorganizing the saddlebag, digging out the waterskin. When I spoke, he froze for a moment.

"It's safer for you here," he said, a slight edge to his voice. He didn't meet my eyes as he straightened.

"I don't have a weapon. Not to mention, I've never been in a fight."

His cheek twitched. "My mind is made up, Savra." With his chin, he gestured to an overhanging cliff of dirt at the edge of the Crease. "The shadows there will conceal you. Keep the cloaks as blankets in case you get cold."

"But—"

A rumble from deep in the earth cut me off. My gaze snapped to Havialo. Had he caused that?

His eyes were cold as he tossed me the cloaks. "The journey ahead is no safer than what we've traveled so far. You must learn to trust my judgment because if we argue at the wrong moment, it could mean our lives."

I winced at his hard words. I hadn't meant to cause trouble. Then again, the sudden edge in his tone bothered me. And the trembling earth. Had it been a threat or my imagination? My thoughts returned to Teppo and the things he'd said about Havialo and my father. Maybe I should be more cautious with my trust.

After a tense silence, I glanced at the cliff at the Crease's base and nodded. "What should I do if you don't come back?"

"I'll be back," he said. "And Savra... I'm sorry. I have no desire to command you or anyone. But my vow matters more than my desires."

With that, he trudged off along the lower flank of the Crease.

Havialo returned in the night. I heard the snorting of horses, the rustle of fabric. A fur-lined cloak fell over the top of me, brushing against my cheek. Still troubled about how he'd acted, I pretended to be asleep.

In the morning, the sight of all the supplies he'd obtained calmed some of my worries. There was clean traveler's clothing, soft bread, dried meats and wax-shelled cheeses—even new boots. I picked up the pair that looked sized to my feet, drawing my brows together at the fur cuffs.

"Will it really be cold enough for these?"

"As I mentioned, you'll soon have the pleasure of experiencing the winds of Guralan. The movement of air has something to do with the Maelstrom—I feel the same taint in the gale as I do in the Cosmali sea tides. In any case, I suspect you'll appreciate a bit of armor against the wind's bite." He paused a moment, fixing me with a pensive expression. "And I got you something else. An apology for my short temper—the difficult conditions of the last days wore on me, despite my best intents."

I hadn't yet seen a full smile from Havialo, but the corners of his mouth twitched as he held out a packet of candied fruit.

"Thank you," I said, accepting the gift. "Now, are you ready to expose me to this ferocious wind?"

I shouldn't have spoken so flippantly. Within the hour, we were making our miserable way through the forests of Guralan, where the frigid wind sliced through clothing and numbed straight to the bone. The widely spaced trees bent away from the weather, their bark dry and peeling on the windward side, branches gathering on the leeward exposure as if to shelter from the gale.

The few travelers we passed wore furs similar to ours. By the looks on their faces, they didn't like the weather here any more than I did.

The sturdy little gelding Havialo had found for me—trying to cheer my spirits, I'd named my mount Breeze—plodded behind Havialo's feisty mare. I kept my cloak pulled tight against the stiff wind. The icy air bit my cheeks and nose, and my toes alternately ached and went numb.

"Is it always this awful?" I asked.

"I've heard of Guralan blacksmiths hanging anvils from chains and judging the strength of the wind by how far it pushes the weight aside. Does that answer your question?"

I shivered. "But if it's this cold here, and Jaliss is even higher into the mountains, how does anyone stand it? I can't imagine living here, much less somewhere worse."

"Well, first off, a Guralaner would tell you that without the wind, they'd be afraid of waking up soft and whining like an Aniselan or Cosmali. The age-old rivalry of the provinces."

"What about the Atal? What do the Guralaners think of them?"

"Same as you, I imagine. They likely avoid thinking about the imperialists whenever they can."

A low hanging bough cut across the trail, needles shivering in the wind. The mage laid over his saddle's pommel to pass beneath it, the branch scratching over his cloak. When it dropped off the hump of his back and slapped his mare's hindquarters, she shied and snorted. Havialo whispered to her, working a rein with each hand, until she calmed.

Once the mare stood quietly, I squeezed my heels against Breeze to urge him forward, ducking beneath the bough. "I've been wondering..." I said. "When Teppo said that Numintown fuels the Empire's dominance, what did he mean? The Maelstrom-metals?"

With a click of his tongue, the mage turned his mount for the trail ahead. "That's right," he said over his shoulder.

I understood why the Empire would need metal for everything from swords to door hinges, but the amounts we delivered weren't enough to provide kitchen knives for every household in Jaliss, much less longswords for the protectors. The metalogists used rings of various metals to channel power, but Cosmal couldn't be their only source.

"It doesn't make sense," I said. "The quotas are too small to make a difference."

He pulled up so we could ride side by side. When I drew even with him, he collected the reins in his far hand and extended the other toward me, wiggling his middle finger with the silver ring. It was the band he'd taken off in disgust after failing to persuade the registrar to list me as a scribe.

"I know metalogists wear rings to channel their power," I said. "You have a rank in argent magic, right? And you use the silver ring to signify your advancement. But there must be silver mines in the Icethorns."

"I'm sure there are."

"Then I don't think I understand," I said, though an idea glimmered in my thoughts.

"That's because the Empire guards the secret carefully. Without the rings—and bracelets, anklets, armbands—there are no metalogists. The magic comes from the metals, not the other way around."

"But not all metals..." I said, understanding. Silver, gold, and black iron were the only required metals in our quotas. Any other nuggets filled in the remainder. Argent, aurum, and ferro mages needed those specific metals for their power, but their magic must have required materials deposited by Maelstrom currents. It was obvious now that I saw it, but the Empire's metalogists were something an ordinary Prov avoided thinking about if at all possible. Plus, by allowing us to fill parts of our quotas with metals like copper and pyrite, the Empire had a screen for their true desire.

He dropped his hand to his thigh as he nodded. "Only the Maelstrom-metals grant the power. And without the metalogists backing it, the throne would never stand. Without the work done by Numintown and the other Cosmali settlements, the Atal Empire wouldn't exist. Or if it did, it would look quite different." His lips twitched in amusement when he glanced at me. "Perhaps we'd see how the geognosts would govern."

Swaying in the saddle, I considered the new information. Numintown had worked the sluices for decades without understanding we were empowering our oppressors. Most likely, snitches reported those who figured it out. If Cosmali Provs caught on to the power they held, another uprising was sure to follow.

But Havialo had claimed that we needed to deliver the ledger to Jaliss to protect Numintown from rationing. Or worse, dissolution. Would the Empire actually starve or kill the people who produced the resource that fueled its power? I glanced sideways at the geognost. I didn't see why he would lie to me. He'd given me my father's letter. I'd seen the smoke rising from town.

But something didn't make sense.

The rutted road curved around a rock outcropping that cut the wind, a welcome respite from the biting cold. I flexed my fingers inside my mittens to work the stiffness from them.

"You never answered," I said. "Is it even colder in Jaliss?"

He smirked. "I don't think anywhere is colder than Guralan Province on a windy day. Not even the most exposed mountain top."

I sighed in relief. "Then I can't wait until we leave this place."

"To tell the truth, if it weren't for the Maelstrom-taint in the wind, I'd consider settling here *because* of the gale. An earth mage practicing with such a ready and predictable source of energy could do quite well for himself. As it stands, I'd rather pull my teeth out than live here."

"So that's all you need? Wind or an earthquake or a rockslide, and you can work your magic?"

"Yes and no. Every time a geognost connects with and changes the natural world, it saps the mage's internal reserves, which require time and rest to rebuild. I must choose carefully when I wish to use my power because I don't want to be fatigued if a real emergency arises."

As the far edge of the outcropping approached, the trees beyond shaking in a fresh gust, even the horses slowed. Before leaving the shelter of the hill, Havialo reined up. "Just an hour or so until dusk. Better to set camp where there's shelter than risk that." He gestured to the howling wind ahead.

After the horses were brushed and watered and a small fire crackled, flames leaping when the wind swirled into our sheltered spot, I gathered my knees to my chest. A small rumble trembled through the earth below, reminding me of home.

"I didn't know Guralan had shakes," I said.

Havialo shrugged. "Been much worse everywhere, lately. On the mainland we don't usually have the small shakes you see on the peninsula. Instead, we have quakes violent enough to open chasms in the land. It wasn't so bad in years past because they only happened every ten or twenty years. But now, it's once every few months. When we get onto the Atal Plateau, we'll ride around rifts so deep you can't see the bottom. Ruins lives when the herding towns get split down the middle. Especially since the Empire won't help them recover."

He dragged over a satchel of rations and started rummaging. Leaning back, I looked at the darkening sky. A few thin clouds scudded overhead.

"Hey, Havialo, why do you owe my father so much?" I asked as he handed me a crust of bread and hunk of cheese. "And even with your differences, why leave Stormshard entirely? It seems you hate the Empire as much as anyone."

Havialo's spine stiffened, and he stabbed the fire with his poker stick. "My disagreements with Stormshard's base philosophy were irreconcilable. They believe everyone has the right to choose their actions. But the problem is, without a strong hierarchy, no single person makes final decisions. Your father believes it's the best way to work, but when there are differing opinions..." He shrugged. "It breaks down."

"And the promise? You've come a long way to bring me to my father. You said it was a favor owed, but it's a big undertaking. Not that I don't appreciate it."

A grim expression settled on his face, the firelight etching lines at the corners of his mouth. "It's a long story. Difficult to talk about if I'm honest. Perhaps in daylight, I'll find it easier."

My bedroll was rolled and tied to my saddle where it leaned against the outcrop near the hobbled mounts. I shivered as I left the fire's warmth to fetch it. As I smoothed the wrinkles from the bedroll and climbed inside, laying my cloak over the top, I watched the geognost at the edge of my vision.

"Do you really think the Empire will cut Numintown off if we don't bring the ledger?" I asked.

He tensed again. I pretended not to notice, fussing with the lay of my covers.

"It's just... what if we fail? I can't stand the thought of Numintowners dying because of me."

Immediately, the mage's body relaxed.

"Not a problem," he said. "We'll be striding into the Hall of Registry within weeks. The clerks won't even look twice at you before handing over your writ and filing the ledger."

"All right," I said. "I'll just have to trust you, then."

I rolled away from the firelight, pulling my covers high. The problem was, I wasn't sure I did trust him after all.

Chapter Seventeen

Evrain
A courier post, Atalan Plateau

Outside the small courier post, Evrain reined up and climbed down from the saddle. His knees cracked when his boots hit the packed earth, reminding him of the passage of time.

Seven long years since he'd seen his family, but that would soon change.

Evrain's horse snuffled at his hair. With a crooked smile, Evrain dug into his pocket and produced a broken piece of carrot.

"Spoiled beast," Evrain said, ruffling his mount's forelock as he held his palm flat for the horse to take the carrot.

The midday sun baked the Atalan Plateau, raising heat shimmers from the gently waving grasses. Before stepping onto the porch of the courier post, Evrain paused and scanned the wide vista. As he did, a cool breeze swirled down from the Icethorn Mountains behind the post. A reminder that even in Highsummer a stray snowstorm could escape the mountains' crest, sending flakes dancing over the plateau.

But not today. And anyway, what was he doing pondering the weather when he should be checking for news of his loved ones? Delaying. That's what he was doing. Because so far, he'd heard nothing, and he feared that the silence meant that when he did receive news it would not be good.

The floorboards creaked as he stepped into the darkened interior of the post. At the counter, the courier, a young woman with Sharder sympathies looked up. Recognizing him, she pressed her lips and shook her head.

Evrain sighed. He told himself there could be hundreds of reasons for the delay. The problem was, so many of those reasons meant trouble.

Chapter Eighteen

Kostan
A cavern, unknown location

"The empire did not wish its Scions to survive beyond
Steelhold's walls. I wonder if you knew that before you ran."

The voice penetrated my mind like a steel blade, cutting into my
awareness. My eyes flew open.

Torchlight flickered off the stone walls of a cavern. A woman sat
by my cot, her dark hair pulled back from a lined face and secured
by half a dozen braids. Straw from the mattress beneath me poked
into my back. I shifted and felt the rough-spun bedsheet against my
bare skin. I'd been stripped of everything but my small clothes. My
hand darted to my chest where I felt the Heart of the Empire still
resting against my breastbone.

"Where am I?" My words fell from limp lips.

"We haven't decided whether you deserve that information. And
as for your necklace, you shouldn't have worried. We aren't petty
thieves."

I blinked a few times. On the far side of the cave, a natural
opening had been enlarged to serve as a door. A curtain hung across
the gap. Above the rod supporting the top edge, I spotted firelight
dancing on the ceiling of another, larger chamber beyond.

"How long?"

The woman stretched as she stood then moved to a trunk against
the opposite wall. She had a lithe figure, strong despite her
advancing years. A bow was slung across her back. "Four days. You
nearly died on the first night."

"Bandits. You were following me. I remember..."

But that wasn't right. Just before I'd lost consciousness, I'd seen the uniform of an imperial protector.

The trunk's lid hit the wall with a muffled thump when the woman tossed it back. She pulled out a tunic with a heavy weave, then squinted as her eyes traveled the length of my body. After a moment, she cocked her head and held up a pair of trousers as if judging them against my size. With a shrug, she bundled the garments into her arms and returned to my bedside.

"Your clothing was beyond repair. Not that a seamstress could have tolerated the smell anyway."

I rolled onto my side. My arms shook as I pushed up to sit. When I reached for the trousers, the realization struck me. They'd removed my pants and boots, exposing my golden cuff and bandage. Bandits or not, I doubted anyone living in the Empire was ignorant about the custom of branding the Scions.

The words she'd used to wake me came back into my thoughts. What had she said exactly? Something about the Empire keeping its Scions confined to Steelhold...

She knew what I was, yet hadn't killed me. Why? I had no illusions regarding the Provincials' opinions of the Empire.

Of course, maybe they'd decided it would be too merciful to kill me in my sleep.

A wry smile twisted her lips, deepening the line at the corner of her mouth. "You're wondering why you're still alive. Simple. Your condition and location cast doubt on your loyalty to Emperor Tovmeil. Given the information we could gather from an actual Scion, it would be foolish to eliminate you too quickly. Besides, the infection in your foot seemed likely to do the job for us." A look of concern crossed her face. "It still might. We managed to calm the wound, but it doesn't appear to be a simple matter to clear the affliction. Our healer seems to think there's magic involved. Is there something you do to care for your brand?"

"Servants clean the wound and change the bandages."

"That's all?"

"There's a salve."

She pressed her lips together. "Perhaps enchanted to both keep the wound from healing—and to keep infection lingering but never thriving. If we could just clear the sickness from the flesh, the burn might finally close. As it is, the edges try to knit only to burst open from the swelling. Our healer has sent word to Jaliss, a discreet inquiry."

Shakily, I shook the wrinkles from the trousers and stuffed them under the sheet to pull them over my legs. When the fabric brushed the bottom of my foot, darts of pain shot up my leg. Compared to what I remembered from the last days, though, I scarcely noticed it.

After sliding the pants over my hips, I considered what she'd said. I'd been taught the brand would only heal on my twenty-first birthday. Until then, the lines in my flesh needed to remain open to reflect the uncertainty of Ascension. Could this have been a lie? Did some type of magic hold our cuts open to keep us dependent on the Empire? If that was true, did our brands and scars even change to reflect worthiness, or had the Emperor's symbol been burned into one of us from the beginning?

"Of course," the woman said, handing over the tunic, "even if we learned how to cure you, many among our group think we'd be idiots to do it. They think we're fools to have spared you. To them, you're a poisoned dart sent from the Hold to dig into our tender flesh."

The Hold. At once, the events of my flight from Steelhold roared into my thoughts. Emperor Tovmeil had been murdered. The other Scions too, most likely. I pulled the tunic over my head, pushed the covers aside and swung my legs over the side of the bed.

"I need to get to Jaliss," I said.

"Apparently, you don't quite understand your situation. By my guess, you can scarcely stand, much less walk. Disregarding that, we certainly wouldn't be so stupid as to let you go."

Chapter Nineteen

Savra
Somewhere in windswept Guralan Province

The outcropping hid the eastern horizon, but I knew dawn was coming when gray lines emerged from the deep shadows in the forest across the road. Curled in his bedroll opposite the smoldering campfire, Havialo was snoring.

Careful not to rustle the blankets, I sat up and folded the top half of my bedroll aside. In the predawn hours, the wind had finally slowed. The resulting quiet was eerie, as if the forest were listening. Waiting. I shivered as the night air cooled my skin.

I pushed up to a crouch, wincing when one of my knees cracked. Across the fire, the geognost grumbled before rolling to put his back to me, a fold of his cloak pulled over his head. I remained motionless until his snoring resumed.

Time to find answers.

After our conversation the previous night, I'd lain awake for hours, thoughts racing. The longer I'd thought about it, the worse my fears became. The mage was hiding information from me, more than his refusal to explain my talent and what it meant. For all I knew, he'd arranged to set that fire. My mother and sister might be in danger or worse. Every time I thought of it, my chest tightened. How could I have run off without asking more questions? Sure, he'd given me the letter from my father—when I squeezed my elbow to my body, I still felt the paper crinkling against my ribs.

But it wasn't enough.

Maybe my father *was* waiting for me somewhere near the capital. But he'd abandoned us years ago, while my mother had stayed to raise us. If I owed allegiance somewhere, it was to her and Avill. I needed to learn where they were being taken. Perhaps more pressing, I needed to learn if this sanctuary even existed.

Gingerly, I stepped off my bedroll and slipped into my boots. In the dark, I couldn't spot the saddles, but I knew where to find them. The saddlebags were near. I might find nothing by looking through Havialo's things, but my search for answers had to start somewhere.

I grimaced and froze when one of the horses snorted at my approach. After a moment, I relaxed when another snore rose from the vicinity of the fire.

"Shh," I whispered, stroking Breeze's neck. His fur was sleek, well-groomed. If nothing else, Havialo had a good sense for horses.

Havialo's saddlebags were twice as heavy as mine. The water, no doubt. Yesterday, he'd kept all the water skins in his saddlebags. I wondered now if that had been a tactic to keep me dependent on him. The shadows against the outcrop were too deep. I moved the bags carefully, cringing when the weight made me stumble, pebbles crunching beneath my feet.

With fingers stiffening in the cold, I worked at the buckles closing the bags. My thumb slipped, the nail catching on a rib of leather and bending back. I stifled a curse and sucked on the injured nail before inhaling and continuing.

Wincing at every rustle and creak of leather, I groped through the contents of Havialo's saddlebags. The water skins were on top, forcing me to lift each sloshing package and set it carefully aside. My hand landed on the scroll holder, and I pulled it out.

"Some people call metalogists by another word: spiritists."

I jumped at the sound of his voice, whirled and caught my heel on a rock. I stumbled backward over the saddlebags and scraped my shoulder blade against the sharp crystals of the stone outcrop.

Havialo stood before me, cloak askew over his shoulders, hair mussed with sleep.

"Wha—what? Spiritists?"

"It's an old term. From before the Atal Kingdom conquered the Provinces."

Awkwardly, I pushed off from the outcrop to stand upright. The water skins were strewn around my feet, and the saddlebag yawned. I couldn't pretend I hadn't been going through his things, but he

106

hadn't mentioned it yet, so I saw no reason to bring it up. "Why are you telling me this?"

The sky had paled enough that the whites of his eyes shone in the darkness. He glanced down at the open saddlebags.

"I'm telling you this because anyone who mistakes a metalogist for a spiritist is wrong." He lifted his left hand, the one with the silver band around his middle fingers. "Metalogists are the corrupted tools of the Maelstrom. Even me, with my single rank. There is nothing innate about their ability, and as a result, they have no innate ability to sense its wrongness. Its cost."

A squirrel chattered in the trees overhead. Flakes from a pinecone began to rain down. Where was the mage going with this conversation?

Havialo dropped his arm to his side. "I'm telling you this because I know you doubt my story. You may even be thinking of leaving. I won't stop you. You are not my captive. Even if it means I never pay my debt to your father, I refuse to keep you against your will. That's the very behavior I hated in the Empire. The reason I joined Stormshard all those years ago."

"I still don't understand what this has to do with the metalogists."

"Actually, I was speaking of spiritists."

Right, he had said that. Anyone that mistakes the two is wrong. "So what's a spiritist, if not a metal mage?"

"You are, Savra. That's what I've tried to keep from you. The thing that metalogists pretend to be with their false abilities and tainted powers. It was born into you. Your father wanted to be the one to explain, but I suppose he'll have to forgive me." He shrugged in apology.

"All right, I'm a spiritist. Thank you for explaining. But it's just a word that tells me nothing about my supposed talent. What does a spiritist do?"

"It's early and it's cold. Shall we warm the fire and see about breakfast?"

I still clutched the scroll holder. Beside me, Breeze stamped his front foot as if impatient.

"I'll explain everything," Havialo said. "I swear. Afterward, if you still don't trust me, I'll try to find someone else to escort you north.

I'll give you directions and coin plus the information you'll need to contact your father. Will you give me this chance, though?"

The coals and their promise of fire certainly sounded better than standing here in the cold. After a moment, I nodded.

"If there's anything the Atalan people can claim as their own, it's earth magic," Havialo said as he stirred the coals.

The sun was rising and with it the wind. As the embers flared, sparks leaped from the circle of stones and swirled into the dawn sky.

"The magic runs through merchant and elite-class families," he continued. "If any magic should have powered the Empire's rise, it's geognosty. Instead, beginning centuries ago, earth mages were forbidden to marry. Our lines withered, though quite a few sire offspring or give birth in secret."

"But why?" I blinked as a speck of dust landed in my eye. Storms, but I hated this wind.

"One of the early kings had an advisor, a mystic and alchemist who discovered the power in Maelstrom-blessed black iron. Others soon took up the study. While granting power, the Maelstrom's energy infected its wielders with a desire for dominance. Soon enough, the Hall of Mages was built, with the geognosts all but forgotten."

"And this is related to my talent?"

He nodded as he laid another branch on the fire. "Stormshard scholars suspect that your talent has always been present in the provinces—Cosmal and Anisel in particular. The old word, spiritism, almost certainly comes from the nature of your abilities. But somehow, knowledge of spiritism disappeared from the land around the same time the metalogists rose in Atal. It reemerged in Anisel a century ago. You probably recognize the event."

I nodded. A hundred years ago, the Anisel Uprising struck the hardest blows the Empire had felt since its founding, leading to— among other things—the Decree of Functions. Fewer freedoms for the Provs meant fewer opportunities to rise up.

"I'm no expert in spiritism. I can't teach you or even explain much about your talent. So if that is enough reason for you to ride away, I cannot offer anything to stop you. But I can tell you stories from the Uprising."

"Such as?"

"Sometimes, it seemed the Aniselans knew the Empire's plans days before the vanguard arrived. Other times, the Emperor's forces fled battles in absolute terror, only to find themselves unable to remember what had frightened them."

"All because of the spiritists?"

"That's my theory, and judging by the actions of the Emperor at the time, he drew the same conclusion. But despite the early victories, eventually Anisel Province lost, and the Empire took steps to make sure it wouldn't be threatened again."

"The Decree of Functions?" I couldn't think of anything else that had happened around that time.

His lip twitched as he absently poked at the coals again. "The Decree is more than it seems. You don't remember everything about your time with the registrar, but be sure she wasn't simply checking her ledger and signing your parchment."

"She asked strange questions. I remember that much."

"Designed to root out many undesirable traits from among the population, but one threat is worse than the rest put together." He looked at me pointedly.

"So the Emperor is afraid of our talent. That's why I'm in danger."

"You would have been taken away and executed had I not intervened." Havialo grimaced as a fresh gust of wind howled overhead.

"Just based on my answers?"

"It happens all the time. There was another girl from a town near yours, Agartown I believe? They usually tell the parents that the young person has received a Function in a different province."

A dart of cold struck my heart. The girl that Avill had spoken of. She'd been given the courier Function—according to her writ, anyway—and her family hadn't seen her since.

"We can't really be that threatening, not against the protectors and metalogists and everything else the Empire controls."

Havialo shrugged. "The rumor I heard was the Emperor at the time of the Uprising had a vision. If Atal were ever to fall, it would be at the hands of a spiritist. I doubt that's true—as far as I'm aware, no one knows the future. But it was clear that the spiritists were a threat. In the Emperor's eyes, that threat was too great."

As the sun cleared the treetops, its rays stabbed my eyes. I raised my arm to shade them.

"Sometimes, Stormshard rescues a suspected spiritist before the registrars come. A few times, I helped with that kind of mission. But the stakes were too great, the consequences too severe when we failed. I forced myself to attend the executions, a punishment for my mistakes, I suppose. When that became too much, I stopped aiding the rescues."

"I can't imagine how hard the deaths must have been to watch. But you were saving lives, too. Why not just stop attending the executions?"

His lips pressed together. "Because I'd missed my own daughter's hanging."

I opened my mouth to speak, but no words came. For a moment, the howl of the wind was the only sound.

"Was she a spiritist too?" I asked.

Havialo's eyes were downcast. He tossed a pebble into the coals as he shook his head. "Just as earth magic runs in Atalan families, spiritists seem to come only from the provinces. Cartilla was like me. Atal elite-class. But you see, where the Empire can be severe when punishing Prov law-breakers, the tolerance for dissent among its treasured elites is simply non-existent. We are supposed to be paragons of imperial virtue. So when word of my involvement with Stormshard reached Emperor Tovmeil, he did the one thing that would hurt me above all else. My daughter was twelve. I heard she was terrified on the gallows. They'd pulled her from her classes at the academy in the Heights district. No explanation. Just took her straight to her death."

"I'm so sorry."

"I could never acknowledge Cartilla openly due to the proscription against geognosts having children. If only I'd just walked away when her mother admitted the pregnancy. Hid myself in the monastery or a faraway land."

When he turned his face to me, his eyes blazed with such a deep hatred it took everything I had not to flinch. I knew his emotion was not directed at me, but rather at the Empire and what it had done to him. After a moment, his rage seemed to drain away. "Thank you. I miss her every day. After her death, I lost all desire to fight with Stormshard. The Empire had gutted my soul. So when Teppo spoke about the Sharders deciding to oust me... I tried to be angry. But really, all I care about is fulfilling this vow to your father so I can leave the Atal Empire for good."

"If you don't mind me asking, how did the Empire find out about you and Stormshard."

A strange ferocity entered his eyes as his lip curled. "Betrayed from within, I assume. Many Sharders never accepted me due to my Atal ancestry. I imagine they passed along the information. As I mentioned, I never agreed with your father over allowing such independence of action among the Sharders." He snapped his gaze to mine. "Don't mistake me. I don't blame Evrain. It's..."

"It's what?"

With a sigh, he threw the stick he'd used to stir the coals into the flames. "It doesn't matter. I no longer care about the Sharders' squabbles. No use unearthing old arguments. So... have I convinced you?"

I considered the question. His story was tragic. But had he put my qualms to rest?

"There's one thing that's been bothering me," I said.

He glanced at me. "I think I might know. Until yesterday, you had no idea how crucial Numintown's work was to the Empire. It makes it difficult to understand how the Emperor could even consider sanctions against the town. But the answer is simple. The Emperor fears losing the Maelstrom-blessed metals. It would be a terrible blow. But there is one thing the Emperor fears more: spiritist power."

Chapter Twenty

With a crutch shoved under an arm—the moment I'd tried to put weight on my branded foot, I'd realized how helpless I truly was—I hobbled across the main cavern behind the woman's graceful stride. She stopped before an unshaven man who sat on a three-legged stool pulling the long blade of a dagger over a whetstone. The steel hissed with every stroke.

At the edges of the room, men and women lounged in piles of furs working oil into leather, stitching ragged hems, and tending to weapons. Suspended over a central cookfire, stew bubbled in a pot and filled the air with a rich, meaty aroma. Behind the man with the dagger, the cavern's wide mouth opened onto a talus-strewn slope painted in the golden light of midmorning sun.

"I see you roused him, Falla," the man—the leader?—said as he inspected me. Behind him, I noticed a stack of folded clothing, the wool dyed the deep red worn by elite protectors. The crest of the order was stitched on a shoulder. That, at least, explained what I'd seen before blacking out. Only Steelhold's clothmakers knew the recipe for the blood-red dye, which meant the uniform must have come from a genuine protector. None of the Empire's elite soldiers would give up their clothing while alive—they'd be hanged for returning without it. My estimation of these bandits rose considerably.

The woman, Falla, stepped aside to let me approach the leader. The man nodded and stood to his full height. Since around the age of fifteen, I'd rarely met someone tall enough that I looked up to meet their eyes. I clenched my fists to push away the faint stirrings of intimidation.

"What's your name?" the man asked.

"Kostan."

"You'd be forced to take a new one if you were to Ascend, correct? Something marking a historical lineage?"

I nodded. "But since I never expected to be chosen, I haven't put much thought into it."

He fixed me with an appraising look. "Any reason you expected to fail?"

"I suppose that depends on whether you interpret escaping the throne as a failure. But to answer your question, I never wanted to Ascend. That alone should have removed me from contention."

"Because your brand would recognize your inner weakness. Yet my healer says the mark on your foot appears to have no magical properties—aside from a festering sickness that is confounding her ability to purge it. In fact, she suggested the pattern of the eventual scar was set the moment the brand touched your flesh."

I shrugged, attempting to keep my face even. "Is your healer a mage? The aurums are responsible for the branding."

The corner of his mouth twitched. A smile? "Suffice it to say, she has an affinity for understanding the workings of magic as well as the humours of the body."

My strong leg had begun to ache. I leaned harder on the crutch.

"Sit," the man said after a moment, gesturing to a heap of cured animal pelts. "Your body has endured much. Taxing your strength will only make the infection flare."

I tried not to let my relief show as I hobbled to the pile.

"My name is Evrain," the man said as he lowered his muscular bulk back to the small stool. Once again, he took up the blade and whetstone, drawing the glinting edge across the stone. He smirked. "And it's unlikely to change no matter where fortune takes me."

"I recognize that uniform." My gaze flicked to the protector's clothing. "It was you that found me."

He nodded. "I did."

"Why did you help me?"

"At first, because you would have died otherwise. I didn't know who—what—you were. As for the uniform, part of living as we do is keeping our immediate surroundings secure. I find that patrolling in the guise of a protector discourages bandits from encroaching on our refuge."

I blinked. "Wait. I thought…"

Falla snorted. "Of course you did. You may have been groomed to rule an empire, but you're surprisingly naive."

Realization struck me. I sat straight and kept my eyes on Evrain. "You're Stormshard." It made sense. The guard at the Chasm Gate had spoken of groups from the renegade movement operating in the mountains.

Setting aside the whetstone and blade, Evrain laid his hands on his knees and stared at me. "There's no point in hiding it from you. I lead our mountain division, insofar as Stormshard fighters follow any one person. We aren't like your Empire. Stormshard is more a philosophy than an army, each of us guided by our morals and hearts."

"I was taught that you operate in isolated groups to keep the Empire from discovering the plans of one band by capturing and interrogating a member of another."

Evrain's expression turned appraising. "That's also true. Many choices have multiple reasons for their making."

At the edges of the room, the other renegades had remained busy while we spoke. But as our conversation took on a sparring tone, they started casting extra glances in our direction.

"But enough of that," Evrain said. "Obviously, you had reason to leave Steelhold. I'd like to know more about that."

I stared at the man across the paces separating us. Did he not know about the Emperor's death? This group was isolated—quite possibly, word hadn't reached this far. Or perhaps the Hold was keeping the situation quiet.

As to his request for information, I needed to think this through. Given my disgust at the Empire's policies, I probably had a lot in common with him and Stormshard. But ultimately, I was an imperial Scion. Falla had already said they'd kept me alive to get information. If I told them too much now, they might decide I'd outlived my usefulness.

"I was led to believe my life was in danger," I said.

"I'd hoped you'd rejected the Empire's practices and had decided to begin a new life," Evrain said with a smirk. "We could use someone like you on our side."

I gritted my teeth. That was exactly the answer I should have given. Too late now. "I didn't say I believe in the Empire's methods. Just that the threat to my life was the immediate reason for fleeing."

Evrain tipped the point of his dagger in my direction, a gesture I took as a token of respect. "A fair point. So you might have rejected them eventually, it's just that these would-be assassins forced you to decide."

I shrugged. "I guess that's one way to put it."

He huffed an amused laugh and returned to sharpening the blade. "It must have been a hasty departure. Judging by your state when we found you, you had little time to prepare. Your leg was hot and swollen to your hip."

"I was woken in the night. As for the infection in my foot, I was taught that it would only heal on the day of Ascension. You claim otherwise."

"I'm sure you were taught many things of dubious value," Evrain said.

"Perhaps."

"What do you know about the threat to your life?" he asked, glance darting to Falla. I could almost read his thoughts. He hadn't known about a move against Steelhold, and this concerned him.

"Less than I'd like," I said.

"It wasn't Stormshard. You should know that. We don't kill young people without cause."

"What about other Stormshard bands?"

He shook his head. "Unfortunately, none of the other Shards—that's how we refer to our groups—have that kind of... competence. My group might manage it, but the odds of success would be low. So, Kostan, you know less than you'd like, but that doesn't mean you're entirely ignorant, right?"

I hesitated, unaccustomed to being addressed without a title. In Steelhold, I'd either been referred to as "sire" or "Scion."

After a moment's consideration, I said, "Emperor Tovmeil told me there were many threats to Atal. He feared for the throne and the Ascension."

"I see." The man stared at me long enough that I felt uncomfortable. Along with the ache in my leg, fatigue was creeping back into my thoughts, fuzzing them around the edges.

"Well, Falla?" he asked. "How do you judge his words?"

The woman detached from the wall and stalked forward before turning. Her eyes narrowed as she considered me. "He's telling the truth, as far as I can sense." She cocked her head. "But he holds back. And there are complications I don't yet understand."

My eyes widened as I searched her hands for silver rings, but she wore none. Like the argent mages, her words suggested she was reading my thoughts. Immediately, I rubbed my thumb against my ring finger, seeking a connection to raise my spirit armor.

The ring was gone.

Falla smirked and reached into her pocket, pulling out the band I'd worn for seven years. She held it up and peered at me through it. "Trust me. You don't want to wear this. Better to have no magic than power tainted by the Maelstrom."

I'd never been good at argent magic, but I still felt vulnerable seeing my ring in her hand. I swallowed, not trusting myself to speak without giving away my nervousness.

She turned the corner of her mouth up in an amused smile. "So, we keep him around for a bit longer, Evrain?"

The Stormshard leader gave me one last considering look. "For now. But I don't like hearing of such... upheaval in Steelhold happening without our knowledge."

I dropped my eyes to the floor before my expression gave me away. If only he knew...

Evrain climbed to his feet and peered out the hideout's entrance as if he could find answers in the open wilderness beyond. After a moment, he turned.

"Ride out. Kei is leading a small hunting group near the Vale Fork. Tell her to head for Jaliss with utmost haste. We need to know what this means."

With a nod, Falla stalked to a rack beside the cave's exit and lifted a long cloak from a hook. She snatched a rucksack from the floor and stuffed a sloshing water skin and an oiled-leather packet of food inside. Ducking out the entrance, she swung the pack onto a shoulder.

Moments later, hooves clattered across scree, fading to a low drumming when her mount gained an earthen trail.

Evrain stared down at me, expression grim. "Consider the next days your chance to prove yourself useful, starting with clearing up those complications which have perplexed my spiritist and healer. When Kei returns with information from Jaliss, I'll make a decision on your fate."

Chapter Twenty-One

Savra
Bellows, Guralan Province

Travelers crossing guralan Province rarely spoke as we passed them, no doubt because one had to shout over the wind to be heard. As Havialo and I plodded along the northward road, we exchanged nods with the few parties we encountered. An acknowledgment of our shared misery more than anything.

In the evenings, we took shelter where we could find it. Even when a dense stand of trees or another stone outcrop provided enough windbreak that we could speak easily, we were too worn out from the constant gale. We hadn't spoken again about my investigation of his saddlebags or the things he'd told me that had persuaded me to trust him. When I looked at Havialo, I now recognized the deep sorrow that gripped his soul. Nothing he could do would bring his daughter back. Sometimes I wondered if her loss gave him more reason to keep his vow to my father.

Sometimes I wondered if he secretly resented me for living where she'd lost her life at the gallows.

Though we passed sidetracks leading to logging camps in Guralan's forests, we rode through only one major settlement between the Crease and the border of Old Atal.

Bellows. When Havialo first told me the name, I laughed, thinking it a joke. But apparently, the Guralaners had a sense of pride about their wind.

As we approached the town, smaller roads joined our track, bringing foot-bound travelers and wagons piled high with timber, hostlers with mule trains in tow. I smelled Bellows before we could see the outermost shacks and the cloud of windblown dust pluming off downwind. It was the scent of humanity, wood fires and manure, fresh straw and baking bread. I'd never visited a settlement other than Numintown and the neighboring villages. That it could remind me of home so easily surprised me.

The differences were just as shocking.

The first building we passed was a blacksmith's. Inside the smithy's darkened interior, the blacksmith pounded hot steel with arms the size of a mule's neck. His eyes glinted in the glow of his furnace. Beside him, a young man worked the bellows. Tacked to the outside of the building were the official writs declaring their metalworking Function. In Numintown, no one bothered to display their writs. Everyone in town was a sluicer. We'd never been questioned about it. I supposed in areas where Functions were more diverse, there was more concern about impostors trying to step outside their assignments.

Farther along, massive windmills rose over the buildings, slicing the air with blades that moaned as they wheeled overhead. I stared in awe at the whirling machines and wondered if one had ever broken free of the mounting.

Deeper into the town, my shoulders crept up so high it felt like they touched my ears. It was overwhelming, all the noise and bustle. Stalls offered skewers of meat for travelers and locals alike. Hooves raised pulverized dust and manure from the street, and I wrapped a scarf around my nose to keep from coughing. A few people clapped and sang on a street corner.

When we finally passed the central crossroads, my nerves started to ease until I thought forward to the weeks ahead. If I felt overwhelmed by the activity in this provincial Guralan settlement, how would I react to life in the capital? By my understanding, Jaliss was many times larger. Inconceivably larger, maybe.

Havialo must have noticed my anxiousness. He nudged his mount closer to mine. "You'll get used to it," he said. "People are the same whether you're in Numintown or some foreign land beyond the Maelstrom."

I cast him a faint smile. I hoped he was right.

At the traveler's bazaar on the far side of town, Havialo bought me a thicker cloak and a leather mask I could wear over my eyes when I wanted a break from the wind. Narrow slits allowed me to see while the mask cut most of the wind. With a scarf wrapped over my nose and mouth, the gale was almost bearable. I didn't even care that I looked like a masked bandit.

Or worse, maybe I looked like the legendary creature used to frighten Numintown children. A Hollow One was supposed to come wearing layer upon layer of clothing. But if a curious child were to pull at the garments, take them off one by one, they'd find nothing inside. Just a great emptiness filling the clothing.

The thought brought a wave of homesickness.

In all, we rode across Guralan Province for eighteen miserable days. Except for the single night we stayed in a sturdy stone inn, I hadn't felt warm since the Crease.

Despite my nervousness, it was a relief to reach the edge of the province. This close to Old Atal, the road was now called the Emperor's Way. In many places, cobblestones armored the track against the constant abuse of horses and wagons. And where it bent and started up the first switchback on the massive slope separating Guralan from the high, Atalan plateau, stone blocks the size of small houses had been embedded in the road's surface. Letters had been carved into the blocks by long-ago masons.

Let all glory in the Empire's rise.

Let all bow before the Emperor's will.

As Havialo's horse clopped over the stones, her tail lifted and the remains of last night's grazing dropped onto the lettering. I wondered whether earth magic gave him the power to speak with beasts, or whether she simply sensed her master's thoughts. Or maybe even the horses understood the evil of the Atal Empire.

My gelding plodded forward without depositing his own opinion on the stones.

According to Havialo, this part of the journey was called Hundred Turn Hill. The road cut across scree and around outcrops, through low brush that clung to the perilous slope. Halfway up the hundred or so switchbacks, a guesthouse perched on a platform cut from the hill. I eyed it nervously when Havialo reined up. Having grown up where the earth shifted and slipped and buildings sometimes toppled onto sleeping families, I wasn't eager to try my luck at this unlikely nest.

The mage noticed my reaction and cast me a wry grin. "Just inquiring about the conditions ahead. The upper turns have a reputation for getting treacherous after rainy weather or a cold snap."

"What exactly do you mean by treacherous?"

"I don't want to alarm you. Perhaps it's best we just wait and see," he said with a wink.

After passing the guesthouse, I stopped trying to count the turns. At a switchback perhaps halfway between the inn and the rim, Havialo rounded the bend and reined up, closing his eyes in concentration.

"What is it?" I asked. I couldn't see anything different about the road ahead.

He shook his head, brow wrinkling. "There is a tremendous locus of stored energy a few hundred paces on," he said as he opened his eyes. He stood in his stirrups, leaning first one way and then the other as he examined the track.

"What does that mean?" I looked to the side, down the dizzying slope to Guralan's undulating sea of trees. From this height, each pine looked like a little floret of broccoli, the greenery gnawed from one side by the hungry wind. An image of tumbling down the mountainside to land, broken, amongst half-eaten vegetables made me shudder.

"Something is ready to give. A boulder about to unbalance. Or maybe a section of cliff is waiting to sheer off the main face. Could happen today or in ten years. In any case, I wouldn't want to be in its path when it happens."

"That's what you meant by treacherous?"

He shrugged. "Among other things." Clucking to his mount, he urged her to the edge of the road and peered down at the switchbacks we'd already traversed. While he examined the slope below, he muttered to himself.

"So what do we do? Find another way?" At the inside edge of the wider area where the road turned back on itself, a small tuft of grass had taken root amongst the piles of loose stone. Drawn by the promise of a quick snack, Breeze sidestepped toward it. I didn't bother to scold him. I didn't mind edging away from the drop, myself.

As he bent to tear a mouthful from the hummock, the rumble started. A low growl, as if the earth were clearing its throat.

"Down. Dismount!" Havialo yelled.

I vaulted from the saddle. Moments later, the first rocks clattered onto the road ahead. The ground began to shudder.

"Don't leave this platform," the geognost called. He'd left the saddle and now ran toward me, leading his mare. Without another word, he handed off the reins and dashed for the road ahead.

Rocks pelted either side of the man as he ran forward. I screamed when a stone the size of a watermelon bounced off the talus above and whizzed for his head.

The missile stopped and hung in the air for an instant before dropping straight to the road at Havialo's side.

The geognost ran on.

After maybe a hundred paces, Havialo stopped in the center of the track. He dropped to his knees, laid hands on the earth.

Rockslides loosed by the shake slid down the hill like rivulets in a pile of sugar. Liquid. Deadly. On the switchbacks below, travelers and caravans panicked. Men and women ran up, down, anywhere to escape the rivers of death tumbling toward them. Mules leaped from the track and tumbled for the forest below. A wagon teetered and fell over the brink, dragging the team of oxen down behind it.

As if time abruptly froze, the shaking stopped.

Fins of hard stone, serrated like knives, erupted from the slope. The rockslides slammed into the new outcrops and channeled aside, streaming away from the scattered parties. With a roar and clatter, the slides fell harmlessly onto the forests below, flattening trees. On the road ahead, Havialo arched his back and threw his hands forward.

Moments later, an area of the bench half a league away gave way, letting go in a slide so massive the dust cloud billowed to touch the clouds.

Havialo collapsed.

All was quiet.

After a few minutes, I led the wild-eyed horses up the road to him.

"As I mentioned," he said, eyes rolling back. "It can get treacherous up here. Mind leading for a while?" His head rolled on his neck. "Seems I'm going to black out."

"Savra," Havialo said, "before I found you, what were your feelings on the Empire?"

Two days beyond Hundred Turn Hill, the geognost rode easily in his saddle. The vast grassland of the Atalan Plateau spread all around, broken only by herders' huts and cracks in the earth that Havialo claimed had only recently opened.

The sun pressed warmly on my shoulders and thighs. Lazy flies buzzed around the horses' ears and eyes, causing the mounts to snort and toss their heads. Every few paces, Breeze snatched a bite from the tall grass hanging over the road. I pretended not to notice his snacking.

"Hmm," I said. "No one in Numintown likes the quotas or the Decree of Functions. But most people would choose to be sluicers anyway."

"And you?"

"I used to daydream about doing something different. I don't know if I would have, though."

The mage nodded. "What about the protectors? What do you think of them?"

I shrugged. "They pretty much leave us alone." I shuddered at the memory of the protector's fist slamming my jaw. The joint still ached when I ate. "Thankfully," I added.

"But you would prefer to have the freedom to choose your destiny, right?"

"Yeah, sure. No one likes the Empire dictating our fates." I turned to look at him. "Are you asking whether I plan to join my father's cause? Become a Sharder? That's what he wants, right?"

A melancholy smile touched his lips. "The thing is, Savra, Stormshard has no idea what to do with you. How to use you. Your father's cause is doomed. He abandoned his family and has led dozens of men and women to imprisonment or death for a fight he'll never win."

I hadn't seen my father in seven years. I couldn't explain the rush of anger when the mage criticized him. But it was there all the same, heating my cheeks and making me dig my fingernails into my palms. "I'm sure he'd disagree."

Havialo inclined his head in agreement. "That he would." He turned away from me, staring at the distant horizon. Somewhere out there, not yet visible, the great snowy crest of the Icethorn Mountains rose up from the plateau. The capital, Jaliss, sheltered beneath their slopes. I tried to imagine what they'd look like, but couldn't quite form a picture, having never seen true mountains before.

"You said father would find a way to train me in spiritism."

The mage's jaw worked as he considered his words. "Yes, I think he will. But I'd like to propose a different arrangement. Please hear me out."

Something in his tone made my belly squirm. "Okay..." I said.

"I've already told you why I left Stormshard. I couldn't handle the failures. Not just the executions I forced myself to witness, but the bumbling maneuvers, too. The movement has so much desire and so little direction. I'd even call them incompetent."

Once again I bristled for the father I lost long ago. Taking a deep breath, I held my tongue. I'd promised to hear him out. And maybe his criticism was valid.

"I gave you the wrong impression about something. When I left Stormshard, I didn't retire from the fight. I simply moved on to a more effective position."

My spine stiffened. After the information he'd withheld before, I shouldn't have been surprised.

"I apologize—again—for not being forthright," he said. "My secrecy is a bad habit, ingrained after years of working against the Empire. The stakes are so high."

I pressed my lips together. I'd promised myself I'd let him finish before passing judgment. "So there's another renegade group?"

He tapped a finger on his saddle's pommel. "I suppose you could call it that. It's a different type of game than Stormshard plays. Higher stakes. The players are... quite powerful. And the objectives rather ambitious. We could use your talents."

"I'm not even sure I want to fight against the Empire. Maybe a scribe's life will suit me. Or maybe I'll convince my father to send me to the sanctuary with Avill and Mother."

A flash of something—anger?—crossed his face. "I'll admit it astounds me that a Prov could grow up under the Emperor's oppression and not want to fight back. Especially when handed the opportunity. After all, my daughter..."

He blinked a few times, then looked away. "Sorry," he said after a moment, voice rough. "Sometimes my emotions gain too much hold."

I took a deep breath. "I understand. But I'm not ready to decide anything. A couple weeks ago, I didn't even know if my father was still alive. I haven't had a chance to talk to him and understand why he made the choices he did."

Havialo kept his gaze fixed on the road ahead. "We'll continue as planned, then. Please forget I mentioned anything."

Unsure what to do, I leaned forward and waved the flies away from Breeze's ears. The silence seemed to flow from the mage, an uncomfortable quiet that gave the sense I'd done something wrong. I just wasn't sure what.

Chapter Twenty-Two

Kostan
Stormshard refuge, Icethorn Mountains

"You'll ride with Falla and me today," Evrain said, handing over a bowl of porridge.

Having escaped my deathbed—for now—I'd lost my bunk in the privacy of the cavern's back room. Evrain had retaken that honor, leaving me to find an open bed in the main chamber. The best spots had already been claimed; overnight, I'd curled up on a set of grain sacks, using a canvas tarp as a blanket. It had been years since I'd slept with anyone else in the room, and I'd expected a restless night. But I scarcely remembered laying my head down.

"Ride where?" I asked, rubbing the sleep from my face. "I'm not much of a horseman." I'd had a few lessons in the narrow alleys of Steelhold, but the confines hadn't given the animals room to work through their gaits. In the months before Ascension, the Scions customarily rode out the Chasm Gate to begin a tour of the Empire. Because the Emperor lived a sequestered life, it was the only time he or she would see the land. But for now, my skills were limited to mounting without falling off and basic signaling of the horse.

"It doesn't matter so much where as why," Evrain said. "I'd like a chance to talk to you where you might feel less... watched." He gestured with his chin toward the other members of Stormshard who looked over maps, repaired equipment, ate breakfast—and stared at me. "But if you're curious, I make a circuit of the surrounding area every few days. An effective operation begins with a secure home territory."

My foot throbbed—Falla had cleaned the wound before I slept, but the ache was a reminder of the sickness that festered inside my flesh. I grimaced before yawning. "I don't think I'm recovered enough for a long ride."

Evrain glanced over my shoulder where Falla huddled with another woman. "Falla would have me whipped if I caused you to relapse after she and the healer worked so hard to beat the infection back. We won't be gone more than an hour or two."

The porridge was thickening as it cooled. Evrain glanced at it. "Best you eat quickly. It's rather disgusting otherwise."

As I spooned the glop into my mouth, I watched the mountain insects, lit by the morning sun, buzz outside the entrance. They looked like swirling sparks.

Yesterday, I'd still been dazed by my illness. But I needed to have my wits about me now. As forthright as these Stormsharders might seem, they were sworn enemies of the Empire. In many ways, I represented everything they hated, so I needed to choose my words carefully. Evrain and Falla had allowed me time to prove myself, but the others might be waiting for an opportunity to put a dagger through me.

Even if I convinced the Sharders I was a friend—and perhaps I still needed to answer that question for myself—I couldn't remain here. I needed to get to the Graybranch Inn and learn what had happened to Azar and Vaness. With Ilishian dead, Azar was the only person I could trust. If I still wished to Ascend and save the Empire from destruction, I needed her help.

But how would I get to Jaliss? Aside from my immediate problem of convincing Evrain to spare my life, I couldn't walk. Surely, the Sharders wouldn't deliver me—and my knowledge of their mountain hideout—to Jaliss. And if I tried to go alone, the infection would finish me before I reached the capital.

The moment I set my bowl aside, Evrain strolled over with a boot for my unbranded foot and a fur mitt to slip over the other. He knelt on the floor and scooted over a small trunk filled with healing supplies.

When I realized the Stormshard leader intended to care for my foot like a common servant, my cheeks went hot. He must have expected the reaction because he looked up and smirked.

"I mentioned earlier that Stormshard's philosophy doesn't include a hierarchy. No member is more important than another, though the opinion of experienced Sharders often carries more weight. The people here listen to me because I've been with Stormshard for many years. Even if we never unseat the Emperor, not one of us lives under another person's edicts. In that way, we've already won."

My eyes flicked to the private back room where he'd slept sheltered from the snores of his fellow Sharders. He noticed the direction of my gaze and nodded. "It's my turn is all. Before we dragged you in, Falla had the bed."

I couldn't help feeling shame over my helplessness as he unwound the bandage from my foot. The inner layers of the bandage stuck to my skin where seeping blood and pus had infiltrated the linen overnight. I dug my fingers into the grain sacks beneath me to keep from grunting in pain as Evrain pulled them away.

He inspected the wound, fingers gentle as he probed the edges. His face was set in something that might have been anger. On my behalf? Or was he thinking of the centuries-long line of emperors who had dominated the land, relying on cruelty and fear to keep their subjects loyal?

"From the moment I understood my destiny, I've wished I'd been born under other stars. On a different night to a different family." I wasn't sure where the words came from, only that I had suddenly felt it important that he knew.

Evrain placed a wad of cotton over the mouth of a flask, tipping it up to soak the white fluff. He dabbed the edges of the brand, working from the outside in and looking up to gauge my reaction. I inhaled at the sting but nodded to let him know I could tolerate it.

"I'm not surprised," he said as he lowered my heel to the ground. "I can't imagine the burden. Outside the walls of Steelhold, we know little of the lives of the Scions. I'm sure it's not a free existence. Nonetheless, your upbringing must have given you some desire to take the throne."

He asked the question casually, as if simply wishing to keep the conversation flowing. But I heard the restrained tension in his voice. By bringing me here, Stormshard had invited the enemy into their home. He must be desperate to know my true feelings.

It seemed unreal, but I trusted that Emperor Tovmeil had believed the vision given by his bracer. Considering the danger to everyone in the Empire, wasn't I obligated to try to Ascend? I could try to explain my whole story to him, but I feared I'd reveal too much. My thoughts whirled.

"You're conflicted," Evrain said. "Falla told me as much." He once again lifted my foot, rotating my leg so that more light from the door fell on the wound. "Storms, but I wish we knew what they did to keep the infection at bay. At best, it seems we can keep you from dying. But we certainly can't help you walk again."

"There was a rosewater bath and some type of salve," I said, hoping to avoid the subject of my feelings for the Empire.

The corner of his mouth turned up at my avoidance of the topic. "Well, perhaps we'll try the rosewater and hope we get good information in the city."

As he started wrapping a fresh bandage around my foot, a woman burst through the door. Evrain jumped to his feet, gesturing at one of the other Sharders, a wiry man, to finish the bandage.

"Evrain," the woman said, nodding her head in greeting. She was breathing hard, and sweat pasted delicate hairs to her neck. She wore simple linen garb dyed in dark blues and grays and had a satchel's strap crossing her chest one way, a longbow and quiver strap crossing the other. Her eyes were as wide as the sky and easily as beautiful.

"Good morning, Kei. Every time I think you'll never best your time to ride to Jaliss and back, you quickly prove me wrong."

The flash of pride on her face was replaced by a somber expression. "But I rarely return with such troubling news. The Chasm Span has collapsed, Evrain. It's gone."

Around the cavern, Sharders abandoned their tasks and turned to listen. The man working on my foot dropped the roll of bandage onto the floor and strolled over.

"How?" Evrain asked.

Kei shrugged. "No one seems to know. It's been six days. Steelhold is locked down. No one in or out, and there have been no statements from the throne."

Evrain's gaze shot to me. I suspected he was adding up the days of my convalescence with the time it took to walk from the Chasm

Gate to the place they'd found me. After a moment, he fixed a glare on the man who'd abandoned work on my bandage. Startled by the reminder, the man hurried back to my side.

"Bind it securely," Evrain said before turning his attention to the new arrival. "Kei, I appreciate the time you've just spent on horseback and regret asking you to mount up again so soon. But please take a few minutes rest and prepare for a patrol. We have much to discuss with the Scion."

The sun was warm on my back and shoulders, but I couldn't enjoy the feeling. I wasn't a very good rider to begin with, and with just one foot in the stirrup, the other leg loosely bound to the girth strap to keep me from falling off, I sat lopsidedly in the saddle. Every step the horse made jarred my tailbone and spine.

But the real problem was Falla riding behind me. I could feel her eyes on my back. Worse, I could imagine her peering into my head. I wasn't sure what, exactly, a spiritist was, but her abilities seemed to resemble an argent mage's. I had to assume she'd know if I was lying. And I knew that Evrain would soon ask some pointed questions.

Ahead of me, Evrain and Kei rode side by side. Evrain led my horse rather than allowing me to guide the animal. Just as well. It took most of my concentration to stay balanced in the saddle. And I was so very tired.

A tremor, another of the small quakes that had been rattling the area, rumbled in the depths of the mountain, setting its skin shivering. A few rocks tumbled down the slope ahead, landing in a stand of low evergreen brush in the narrow valley below. I couldn't help tensing. The trail we followed could hardly live up to the name. Only slightly more level than the slope above and below, it traversed up and over the flank of the mountain, sometimes crossing areas of sparse grass, sometimes winding through fields of scree and boulders. On the horizon line, a tower of rocky rubble blocked the view around the corner. On its summit, a pair of mountain goats capered.

"The Chasm Span... gone... I find it hard to believe," Evrain said.

"Not a stone left," Kei said, her voice clear in the mountain air. "At first I thought I was mistaken. Fatigued from the hard ride."

"So, Kostan," Evrain called over his shoulder. "Did you know of this?"

Once again, I jerked in surprise at hearing him address me without a title. The only other person who'd regularly called me by my first name alone had been Vaness.

"I—yes. I... well, I was crossing it when it started to collapse." I cringed at the memory of stone blocks giving way beneath my feet.

Kei turned and arched an eyebrow. Now that she'd relaxed from her headlong ride, her face had settled into a content and confident expression. She didn't look much older than me, but the ease with which she seemed to move through the world was captivating.

"I'm sure that was startling," she said.

"That would be one way to put it."

"Whatever you two do," Falla said, leaning around me to speak to her fellow Sharders, "don't ask if he screamed like a frightened child. I'll know if he lies."

Evrain laughed. "I wouldn't dream of it."

When I turned to look at Falla, she winked.

"As a matter of fact, I did not," I said, glad for the distraction. The more I could steer the conversation away from the events inside Steelhold the better.

The trail reached a small, level area of exposed rock where a path led onto the fin of broken stone that had blocked the view earlier. I imagined the little spire gave an expansive vantage of the surrounding valleys and slopes, a good point from which to inspect the terrain. Evrain nudged his mount into a tight turn, the horse's feet clopping against the smooth granite. As he did, another small quake growled in the mountain's heart, a reminder of the Breaking and the danger it posed to the Empire.

A stirring of fear in my stomach answered the mountain's rumble. If I didn't find a way back to Jaliss, the tremors would get much worse.

"Kostan," Evrain said, face now quite serious. "Make no mistake. I like you. But I will kill you if we don't get what we need from you. Why didn't you mention the Chasm Span?"

I knew Falla was watching every word. I couldn't outright lie. "Well, to start, I'm afraid that once I tell you everything you want to know, you won't have a use for me."

He seemed to consider this, the stark mountain sun deepening the shadows in the crow's feet around his eyes. "That's a fair point. So allow me to restate my position. I don't wish to kill you. And you are worth far more than the information you might share. A future ally with ties to Steelhold would be a major benefit to us. However, you will have to prove that allegiance. Perhaps you could start by speaking more freely."

I shifted in the saddle, trying to take more weight off my injured leg. There seemed little I could do to avoid saying more. "Some time ago, probably close to twenty days now, the Emperor summoned me. I'd never spoken to him before nor seen him at a distance closer than one hundred paces. He told me there was a grave danger to the throne and the Ascension. I believe those enemies were the same which caused Ferromaster Ilishian to wake me in the dark of night with word that I must flee. But since Ilishian fell to his death when the Chasm Span collapsed, I know little about the extent of the threat."

A considering look fell over the Stormshard leader's face. His eyes flicked to Falla, and after a moment, he nodded. "My spiritist believes you, which is the best proof I'll likely receive."

I kept my back straight, careful not to let my relief show. If questioned directly about the Emperor's death, I might be able to deny knowledge—after all, I hadn't seen the body. But I didn't wish to test that, and my instincts told me I needed to keep the information to myself.

Evrain folded his hands over the saddle pommel. "As a gesture of good faith, I'll share something with you. Falla told you that the infection in your foot appears unnatural. It's been held to simmering most likely by the salve which you described. What we haven't yet shared is we believe we know the cure."

I raised my eyebrows. "And?"

"Your ankle cuff. It's wrought from Maelstrom-gold. As you're surely aware, the gold from Cosmal grants power over the wearer's body. Usually, that enables great feats of strength or quickness. In this case, that power is more a curse, holding the sickness inside your flesh. If we cut the cuff off for you, the ordinary methods for clearing an infection will almost certainly allow you to heal as normal."

I blinked, in shock at his words. It made sense, I supposed. In our training in the Hall of Mages, we'd learned about the powers of Maelstrom-gold, but we'd never been instructed in bonding with the metal. Maybe that was because no one wished us to learn the true purpose of the cuffs.

Evrain narrowed his eyes at me, watching my reaction. What should I say? If I hesitated at the thought of having my cuff removed, Stormshard might see it as a hidden loyalty to the Empire and the Ascension.

In some ways that was true. I needed to Ascend. It would already be difficult, dangerous, and maybe impossible, to return to Steelhold and reclaim my position. I wore the Heart of the Empire, but that proved nothing. Only the Emperor and a select few advisers knew of the relic.

If I didn't even have a cuff to mark me as an imperial Scion, how could I expect to be recognized? Because we'd been kept sequestered, few would recognize me. A scar on my foot would prove nothing but my willingness to injure my flesh to impersonate a Scion.

"Well?" Evrain asked. "You're clearly surprised. Yet there's none of the elation I expected."

I grasped the saddle's pommel with enough force to press the blood from my knuckles. "I was only considering the repercussions. You just mentioned the advantage in having an ally with access to Steelhold, but without my cuff, I have no proof of my status as Scion. Until I know who threatened my life, I believe it would be against our best interests to cut it off."

Kei's mouth turned up at the corner, creating a charming dimple. "Our interests?"

I blushed. I had said that, hadn't I. "I've never cared for the treatment of Provincials under Emperor Tovmeil and the rulers before him. I swear it. You all are asking a lot for me to commit to an allegiance. I've only just escaped an attempt on my life. This is my first real experience beyond Steelhold's walls. So I hope you'll understand my plea for patience while I try to understand what I want. But yes, I believe we desire similar things."

Evrain draped his reins over his horse's neck and swung down, feet crunching on the grit that strewed the granite beneath. "Feel up to a short trip out there?" he asked, sweeping his arm toward the narrow trail that edged out the fin of stone. No more than the width of my foot in some places, the spire dropped off precipitously on both sides, the plunge ending in a jagged boulder field far below.

I licked my lips. "It might be a challenge one-footed."

He strolled over to my side and tugged on the loose end of the slipknot fastening my injured leg to the saddle strap. "Consider it a chance to build trust."

The big man grasped my wrist and helped me down. At his touch, I couldn't help stiffening. The truth was, as a Scion, I'd had little physical contact with others. Occasionally, the other Scions had nudged me with an elbow, pushed a fist against my shoulder. And there'd been the kiss with Vaness, her surprisingly soft body and lips pressed against mine. But situations like this, where someone offered me help, had been so rare I couldn't remember the last one. It felt nice. Once again, I glanced at Kei, her eyes sparkling in the sunlight.

Maybe I should trust these people after all.

Chapter Twenty-Three

Parveld
In the Icethorn foothills

The way Jaliss crashed against the base of Steelhold's sheer-sided pedestal, washing around the edges and even spilling into the chasm that separated the Hold's spire from the Icethorn Mountains reminded Parveld of his long-ago boyhood. There'd been a girl. Lilik. At low tide, they'd played around the bases of pilings at the fishermen's docks near the mouth of Istanik Harbor.

So long ago. Yet he could still see her smile, hear her laugh dancing out across the water.

He dipped his hand into the pocket of the duster coat he wore against the chill mountain morning and touched the silver-and-gold bracelet. Truesilver. Truegold. Not the tainted metals this Empire craved. Like other civilizations before it, greed would bring Atal down. Or so he predicted, particularly given the convergence of events here with the visions he'd had centuries in the past. Even now, he remembered drowning in an aquamarine sea of magic, glimpses of the future slapping his mind as water filled his lungs. So many visions, yet it seemed all of them led here.

He leaned back against the dry-stacked stone wall of the shepherd's hut. Perched on a grassy terrace an hour's climb into the foothills east of Jaliss, the small shelter did little to cut the night's chill, but it hid him from sight when patrols of imperial protectors passed on the road below. Plus, if anyone happened to spot him, they wouldn't question his presence. He'd given the previous shepherd enough real coin—not that tin scrip the Empire stamped in their presses and doled out to Provincial subjects—to fund a journey to the Aniselan ports and away to some free land. Parveld knew nothing about caring for sheep. He figured they wouldn't starve on this well-grassed terrace. At least not until Deepwinter approached. Before finishing his time here, he'd find someone to take over their care.

As if to remind him of that vow, a young member of his flock butted him with hard nubs of emerging horns.

"Ow!" Parveld said, smiling as he laid a hand on the wooly head. He scratched around the animal's ears, causing a rear hoof to paw the air in reflex.

The mountain sun shone strongly on Parveld's chest and face. He was about to lay his head back against the wall and close his eyes when he felt the first glimmer of sparks crossing the fringe of his perception. As always—even when sleeping—he kept a portion of his awareness focused on the mystical aether surrounding him. Over the last twenty decades, he'd learned that his spirit sense extended to a distance of around ten leagues in any direction. A couple day's walk at a reasonable pace. Ordinarily, he'd ignore newcomers until they were almost directly beneath his perch.

But these sparks were different. One glowed like a bonfire. Like the sun fallen to earth.

The girl approached.

Chapter Twenty-Four

Savra
Nearing Jaliss on the Atalan Plateau

According to Havialo, we were just a couple days' ride from Jaliss when we turned off the road in search of his acquaintance who would alter the ledger. A narrow trail pressed through deep grass and willows to reach a rickety shack that crouched on the edge of a large pond as if hoping to catch minnows. We hobbled the horses at the rear of the building then circled the structure. A man in a courier's uniform lounged on the porch that overlooked the water, feet propped on the railing.

"Havialo," he said when we came into view. "I received your message—"

"Then there's no reason to discuss it," the mage said, cutting him off with a glance in my direction.

The courier shifted his gaze, looking me up and down, before returning his attention to Havialo. "You never were much for pleasantries."

"And you never were much for duty when you can stare at a puddle," Havialo said as he gestured to the pond. A stand of cattails grew at the far side of the porch, and dragonflies hovered among them.

I'd kept behind the geognost when he stepped onto the porch, and now I was glad for it. Havialo had a knack for irritating so-called friends, it seemed. At least there weren't any protectors around for the courier to summon.

The courier rolled his eyes. "I do everything required by my Function and run a discreet business on the side. If I take a moment now and again to enjoy my surroundings, I'll not feel guilty for it. Anyway, I certainly hope this document is less complicated than the last. I thought you'd never be satisfied with the—"

Havialo stepped forward, raising the scroll tube in an almost threatening manner. "It's just a single entry. Savra Padmi's Function needs to read 'scribe.'"

Dropping his feet to the porch, the courier yawned and stood. "I'll just be a few, then." He snatched the scroll tube from Havialo's hand as he yanked the door open. When the geognost made to follow, the courier shook his head. "Take some time to enjoy my puddle. Storm's fury, but you could stand to relax now and again."

"I'd rather assure you complete—"

The man shook his head. "No good forger reveals his methods."

Havialo looked ready to battle his way into the cottage. With a deep breath, he forced himself to relax.

"Please work quickly. We'd like to cover more distance before we camp. Savra here has never seen the Icethorns."

The courier sighed. "As you say."

Before the sun dropped a finger's width down the sky, we were underway again. It was official. My Function was scribe. Yet while I should feel relief at moving a step closer to my writ and my father, I couldn't shake the feeling I'd missed something important in the men's interaction.

A day later, I finally saw the Icethorns. Like jagged clouds, they soared over the grasslands. Never in my life could I have imagined something so beautiful—and forbidding. As we drew nearer, details emerged. Ragged cliffs punctured the snowfields, and narrow vales held dark strips of trees. It was all I could do to keep my eyes on the trail ahead. When the road turned to parallel the range, I gave myself a stiff neck by turning my head to the side so often.

As we rode beside the steep foothills, I imagined I could smell the snow that plastered their crests. Sometimes during Deepwinter, frost left long, white crystals on the brush near the spine of the Cosmal Peninsula. Once, Avill and I had begged off our tide picking duties and hiked inland to pluck the flakes from the leaves and watch them melt on our hands. But I could only guess what actual snow felt like. And the smell—the fresh air that sank from the mountain tops made me think of clean sheets, just laundered and dried in the sea breeze. Only cleaner.

After a camping one more night on the grassland, we drew within sight of the capital. The city of Jaliss surrounded a massive stone pillar like a besieging army. Sprawled beneath the towering monolith, the capital was a dark blanket of angular buildings and crooked streets. Even at midday, chimney smoke hung in a layer over the enormous settlement, deepening the shade that pooled in the streets.

Crowning the stone spire, the fortress was like nothing I had ever seen. Though the walls and buildings within were too far away to make out details, the Hold looked as if it had been carved from the mountain itself. The work of a master sculptor on an inconceivable scale. Even standing directly beneath the pillar, the actual fortress would be as far away as the distance between Numintown and the next nearest settlement. An hour's climb from the city, at least.

On the side of the pillar facing the grasslands, a dark cut switchbacked up the sheer wall of the spire. I assumed it was an ascent trail carved into the mountainside. I shuddered at the thought of trying to navigate the trail.

Every few minutes we passed travelers walking or riding the other direction. Less frequently, mounted men and women trotted or galloped past us toward the city, casting incurious glances our way as they passed. Our horses' hooves made hollow tocks against the cobblestone road.

Our arrival at Jaliss both excited me and struck fear in my heart. My new life would begin somewhere in its wide spread of streets. As we drew closer, I noticed that the buildings nearest the stone pillar were the largest. Likely home to the Atal elite. Whereas down on the grasslands, shanties crowded together. I had few illusions on where I'd end up living—if I stayed in the capital, that is—but I also imagined I'd be called to the upper districts to scribe letters and documents for the wealthier citizens.

Of course, I might not end up a scribe at all. Once Havialo helped me find my father, maybe I'd join up with Stormshard. The thought gave me a little thrill, though I hated to admit it. But I could also

141

imagine Avill's reaction at the idea. I'd already failed her once by fleeing Numintown. Why should I be the one to fight the Empire when my little sister needed me? My best choice—my most responsible choice—would be to demand that my father send me to the sanctuary. Maybe he'd join us, even.

As for Havialo's offer to join his new renegade group, I couldn't see a reason to choose that over my other options. He hadn't mentioned it again, but I'd caught him appraising me more than once. I knew he still hoped. And somewhere down inside, I had a niggling fear of how he'd react if he asked and I refused.

As we drew closer to the city and the Hold, I squinted, searching for climbers on the path. It didn't appear that anyone was making the climb—I wondered whether that was common. Another strange detail caught my attention: on the back side of the pedestal, it appeared there'd been a recent rockfall from the mountainside opposite Steelhold. A large patch of stone had fallen away, leaving behind rock much lighter in color. Judging by the size of the scar, it must have been a massive collapse. I hoped no one had been traveling through the chasm below.

I pointed it out to Havialo, and he reined up, staring in shock. I'd never heard him curse, but the words that fell from his mouth made me blush.

"Do you know what happened?" I asked.

"The Chasm Span. It's gone." Holding the reins tight, he continued to stare, muttering another epithet.

Traveling the other direction, an elderly woman approached, a herbalist judging by her basket filled with packets of dried plants. Master Havialo raised a hand, asking her to stop. She turned weary eyes to him.

"What happened to the Span?" he asked, gaze flitting between her face and the scar where the bridge had apparently peeled away.

The woman shrugged. "Not a soul in Jaliss knows. Or if they do, they won't say."

"No explanation from Steelhold? Someone inside the fortress must have seen."

The woman snorted. "Likely you're right. But since the gates have been shut since the bridge came down, I wonder if we'll ever know the truth. Some claim they heard the alarm gongs the night it fell, but that's just gossip mongering if you ask me."

"Closed? Entirely? I don't remember a time when the gates were shut," Havialo said.

As they spoke, my gelding eyed the grass at the edge of the road. For once, I tugged at the bit, discouraging him. The woman's gaze flicked to me, but she quickly dismissed me as uninteresting.

She sucked her teeth, shrugging. "Anyone who reports for their Function inside the walls has been turned away. No scrip for their efforts in making the climb, and of course the grocers and butchers won't hand over their wares without scrip. There are stirrings in the Splits about raiding the imperial stores. Everybody has to eat, you know, whether or not the Empire wants us to perform the Function they've forced on us."

As he took in the information, Havialo ran his hand through his hair. "Well, I'm grateful to you for the news."

She said nothing in response, simply ducked her head and trudged on.

"If you don't mind," the mage called after her. "Where are you bound?"

She turned and gave him a gap-toothed grin that struck me as strangely ironic given the sadness in her eyes. "Think I can make Anisel before I die? Because I tell you, there's a storm coming. And if I'm going to be swept up, I'd rather see a few different faces before I go."

Havialo inclined his head and dug into his pants pocket, flipping her a steel coin. "Best of luck, my friend."

Ahead, a simple wooden building stood at the side of the road. On the single step leading from the ground to the door, a woman with the courier's crest on her sleeve leaned against a post, looking bored. In front of her was a flat-topped podium.

"Wait here," Havialo said, dismounting and handing off his reins. I started to ask why, but he was already gone.

The woman watched Havialo's approach with mild interest. I couldn't make out his words as he spoke to her, but after a moment she nodded and hurried into the small building. When she emerged, she carried a satchel, sheet of parchment, and a quill. From inside the podium, she fished out an inkpot. Stepping aside so Havialo could use the podium's surface to write, she assiduously kept her eyes off the paper. Or at least, she pretended to. I caught a few sly glances in his direction.

When the mage finished writing, he folded the paper, dripped a small puddle of wax on the seam, and marked it with a sigil pulled from his pocket. He handed over the letter.

The woman hurried around the other side of the building. Moments later, she was thundering down the road on her horse.

I didn't meet Havialo's eyes as he returned. Whether he believed he was protecting me or not, I was tired of his secrecy.

"Now what?" I said, scanning the snowcapped ridge.

"Now we wait. Your father will be here soon." As he spoke, his gaze slipped to the side.

If I wasn't mistaken, he was lying.

Chapter Twenty-Five

Kostan
On a Sharder patrol, Icethorn Mountains

Muscles in my lower back tightened at the dizzying drop on either side of us. Even seated beside Evrain upon a sturdy and flat bench of rock, the heights seemed to tug at me.

I planted my palms on the stone beside my thighs and felt a little better. Just a little.

"I wanted to tell you how I ended up with Stormshard," Evrain said. He sat easily on the stone, legs outstretched and crossed at the ankles. "You probably judged by my appearance that I'm Prov by birth."

"Cosmali, I'd guess?"

He nodded, then pointed to a pair of circling ravens. "We assign so many ill portents to those birds," he said. "At least, Provincials do. And yet, we revere the eagles and ospreys. The solitary, selfish killer placed above the clever scavenger who mates for life and will defend his love and home against all comers."

"Atal have the same superstitions. That's one thing we have in common with the Provs, I guess."

"And how do you see yourself? As a hawk or a raven?"

One of the black birds cawed and rolled in the air, a playful display for his mate. I thought of Vaness. We'd had camaraderie, but nothing like that.

"I don't know. I've never had much opportunity to make choices. Am I a killer? A lover? I don't know. All my life, I've been a Scion. No more and no less."

"Believe it or not," Evrain said, "most people your age are still figuring out who they are. So don't feel as if your task is hopeless. But I am hoping you'll discover a revolutionary heart beating in your chest."

Out of Evrain's sight, my hand curled into a fist, knuckles pushing into granite. I couldn't be a Stormsharder. To save my people, even the man seated beside me, I had to become what I most hated.

As if agreeing with the thought, a small cloud slid across the sun, bringing an instant chill to the air.

"Back to my story," Evrain said, "I once lived in a small settlement on the Cosmal Peninsula. I was a placer miner, working the sluices every day. Happy, even. But a few years before, a friend of mine had given me a warning. He had a son. The boy was strange, given to fugues where he claimed to look into the souls of his neighbors. No one paid it much mind until the registrar came. Instead of receiving the sluicer Function, the boy was dragged away. Officially, his Function was listed as hostler, but he knew nothing of horses.

"After a year with no letters from his son, my friend paid a wagoneer known to have contacts with renegade groups. He wanted to know where his son had ended up, but when he received the answer a few weeks later, he wished he'd never asked."

Even though his tone hinted at the truth, I couldn't help my question. "What happened to the boy?"

"Executed as a threat to the Empire. He hadn't even lived a week after they took him away. After my friend learned the truth, he started asking around the peninsula. There were similar stories through the generations. So when my daughter started having strange nightmares and visions, I knew I had to do something. I left within the month. Didn't even say goodbye out of fear I'd endanger her. Better my family had no knowledge if questioned about me. I already had minor involvement with Stormshard, but I committed to full membership. I've been a Sharder ever since."

As Evrain had spoken, I'd become so caught up in his story that my discomfort with the heights had vanished. I picked up a small rock and threw it over the edge. A few long seconds later, it clattered distantly against the boulders.

"Forgive my saying this, but short of unseating Emperor Tovmeil, how does this help your daughter?"

"In truth, I'd hoped to have done more by now—my daughter's Function assignment would happen this year and I can't let her be found. It's been seven years since I left home—my younger daughter probably doesn't even remember me. I had grand visions of unseating the Emperor and bringing a new era to the Empire. But I've learned much in the years since. True change will come, but it may take more than my lifetime. In the meantime, I sent a trusted friend to rescue my family. The friend is an imperial courier with ties to Stormshard—her Function will allow her to travel Cosmal without raising suspicion, whereas the protectors have learned my face over the years. In any case, my friend will escort my wife and younger daughter to a port in Anisel and buy them passage to a land far from here. And as for my older daughter with the... ability so hated by the Empire, I've asked to have her brought to me. I can keep her safe in these mountains. And maybe, with her talents, we can work together to change life in the Empire."

"You wouldn't feel better sending her with your wife?"

Evrain sighed, and I couldn't help but notice the tension in his face. "I wish I had, to be honest. I expected to hear from the courier and my daughter by now. They're likely just delayed by the recent earthquakes, though. The Cosmali Crease is difficult to traverse. Sometimes travelers get held up for weeks waiting for repairs to the road."

For Evrain's sake, I hoped that was true. I hadn't heard of any major collapses in the Crease, but not all reports from the Empire reached the Scions.

"What's your daughter's name?" I asked.

Evrain cast me an amused smirk. "We aren't on that close of terms yet, I'm afraid."

I nodded, chastened. Of course he wouldn't tell me her name. He might as well be handing her over to the protectors if I betrayed him.

"In any case," he said, "I'm telling you this because I believe it will help you understand our position. Surely you have someone you care about as well. That's one thing we all have in common."

Immediately, my face burned with shame. I looked away to hide it. Yes, he might assume I had someone to care about—someone who cared about me. In truth, Vaness was the nearest person I had. And we'd hardly been close.

"Makes sense," I said, clearing away the catch in my throat.

"We should get back," Evrain said, looking over his shoulder. "Falla is not the most patient of women. But there's one more story I want to share. I think it's important you understand why I, in particular, am cautious with my trust."

I glanced back at Falla and Kei. While the older woman was showing her impatience by fiddling with her saddle ties, shading her eyes to scan the horizon, and throwing rocks down the hill, Kei had taken a seat a few paces uphill from the trail and leaned against a stone to soak in the sun. With the warm rays on her skin, she looked entirely content.

"They'll be fine," Evrain said with a fond smile. "Even Falla. As her husband says, she has as much bluster as a Deepwinter blizzard, but none of the bite."

"If you say so..."

The man chuckled. "In any case, when I was new to Stormshard, I befriended a geognost named Havialo. He was five or ten years older than me, elite-born Atal, but we understood each other well. Personally, anyway. But we didn't agree on the best way for Stormshard to reach its goals. I had no taste for violence or dominance. But Havialo believed that the Empire would never be defeated without sacrifices, even of innocent citizens. He felt that the Sharders needed a firm hand and leaders ready to take radical action. Havialo was nice enough and fairly persuasive, but among our peers, more Sharders agreed with me."

"Have you ever considered *choosing* a leader? Someone to reflect the will of everyone in the group rather than dictate direction?"

Evrain's expression was thoughtful. "I have. And I understand what you're saying. But we've lived so long under the Empire, the protectors, the snitches. We need our freedom before any of us is ready to hand over their choices to someone else. Even if that means we take longer to achieve our goals."

Somewhere on the sparsely forested slope below our perch, a jay chattered. A light breeze swirled up from the valley, carrying scents of pine and sun-warmed lichen. The heights reminded me of patrols around Steelhold's wall. There, I'd stood and surveyed the domain that might someday be mine. But up here, Evrain looked over a wild territory that didn't truly belong to anyone but the birds and hunting cats. And rogue groups hiding out in hillside caves.

"Havialo was impulsive, and he decided to take a drastic step to prove his methods were better. He intended to burn the Hall of Registry. If the Empire's copies of the Function writs were lost, he believed Provs would rise up and burn their own copies as a first step in casting off the Empire."

My eyes widened. "But the Hall is right by Lowtown and Tanner's Row. The buildings there don't even have slate roofs. The fire would tear through the slums. It's an issue the Ministry has considered addressing."

Evrain nodded. "Exactly. But since I had no authority to stop Havialo short of turning him in, I decided the only way to spare the innocent residents of the Splits was to get inside the Hall and steal the records first. If there was nothing of value to burn, I believed Havialo would give up on his plan.

"Unfortunately, Havialo was so desperate to prove himself he decided to act days before he'd initially told us he would. We had no way to know, but both my group and Havialo approached the Hall on the same night. Things got messy with so many Sharders working at cross purposes, and the short story is that Havialo was spotted."

"The protectors captured him?"

Evrain shook his head. "Because he was elite-born, word of his betrayal traveled straight to the Ministry and Emperor. No offense, but I don't know whether cruelty is bred into the Scions or if it comes from your training. Instead of punishing Havialo directly—that may not have ended well for the would-be executioner anyway, given his talents as an earth mage—the leadership sent a cadre of protectors to his young daughter's academy. She was dragged through the streets with no explanation. Hanged for all the city to see."

Revulsion swirled in my belly. Staring over this rugged corner of the Empire that I hoped to rule one day, I wanted to throw myself off the outcrop for having been born under the stars that declared me fit to control it. I didn't know what to say. A child, killed in the center of Jaliss for no other reason than having the wrong father? It was disgusting.

"I can't imagine..." I said. With no bonds of the sort experienced by a parent and child, I honestly couldn't understand the man's grief. Still, I felt sick inside.

"I doubt any of us can truly imagine his anguish unless faced with a similar loss," Evrain said. "In any case, we lost Havialo after that. He never cooperated directly with us again. In particular, he never cooperated with *me*. Sometimes I've suspected him of working to sabotage me, though I'm not sure I could prove it. And the truth is, I sometimes wish he would succeed in undermining me. It was an accident that we arrived at the Hall together and got tangled up. Still, I can't help feeling I'm to blame for his daughter's execution. I don't think I'll ever escape that."

"To answer your question..." I said.

"Which question?"

"You wondered whether we're born cruel or taught the behavior. I hope the answer is 'neither' in my case. And there's another Scion. She's... well, I don't really know. For a long time, I thought we shared a hatred for the Emperor's brutality. Recently, something she said made me wonder, but I can't imagine that she's irredeemable."

"You're probably right. No one is born evil, and no amount of conditioning can change a pure heart." Evrain clapped me on the shoulder. "So, I imagine that foot of yours could use time propped up on pillows. Should we head back?"

"One question," I asked. "Do you know who was directly responsible for her execution? I'd like to know in case I'm ever in the position to... make them atone."

Evrain stood, extending a hand to help me up. "According to the palace, all orders issue from the Emperor himself. I don't know if that's true. But there was a minister who publicly attended the execution. Minister Brevt."

I nodded, hiding my reaction. Minister Brevt, the same man who'd been involved in the Emperor's murder and the threat to my life. Why wasn't I surprised?

We returned along the narrow fin of rock, Evrain's steady hand guiding me. When we neared the women, he turned and spoke in a low voice.

"You know what Stormshard means to me now. There's little else I can say to help you decide. I'll want to know where your allegiance stands by sundown. Removing that cuff would prove your intent, I think."

Chapter Twenty-Six

Savra
An hour's ride from Jaliss

We retreated from the road, cutting a path through the tall grass. Near the base of the mountains, Havialo hobbled the horses and flopped down on the grass. I didn't feel like relaxing.

"I feel I should ask again, Savra," he said casually. He lay with one ankle crossed over the other, head pillowed on his hands. "Would you consider using your talents for a cause with a real chance at success?"

Should I confront him? I knew he was still hiding some truths. A gut feeling, but I trusted my instincts. What would confrontation gain me? I doubted it would produce answers.

"I don't even understand my talents, much less how to use them," I said. "I appreciate everything you've done for me, but I don't want to make important choices until I see my father."

Above our stopping place, the hill rose steeply to a flat terrace. A crude hut stood near the edge of the platform. Sheep wandered nearby, grazing and bleating.

Havialo's mouth turned down at one corner. "In truth, I don't believe anyone knows the extents of what a spiritist can do. The Empire's practice of exterminating your kind has limited the exploration of your abilities. Surely that must anger you. Don't you want to get even? Neither your father nor Stormshard can help you do that."

I shrugged. "Until a few weeks ago, I'd never heard of spiritism."

He plucked a long stalk of grass and pinched the seedhead between thumb and forefinger, stripping off the grains. "Well, think about it. We have time to wait."

Wait until what, though? "How long will it take my father to get here?"

He didn't look at me and didn't answer. After a while, I got tired of standing and sat a few paces away.

As the clouds drifted over the sky, I wrapped my cloak tight around my body. The sun here was so strong it made one forget how quickly the air gave up its warmth without the rays. Movement on the hill above caught my eye, and I craned my neck to see the shepherd making his way down the steep slope. He carried a walking stick in one hand and used it for added stability as he descended.

"What do you think happened to the Chasm Span?" I asked. "And aren't you worried about Steelhold being closed?"

Havialo had draped his forearm across his eyes. When I spoke, he yawned and propped his body up on his elbows. "Interesting you should ask that. I may indeed know about actions taken against Steelhold, likely leading to the fall of the Span. But you see, without a commitment from you to work against the Empire which has hurt you and your kind again and again, I see no reason to share anything more."

The venom in his voice surprised me. Over the weeks of our journey, he'd at least attempted to keep a reasoned tone.

"What about your vow? If I were to join you rather than my father, wouldn't you be breaking your promise?"

"That's not for you to worry about. There's not much time, Savra," he said again. "Think hard."

I pulled a stalk of grass and bent the stem into a knot. In Numintown, the only grass was a short variety that tolerated the salt breezes. At once, I missed home with a fierceness that surprised me.

I thought of Avill's laugh and my mother's bemused smile. But Mother and Avill weren't in Numintown anymore. Most likely, none of us would ever return.

Overhead, the clouds continued to build over the mountains, growing ominous. A storm waited to pounce. Wind began to skirl down from the heights carrying a breath of frost.

"Should we put up the tarp?" I asked. Though not a proper tent, we'd traveled with a sheet of canvas and a pitchpole that came up to my ribs. The resulting shelter was hardly comfortable—during the few nights we'd used it, I'd felt as if the tent's ceiling would suffocate me. But it would be better than a drenching rain. Or worse, snow.

Havialo shook his head and pointed. Leaving the road, a trio of riders eased their mounts from a gallop to a trot. The geognost scrambled to his feet. As I stood from my patch of flattened grass, I noticed the shepherd had continued his descent. It seemed strange that he'd left his shelter with a storm looming. He must have had his reasons, though.

Havialo raised a hand in greeting as the riders reigned up.

None of them were my father.

"Havialo," said the man in front. He had a painfully thin face, sunken cheeks beneath cheekbones so sharp they could cut. His eyes were small, darting flecks of brown hiding in the shadow of his brow.

"Where is my father?" I asked.

Everyone ignored me.

"I didn't think your master would expose himself by sending you so openly, Biallist," Havialo said. He then turned to the other newcomers, a stout woman with a hooked nose and a permanent sneer, and a leather-armored man with flinty eyes who struck me as a hired guard.

"As you may have heard, there were difficulties with our initial operation," the man, Biallist replied. "We've been forced to proceed in a manner uncharacteristic for our organization."

As he spoke, his gaze briefly landed on the stone spire where Steelhold presided over the surroundings.

"What went wrong?" Havialo asked.

The woman nudged her mount forward. The movement of her hand on the reins caught my attention, and I noticed a silver band on her finger, similar to Havialo's. On her other hand, a gold ring encircled her thumb.

A rank in argent magic and another in aurum. Was she a true metalogist, or a dabbler like Havialo?

"You know as much as we do. The last Biallist heard from Minister Brevt, everything was in place. The... recruits were drilled and drilled again on the plan. Seeing as most of them were your responsibility, we were hoping you had some insight."

Havialo's eyes darted to me. Did he just now remember that I had ears? "Perhaps we should talk about this later," he offered.

The woman stared at me for a moment. "I don't see much purpose in inserting her via the scribe's Function at this point," she said.

I took an unwitting step back. Havialo sidestepped between the newcomers and me. He snatched the reins of the woman's mount, holding them near the bridle. "Here, Venna, let me help you down," he said as he held out a hand. "As I mentioned, I think we should discuss the particulars of the operation later."

Venna's mouth twisted in annoyance. "Avoiding the subject won't make up for the failure." Ignoring his offered hand, she swung her leg over and dropped to the grass. The armored man followed her lead.

"I brought some of that aged cheese from the Guralan coast," Havialo said as he stepped to his hobbled mount and began rooting through the saddlebag. Meanwhile, Biallist dismounted, watching the woman as if waiting for a signal.

I continued to retreat. Whatever this was, I didn't want to be part of it. When the backs of my legs brushed the tall grass at the edge of our trampled area, I glanced back to judge the distance to Breeze. My gelding was still hobbled. Unfastening the leather cuffs on his forelegs would slow me, but I might free him and ride off before they caught me.

Savra.

A bolt of ice shot through me. Though my name sounded as if it had been spoken aloud, I knew the voice had been inside my mind. Even so, I searched my surroundings for the speaker. Biallist and Venna continued to approach Havialo, forced courtesy hanging over their bodies like frozen clothing.

Please don't be frightened, the voice said. Not of me.

Don't be frightened of a voice suddenly echoing in my own skull? My fingernails dug into my thighs. Swallowing the sudden stone in my throat, I nearly coughed.

"Who?" I whispered, just a breath of air escaping my lips.

Don't speak aloud. You must not alert the others.

Standing frozen, I ran my eyes over the area. Still, neither Havialo nor his friends seemed to have noticed someone else speaking. The guardsman stood a few paces back from the other pair, while Havialo pasted on a smile and handed over a wedge of wax-encased cheese.

"A thoughtful gift. But it doesn't change the situation, Havialo," Venna said. "Given the lack of results from the original plan, there are some who want to proceed with the alternative."

Havialo's spine stiffened. "Even considering the cost?"

"They believe some of the loss of life can be prevented." Venna gestured toward me with her chin. "But that still leaves the problem of your new acquisition. Her value has dropped considerably in light of recent events. If she's unwilling, at this point she's more of a liability."

Look uphill, the voice said.

I dragged my attention from the group and glanced up the slope. The shepherd had come within a hundred paces. When our eyes met, he nodded.

As Havialo turned to look at me, his face hardened. "She'll obey."

"Why is that?" Venna asked. "She looks ready to flee already."

"Because my men hold her mother and sister hostage." He cupped a hand around his mouth. "You hear that, Savra? There is no sanctuary. Your mother and sister are in a hidden location near the Crease. My men are keeping them secure and fed, and they'll continue to do so as long as you cooperate."

It felt as if my heart were shattering at the confirmation of my fears. Mother and Avill must be so frightened. If only I'd refused to go with the mage in the beginning.

"Wouldn't you be just as content to see her... exterminated?" Venna asked. "I seem to remember you speaking of that."

He shook his head. "Despite Evrain's actions, I don't wish to see his daughter die. Savra is innocent of her father's sins, and she's shown integrity during our travels."

Die? Sins? My heart thumped harder. As if in answer, the storm winds lashed, flattening the grass around us.

You can't outrun them, the shepherd said into my thoughts. And he's lying about your mother and sister. At least partly. Anyway, you'll do neither of them any good if you die here.

I shook my head, still wondering if his words were part of my imagination.

If you turn to flee, the thug will send a crossbow bolt through your back, he continued.

I stepped to the side to get a better view of the guard and saw that he did, in fact, have a small crossbow holstered at his belt.

Good. You're starting to believe. A natural. When I first heard voices through the aether, it took days for me to acknowledge them as real.

Biallist curled his lip in disgust, skin sliding over the bones of his face. "I forgot this one was personal."

"Evrain's flawed views cost my daughter her life. "

"Wait," I blurted. "I thought you said one of the Sharders betrayed you because of your Atal birth."

The geognost turned to me, a wild look in his eyes. "And if I'd explained that your father was responsible, would you have believed me? You see, Savra, I've tried over and over to convince you of the proper choice. But you're just as stubborn—and faithless—as your father. I never wanted to use your mother and sister against you. If you'd seen the righteousness of my cause, they'd have gone on to the sanctuary without you ever knowing. Now, you'll need to be forcibly trained to accept our mission."

"But my father asked you to rescue me... You'd forgiven one another for past quarrels..." The words sounded stupid, even to me. Of course my father hadn't sent him. If he had, Mother and Avill would be safe. Most likely, I never would have been separated from them.

Havialo sneered. "I doubt your father remembers telling me about you. We were deep into our cups soon after he left Cosmal. He feared you might have the spiritist talent, you see, and had a foolish hope of joining the Sharders and ending the executions before you came of age. But like all dreams, that faded. He *did* send for you, though. Unfortunately, the courier tasked with escorting you away from Numintown was... waylaid. Evrain will never know why you failed to arrive—I doubt he remembers discussing your nightmares and aura-sight with me."

My hand fell on the pocket where I'd kept the note since Havialo had given it to me.

The mage smirked when he noticed the motion. "You remember the ease with which my friend changed the ledger."

The letter was a forgery—I should have known. A wave of disgust struck me. I'd been treasuring a piece of paper that had been nothing but a lie. The back of my tongue tasted like chalk as I pulled the letter out and dropped it on the grass before me.

"If it's any consolation," the geognost said, "I did hope to see you join the cause willingly. I never wanted this to happen."

"Tell me how to find my mother and sister," I said. "Maybe I'll reconsider your offer."

The woman, Venna, laughed. "She thinks she's clever. Frankly, Havialo, I doubt this one can be bent to our cause. Easier to dispose of her than force her through the pain of a failed indoctrination. Even with the more... pliable young spiritists you've brought us, our success has been less than we'd hoped."

"What she's saying is we've had to kill half the young people you rescued," Biallist said with an exaggerated sigh. "The stakes are too high to use anyone in whom we have less than absolute trust."

As the man's words sank in, the guard stepped forward. "Ready for your orders, Mistress Venna, Master Biallist."

The woman stared at me as the first raindrops sliced down. Finally, she made a shooing gesture in my direction.

My breath froze as the guard raised his crossbow. Panic clamped my throat shut.

Abruptly the world faded, my aura-sight flaring to life. Spirits sprang into my vision, phantoms against a misty world. The guard had a subdued aura, drab like rain-soaked pine needles. Beside him, Venna was a swirling mass of color, blue determination with just a hint of regret. Havialo was... a morass of wildly shifting emotions, while Biallist pulsed with orange greed.

I'm sorry for this, Savra. The shepherd's voice cut through my mind, shattering my aura-sight like a hammer strike on a skim of ice. I staggered, only to feel as if my lungs were being sucked from my chest. I gagged, bending over.

Across the clearing, the others folded over their stomachs, groaning in agony.

"Impossible," Havialo croaked. "She's not trained. I'm certain—"

"Obviously, your certainty isn't worth a piece of imperial tin scrip," Venna said, her voice tight. "Shoot her, Krens."

The crossbow snicked, but before the bolt struck me, an unseen force shoved me back. The bolt flew over the top of my head.

Once again, please accept my apologies for the rough treatment, the shepherd said as I landed on my rear.

"What is going on?" I yelled, turning my head toward the shepherd. Now about fifty paces above us and sidestepping down the slope, feet skidding, he waved my attention away.

"Savra," Havialo said. "You must control your ability. You're gathering energy from our spirits. If you wish to convince these people you aren't dangerous, you must cease."

"But I—" Suddenly, it started to make sense. The shepherd must be a spiritist. None of the others had noticed him, and Havialo was attributing the man's power to me. "—why should I? This woman just tried to have her guard kill me."

"A mistake I'm sure," the mage said. Still hunched over his belly, he turned to Venna. "You've been hasty, old friend. You see, she's more powerful than we expected. Imagine how it could help our cause."

"Our cause?" Venna said, forcing out the words. "You may have cared at one point, but now you're just a wounded animal. Lashing out in all directions."

Havialo's face went purple with rage. As the wind gusted down from the mountains, I winced, preparing to be struck dead by a bolt of lightning flung from the sky. But an instant later, the ground shuddered and shook. Earthen tongues rose from the land, tearing grass up by the roots, dribbling soil from their tips. Above, the storm weakened—the energy redirected for Havialo's conjuring.

One of the dirt tentacles thickened at the end as rocks from the stalk rolled up and formed a stone fist. Venna eyes went wild with anger as she pinched the gold ring on her thumb. Like a whip slicing the air, she sprang, crossing the distance between her and Havialo in an eye blink. Her thumb jabbed the hollow of the geognost's throat.

I truly hate violence, the shepherd said. The human tendency toward it is surely our greatest fault. Steel yourself, Savra. This will hurt.

I screamed as the burning pain in my lungs and heart became searing agony. I felt pulled, torn, turned inside out. It seemed like time froze, leaving nothing but endless hurt.

And then, with a thunderclap, the pain stopped.

I stared, disbelief numbing my tongue.

Where the three newcomers and Havialo had stood, there was nothing but flattened grass and plowed earth. Beyond, the horses snorted, eyes rolling.

I saw sparks at the edge of my vision—I'd been holding my breath for too long. Wheezing, I sucked in a lungful of air.

When I looked up, the shepherd stood before me, hand outstretched to help me to my feet.

"I'd hoped our first meeting would have gone more smoothly."

Tentatively, I accepted his help. Once on my feet, I realized he didn't look over twenty-five or thirty. When he'd spoken into my mind, I'd had the sense he was much older.

"I don't understand what just happened," I admitted.

"No, I wouldn't expect you to," he said. "And the things I have to tell you will likely just make you more confused."

I blinked. "How did you know my name? How did you say it into my thoughts?"

The corner of his mouth turned up, a charming expression that was somewhat sheepish. "Just so we're even, I'll tell you mine. Parveld, though I wasn't always known by that name. And to answer your questions, in some ways it seems like I've always known who you are. That's not precisely true, of course. For the first seventeen years of my life, I had no idea we would meet. It's just the two hundred years since are such a long time in comparison."

I shook my head, unable to handle any more revelations. My knees wobbled.

"You're pale," Parveld said. "Why don't you sit back down."

Chapter Twenty-Seven

Kostan
On a Sharder trail, Icethorn Mountains

When we reached the part of the return ride where two horses could travel abreast, Kei reined her mount back and rode beside me. The trail had dropped closer to the valley bottom, and the twisted evergreen trees gave the air a warm scent that invited calm.

"I get what you're saying about the cuff," Kei said. "Without it, you'd have a much more difficult time convincing a strange gate guard to allow you past. But would you really be comfortable knocking on one of Steelhold's gates? People in the Hold tried to kill you, right?"

"Maybe not. But I don't want to limit my options without more information. Did you hear anything else about the Hold?" I'd been thinking about the locked gates. What did it mean? More fighting within the walls? Were the conspirators trying to determine their next action?

She shook her head. "I didn't linger long. The whole city is on edge—without the flow of scrip and information, people are hungry and afraid."

I curled my lip. "The Emperor should have made provisions for something like this. Provs shouldn't suffer when the palace endures an inner crisis."

"Agreed. Though the Provs could try harder to solve things themselves. Even without the palace and elite paying out scrip, there's no actual shortages—yet anyway. Why not barter amongst themselves to get what they need?"

Did she really not know? Or was she testing my opinions of imperial policies? "Because their Functions forbid it. Even I've seen what the protectors do to people who violate their writs."

Kei snorted. "True, I suppose. It's easy for me to forget life as a Prov slave. They're more likely to take their anger out on each other than risk the protectors' cudgels."

"Where did you live before you joined Stormshard?" I asked. Her blue eyes and light hair made me think of Anisel Province, but I couldn't be sure.

Her mouth twisted in amusement. "I'll consider telling you my story once I know where your loyalties lie." At that, she glanced pointedly at my ankle.

"The cuff won't come off without the key. Or a hacksaw, I suppose."

"Falla told me about your infection. You were a breath away from death. Is the risk worth keeping your options open?"

"I guess I still feel a sense of duty to the Empire. Not to the throne. To the people. What if I could change things? Give Provs the freedom Stormshard is fighting for?"

Her bright laugh tumbled through the forest. "I can only imagine how that would irk some of my fellow Sharders. Years of fighting only to have a Scion accomplish their goal."

I tried not to flinch. "Would they still hate the idea if I struck down the Decree of Functions and abolished the Order of Protectors? There are better ways to lead the Atal Empire. I'm sure of it."

"I like you, Kostan," she said. "And I'm sorry to say this. But unfortunately, some Provs won't be content until the Empire is obliterated. In their fantasies, the Atal are the servants for a few generations."

A breeze pressed through the forest, stirring the hair around her face. Kei sat so easily in the saddle, her hips rocking with each step of her mount. A melancholy smile teased her lips.

"Anyway," she said after a moment, "cuff or not, I don't see how you'd undo centuries of Atal oppression single-handedly. You're a fugitive existing on the goodwill of a Shard of mountain rebels. Meanwhile, people inside Steelhold want to kill you, and your only trusted ally fell with the Chasm Span."

"There's one other person I could trust," I blurted. "The man who helped me escape believed her to be loyal."

I sat straighter, annoyed at myself. Maybe the time on horseback had stolen my wits. More likely, the presence of an attractive young woman had loosened my tongue.

The impulse to tell the Sharders my full story flared to life. At the rate I was messing up, it seemed likely to come out anyway. I clutched the saddle pommel as I remembered another detail from my conversation with the Emperor. He had warned me of a betrayal. Likely at the hands of a woman. Maybe Kei would be my downfall.

"Oh?" she asked, arching a delicate eyebrow.

I swallowed. Avoiding an explanation would just raise suspicion. "She's a ferro mage. Azar. We were supposed to meet at an inn in Jaliss after we fled. I asked her to rescue my friend, Vaness. But then the Span fell."

"Did Azar make it out?"

I shrugged. "Not across the Chasm Span. She was still within the walls."

"Well, you won't be traveling to Jaliss soon. You're swaying in the saddle after just a couple hours. You should think hard about getting that cuff off."

In truth, I was considering it. It would be so much easier to abandon my responsibility. I could live here with Stormshard. Patrol the area. Forget the throne. "Maybe. Or maybe your healer's friends in Jaliss can find out what was in the salve that kept the wound healthy. I can handle the waiting and the aching foot a little longer."

Kei rolled her eyes. It was charming. "Just like a man. Too tough for your own good. Anyway, I have a hacksaw when you're ready to join us."

At that, she clucked to her mount and trotted off, ponytail swinging. I stared at her retreating back, savoring the fantasy of starting a new life as an ordinary Sharder.

"Hey, scout that last exposed section for us, will you Kei?" Evrain called ahead. "I'd like to pass unnoticed."

"Always making me work for my keep!" the woman called back, voice full of cheer. Clucking to her horse, she trotted from the forest, sunlight kissing her head and shoulders.

Moments later, a violent tremor roared from the mountain's belly. The quake hurled me from the saddle, torquing my bound foot until the knot slipped free.

As I slammed into the earth, I heard Kei scream.

Chapter Twenty-Eight

Savra
A circle of upturned earth, Atal grasslands

In the center of the trampled area, mounds of loose earth were strewn with uprooted grass and small stones. The devastation proved that I hadn't imagined Havialo's conjuring. Nor had I imagined the three people who had arrived to meet him. They'd been here, solid and real, and now they were gone. Vanished in a thunderclap.

Were they dead? My lip trembled. Maybe I didn't want to know.

"They're alive," the man, Parveld said. After gesturing to a low hummock of earth where I could sit, he'd backed off a few paces, moving slowly as if I were a spooked rabbit. "Even after all these decades, I can't Want to kill someone, no matter what terrible things they've done. I can't help seeing the true nature of their sparks. Almost everybody believes their actions to be righteous."

The horses were still pawing at the ground and blowing, eyes white rimmed. Clucking his tongue, Parveld approached the small herd and raised a hand toward Havialo's mare. She shied away.

The man shook his head, chuckling to himself. "Maybe in another century I'll learn the trick of horses."

"Do you read thoughts?" I asked. "How did you know I was worried you killed them?"

All the horses had sidled away from him now. With a last shrug in their direction, he strode to another grassy hummock and sat. Near me but not too near.

"I *can* read thoughts, yes. But I prefer not to. Everyone has a right to their privacy. Just now, I simply thought of the first question

I'd ask if four people suddenly vanished. I'd want to know what happened to them. And the answer is, I sent them away. They're at an oasis a day's walk into the Sandsea."

"You can look into peoples' minds, but you're not an argent."

He held up his hands to show his fingers were bare of rings. "Not an argent or any kind of metalogist."

"Havialo thought I was using my magic. Are you a spiritist?"

He inclined his head. "I've traveled to many lands. Magic is slightly different everywhere. Talents go by different names. But yes, my abilities are close to spiritism. To yours."

"I still don't understand how you know so much about me." The more I thought about it, the more my nerves prickled at the situation. Sure, this man had rescued me. But so had Havialo. I crossed my arms over my chest, hugging myself tight. If only I could go back to that last morning with Avill. I'd run away before the boy summoned me to the registrar.

He sighed. "I speak in riddles—I'm sorry. And I forget as many things as I remember. Both are effects of living far longer than anyone should. Long, long ago, I learned of you through a vision. But I can also sense your power. Spiritist to spiritist. You are a bonfire."

"This vision told you I was coming to Jaliss? Did you expect Havialo to betray me?"

"Nothing so specific. I couldn't even be certain you existed until I felt your spark."

"Spark?"

"Your spirit... it glows in the aether."

I glanced at Breeze. Still hobbled, he'd calmed enough to begin grazing again. Good. I wasn't sure I wanted to stay here much longer, but I didn't want to ride a spooked mount.

Overhead, the storm continued to break apart. Silver lined the edges of the tattered clouds. As I looked up at the vast sky, my vision went blurry. What was I going to do? Here I was, talking to a strange man many weeks' travel from the only home I'd known. I'd learned much in my journey with Havialo: how to set camp, where to fill water skins, the geognost's opinion on imperial politics. But I had no idea what to do next. Try to find Stormshard and my father?

Follow the road all the way back to Cosmal Province and—assuming I made it safely—attempt to find my mother and sister.

For that matter, why should I even believe they were still alive?

I bit my lip. Hard. I would not cry. Not now, in front of a stranger who—for all I knew—just wanted to manipulate me into serving *him* instead.

"Thank you for saving me," I said, for lack of other words to fill the silence.

"I'd like to do more. I'd like to help you. Teach you."

"You just rescued me from the last person who said that."

"I know. And I can't offer anything besides my word."

And this, he continued in my head. As he spoke, emotions joined his words. Reassurance. Hope. Resolve. Kindness.

It was too much. A tear spilled down my cheek.

"Why?" I said. "What's so important about me?"

"Terrible things are coming to Atal and the Provinces. I'm afraid we can't stop that. But without you, the suffering will be immeasurable. Inconceivable."

"I don't understand. I'm just a Prov from Cosmal Province."

He shook his head, eyes seeming to plead. "I don't know, Savra. I wish I did, but all I had were glimpses."

I hugged my knees tighter. "Havialo was bringing me here to be a scribe."

Parveld's face lit. "I knew it! I saw you with a quill."

Of course he did... I didn't know whether to laugh or cry. "Well, that opportunity is gone now..." Except it wasn't. Maybe I should just follow through. I had the ledger.

"You were heading into Jaliss?" he asked.

I nodded. "Havialo had a plan to get me my Function writ."

"It's the right path," Parveld whispered, almost to himself. He jumped to his feet and started pacing. "You should continue."

Just ride into Jaliss with the scroll tube and hope it worked out? What about the unrest with Steelhold's closure? I ducked my head and ran my hands through my hair, frustrated and wrung out.

When I looked up, Parveld had snared Breeze's reins. Though my poor gelding rolled his eyes at the strange man, he followed reluctantly.

"The Graybranch Inn. I have an account with the proprietor, Fishel," he said, setting the reins on my lap. Giving a quick glance at Breeze's hobbles, he seemed to think better of stooping to unfasten them. "In my visions, your writings moved the Empire. Even more than your magic."

"People said the city is dangerous right now."

"A sickness that quickly spreads across the Empire. Soon, nowhere will be safe. The Graybranch is a haven. There are few others."

I grabbed the reins and stroked Breeze's front leg, stopping at the buckle for the hobbles. My gelding snuffled at my hair then nudged my head with his nose.

Even before Havialo had admitted to kidnapping my family, I hadn't been sure I wanted to be a scribe. I appreciated Parveld's kindness, and he obviously worried about my future. But all I really cared about was my family.

I glanced at the sun. It would be dark in a few hours. I needed to choose: stay here and spend the night exposed, or look for shelter in the city. Regardless of the unrest in the capital, a door with a lock would be safer than a tent in the grasslands. In the morning, I could consider my predicament with a fresh mind.

"One question. If I'm so important, why aren't you insisting I stay up there where you can protect me?" I gestured up at the shepherd's hut.

"Every instinct screams at me to do just that," Parveld said. "But it's not time. Not the right path."

I finished removing the leather cuffs from Breeze's forelegs. When I stood, the horse laid his neck over my shoulder. At least I'd made one true friend on this journey. Scratching his withers, I lifted a foot to the stirrup and swung up into the saddle. I didn't meet the man's eyes—the whole situation made me uncomfortable.

I'd heard stories of strange magic in distant lands. The notion that he'd seen me in a vision, even centuries in the past, didn't seem impossible. I'd heard the monks in the Jalakyrisi Spicelands lived for thousands of years. And some Provs claimed to have visions of the future. But even if I believed Parveld, I wasn't ready to put my fate in someone else's hands.

"I won't beg you to trust me," Parveld said, once again seeming to read my mind. "You're clever enough to make your own decisions. But I do think you should take these."

I blushed when he held up Havialo's saddlebags—including the scroll holder containing my ledger. Money. Supplies. Havialo hadn't even trusted me with a waterskin, yet I'd planned to ride off into a strange city with the meager contents in my panniers. I wasn't thinking clearly.

"Thank you. And I'll think about what you said about training." I laid the saddlebags over my lap. It would be easier to ride if I sorted through them and took what I needed, but I wanted to get going.

Parveld tucked his hands into his pockets. "The Graybranch sits on the border between the Splits and the Merchants' Quarter. Fishel keeps a stable, a difficult find in the city."

I took up the reins and settled my weight in the saddle. After weeks of riding, it felt as comfortable as any other seat. "Graybranch near the Splits. Got it." I'd consider it, anyway.

"I'll stay here until Chilltide deepens," he said. "After that, I'll leave a note with directions to a warmer shelter. Come find me when you're ready."

Nodding, I pressed my heels to Breeze's sides. I felt Parveld's eyes on my back as I rode away.

The sun hung a few fingers off the horizon when I passed the capital's first outskirts. I kept Breeze to a light trot, not wanting to waste time. As I passed into the bustle of the city's inner districts, I slowed to keep from trampling the foot traffic clogging the streets. Careful to avoid looking like a wide-eyed Prov, I pulled my cloak's hood over my hair and tried to sit casually, eyes examining the signs for inns or guesthouses.

When the ground trembled, I stiffened. The rumble grew. Around, people dropped to crouches.

Breeze tossed his head, wild-eyed, as the quake swelled to a violent rocking. Moments later, the earth heaved and sent him down on one knee. One of us screamed as I flew from the saddle.

Chapter Twenty-Nine

Kostan
During a catastrophic earthquake, Icethorn Mountains

The mountain rolled beneath me, throwing stones into the air. Trees toppled, crashing down, roots tearing from the earth with a roar. Rocks bounced down the hillside, careening across the trail ahead.

I couldn't see the others, but I heard Evrain yelling. The horses were gone, bolted or fallen down the slope. A few paces downhill, a flying boulder smacked a tree, snapping the crown from the trunk.

I couldn't hear my own scream as I crawled forward.

One elbow and then the other, knees against the shuddering earth, I made for the open area ahead. The place Kei had ridden ahead to scout.

The source of her scream.

Somewhere high above, a dust cloud billowed as a section of cliff gave way. I couldn't see the slide, could only hear its growl and thunder.

Hands grabbed me under the armpits, dragging me upright. Dust and grit blurred my vision. Blinking, I spotted Falla to one side of me. Evrain stepped to the other. The Sharders draped my arms over their shoulders. We staggered forward together.

When we reached the open slope, my companions stopped short. From the morning's ride, I remembered a solid mountainside dotted with brush, stones, even wildflowers. Now, a moving river of soil raged before us. Boulders floated in the torrent, and trees tumbled roots over branches.

Dry-mouthed, I staggered backward with the others, then let them steer me downhill, through the crumbling forest toward the valley bottom.

We slipped and slid. No matter their efforts, my brand hit the ground again and again, sending agony streaking up my leg. Trees leaned and fell, roots tearing from the slope. I felt certain we wouldn't survive. Yet somehow, as we reached the steep ravine where the mountain slopes converged, the trembling began to subside. I huddled between the Sharders, still waiting for the valley walls to roar down and crush us.

Eventually, the rumbles ebbed then ceased. Somewhere in the ragged forest above, a lone bird chirped. A few paces from us, a small stream burbled.

Falla shifted, a moan from her throat quickly stifled.

"Falla?" Evrain asked. The big man hurried around me to her side.

I uncurled from my awkward crouch, accidentally knocking my injured foot against a fallen branch. Pain shot from the wound, traveling up my bones and setting my spine shivering. Beside me, Falla breathed through gritted teeth.

"Broken," she whispered.

Her right arm hung limply at her side, the fabric of her sleeve torn. A livid bruise had already bloomed, purpling her flesh from elbow to shoulder. Her left hand hovered protectively over the injury.

"What happened?" Evrain asked.

"Rock. Came down early on. Right after Kei screamed."

I blinked in surprise. Even injured, she'd still carried half my weight down the slope. Then her other words struck me.

Kei...

Evrain must have had the same thought; he jumped up and scrambled downstream, peering. After a moment, he returned and crouched beside us, face grim.

"Well?" Falla asked, voice tight.

Evrain shook his head.

What did that mean? Had he seen her body? I licked my lips to ask when a branch snapped behind us. A horse plodded out of the forest. His head was low, reins dragging. Bleeding scratches covered his neck and chest. As for the saddle, nothing remained.

A smile touched Falla's lips. "Always said Chaser was the most stubborn among us. Hey, old friend."

Slowly, Evrain stood. He clucked to the animal as he approached and gathered the reins. After allowing the horse to smell his hand, he stroked Chaser's neck. "I don't know who's more stubborn, you or your mistress." The Stormshard leader stood with the animal for a moment, forehead pressed against the sorrel-furred cheek before turning to us.

"We'll splint Falla's arm. Kostan can ride. Agreed?"

I pushed away the urge to protest. My pride could suffer for now. Instead, I nodded and clambered to my feet. Falla pulled out her belt knife, and after a moment's hesitation, she held it out.

"You try to stab me with that, I'll tear out your windpipe with my teeth," she said, attempting a smile. "I need you to cut fabric strips for the splint."

"You've nothing to fear from me. I forgot I was supposed to be your enemy," I said, accepting the blade.

Between the three of us, we had nothing but the clothes on our backs. With Falla's fresh injury, she'd need any warmth we could provide. My tunic then. As I started to untuck it from my trousers, Evrain laid a hand on my shoulder. He'd already removed his shirt, baring a muscled chest with a thin furring of gray hair and the scars to match his years as a Sharder.

Falla smirked. "Can't resist a chance to show up the strapping young lad, eh, Evrain?"

The leader rolled his eyes at her as he handed over his shirt. I slipped the knife into the stitching and cut away a sleeve. As I tore strips from it, Evrain gathered sticks to hold the injury rigid.

Falla hissed when we cinched the splint to her arm but otherwise bore it stoically. Afterward, she swallowed, eyes turning downstream. The joking must have been her way of avoiding thoughts of what lay ahead.

A mountain had come down on Kei's head. No one could survive that.

The landslide had created an earthen dam across the narrow valley. At its lowest, the berm was deeper than the height of two men. Already, the stream that tumbled down the ravine had begun to pool. In a few days, a small lake would fill the valley bottom.

Falla's stalwart horse huffed as he struggled up the loose soil and rocks, and I patted his silky coat to reassure him. Ahead, Evrain trudged with head down, reins held loosely in his hand. Behind, Falla marched with lips pressed together, breathing heavily through her nose.

Coldness filled my chest, slowing my heart. Somewhere beneath our feet, Kei's body lay in an early grave. So much hope and joy snuffed in an instant.

I laid my palm over the Heart of the Empire, felt the hard metal and stone against my breastbone. If the Breaking continued, Kei's spirit would be joined by thousands killed by the land's wrath.

And Emperor Tovmeil had believed only I could stop it.

Beyond the landslide, the trail resumed, damaged but usable. We moved in a slow procession over the uneven surface, scarcely speaking. I couldn't get Kei's smile out of my head.

"At least she died free," Falla said after a while.

"Indeed," Evrain agreed. "And someday, no Prov will have to bow to the Atal Empire."

"I hope it comes to pass," I said. "I would like to see an Empire that treated Provs and Atal equally."

In response, Falla spat. "No offense, Kostan, but I'd advise you to avoid statements like that. Half the Sharders in the band would slit your throat for suggesting it. As far as they're concerned, death is better than being part of Atal."

I winced. It seemed Kei hadn't been alone in her appraisal of her fellow Sharders. "Thanks for the warning, I guess."

She smiled, but it lacked any real joy. "Seen enough death for today, my friend."

At the reminder, silence once again cloaked us. I stared at the trail ahead, frustrated and wondering what would become of us all. We were a somber group as we approached the final turn before Stormshard's home cavern.

When we rounded the bend and saw the piles of rubble where the cavern had collapsed, Evrain fell to his knees. His gaze flew to Falla. Had her husband been inside?

"Anyone here?" Falla yelled, a desperate edge to her voice.

From behind a boulder, a single figure emerged. Staggering and bleeding, the man limped to us. His eyes were hollow, grief-stricken. He shook his head.

Chapter Thirty

Savra
Amongst toppled buildings in the outskirts of Jaliss

A man wearing ragged clothing and a desperate snarl leaped for Breeze's bridle. My gelding squealed and lashed out with his front hoof, striking the man in the thigh. Clinging with my knees, I leaned hard over the saddle as we trotted down another ruined street.

Jaliss was in shambles.

Shadows filled the buildings. Silence gathered in the streets—those who'd been out when the quake struck had quickly melted away. I was in a warehouse district; the wood frames of the structures had fared well, but many stone chimneys had toppled.

Evening had descended, and despite the gloom beneath Jaliss's pall of smoke, few lamps and torches had been lit. Distant shouts peppered the air, and far away, beyond the immense shadow cast by Steelhold's spire, angry tongues of fire licked the air. Steam billowed from the fire's heart; by the looks of it, it wouldn't be long before the flames were doused.

After putting the desperate man well behind me, I paused and stroked Breeze's neck. I was hopelessly lost. Somewhere, a street should lead away from the city. I'd come in from the east. With luck, I'd find a way back to familiar territory.

But would the open grasslands be any safer? Parveld's words echoed in my mind. The Graybranch Inn was a haven. It had to be a safer bet than aimlessly wandering or pitching a tent just outside a devastated city.

What about leaving the city and riding through the night? To where? I might distance myself from the immediate danger, but I'd face another difficult choice in the morning.

While I was here, I should at least attempt to find this Graybranch Inn. In the morning, the worst of the danger would have passed—I would think, anyway. I could take my time in making my decision, choose the best course rather than react in a panic.

Nudging Breeze with my heels, I turned him toward the center of the city. No doubt someone would give me directions to the Graybranch.

Deeper into Jaliss, cobblestone pavement replaced the earthen streets. Unfortunately, the stones had been tossed like beans in a skillet and were a jumbled puzzle, making footing treacherous. I dismounted to allow Breeze to pick his way forward.

I kept the hood of my cloak pulled over my hair, my face turned down. More people were out in this area, many with dust-streaked faces and scratched skin. When I reached another cross street and looked up, my throat caught.

Built of stone rather than wood, many walls had collapsed, baring the insides of buildings for all to see. Families huddled outside their homes, clutching injured limbs, eyes wide with shock. Glancing up and down the streets, I spotted protectors moving in small knots, torches high against the falling night.

I kept close to my gelding's side, eyes alert. The western horizon still glowed, but full night would soon fall. At least here, the crowds provided some defense against attackers. Better than moving alone through the darkness of the outskirts.

At the next street corner, I spotted a mother and her daughter huddled beside a still-standing building.

"Excuse me," I asked. "Can you give me directions to the Splits?"

The woman shook her head and pushed her little girl behind her.

I swallowed and walked on, my nostrils filling with smoke. Ahead, the stonework on the buildings changed from the native granite to deeply veined marble. Massive slate blocks paved the streets, too large for even an earthquake to shift. A line of protectors two deep stood shoulder to shoulder, defending the district. I tugged on Breeze's reins, steering him away from what I assumed were the homes or businesses of elite-class Atalans.

Deeper into the city, people screamed. Glass shattered as fire leaped into the darkening sky. I glanced back at the protectors guarding the wealthy district, expecting some might run to help with the fire. Jaws set, eyes locked directly ahead, not one moved.

As I started forward again, muffled thumps emerged from an alleyway ahead. I hesitated, scanning the fronts of nearby buildings. Fewer walls had crumbled here. Most doors were shut and padlocked, and wooden shutters covered the windows. Placards hung over entrances, advertising tailors and clothiers.

Nudging Breeze, I crossed the street to the side opposite the alley mouth.

As I hurried past, I heard a shout. "Hey!"

I quickened my pace.

"Girl! I'm trying to talk to you!"

It took all my willpower not to glance back over my shoulder.

Something whistled over my head. The cobblestone smashed the front of the building beside me. Breeze started, tossing his head. My heart sledged against my ribs as I broke into a run, hoping Breeze could keep his footing.

When a pair of men stepped into my path, I stumbled. One grinned, exposing straight teeth with a hint of staining from the tobacco favored by Atal elite. He wore an expertly tailored waistcoat with silver buttons. His companion, another Atal, twirled a broken chair leg.

"I believe my friend back there asked to speak to you," the leader said, running a hand over hair slicked down by wax. When he pushed back the sleeve of his waistcoat, muscles rippled in his forearms. This man might be a privileged Atal, but he shared their obsession with strength. "You're lost, aren't you? A stranger here, perhaps. Don't you know the Heights and Merchant's Quarter are off limits to Provs without a writ stating your business." He held out his hand as if waiting for my document.

"I came to the city to receive my writ," I said, raising my chin. Behind me, I heard the others advance. I guessed there were at least two more, but I couldn't risk taking my eyes off the men in front of me.

The leader raised an eyebrow. "Interesting, considering you stink of Cosmal."

"If I'm not allowed here, maybe you can give me directions to the Provincial areas." While I spoke, I passed Breeze's reins to my other hand and stepped back alongside the saddle. My standing leg tensed as I unweighted the foot I'd need to jab through the stirrup's iron ring to mount.

"We'd better give you an escort," he said, covering my body with a leering gaze. Behind him, his friend sneered, raising the chair leg.

I moved, shoving my foot into the stirrup, but it was too late. Hands fell on me from behind, grabbing me around the ribs. As the scream rose in my throat, the world receded.

No. Not now.

Despite my mental protests, my aura-sight flared to life. At once, I saw their spirits. Lechery pulsed, a deep reddish-purple, through their thoughts. I had no doubt what they intended, nor that they'd probably leave me dead afterward to protect their reputations. Not that they needed to worry about an accusation from a Provincial girl who hadn't a single friend in the city.

As more hands fell on me, pulling me away from Breeze, their voices entered my mind. I stiffened, revolted and terrified. Like the night whispers that sometimes seeped into my thoughts, the men's desires babbled in my thoughts.

Somewhere in the midst of my panic, resistance sparked. I couldn't let them do this. I *wouldn't* let them do it.

With all my focus, I reached my awareness for their spirits and voices. Grabbing handfuls of their auras, I yanked and twisted, yelling into their thoughts.

NO!

At once, the world snapped back into place. Jagged cobblestones bludgeoned my hip and elbow as I crashed down. The men stepped back, wide-eyed in terror, bent over their bellies as if pained.

Scrambling over the uneven terrain, I snatched Breeze's reins and took off at a sprint. Snorting and blowing, he followed, sturdy legs finding safe points for his hooves.

As we hurried away, I glanced over my shoulder. What had I just done?

A few blocks on, the buildings became dingier. I stopped and leaned forward over Breeze's mane.

Where was I going to go?

As if carried on a warm, Highsummer wind, the words entered my mind along with a sensation of someone near.

Hurry to Fishel's, Savra. The Splits. You're nearly there.

"Parveld?" I asked. But the voice and presence had vanished.

I rubbed my forehead with the heel of my hand. A block to my right, a fire burned in an immense iron basket. A man wearing the crier's crest stood near, calling through a speaking horn.

"By order of the Emperor, Jaliss is under curfew. Please return to your homes and await direction from Steelhold!"

Beyond him, someone yelled. A man staggered from an alley carrying an injured woman in his arms. Blood streamed from her forehead, and her eyes stared blankly. She might already be dead. The man paused long enough to kick a stone toward the crier.

"To the Gray Gorge with your precious Emperor," he yelled.

Unfortunately for the man, he hadn't noticed the pair of protectors farther down the street. The Emperor's soldiers marched forward and stripped the body of the woman from the man's arms. I looked away as a series of thumps ended with a loud crack. When I balled my fists and lifted my eyes, the protectors were dragging the man between them. His head lolled as they dragged him around the corner and out of sight.

I tugged Breeze toward the crier, drawn by his official-looking uniform.

"I need to get to the Splits," I said.

He looked at me as if I were a piece of garbage. "The Splits?" he said, lip twitching. "If you value your virtue, I'd stay clear."

Despite his words, he jabbed his thumb toward a street that descended toward the right. Squinting into the torch-lit smoke, I saw ramshackle buildings huddled together. "Is the Graybranch Inn down there?" I asked.

The man spat on the ruined pavement. "If the protectors haven't razed it as a breeding ground for rats and revolutionaries." He scanned me up and down. "Come to think of it, you have an unseemly look about you. Sharder?"

I stepped back, shaking my head. "Just a weary traveler. I should move on."

He narrowed his eyes. "Or maybe you should stay here until my protector friends get back to ask you some questions."

I shook my head again and stepped away. I'd been foolish to name my destination. But as I started down the street, I heard him laugh to himself. He'd just been trying to scare me.

I hoped.

Chapter Thirty-One

Kostan
Beneath the shelter of tree branches, Icethorn foothills

The hammer struck the chisel with a ringing blow that sent agony up my leg.

"Sorry," Evrain muttered. "Just hold as still as you can."

As he set the chisel again, laying it against the padding that protected my shin and sliding the tip into the groove the first blows had etched in my cuff, I bit down hard on the stick Falla had shoved between my lips.

With the next hammer strike, black fluttered at the edges of my vision. Above, the overhanging boughs of a pine reached down like claws. The lone Sharder who'd survived the cavern collapse patted my cheek to keep me from passing out.

"It's okay, Shaw," Evrain said. "If he blacks out, this will be easier anyway."

"As you say." Shaw clapped my shoulder then stepped aside. He'd been out front of the cavern when the quake struck, working on some tool repairs at the anvil. A rock had struck his head right after the shaking began, and when he woke, the cave was gone. He'd spent the time between his recovery and our arrival digging. But it was no use. Not a sound came from within the collapsed hideout. With no food or water, we couldn't remain out in the elements. We'd begun a slow, hobbling descent out of the mountains—Stormshard had a refuge somewhere near the border with the plateau.

"All right, Kostan," Evrain said. "Another few blows. You sure this is what you want?"

I gritted my teeth and nodded. During the march away from the destroyed cavern, Falla had been stoic despite her broken arm and lost husband whereas I'd been forced to ride the horse like a weakling. Once I'd seen the chisel among Shaw's supplies, I'd made up my mind. I'd fled Steelhold under the threat of murder. I had the Heart hanging around my neck. Wearing a gold cuff under my trousers would make little difference. And besides, I couldn't stay dependent on Stormshard to tend my wound. I couldn't even *stay* with Stormshard.

Not anymore.

"Go ahead," I said.

The leader gave a curt nod before resetting the chisel. He struck again, and the bite stick fell from my lips. My head spun. Everything went black.

The moon was up, a ghostly orb casting wan light through the pine branches overhead. Beside me, the three Sharders lay close together, conserving warmth. I took a moment to realize they'd piled everything warm on top of me as insulation. Squinting in the dimness, I spotted Shaw's rucksack and canvas tool holder, Evrain's tunic, and a saddle blanket recovered from outside the cavern.

Guilt tightened my chest as I stood and crept from beneath the tree. Beyond the spread of its boughs, the silver light was bright enough to see clearly, and I scanned the trail ahead. Only once I'd taken a couple of steps did I realize: my foot hardly hurt.

Immediately, I dropped to the ground and propped my ankle on my knee. I wiggled a finger through the folds of the bandage and probed the wound. The flesh was still raw and sensitive, but the area around the gashes was no longer swollen. I'd believed Falla's theory about the cuff, but I hadn't realized how quickly its removal would cure me.

Unfortunately, I had no second boot. I glanced back at the tree then shook my head. Bad enough that I planned to steal their only horse. I couldn't bring myself to take one of their boots, too.

Besides, I doubted I could get it off without waking one of them.

In the grass beside the trail, a rodent dug at the earth. When I stepped toward it, little black eyes stared up at me. Walking on just the ball of my injured foot to keep the bandage clean, I moved past the small creature. The horse grazed on tough mountain grass a few paces down the trail. Scratching between his ears to soothe the animal, I unwound the reins from a tree branch then led him downhill.

When I'd passed out of sight of the drooping branches where the Stormsharders slept, I turned and whispered an apology. Maybe I'd meet them again someday. With good fortune, I'd be able to prove that an emperor could be both strong and noble. At the very least, I hoped for the chance to beg forgiveness.

For now, I'd just have to live with my guilt. They were resilient people, and I had no doubt they'd arrive at their shelter safely.

Well, very little doubt anyway. But a would-be leader needed to make hard choices, especially when lives were at stake. As I grabbed the horse's mane and awkwardly mounted, prompting a stamping of feet and rolling of eyes, I thought of Kei's ponytail.

Maybe that's what Emperor Tovmeil had prophesied. A woman would betray me. Kei had made me believe, just for a moment, that I could be someone else. A Sharder and free man. But then she'd died and reminded me of everything I could never have.

Settling the reins in my hand and shifting my weight over the horse's bare back, I swallowed and squeezed my heels to his ribs.

I had an Empire to win.

Chapter Thirty-Two

The Graybranch Inn had survived the quake intact. Unlike most of the surrounding buildings, the siding had few splinters and fewer gaps. A wide porch ran the length of the front of the building, and though the foundation was stone, the mortar looked to have survived the shake.

Unfortunately, the door was barred with a curtain drawn across the small glass window beside it. No light came from the upper windows either.

As I stood on the packed-earth street, holding my gelding's reins and stroking his mane, I trembled. A few hours ago, I'd imagined starting a new life. Finding my father or rescuing my mother and sister or simply taking up the scribe's Function.

Now I wondered if I'd survive the night.

As I'd followed the winding streets to the Graybranch, more criers had started calling out the curfew. The city grew emptier and emptier as its citizens drained away into whatever refuge they could find. I'd glanced at many promising heaps of rubble or ruined buildings. But I'd moved on every time, encouraged by Parveld's promise of safety.

But the Graybranch offered no refuge. The inn was deserted. As if to kick the last hope from my heart, my stomach rumbled. The inside of my mouth was tacky with thirst. I hadn't eaten since breakfast, and I'd last drank while waiting for Havialo's friends. Soon enough, hunger and thirst would become as big a problem as the curfew and bands of protectors enforcing it.

"What do you think, Breeze? Can we escape the city after all?"

Glancing along the edge of the porch, I spotted a trough. Despite the violent quake, water stood a few knuckles deep in the bottom of the wooden box. Though the smell of the water turned my stomach, I knelt and prepared to drink after Breeze finished.

"Are you trying to get tossed in the lockup, Prov? Curfew went into effect half an hour ago."

The gruff voice sent ice down my spine. Swallowing, I turned.

With a smirk, the man stuck out a meaty hand. "Name's Fishel. And you are?"

"He'll be secure in here," Fishel said as he latched and locked the stable door. When the man gestured toward the rear door of the inn, I hesitated, glancing over my shoulder at the wooden building we'd just left. Breeze was secure in a clean stall, a tin water pail hanging in the corner, but I hated to leave my only friend. Nonetheless, I followed the innkeeper into the main building, squinting in the near dark.

"A moment," he said. Flint struck steel, and sparks flared in the air. After a couple tries, he coaxed a flame from a small kerosene lamp then fitted the glass chimney over the base. "Few guests tonight, but they've all received the same instructions. No fires until we know the ground has stilled," he explained. "After we settle you into a room, you'll do the same."

"I—yes, sure." That explained why I'd seen no light coming from the windows.

The floorboards creaked as he strode, hardened leather boots scuffing against the floor, to a counter in the inn's common room. A row of small wooden casks stood on a table behind him, copper taps plugged into the bottom. Most nights, this room was probably full of travelers drinking ale. Foreigners, even.

"My writ allows me flexibility in what kind of payment I'll accept," Fishel said as he pulled out a heavy book and plucked a quill from the counter. "Your accent is Provincial, so I gather you'll pay in tin scrip."

"I—well, I'm not sure what I have." I lifted Havialo's saddlebags onto the counter—before entering the city, I'd switched my panniers for them, keeping just the cloak and my small knife from my old bags. But I hadn't sorted through Havialo's possessions because sunset had been so near. I unbuckled the leather straps and started rummaging.

The proprietor's face immediately stilled. He laid the quill on the counter. "Now I'm a respectable man. I'd hate to turn a girl away on a night like this. But you're not the only one at risk here."

I chewed my lip, confused. Did he think I was trying to sell something else? My virtue maybe? My fingers brushed the small blade Havialo had given me. Though scarcely larger than a fish-scaling knife, the handle was made from mother-of-pearl, and I figured it'd be payment for one night. I pulled it out and laid it on the counter. "The person who gave me this said it was good steel."

Fishel laid his palms on the counter. "You're new here, a Prov. That much is obvious. But surely the rules are the same in your home. Scrip or foreign currency for services. Everything else is black market."

"I suppose I hadn't thought of it. We only have tin scrip back home."

He shook his head. "If the inspectors turn up tomorrow and I've let you stay without paying real scrip or coin, I'll have my writ revoked. My choices will be exile or starvation."

He cast me a pitying look as he shut the book. "Best I can offer is to let you shelter behind the building. If you're quiet, you may escape notice until dawn."

I gritted my teeth as I set the knife aside and started pulling everything from the saddlebags. Travel rations. Waterskins. A length of ribbon—his daughter's? I thought back to the steel coin Havialo had flipped to the traveling herbalist. He'd pulled it from a pouch inside his tunic. My hopes pooled at my feet—why had I even imagined he would have carried his money in his saddlebags?

"Would it matter if Parveld sent me?" I asked, out of ideas.

At once, the man's eyes lit. "And that, my girl, is the best news I've heard all day. He told me his sister would be arriving before Chilltide. You must be so weary after journeying all the way from Ioene! Fortunately, I've been holding your room since he first laid down the coin for it. I hope you don't mind a cold meal."

I stood frozen. Sister? Ioene?

Fishel hurried around the counter and laid a hand on my back, urging me toward the stairs. "If anyone bothers you—imperial inspectors for instance—speak of the wonders crafted in Ioene's forges. It never fails to impress. I hear your home estate with the nightvining wine grapes is lovely."

Recovering from my shock, I took a hesitant step toward the stairs. Why hadn't Parveld told me the extent of his arrangements? Should it worry me that he'd planned this so much in advance? And even if it did, were the streets a safer choice?

The questions whirled, but a shout and thump from outside decided me. "I—yes. My family has done quite well as wine makers. Parveld has been searching for export contracts with the Atal elite. I'm looking forward to hearing about his progress."

Fishel smiled as he passed me to take the lead up the stairs. "Wonderful. I believe you'll do well here once the dust settles. So to speak."

Chapter Thirty-Three

Parveld
Beside the remains of a simple shepherd's hut

Full night cloaked the land, hiding the reminders of the evening's earthquake. Parveld sat near the pile of toppled stones that had been his shepherd's hut a few hours ago. Before him, a small fire crackled.

He held the silver-and-gold bracelet on his lap. Age burnished the metal, tiny scratches marring the surfaces. Despite his regular efforts with a polishing rag, tarnish gathered in the creases where the strands of metal entwined. He ran a finger over the curves then turned it over. As he watched, the word *Savra* appeared, etched into the metal.

I know. I should have given it to her. There was so much happening, he said into the aether.

Centuries of practice, yet you're still such a terrible liar, said the spirit of the woman infused into the metal. A tendril of affection curled out from the bracelet, wrapping him in an ethereal hug. Another presence offered friendly amusement, the sort of teasing only trusted friends could get away with.

Parveld smiled. *Okay fine. I tried. But I just wasn't ready. You two are all I have, now.*

It's not forever, two voices spoke at once, echoing in Parveld's mind. The woman laughed and continued alone. *Besides, Savra is pretty. Maybe you don't have to be alone in the mortal realm either.*

"Right..." Parveld said. "If the centuries haven't helped me learn to lie, they've taught me even less about speaking to women. Savra was nervous around me, to put it mildly. Anyway... I saw a different future for her."

A potential future. Nothing is certain with the tides of fate.

It isn't going to happen, Lilik. You know that. And I'm okay alone.

A wave of acceptance flowed from the bracelet. *Fair enough, my friend.*

Back to the issue, tonight was too close, the man inside the silver strand added. *If she hadn't made it to the Graybranch...*

Do you think I should have pressed her to stay with me? Parveld asked. *She even asked why I didn't. But she was so guarded... And it felt right for her to continue into Jaliss.*

I think you should have given her the bracelet as we agreed one hundred eighty-seven years ago, the woman, Lilik, said, *sending a thread of amusement into his mind along with the thought.*

Parveld pressed the metal band close to his heart. *All right. But promise me you'll be safe. I mean to join you both in the aether someday.*

Silence followed his words. Somewhere on the grassy terrace, a sheep bleated.

I can't promise. But I can't wait to be together again. As long as there's a sliver of hope, I won't stop trying. Even after that hope vanishes, in fact.

Heart aching over the coming goodbye, Parveld stood. He grabbed his walking stick from beside the fire and poured a measure of water over the blaze.

One step at a time, he started the descent to the plateau and the city upon it.

Chapter Thirty-Four

Kostan
In the streets of Jaliss

Though I needed only my fingers to count the number of hours I'd spent in Jaliss, the devastation in the city was a sword thrust through my heart. Remorse draped me like a cloak of lead. I'd spent my life hating the Empire and disdaining the idea of ruling, but now I felt as if the suffering in Jaliss was my responsibility.

My time in the mountains had changed me. The citizens of Jaliss were no longer subjects of the Empire. They were mine. My vassals. My responsibility. I had no choice but to Ascend the throne, and every moment between now and that ascent was my burden to bear. Every blow from a protector's cudgel would be as if I'd swung the club myself. Every rattle and tremor of the earth's Breaking was my fault.

Until I'd restored the Heart of the Empire to the throne, I would not sleep easily. Kei's death had taught me the consequences of shirking my responsibility. The collapse of Stormshard's cavern had only sealed my destiny.

I had to take back Steelhold. Starting by visiting the Graybranch Inn in hopes of finding news from Azar.

At the edge of the Merchant's Quarter, the street known as the Corridor of Ascent led to the trail that climbed Steelhold's spire. I stopped to regard my rightful home. The rising sun glowed on the fortress's walls, giving the impression that the Hold burned. And if I needed to torch the fortress to unseat the conspirators, I would.

Patting my horse's neck, I clucked to him and turned his head for the Splits.

As we descended through the city, exhaustion fell over me. I could only imagine how my mount—Chaser, Falla had called him—suffered. We'd been riding at full gallop since I'd abandoned Evrain and his friends. The overhanging tree hadn't been far from the boundary between mountains and grassland, and I'd spent most of the night on the open road, chasing the moon across the Atalan Plateau. When the sky behind me paled with predawn light, sweat had dripped from Chaser's flanks. But he'd never hesitated. Even now, he plodded with steady feet across the rubble-strewn streets.

I shook my head at every fallen wall and overturned cart we passed. It would take months to rebuild Jaliss. How long until the next quake? Or worse, what would happen when a gash like the Gray Gorge opened in the city's heart?

I had to stop this.

If the despair had been palpable in the Merchant's Quarter and the wealthier residential blocks, the mood in the Splits was abysmal. Men and women sat on stoops, staring blankly with hunger obvious in their sunken cheeks. If they were curious why a young man wearing just one boot was riding bareback through the Splits, they didn't show it. By cutting off Steelhold, the Minister Brevt and his allies were strangling the city.

What was their purpose? Were they waiting to complete their coup until the Provs were too hungry and desperate to care who sat on the throne as long as the flow of scrip resumed?

Anger simmering in my chest, I nudged poor Chaser on.

Despite my expectations, the Graybranch Inn looked more suited to the upper districts than the squalor of the Splits. I understood why Ilishian had chosen the establishment. The construction was sound. No doubt the rooms were secure and clean.

When I reined up out front, the fatigue that had been chasing me slammed into my body. I swung my leg over Chaser's hindquarters and dropped. When my feet touched the ground, my knees buckled. I landed hard and sprawled. Flat on my back, I stared into a clear, Atalan sky marred only by the imposing lines of Steelhold.

I rolled onto an elbow and slowly gained my feet. My knees wobbled and ached. The first steps were agony. I looped Chaser's reins around a post supporting the porch awning then stared at the intimidating rise of the steps.

I took a moment to rub the white blaze on Chaser's nose. He snorted in appreciation before lowering his muzzle to the trough before him. Making a silent vow to find him a bucket of the finest oats, I took a deep breath and planted a foot on the first stair.

Chapter Thirty-Five

Savra
The common room of the Graybranch Inn

Fishel nodded when he exited the inn's kitchen. "Good morning, Savra. Your brother came by in the night. He dropped a package through our courier slot."

A dart of paranoia sent me sitting bolt upright. "He what?"

"The letter explained that he expected a busy week of negotiations. With the quake, many Atal families have suffered losses in their wine cellars. He didn't wish to wake you, but wanted to return the bracelet he brought from Ioene to remember you."

I was seated at a simple table in the common room, the scroll case with my ledger placed before me. Before leaving the simple room I'd been given the night before, I'd adjusted the straps on a saddlebag. It made a workable satchel, though if not for the chaos in the city, I guessed it would draw a few stares. At the moment, I was trying to figure out whether I should tuck the scroll case inside—it was too long and would jut out the top—or whether to remove the ledger from the case and fold it to fit in the saddlebag.

After waking, I'd thought about my next steps. My father was close. I'd come this far. If I couldn't find him or contact Stormshard after a week or two of searching, I could still try to find a way back to Cosmal Province. It had been weeks since I left Numintown—I doubted I'd gain anything by rushing back to hunt for traces of my mother and sister. Better to learn what I could of my father first. Plus, it would give me time to think about Parveld's offer of training.

Along with a wooden bowl filled with porridge, Fishel set a bracelet on the table. Formed of strands of silver and gold twisted together, the band had a flat area stamped in the middle. A picture of an island had been etched on the disk, a steep-sided mountain with something spraying from the top. The metals had been pressed such that the areas of silver were the sea while the flattened gold strand ran through the sky. Fire and water. Vitality and tranquility.

"Reminds you of home, I'm sure," Fishel said, pointing to the picture on the disk. "I hear Ioene's eruptions are amazing on dark nights. Not dangerous—the lava never spills more than a short distance down the mountain. But with the aurora flaring above, it's supposed to be a wonder that an adventurer never forgets."

He stared at me pointedly. After a moment, I nodded. "Ioene. Yes, it does remind me of my home."

With a nod of approval, Fishel folded his hands before him. "I apologize for the limited fare. I've had a hard time getting fresh produce since the... incident at Steelhold. I imagine things will only get worse. Fortunately, I have an expansive food cellar. As long as you don't mind oats and pickles. Oh! I nearly forgot."

With a flourish, Fishel deposited a spoon on the table, then winked. "There's a pitcher of water and cups on the counter. I'll have tea out shortly."

As he turned for the kitchen, I glanced at the spoon but my attention snapped back to the bracelet. I wasn't sure whether to put it on, throw it away, or hide it where I wouldn't have to think about it. As I peered closer, I noticed writing where the bracelet could be squeezed together for a tighter fit.

Savra.

I dropped the bracelet as if it had burned me and snatched the spoon, scooping a thick measure of porridge. The sooner I got to the Hall of Registry and took control of my life, the better.

As I slipped the bite into my mouth—despite Fishel's apologies, the porridge was quite good—the door opened. My eyes widened when the young man stumbled through the door. He looked so exhausted that another step would send him sprawling on the floor.

The squeal of my chair against the floor sent a shiver crawling up my spine. Despite it, I ran forward to catch the newcomer if he toppled.

He looked up.

My heart stopped.

I felt like I'd known him forever, though I'd never seen his face before. The man blinked and sagged against the door. Bells jingled merrily as the latch clicked shut.

I was still staring when Fishel banged his way out of the kitchen, tea set on a tray.

"Welcome to the Graybranch Inn," he said, setting down the tray and stepping around the counter.

Fishel made three paces before the young man toppled to the floor.

Together, Fishel and I wrangled the new arrival off the floor and helped him toward the table where I'd been eating breakfast. As the man stumbled forward, arm over my shoulder, I noticed he was wearing just one boot. A dirty bandage wrapped the other foot though it seemed to bear weight.

Once seated, he slumped forward, elbows planted on the table, head loose on his shoulders.

I couldn't stop staring and blushed when Fishel caught me at it.

The innkeeper pulled out a chair and sat, stretching his legs out. "Well then, you're the second traveler who's arrived at the Graybranch since the quake—and looking even worse off than this young lady did. I can't understand why anyone would deem it a good idea to enter the city right now."

"I'm looking for someone," the arrival said. I got the sense that the effort of moving his lips was almost more than he could manage. With an obvious struggle, he pushed off the table to lean back in the chair. The weight of his head followed behind, rolling up off his chest. As it did, his simple tunic tugged to the side, exposing a silver chain encircling his neck.

When our eyes met, his widened. The newcomer held my stare, and it was all I could do to force my gaze away. He had dark eyes, typical Atal, and chestnut hair streaked with hints of blond. Why did I feel I knew him? Again, I felt blood coloring my cheeks.

After a moment, Fishel snapped his fingers in the man's face. A flash of surprise crossed the man's weary features as if he'd forgotten the innkeeper was there.

"Other than Savra here, my remaining guests left early this morning," Fishel said. "Bound for Anisel's ports and trading prospects in cities not toppled by a recent quake. So if it was a foreign merchant you intended to meet, I suggest you climb back on your horse and ride for the Provinces. Not that you're in a condition for it."

"I'll take a room, then," the man said. His eyes had returned to me.

Fishel sighed. "Will you be paying in scrip, steel coin or foreign currency? You're Atal if I were to guess, but as long as you can provide papers that verify a foreign birth, I'll accept whatever currency you're offering. I'm no clerk, so don't expect me to recognize a forgery. And that's exactly what I'll tell the inspectors."

As if Fishel's words reached the man from some great distance, he blinked, slow comprehension dawning on his face. After a moment, he patted his pockets.

Fishel rolled his eyes. "Let me guess. You don't have any coin."

"Well... I—"

"Sorry, friend. I can offer you water before you leave."

"I lost everything." The young man turned desperate eyes to me. My heart ached. I couldn't let him face the city. Not like this.

"He's my betrothed," I blurted. "Just arrived from the ports in Anisel. Darling, I didn't expect you to follow so soon—the seas around Ioene are treacherous this time of year! I told you I'd be safe."

Chapter Thirty-Six

Kostan
The common room of the Graybranch Inn

Betrothed? What was this?

"I suppose your... brother will pay for your betrothed's stay as well, Savra?" the innkeeper asked, rolling his eyes.

The young woman's green eyes flicked to mine again, and once again I felt the surprise in my chest. She inhaled and swiveled in her chair to face the innkeeper.

"Yes, Fishel, thank you," the young woman, Savra, said. The pair locked eyes. After a moment, Fishel scooted his chair away from the table and paced to the counter at the back of the room.

I swallowed. Clearly, Savra had mistaken me for someone else. But how? How could someone be confused about the face of their betrothed?

"I—I've had a long ride," I said. "My horse... needs grooming and food. He served me well in reaching here."

My mind was drifting on a sea of fatigue, and I wondered whether this was some strange dream. But when Savra's warm hand fell over mine, little shocks traveled up my arms. That didn't happen in dreams, did it? As quickly as her touch had come, she pulled away, shy. Once again, our eyes met.

A heavy book slammed down on the table between us, falling open to a page filled with a scrawled guest list.

"Your future brother-in-law's account will cover your stay for quite some time," the innkeeper said, a trace of sarcasm touching his words. "Now, will it be one room or two?"

Savra opened her mouth to speak, swallowed, then started again. "Two, please. We aren't yet wed, Fishel."

With an exasperated sigh, Fishel leafed through the guest list to the first page with blank lines. He lifted a quill and looked at Savra with a smirk. "And your betrothed's name is?"

"Kostan," I said, rescuing her before exhaustion took me and I slumped forward onto the table.

Chapter Thirty-Seven

Fishel latched the man's—Kostan's—door with a quiet click. It hadn't been easy to wrestle his big frame up the stairs and onto the narrow cot, and a drop of sweat trickled down my cheek. But the heat in my cheeks was from something else entirely. As the innkeeper stepped around me, heading back downstairs to busy himself with whatever chores Kostan's arrival had interrupted, I kept my eyes on the floorboards.

What had I been thinking, declaring Kostan my betrothed? The impulse had been so sudden; I hadn't considered the reasons... or the consequences. I mean, yes, he'd seemed to need help, but he was a complete stranger. And an Atal at that.

Maybe he wouldn't stay long. I wasn't sure I could face him and handle the embarrassment of what I'd done. But the thought that I might not see him again terrified me. What was wrong with me?

Now that the door hid him from sight, at least I wasn't plagued by the nearly irresistible urge to stare. I needed to continue my day. First, I'd locate the Hall of Registry. If the doors were open, I'd attempt to present the ledger declaring my scribe's assignment. If not, I'd spend the day getting familiar with the city.

I traced a finger over Parveld's bracelet. During Kostan's shocking arrival, I'd slipped it onto my wrist. It felt comfortable there, warm against my skin. I guessed it wouldn't hurt to leave it on for now.

Downstairs, my saddlebag-turned-satchel still rested on the table with the scroll holder beside it. Snatching them both up, I stuck the leather tube down inside the bag and slung the arrangement over my shoulder. As I walked to the door, I heard Fishel's boots behind me. Setting my hand upon the latch, I turned to look at him.

"Could you give me directions to the Hall of Registry?"

He folded a tea towel over his arm as he looked at me. "The registrars? Why?"

Right... foreigners didn't receive writs. Fishel knew I was a Prov, of course, but he needed to be able to deny it if an argent mage questioned him. "Well, depending on how the negotiations go between Parveld and the elites, I'll need to hire a few caravaneers to transport the casks of our wine, correct?"

He sighed. "It's not a good time to be out, Savra. Better you rest here until the city returns to normal."

"How soon do you expect that will happen? I can't delay my business indefinitely."

He pressed his lips together but seemed to recognize my determination. "Follow Spire Street until you pass the leatherworker's with a hardened jerkin hanging from the sign. Take a left, wind your way up toward the Heights. The Hall of Registry is near the juncture where the Merchant's Quarter meets the Splits and Tanner's Row. If you reach the iron gates at the entrance to the Heights, you've gone too far."

"Thank you."

"Savra," he said as I squeezed the latch. "Parveld... he's a good man. I owe him much and don't wish to disappoint him by failing to protect you."

"I'll be back by midday," I said. "It's just a single errand."

Out in the street, I stopped and turned a slow circle. When covered in darkness, the city had appeared damaged but reparable. The harsh light of morning showed the true devastation. In the Splits, earthen streets had been a small salvation. Unlike the destroyed cobblestones in the wealthier areas of the city, the ground beneath my feet was merely cracked and uneven. I glanced back at the stable and wondered whether I should saddle Breeze.

No, that was just my selfish desire for comfort and companionship. Once back to the cobblestone areas, it would be just as hard for him to pick his way through the rubble as it would be for me to trudge across it. Maybe harder.

Hitching up my satchel, I set off up Spire Street.

Along the narrow passage, children lingered close to the stoops of shanties and shacks. Occasionally, I spotted eyes peering out at me from behind shuttered windows. Where houses had toppled, no one remained. I wondered where they'd gone. To friends? Out of the city?

Jumbled cobblestones marked the transition into the Merchant's Quarter, and I kept my eyes alert for the leatherworker's sign. Patrols of protectors marched through the area, eyes hard. Though the doors to shops were shut and barred, I suspected the chaos made extra opportunities for thieves.

Which made me wonder whether I should try to contact Stormshard now. From Havialo's accounts, they were something of a band of thieves themselves, though with more noble intentions.

But how? Should I stand on a corner and yell for a member of the a renegade group? Clearly, that wouldn't work. Better if I could attract their attention in other ways.

In any case, first things first. The registrars.

When I spotted the leatherworker's shop, I turned left. As Fishel had mentioned, the road began a winding ascent toward the Heights and the massive homes of the Atalan elite. As I climbed, the streets became less deserted. A few cloth sellers had braved the toppled buildings and rubble-strewn alleys and called out as I passed.

"Tin scrip, steel coin, foreign currency. All accepted with a writ to prove legality!"

"Finest silk from faraway islands!"

"Get your clothing sewn while you wait!"

Further on a jeweler stood outside his store, holding a few necklaces high. "Low prices for our troubled city. Get them now before Steelhold reopens and increases demand. Almost a steal!"

And when I passed closer, he hissed and looked sideways. "Have a few pieces of Maelstrom-gold in the back room," he said in a false whisper. "And a mage who can attune them. Get yourself an advantage, no matter your Function."

Snapping my head away, I hurried on. I'd seen enough Maelstrom metals to last a lifetime. I wondered what the jeweler would think if I told him.

Finally, I spotted a marble-walled building with the words Hall of Registry carved into the facade. I certainly hadn't needed to worry about passing it. Fishel must have truly been concerned for my safety to tell me when to turn around. What happened to Provs who wandered into the Heights?

Unfortunately, the doors to the Hall appeared locked. I mounted the steps anyway, earning a few strange looks from the street sellers and the scattered pedestrians braving the city. The massive doors were iron-bound and carved from dark hardwood. Glass windows had been set in the wood. Cupping my hands at the sides of my face, I peered through.

In the darkened interior, a clerk glanced up from a desk.

I waved.

He stared at me a moment before continuing his work. I rapped on the door. He ignored me.

"Excuse me," a gruff voice said.

A pair of protectors stood behind me. One laid a hand on his sword's hilt. The other pulled out his cudgel. He slapped the end against his opposite palm.

"Yes?" I said.

"You're violating curfew."

I blinked. "I thought the curfew ended at dawn."

"Don't play stupid. What's your business?"

"I—I came for my writ. I received my assignment and traveled here from Cosmal." I reached for my scroll holder. "I'm to be a scribe."

The cudgel came down hard, cracking against my knuckles. "Doesn't matter what your Function is. You're out when there's a curfew."

"But I—"

Again the cudgel came down, thudding against my shoulder. I staggered and nearly fell.

"Okay, I'll go back to my... lodgings," I said, hands up to defend my face.

"What do you think?" the man with the cudgel said. "Shall we take her in?"

"Where are you staying?" the other asked. "We'll have to investigate. And I'll need to see your permission to enter Jaliss without a Function writ."

"But I came to the Hall to get my writ."

"It's no excuse." The cudgel-bearer shook his head. "She's got the look of a Sharder about her, wouldn't you say?"

He didn't look at his partner as he spoke, but rather pinned me with his dead-eyed stare. I raised my hands in a plea. "Listen, I'll go. I didn't mean to disobey. I didn't hear the curfew had been extended."

"You know," the other protector said, moving his hand from his sword pommel to a pair of iron handcuffs. "I think we'd best just take her to the holding cells until we sort this out."

I didn't know what else to do.

I ran.

Bounding down the stairs, I bit my lip and willed my feet to land on sturdy blocks. After the quake, the steps might be unstable, and if I went sprawling, I was caught.

I exhaled in relief when my feet landed on blocks of slate at the bottom of the stairs. Kicking away a stray cobblestone, I lunged forward, heading down the street. Behind me, the protectors shouted for help.

I risked a glance over my shoulder; the men were coming down the stairs.

An arm came out of nowhere, smacking me in the ribs, lifting my feet off the ground. I screamed as the smell of an unwashed body entered my nose. Laughing, the man cracked knuckles against my head.

"I sure hope there's a reward," my captor said. He'd been hiding in an alley beside the Hall—his cloak still pooled in the darkened recesses. He leered, exposing yellow teeth. Food crammed the crevices at his gum lines. "Never thought I'd be helping protectors, but without the flow of tin scrip, and my home fallen in atop me, guess I'll do anything for the coin to buy a mug of ale."

He held me with one arm, my body tucked against his waist while I squirmed. Jabbing out with my elbow, I connected with his gut, but he just laughed. I heard the protectors' approach, metal clicking, leather creaking.

Another crack as the cudgel came down, and I winced, waiting for the flood of pain. But the arm around me loosened. I fell to the ground as my captor crumpled, head bleeding from the growing knot where the club had hit him.

"Now," the protector said, staring down. "As I said, we'll just take you to the holding cells."

Chapter Thirty-Eight

Kostan
A simple bedchamber

When I opened my eyes, I was tucked into a narrow bed in a room smaller than my palace closet. I didn't remember lying down. Savra and the innkeeper must have all but carried me to bed. I groaned in dismay, thinking of the extra effort I must have cost them. I sat up and groaned again—it felt as if every muscle in my body was afire.

How long had I slept? Guessing by the bone-deep fatigue that still pressed on me, just a few hours.

Wooden shutters were closed over the window. Yawning, I unfastened the latch on the shutters and let them swing open. An inn like this couldn't afford glass for the upper story, and smoky air flowed into the room, already warm and tinged with scents of the Splits. A square of hot sunlight fell on the blankets covering my lap.

Another waft of air puffed through the window, smelling of garbage. I wrinkled my nose and clapped the shutters closed again.

On the small table beside my bed, a candle lantern burned. A tin pitcher and ladle stood beside it. Otherwise, the room was empty except for my single boot which stood on the floor next to the bed. I stared at the leather, once polished daily by palace servants, now scuffed and scratched. A man with one shoe. What was I going to do? March up to Steelhold and demand another boot along with the title of Emperor?

I shook my head. Despairing would do no good. I *would* find a way to retake the throne. Starting by learning more about the situation in Jaliss and searching for information on Azar.

My body protested as I stood. My bed called me back to sleep. I took a deep breath to give me strength. I wouldn't waste daylight hours, not with every citizen of the Empire counting on me.

My thoughts were still fuzzy as I nudged the door to my room open. The hallway had no windows, no lamps burning. At the end where a staircase descended, daylight gave the woodwork a warm glow. Walking heel to toe, I moved the length of the hall. Something felt strange as I padded along the wooden floorboards, but I couldn't place the sensation.

When I stepped down the first step, I realized what had been nagging me. My foot didn't hurt—it hadn't since I woke beneath the tree branches with Evrain and Falla. And now, the sensitive areas around the brand felt... almost numb. I sat on the top of the stairs, ignoring the burning protest in my thigh muscles, and stripped the now-filthy bandage from my foot. I ran fingertips over the brand, no longer an open wound, but a series of smooth ridges. My fingers lifted away—I wasn't sure how to feel about the change. The unhealed brand had been a part of me for so long that I'd come to think of it as a facet of my identity.

But that was over now, like so many other things. Bundling the bandage in my fist, I descended to the common room, knees aching.

The proprietor, Fishel, sat at a guest table. A bucket of peas stood beside his chair along with a pail for the pods. On the table, the shelled peas were collecting in a wooden bowl.

"Thank you for helping me to a room," I said.

He started when I spoke. "Huh? Oh, yes, of course."

"About the payment..."

"Taken care of," he said, waving away my statement. Fishel plucked another handful of full pea pods and dropped them on the table. Staring at the door, he snapped off the stem end from one and peeled away the string. Cracking the pod open, he dumped the peas into the bowl.

When I crossed the room, he kept his eyes fixed on the door.

"Everything okay?" I asked. He seemed nervous, busying himself shelling peas as a distraction.

"I—well, I suppose so. I shouldn't be so concerned with the business of others. I'm sure Savra—" He shook his head as if to clear his thoughts. "I'm sure your betrothed can take care of herself."

212

I pulled out a chair and sat beside him, grabbing a handful of pods. Dozens of questions about the young woman sprang to mind. As did those startling green eyes. But if it wasn't Fishel's business to wonder where she'd gone, it certainly wasn't mine.

Chapter Thirty-Nine

Savra
The lockup, Jaliss

The lockup wasn't what I'd expected. Instead of a stone-walled building with cells, a fence of wooden stakes bounded a wide-open area. Around two dozen men and women were scattered in the enclosure, sitting idle and looking as if they wish to avoid attention. In one corner, a small group huddled. As the protectors unlocked my cuffs, stripped me of my satchel, and shoved me through the gate, the huddle turned to look at me.

One, a man with a dark shock of hair hanging into his eyes, snarled.

Blowing through my lips, I hurried across the enclosure. I wanted the far wall at my back. Unfortunately, when I turned to survey the yard, the morning sun shone into my eyes. I squinted against the glare but couldn't see anything.

Only once I shaded my eyes and peered did I spot the approaching shadows. A semi-circle of six men trapped me against the wall.

I edged sideways, and the arc tightened in that direction, shoulder to shoulder.

An attempt to dart the other direction caused the men to close ranks and stop me.

My heart choked off the flow of air through my throat.

"What do you want?" I asked.

The largest man and apparent leader—the one with hair in his eyes—sneered. "What do you think? Just a little companionship.

Been in here since the Chasm Span fell. The protectors are looking for someone to blame."

"I was just trying to visit the registrars. I did nothing wrong."

This brought a laugh from one of the other men, a ruffian with patched clothing and filth in his scruffy beard. "Besides being born a Prov, you mean. Well, you're in good company. Care for a snuggle?"

As I winced and edged away, he laughed.

"Hey!" a woman's voice boomed. My harassers tensed.

"You step away, Grassle, or I'll knock your head off!"

The leader turned to speak to the woman behind him. As tall as most men, her muscles spoke of both strength and speed. Her high cheekbones gave her an imperious look while the light brown braid down her back showed that she favored practicality over vanity.

"Come on, Sirez. We've been in here for days with no entertainment."

"No entertainment besides forcing those boys to fight like boars in a ring. Cost one of them a tooth. I warned you already. Bother any more innocent kids, and I'll have my... friends visit your home as soon as this is over."

"Look," the man, Grassle, said. "I've got no reason to make enemies with Stormshard."

My eyes shot to the woman. A Sharder! She could help me find my father.

"I never said I was a Sharder. And you're making enemies fast. So either step away, or the rest of us will have to remove you." As the woman spoke, I noticed other prisoners approaching.

Grassle rolled his eyes. "I don't see what's wrong with you people."

"We *people* have a sense of common decency," Sirez said. "Which is unfortunately beyond your comprehension."

Hawking a gob of mucus from his throat, the ruffians' leader spat on the ground. With a twitch of his chin, he signaled his lackeys to leave me alone. A few cast longing glances over their shoulders as they stalked away.

"Thank you... Sirez, is it?" I said.

She looked me up and down. "It worked this time. But if you're smart, you'll find a way to escape. You're far too young and too pretty to be safe here." With that, she turned to leave. The other prisoners had already backed away and were leaning against walls, tracing lines in the dust.

"Wait," I called. "He said you were a Sharder. I'm looking for someone."

The woman whirled on me, eyes blazing. "That man has no idea who I am. And if you value your life, I'd think again before asking about Stormshard. Without direction from Steelhold, the protectors are eager to find scapegoats for the chaos. Any old Prov will do. Better if they have known ties to renegades."

"But it's important. His name is Evrain. He's... an old friend."

I thought I saw a flash of recognition in her eyes. She stomped close and raised a hand as if to slap me. "I said no discussions. If you get out of here, who you contact is your business. From now on, you won't speak to me again. Understand?"

I nodded.

"Good." Once again, she turned to walk away.

"Thank you again," I said. "For getting those men away from me."

She shrugged a single shoulder. "I was young once. New to the city. No one was there to help me. Couldn't let the same happen to you."

It took until midday for my predicament to sink in. As the sun reached its zenith, a pair of protectors let themselves in through the gate. Examining the scattering of prisoners, they spoke with heads leaned together.

After a moment, they seemed to reach an agreement. With a nod, one of the men stalked across the yard, armor creaking, and hefted a young man by the scruff of his tunic. The man—more of a boy I realized—yelped and cried out for help.

Everyone averted their eyes. Everyone except me, of course.

Dragging him to the center of the arena the guard dropped him in the dust and delivered a swift kick to the boy's gut.

"That's for yelling," the man growled. He looked up. "Now! We need information. You know the drill. As soon as you volunteer something of use, this punishment stops."

He kicked again, catching the boy in the back of his elbow. On hands and knees, the joint had been bearing a large amount of weight. It snapped with a hollow sound.

My stomach heaved.

"Anyone?" the other guard yelled.

Across the yard, someone raised a hand. "I already told you what I know. But I'll repeat it if you'll just spare the boy."

The guard stomped over the man and grabbed him under the armpit, pulled him through the dirt.

"We're listening..."

"I was traveling through the chasm. Home too late from the pubs. I was trying to take a shortcut. I heard an alarm gong."

The guard attacking the boy curled his lip and brought a metal-armored fist down on the boy's back. "Useless."

The confessing prisoner raised his hands in a silent plea. "But there's more. When the Span fell, I saw a body."

"A body," the guard sneered. "Right."

"A man. He screamed and fell with the bridge. If you find the body, you may learn more about the collapse."

The guard laughed. "I guess I'll spend the rest of the day digging through rubble, then." He turned to his friend. "Seems we haven't made enough of an example, eh?"

"Seems so."

As one, the protectors drew swords. When I realized what they intended, I screwed my eyes shut.

The blackness behind my eyelids faded as auras leaped to life in my vision.

I could see the red terror of the boy. The emptiness of the guards. The sorrow of the man who'd tried to have the boy spared.

And suddenly, blazing heat surrounded my wrist. I gasped, terrified of the burning.

You can stop this, a male voice said in my thoughts.

"Parveld?" I asked.

A strange amusement flooded my thoughts. *I wouldn't be caught dead...* the voice said. *Oh, wait.*

She's not ready. A woman spoke this time. *And this is not a laughing matter, Raav.*

"Who are you?" I asked.

So we're just going to watch those rotted men kill that boy? the man asked.

What choice do we have? the woman said.

We could trust her abilities. A tendril of warmth joined the man's thoughts.

"Trust me with what?" I said aloud. Though part of my mind recoiled at these strangers conversing in my head, a lifetime of night whispers and aura-sight made it easier to accept.

Fine, the woman said. *But if this goes wrong, I'll make the rest of the decisions.*

"Excuse me," I said, a hint of frustration creeping in. "But if it's regarding me, I'll make the decisions."

Savra, the woman said. *You need to Want to stop this.*

Of course I wanted to stop this. I shrugged, frustrated.

Open yourself.

"Open how? And have you considered telling me who you are first?"

I will. We will. But they're going to take his head.

My attention snapped back to the auras. Yes, the boy's terror had gone from red to pure, black dread.

"Yes, okay. Introductions later."

And don't speak aloud. You'll draw attention.

True to the woman's words, I noticed a flicker of aquamarine curiosity in one of the protector's auras. He had moved ever so slightly closer to me though most of his attention remained on the boy. I nodded.

Now, reach for the sparks.

Sparks? I shrugged my shoulders and hoped she'd catch the meaning.

The lights. The colors. Do you understand?

She must have meant the auras. The memory of what I'd done before, grabbing the auras of my attackers, surfaced. As I had then, I stretched my awareness.

Nothing happened. As I tried again, the world began to sink back into place. My feet were rooted to the dusty earth once more. The smell of sweat and sun-warmed wood entered my nose. Distracted by the voices in my head, I'd lost the panic which had caused the aura-sight to flare.

The sword swung, catching a moment of sunlight on its blade before taking the boy in the neck. I couldn't help it. I screamed.

Run. The gate.

The voice was so faint now. As the protector raised his sword again, I swallowed the vomit in the back of my throat and looked toward the gate. Chaos had erupted in the yard, half the prisoners running toward the protectors in anger, half fleeing for the fence.

And one, Sirez, stood at the gate, hands behind her back. As she stepped aside from the lock, the chain fell open. With a nod at me, she slipped to the side and stalked toward the protectors. Once near, she picked up a rock and shouted to grab their attention.

I ran.

Feet pounding hard earth, all I could think of was the sight of steel cutting flesh. Again my stomach heaved. Moments later, the gate stood in front of me. I shoved it open, stumbled into the street. Skidding to a stop, I pulled the gate shut behind me. With luck, the protectors wouldn't even realize I'd escaped.

A pile of confiscated belongings was heaped beside the outer wall of the fence. Spotting my satchel, I sprinted for it. As I snatched it, I peered through a gap between the wooden uprights of the fence. A man cowered against the wall.

"Graybranch," I said, hoping he could hear. "Tell Sirez. And tell her I said thank you."

With visions of blood and a dead Prov boy pounding the inside of my skull, I turned and sprinted away from the horror of life in the Atal Empire.

Chapter Forty

Kostan
Common room, Graybranch Inn

Fishel paced the common room back and forth. He kept glancing at the table as if wishing he had another bucket of peas to shell.

Around midday, he'd disappeared into the back rooms of the inn, returning with a pair of boots. "They're old," he'd said. "I've only kept them for mucking out stables. Seems you could use them though."

I wore them now. The heels were rounded and worn from use, and a crease in the leather rubbed the top of my right foot. Still, they were the nicest gift I'd ever received. I wondered what he would do if I admitted to being a Scion. Rip them from my feet before throwing me out the front door?

As I watched him pace, I fought the urge to do *something*. After he'd given me the boots, I'd walked through the Splits to get a feel for the city's situation. Plus, I figured Azar might have people watching for my arrival. I had discovered little and yearned to march on Steelhold now, but I knew I'd accomplish nothing alone. Patience would serve me best. If I hadn't heard from Azar within a day or two, I could start looking for allies within the city.

Fishel stopped at a window and brushed aside the curtain. Afternoon light baked the packed-earth street. He huffed in dismay and resumed his pacing.

"Hello?" Savra's voice came from the inn's back rooms. "I hope you don't mind. I came through the kitchen."

Fishel whirled, relief so plain on his face she might have been his lost daughter.

"What happened?" he asked, rushing to her.

"You were right to caution me," she said, eyes downcast. "But I'm all right now."

Dust smudged her clothing and cheeks, unsurprising given the state of the city. Her braid had come loose, and she carried a saddlebag over a shoulder.

Fishel cupped her elbow, and she sagged against him, weary but unafraid to accept comfort. I wished I had such trust in other people.

The innkeeper led her to my table in the corner. She hadn't yet noticed me, and her eyes widened at the sight.

"Hello... uh... my betrothed," I said.

Her cheeks went such a bright shade of red I almost felt bad. But the color was so striking with her auburn hair and green eyes that I couldn't make myself regret it.

Storms, but this was confusing.

"I'm sorry—I—" she began before I hurried around the table and pulled out a chair.

"Why would you be sorry?" I asked. "Without you, I'd have slept in the streets. If I'd survived the night."

"Now that you lovebirds are reunited, I'll see about dinner," Fishel said with a bow and a smirk.

"I don't know what prompted me to say we were betrothed." She rubbed the back of her hand.

"Kindness is rare in the Empire. I'd like to learn how a young woman like you survives in Atal without having the goodness struck from her." I winced. I was talking too much.

Fortunately, my words sparked something in her. When she looked up, a faint smile touched her lips. "To tell the truth, I was just passing along the good fortune. If it's not obvious, I'm not from Ioene."

Somewhat tentatively, she lowered the saddlebag down beside her chair. As she moved, a faint scent came off her hair. It reminded me of the open air I'd loved to breathe from atop Steelhold's walls, brushed with hints of grassland flowers and mountain snows. I fought a maddening desire to touch her.

This was definitely not how a Scion of the Empire behaved. Much less an emperor.

"Fishel looked outside," she said. "He couldn't find your boot anywhere."

The corners of my mouth drew back in a smile. I hadn't felt this at ease with anyone besides Vaness. Kei had been an intriguing person, but her allure had been in the... promise of adventure I supposed. She'd represented the freedom I could never have, and I'd been fascinated by her because of it.

"He was kind enough to give me a pair," I said as I sat and raised a foot for her inspection.

"So what brought you here wearing just one shoe and ready to collapse?"

I tensed then summoned my Scion's mask. What could I say? Not the truth, certainly. But I hated to lie to her. "I was in the mountains when the quake struck. It was a difficult journey back to safety... not that I'd call Jaliss safe at the moment. And what brings you here?"

For an instant, I thought I saw my hesitation mirrored in her eyes. She swallowed then spoke. "I came for my Function writ. Scribe. But the Hall of Registry is closed."

"They didn't issue it when you received your assignment?"

"No, well—the registrar changed her mind. I was supposed to be given a different Function, and she didn't have the proper writ." She chewed her lower lip and looked sideways. "I didn't get a chance to see Jaliss before the shake. I imagine it was even more impressive."

"People used to say Jaliss was the jewel of the Empire. I... I wouldn't know. I haven't seen any other cities."

"How about your home? Is it in the mountains?"

I shook my head. "My recent journey was my first into the mountains. I grew up near here, but I can't return to my home just yet." This conversation was still dangerously close to topics I had no wish to discuss. But I couldn't seem to find my wits with this woman sitting across from me.

She sighed. "Damaged by the quake. I'm so sorry. Well, my hometown isn't anything to compare against. We had twenty or so families. A couple of buildings. Sluices."

Cosmal Province. That explained her accent. As part of my lessons, I'd often been given the task of conversing with couriers from the Provinces. But Cosmal was so isolated. Not to mention, anyone bred there was an asset to the Empire. Cosmali were almost always assigned the sluicing Function. She must have shown an extraordinary talent for scribing.

Both Savra's hands were laying on the table, and her index finger tapped the wood over and over. Nerves? I could only imagine the shock of leaving Cosmal Province only to arrive during the worst disaster ever to strike Jaliss.

I swallowed, searching for something to break the tension. "In any case, about our wedding..."

She blushed again and covered it with a small laugh. "Perhaps we should wait until the streets are cleared of rubble and order is restored."

A strange sadness crossed her face, and her fingers strayed to the bracelet she wore. I doubted she'd seen the kind of poverty and hunger currently plaguing the city. My heart panged. I wish I could have spared her this. When I took the throne, I would improve things. I swore it.

But when I took the throne, I'd never speak to her again.

"Dinner is served!"

When Fishel's voice boomed from the kitchen, I felt a wave of relief at being rescued from the conversation. I wanted to spend hours talking to Savra, but it seemed that everything I said just brought up topics best avoided.

"You've done so much," I said as I stood. Wiping my hands on my pants—my palms were embarrassingly sweaty—I strode to the man and relieved him of one of the trays.

"Least I could do for my friends from Ioene," he said with a wry smirk. "I realize the accommodations are nothing like what you must be accustomed to on your estate."

I thought back to what I'd learned about Ioene. The island was supposed to be a haven for mystics. The cities were unlike any other. But the estates? I had no idea.

"My betrothed doesn't live with us yet, Fishel. That would be highly inappropriate," Savra said. "His family is in shipping, and they keep a fine home in the city."

The innkeeper smirked. "Right. Living together already... How could I have assumed such a thing?" The man seemed to be enjoying this, watching us fumble for stories. If only he knew my real identity. Fugitive imperial Scion would certainly beat shipping magnate from Ioene.

I followed Fishel to the table and set the tray before Savra. There was bread, a vegetable stew, and steamed peas from the afternoon's shelling.

"Looks like the both of you could use a calming herbal tea," Fishel said with a wink. "To soothe the nerves."

Chapter Forty-One

Savra
Common Room, Graybranch Inn

The arrival of dinner saved me from trying to answer any more of Kostan's questions without lying. I hated to speak in half-truths and evasions, but what other choice did I have? I couldn't explain what had really happened with the registrar and Havialo, much less my hope to find Stormshard and my father.

But I wanted to. Kostan made me feel so comfortable I wanted to tell him everything about my life.

As our plates emptied and Fishel bustled about, tidying the common room and refilling our tea, memories of the afternoon crept back. The boy. The protectors' swords. The screams of fear and fury from the prisoners.

No matter how I wished to start a new life in Jaliss, become a scribe and get to know Kostan better, I now knew I'd stop at nothing to find my father and join Stormshard. Regardless of Havialo's judgment of the renegade group, I believed in my father. I would use my talent to help Stormshard undo the Empire for good.

It took all my willpower to wrench myself away from the meal. When I abruptly stood, Kostan looked up at me with no attempt to conceal his disappointment.

"I've had a terribly long day," I said, a pathetic excuse.

His expression softened. "I understand. It's been hard on all of us. Maybe I'll see you tomorrow."

"Maybe," I whispered. And though I knew it was hopeless, I found myself eager for the morning.

Chapter Forty-Two

Kostan
The common room by morning

A couple of hours after dawn, I was sitting in the common room when Savra descended the stairs looking like the sunrise itself. I jumped from my chair before I realized she might not wish to join me.

As she stepped off the last stair and yawned, Fishel backed out of the kitchen. "I'm brewing coffee to go with your rolls. Don't expect this to happen again until Steelhold remembers those of us outside the wall."

Savra turned the man a gentle smile. "You're too thoughtful."

He shrugged. "Gives me a reason to feel useful."

As Savra shuffled to the table, rubbing the sleep from her eyes, my heart beat faster. So she would join me after all. She pulled out a chair and sat across from me.

"I'm sorry for leaving dinner so suddenly," she said. "I didn't tell the whole truth because it was so awful. I saw the protectors slice the head from an innocent boy yesterday."

Her words were like a kick to the throat. "Storms. Savra, I'm so sorry."

I wanted to reach out and touch her cheek. But a flood of self-loathing squashed the impulse. Those protectors were my responsibility. How could I even think of offering comfort when I might as well have swung the sword?

And to think, in the minutes just after I'd awakened, I'd considered telling her my whole story in hopes she'd accept me anyway.

As I sat back in my chair, wondering if I even deserved the meal Fishel was preparing, the bells on the door latch jingled.

The door swung open revealing Azar, Vaness... and Ilishian.

Chapter Forty-Three

Savra
The common room by morning

Kostan's chair flew back when he stood, almost toppling before he caught it. Feet pounding the floorboards, he ran to the newcomers.

There were two young women and a man whose age I didn't wish to guess. Their cloaks were stained, the hems ragged. One of the women, a striking figure with coal-spun hair and eyes like the deep blue of an iceberg had boots so scuffed at the toe that I could see her socks beneath. More, the boots were obviously mismatched, one at least two knuckles longer than the other.

Still, was it their bearing that made me think they were anything but the beleaguered travelers they appeared? Or just an instinct?

When Kostan swept the blue-eyed girl into his arms, clutching her tight and whispering in her ear, my gaze fell to the table. Of course he had someone already. What had I been thinking?

Fishel snorted, clearly finding humor in my "betrothed's" reaction to the girl's arrival. Meanwhile, it was all I could do to keep tears of shame from welling.

"Well then," Fishel said as he set a tray with a teapot and cups on the table where Kostan sat with his friends. At least he hadn't given them my coffee. "Anyone for barley porridge?"

The man who'd arrived with the newcomers pushed back the hood of his cloak, exposing a bald pate and gray eyebrows. "We aren't staying long."

At this, the innkeeper bristled. "Pardon me if I ask whether you'll be paying for the tea, then."

The second young woman, a light-haired girl, laid a hand on the man's arm. She pulled a small purse from beneath her cloak and plucked out a steel coin. "Of course, sire. And a question: do you have a private chamber where we might speak to our friend?"

Meaning, could they please talk to Kostan without me, a wastrel Prov, listening in? "Oh, you can have the whole common room for your... private conversation," I said, chair squealing against the floor when I stood.

"Savra, wait," Kostan said. He stood and took a step towards me. "These are my companions from..." At this, he seemed to struggle with his words, eyes darting over his friends' faces.

"This ought to be good," Fishel muttered.

"Members of the Merchants' Guild need not explain their interests to every acquaintance we make," the man said.

"From the Merchants' Guild," Kostan finished limply.

"Pleased, I'm sure," I said, putting all the dignity I could into my words. "I wish you well in your endeavors. Perhaps your merchant friends can find you accommodations fitting your station."

With that, I stood and headed for the stairs, my wounded pride throbbing in my chest.

"Savra, can we talk later?" Kostan asked.

Steel-gray eyes looked up at me from beneath his wavy fringe of hair. I wanted to nod. But instead, my gaze shot to the blue-eyed girl. "I wouldn't want to distract from your reunion."

A look of confusion crossed his face, followed by comprehension. "No, wait. It's not—"

"Kostan," the girl interrupted, "you aren't safe. It's just you and me now. The others... They're gone. You need to get out of sight."

The man gave a sharp hiss to cut off her words, but the girl shot him a glare. She laid her palms on the table and stared the man down. "Considering the situation, I hardly think being overheard by an innkeeper and a tavern stray will put us in more danger than we're already facing."

Danger? Her words were starting to penetrate the angry buzzing of my thoughts. What danger could the Merchants' Guild be in? Looters and opportunists taking advantage of the city's disarray?

Only after those questions surfaced did I realize what she'd called me.

A tavern stray.

I'd had lots of practice dealing with bullies in Numintown. The best choices were to either ignore them or to strike back with such strength they ran away squealing. As I gripped the banister, squeezing the blood from my knuckles, I tried to summon an insult to match hers. But back in Numintown, I'd never succeeded at striking back. I just wasn't good at hurting others. Instead of spitting out words I might later regret, I raised my chin and turned away.

"Kostan," the man said, "Vaness may lack discretion, but she's right. We have a safehouse—and a plan. Do you need help paying your tab here? If not, we should go."

As I set foot in the hall above, I heard Kostan's reply. "Pay the innkeeper twice the usual rate. I've received far more kindness here than I have a right to expect."

I'd intended to storm into my room and slam the door, but as I heard the chairs scoot back from the table, my feet stopped moving. I clenched my fists. Why did I care what happened to Kostan or where he went?

I couldn't answer that question, but the truth was, I did. Instead of seeking refuge in my room, I forced myself to watch as the woman with the coin purse handed over enough steel coins that Fishel wouldn't need boarders for a month. As she did, she spoke in low, almost threatening tones.

Soon after, the party filed for the door. A pace from the exit, Kostan paused and looked up. His eyes were pained as he raised two fingers in a wave of goodbye.

Chapter Forty-Four

Evrain
A trailside refuge

The blisters on the bottoms of Evrain's feet had broken, sealed, and broken again. They bled, soiling his socks. At least the conclave would give him a day's rest. With luck, he'd come out of it with a fresh mount, too.

Inside the small wayside hut, a refuge built long ago when the Empire actually cared for its prospectors and caravaneers traveling into the Icethorns, four faces greeted him. It was a strange comfort to see them, these people hardened by existences lived outside the law. For near to a decade, they'd been friends to him. More, they'd been closer to family.

According to the rules laid down when the founders conceived of Stormshard, only one representative of each Shard knew the location and plans of the other Shards. It was safer that way. But it meant that important decisions needed a conclave like this.

"You look terrible, Evrain," Sirez, the leader of the Jaliss Shard, said. "Like your Shard's been using you as a combat practice dummy."

Evrain swallowed, holding in the flood of grief. His Shard. Gone, except for the scattered few who'd been on patrol. And even then, he didn't know who'd survived. After that feckless Scion had abandoned them, he and Shaw had all but carried Falla the rest of the way down the trail. Those two were safe now—at least as safe as a Sharder ever could be—holed up in the hunter's lodge near the foothills. Maybe more stragglers would turn up; the Shard had always planned to retreat to the lodge in case of a rout or disaster. They'd just never had to test the contingency.

Meanwhile, Evrain had stumbled the distance to the courier post. Showing a forged writ, he'd sent coded messages to all Shard leaders who could make the journey to this small shelter within a day. If he could convince them to support his call for an offensive, it would be close enough to a majority to count as a successful vote.

"Evrain?" asked another woman, Ain. Her Shard worked the small settlements around the First Rift, filching from imperial collectors and sabotaging the flow of directives from Steelhold.

He cleared his throat. "It's—I regret to report that my Shard fell. The quake... almost all of them were inside the cavern when it collapsed."

"Oh, frozen wastes, Evrain. I'm so sorry." Sirez jumped to her feet. She wrapped him in an embrace, her body softer than it looked. Despite everything, Evrain couldn't help noticing the press of her breasts against his chest. A flash of guilt joined his sorrow. It had been seven years since he'd seen his wife. When he'd left, he'd imagined they'd reunite before the season turned, even if just long enough for a proper goodbye.

He patted Sirez's back before politely stepping away. When he glanced at her face, Evrain's brows raised in concern. "No offense, but you're not looking as hale as usual."

Sirez sighed. "It's been difficult in the capital. Not much food with Steelhold abandoning us. No scrip. The suppliers aren't getting their usual directives from the leadership, so food is spoiling in warehouses out on the plateau while they wait for orders—and payment."

Evrain touched a line on her cheek, scabbed over now, but it looked as if a whip or sword had slashed her. "And this?"

She shrugged. "I spent a short stint in the lockup... Escaped when I got your message. Until then, I'd been sticking around to protect as many innocents as I could. Speaking of, I met a young woman inside. Prov. She claimed to be an old friend of yours."

An old friend? Who? Evrain thought through his list of acquaintances. In his business, he'd made many friends among families who received what he stole from the Empire. But few knew him by name.

"Did she tell you her name?"

Sirez shook her head. "But I intend to follow up. She intrigued me. Don't worry, though. She'll hear nothing about you from me until I know whether she can be trusted."

The other Shard leaders were watching the exchange with mild interest—and a hint of impatience. With a nod of apology, Evrain limped to the table. "Thank you for coming," he said. "I have a proposal."

One of the men, a square-jawed drover from Guralan Province, scratched his stubbled face. "We figured as much. Sorry about your men."

"And women," Evrain reminded him. Of the Shard leaders, Joran was the worst about clinging to old ideas on who made the best Sharder. It had been close to a half-century since the organization opened up to women and adolescents.

"Of course. Pardon the omission." Joran's tone remained even, but his thick fingers, laying relaxed on the table, curled slightly.

Evrain drew breath into lungs tired from his march out of the mountains. He glanced at Sirez, who—not unexpectedly—was glaring daggers at the drover. "Shall we sit, my friend?" he asked. "Your opinion on my proposal will carry the most weight, as it concerns Jaliss."

Her expression softened as she took a seat beside Evrain, a move calculated to insulate her from Joran, no doubt. "The city is a disaster. I imagine anything you propose will improve its situation."

Evrain smirked. "I wouldn't be so sure."

"Oh?"

"For a century, Stormshard has nibbled at the Empire's interests, striving to give Provs and even merchant-class Atal a better life. And while I think we've succeeded in that, I don't believe we can continue as we have. We need to do more than raid caravans and eliminate an imperial agent or two."

Sirez smirked. "So what are you saying? We storm Steelhold and assassinate the Emperor?"

She was joking; that was clear in her tone. But Evrain turned to her, setting his face in a serious expression.

"That's exactly what I'm saying."

Chapter Forty-Five

Kostan
Lowtown, Jaliss

As we trotted through the streets, Vaness kept staring at my matched set of boots. I knew she wanted to ask about my brand, and I didn't plan to hide anything. Ilishian would be displeased with me for having the cuff struck off. At this point, I didn't care.

In fact, all I could feel right now was anger at these people for how they'd treated Savra. Even Vaness. A tavern stray? Just the memory of her words made my blood run hot. But I needed them, especially the mages. And of my childhood companions, only Vaness still lived. I hadn't been close to the other Scions, but still I mourned their loss. I shouldn't push away my remaining friend. So I breathed deep when the anger rose, forced it away as my Steelhold upbringing had taught.

In the chill morning air, we wound through the streets of the Splits, passing families living beneath canvas tarps, their homes reduced to rubble. Campfires burned in the middle of the streets, some of the only terrain not covered in splintered wood and scattered stone. Where buildings still stood, shutters were locked tight across windows. I could only assume that bars had been placed across the doors on the inside. Hunger showed in tight faces and greedy eyes. And the Empire's leadership had done nothing to help.

The city might still be calm, people more concerned with digging out and taking stock, but it wouldn't last. Steelhold might believe itself secure behind iron gates and atop a soaring pedestal of rock. But a swarm of biting ants could overwhelm the most fearsome beast. Without imperial representatives to take control of the situation—and especially, to resume the flow of tin scrip and steel coin which allowed the city to function—the Provs would rise up. Maybe even the merchant-class, too.

If it weren't for Emperor Tovmeil's warning of the consequences of Atal's fall, I would join them.

At the border between the Splits and Lowtown, a muddy stream called the Silty flowed through the city. In the Heights, the Silty cascaded down low tiers of stone, confined to its channel by mortared walls and culverts. But here, it spread wide and stinking, carrying sewage and trash and other foul items. During the quake, a decrepit bridge had collapsed into the flow, damming rivulets and creating new channels on the banks. The residents of the slums had replaced the bridge with a set of planks laid from stinking islet to algae-slimed stone. As we crossed, the planks teetered. Filthy water lapped at my boots and seeped in through the tongues.

Still, I fought back my disgust. Some people had to live near the Silty. The least I could do was bear the smell without complaint.

Despite the surrounding shambles, a few enterprising Provs had emerged from their shanties to line the Lowtown streets. Ordinarily, protectors would make regular patrols through the area, demanding writs from anyone trying to peddle wares. If not that, the snitches would be tattling on violators, hoping for a chance to earn their way up and out of the district. But the ordinary ways had already fallen aside. A woman tugged on my trousers and pointed to her ragged cloak.

"Cold? Need a cloak to keep out the night? I'll trade for scrip or food. Or anything else you might desire," she said, trying to look comely.

I tapped on Azar's shoulder and stopped walking. "Give her one of those coins," I said.

"Kos—we can get you a cloak that actually fits," Vaness said.

I shook my head. "I don't want the cloak. I just want to spare her selling the last of her pride to put food in her belly."

The woman's eyes fell away. "I have a little boy. His da died in the shake."

Ilishian's mouth made a hard line. "Just do it, Azar. Better than standing here attracting attention. We can discuss this later."

With eyes darting back and forth for threats, Azar reached into her jacket, rummaging for her purse. Ilishian closed ranks as the young metalogist plucked a steel half-talon free. The smallest coin she carried, no doubt.

But the beggar's eyes lit. She scrambled to her feet and reached for me, gratitude shining in her face.

"Back off!" Ilishian hissed, sliding like a shadow to stand between us. "Leave now. And if you speak of this to anyone, you will be found."

I wanted to protest but kept quiet. Angering the ferromaster would only bring his wrath down upon the woman.

As she scurried off, Ilishian turned to me, eyes narrowed. "Another episode like this and we may just leave you to your fate."

The so-called safehouse was a blacksmith's workshop in the part of Lowtown where the slums washed out onto the plains. Unlike many nearby buildings, the low walls of stone topped by rickety wood framing had come through the quake intact. But still, this place seemed no safer than the Graybranch Inn.

I'd held my tongue during the rest of our trek. But when Azar shut and barred the door behind us, I wouldn't keep silent any more.

"Some safehouse," I said, not caring that my annoyance showed.

Ilishian shrugged and stood back as Azar fished a black-iron statuette of a bird from her pocket. She closed her eyes and coaxed sparks from the metal figurine, guiding them to a lantern's wick. Ilishian nodded in approval.

"Seeing as I got the key from the owner's corpse," the ferromaster said, "I'd say we have adequate privacy here."

"Another person you murdered just to be safe?" I snapped. "You know what? I don't want to be here. I was doing fine on my own."

"Actually," Vaness spoke up, "we found you by following the assassins sent by the Ministry. They'd tracked you to the Graybranch and were watching from posts across the street."

"Then I need to go back and warn Savra and Fishel."

Ilishian curled his lip. "Your new friends will be fine. Once we'd confirmed that they were stalking the proper young Atal man, we took care of them."

I closed my eyes. Of course they had. How had I let myself forget how easily these people killed?

"And no," Ilishian said. "I didn't kill the blacksmith. The Chasm Span did. He made the unfortunate decision to travel through the chasm that night. I'm not sure what circumstances led him to be out so late, but he had no chance of avoiding the stone fall. Lucky for me he wasn't completely buried."

I took a deep breath as I sank onto a crate. "Well, there's that at least. How did you know which door the key fit?"

Ilishian smirked. "You may recall I'm a ferro mage. That means I speak to the dead, among other things. Or did that part of your lessons not take?"

I refused to let his barbs embarrass me. Yes, I should have figured that out. But considering everything that had happened, I doubted it would be the first stupid question I asked today. My head swam with dizziness, and I planted my hands to steady myself.

"Speaking of the Chasm Span..." I said.

"You thought I died in the fall. That's good. It's my hope that everyone else believes it, too."

"And the reason you didn't?"

"Ancient ferro secrets."

I knew that wasn't true. Despite my question from a moment ago, I had been paying attention to my lessons on the different abilities of ferro, aurum, and argent mages. Ferros specialized in imbuing black iron objects with special magic derived from the spirits of the dead, not in surviving thousand-story drops. If anything, I suspected that Ilishian had a relic which granted protection.

"You said you had a plan," I said, turning to Vaness. Ilishian sniffed at the snub.

"Aren't you interested in hearing how Azar and I escaped?" she asked, sounding faintly hurt that I hadn't asked. I understood, I supposed. Before meeting the Sharders, Fishel, and Savra, Vaness had been my only real friend. A bit more than that, even. I'd pressured Ilishian to save her, but now I scarcely seemed to notice her. Her comment about Savra had angered me, but I needed to give her a chance.

Ignoring the ache in my legs, I moved over to sit beside Vaness on a lumpy sack. "Of course," I said, knuckling her in the shoulder. "You don't know how relieved I was to see you. When I was in the mountains, I got sick. I had fever dreams. You were there."

As I spoke the memories came flooding back. If not for my hallucination of Vaness walking beside me, egging me on, I might not have survived.

The corner of her mouth twitched in a slight smile. "Sick from your brand?"

I nodded. "Infected."

"Me too. I fell ill a day after we escaped. Azar got word into the Hold. The aurums are on our side. The Trinity sent a recipe for the salve. Apparently, we need it to keep infections away. It's..." She trailed off as she looked at my matching boots.

"I know. You have to remove the cuff to get rid of the sickness."

"The Trinity's message explained that," Azar said. "But they said it was strictly forbidden. No Emperor can Ascend without the cuff and brand."

As Azar's eyes darted to my feet, I pressed my opposite toe against the boot's heel for leverage and pulled my foot free. I straightened my knee to show her the sole of my foot. The young mage snapped her gaze away, cringing.

"And your opinion?" I asked, taking in the others with my gaze. "Is it critical we hold to an ancient tradition designed to control us? Because if you won't support my claim to the throne, I might as well leave now."

Silence gathered in the room while Ilishian stalked forward to look down on me. I considered standing but decided I didn't need to intimidate him with my height.

"I mean to Ascend regardless of your involvement," I said simply.

"The Ministry will oppose you. As will the argents and the rest of the ferro order."

I shrugged. "And? They are just men and women. Emperor Tovmeil named me his successor. You were there. If you refuse to acknowledge his words, I will find others to believe in me. I'll go to

Stormshard to gather an army if I must." As I spoke the last sentence, I stilled my expression. I didn't really believe the renegades would support me—or anyone—in a bid to rule both Old Atal and the Provinces. But Ilishian didn't know that.

"What do you mean, Emperor Tovmeil named you?" Vaness said. Trained to hide her emotions, she kept her face even, but I could imagine what she was feeling. The other Scions were dead. Somewhere, deep in her heart, she must have hoped that had raised her chances of ascending. And since neither Ilishian nor Azar had deigned to tell her differently, her suddenly smashed hopes must have been slicing her apart inside.

Ignoring Ilishian for the moment, I took her hand. She stiffened, and I remembered how shocked—and comforted—I'd felt when Evrain had touched me. We were Scions. We weren't supposed to be loved.

"I wanted to tell you," I said. "Emperor Tovmeil claimed that if I don't sit on the throne, the Breaking will shatter the land. This last quake will be nothing in comparison. Vaness, I've always thought you would be a better leader than me, but what should I do? Ignore his warning?"

Her jaw worked silently, the muscles rippling in her cheeks. Her full lips were set in an emotionless line. I remembered the feel of them, but the recollection no longer sent heat through my body. Now I felt only gentle affection. I didn't want her to hurt, but I could only do so much to console her.

After a moment, she slipped her hand away and turned on the mages. Standing to her full height, she fixed them with a look of disapproval nothing short of imperial.

"You should have told me," she said.

Ilishian stared back. "I'll be frank. You are only alive because Kostan demanded it. I owe you nothing. Now, I'll admit that saving two Scions gave us a tremendous advantage against the Ministry. The ministers are terrified their plot will be revealed—it's surely the reason for the lockdown on Steelhold. They can't declare their intent to rule while either of you lives. To do so would only doom their cause—the moment either of you showed yourselves, the Empire's power structure would rally against the usurpers. But you, Vaness, certainly weren't saved for any virtue you held over your fellow Scions."

At this, I stood. Ilishian may have saved my life, but he wouldn't treat Vaness this way. "Do you know the Emperor's Mark?" I asked.

The question set him off balance. The ferro mage blinked. "Everyone among the Atal elite does. Perhaps other citizens know as well, those who have bothered to educate themselves on their ruler."

"Get down on your knees and examine my brand."

His look of offense reminded me of an insulted cat. "Excuse me?"

I pulled the Heart of the Empire from beneath my tunic. Both Azar's and Vaness's eyes widened upon seeing the amulet. I doubted either of them knew what it was, but the brilliant banding in the agate was enough to impress anyone. "You gave me this because your fealty lay with Emperor Tovmeil. It still does, which is the only reason you are—in your imagination—lowering yourself to play nursemaid to a Scion two years from his Ascension."

"Exactly. You are not the Emperor. Yet. I vowed to protect you and guide you to the throne. That's all."

"And I'm saying this: examine my foot. Tell me there's no Emperor's Mark upon it. If you're correct, I'll accept your authority while we decide how to proceed. But if you see the Mark, I demand you recognize my dominion."

In truth, I had no idea whether I'd been branded Emperor from the beginning. But if my foot bore the Mark, it would be much more difficult for Ilishian to defy me. I wouldn't lose anything by failing, not when he considered me nothing but a Scion anyway. But I had everything to gain.

The ferromaster couldn't easily refuse, not when I'd used Emperor Tovmeil's name to remind him of his allegiance. Not with Azar and Vaness watching so avidly. With a reluctance that could have been measured in hectares, Ilishian lowered himself to the dusty floor. His cheek twitched as I lifted my foot.

He stared at the sole, filthy after my journey out of the mountains, and no doubt still reeking from the seepage of water from the Silty. The moment stretched on and on. Finally, he bowed his head, pressed up off his knees and stood.

"You are indeed Emperor of Atal. Please accept my loyal service from now until your abdication. Long may you reign."

Chapter Forty-Six

Savra
A simple bedchamber

My small room felt safe. No one could see me hug my knees to my chest or bury my face in my hands. A tavern stray. I shouldn't let that girl's words get to me. But I was so tired. So alone in Jaliss. And for a few hours, I'd felt like I'd had a friend.

"Whatever those three wanted with him, I'm sure he'll be back," Fishel had said while clearing away the tea settings used by Kostan's friends.

The innkeeper was wrong. Kostan was an Atal merchant. He had no reason to return to the Graybranch. Certainly not to spend time with a Prov girl from the Cosmal Peninsula.

Flopping onto my narrow bed, I traced a finger over the bracelet. As I did, I attempted to open my mind as the voices in the bracelet had suggested. I closed my eyes, even tried to imagine the sensation of the world fading when fear summoned my aura-sight. Nothing happened, and I soon gave up.

"Whatever Parveld believes about me, he's wrong." I muttered, looking at the bracelet.

It felt as if the metal warmed against my skin, but no voices entered my thoughts. I was certain the people who'd spoken to me in the lockup were real and that they'd used the bracelet to reach me. But how?

The Empire's ferros infused black iron with all sorts of powers, but this seemed to be something different. Maybe Parveld had worked spiritist magic into the bracelet, allowing his friends to speak to me. In any case, it wasn't working now.

Clutching my chin, I stared at the wall and wondered what I should do.

When something tapped against the wooden window shutter, I jumped. As I shifted away from the wall, the sound came again. A definite tap as if someone were tossing pebbles at the shutter. Kostan? I couldn't think if anyone else who would try to get my attention. Maybe some kids from the Splits were testing their aim.

Edging across the bed, I put my eye to the crack between shutters. Outside, the midday sun pressed down on streets still cluttered with rubble. I saw little through the slit and was preparing to give up when a woman strolled into view. Partway across the street, she paused and with a flip of the wrist sent a small stone flying toward my window.

I flinched as the pebble cracked against the wood. How had she managed such accurate aim without even looking? Not that she could have seen the window anyway—a wide-brimmed felt hat hid the woman's face. But I recognized her confident stroll and the long brown braid hanging down her back. Sirez, the Sharder woman.

I dashed from my room, careened down the stairs, and shoved out the inn's front door into the midday glare.

The street was deserted.

Looking left and right, I balled my fists. Where could she have gone?

In my haste, I'd forgotten my boots. Stepping carefully in stockinged feet, I edged around the building. Sirez wasn't along the south wall either, so I kept going, turning into the narrow yard between the inn and stable.

A leather-gloved hand fell over my mouth while a dagger pressed against my windpipe.

"This way," Sirez whispered into my ear, nudging me toward the stable. How had she gotten behind me? "I'd like to discuss some things with you, but I'll slit your throat if you make my life difficult."

The blade's edge was wickedly sharp. I didn't struggle as we stepped across open space to the stable door. Sirez kicked the thin wood, setting the door shivering. Moments later, the latch clicked open, and the door swung wide.

The stable's interior was nearly pitch black. With a grunt, Sirez forced me forward. I blinked, squinted. Whoever had helped Sirez was a shadow in the dark. A large shadow.

Across the stable, Breeze nickered a greeting. He didn't seem upset by these intruders. Did he know something I didn't or was he just too trusting?

When the door shut behind us, snuffing the last of the light and fresh air, I finally remembered to breathe. My pulse raced in my neck, pressing tender skin against the knife blade in a regular throb.

"I won't give you any trouble," I whispered as the woman removed her hand from my mouth.

As my eyes adjusted, I picked out more lurking shapes. One by one, Sirez's friends detached from the walls and slid closer. The whites of their eyes glinted in the faint glow filtering from the ceiling, but I didn't see a single flash of teeth. No smiles, but no snarls either.

"So," Sirez said, "you were interested in Stormshard... Perhaps too interested."

The dagger at my throat kept me from either nodding or shaking my head. With a small noise that sounded like a newborn kitten, I pointed at her knife hand. "It's not necessary," I squeaked.

"I suppose you're right, considering I could snap your neck before you reach the door," she said. The dagger still hadn't moved. "Then again, perhaps you have some hidden abilities of your own. One of my associates in the lockup claimed to have sensed something from you. What do you know of spiritism?"

I licked my lips. Havialo had told me the Empire hunted people like me. How did Stormsharders feel about my kind?

"Not much," I said. It was an honest answer. "Until recently, I'd never heard the term."

The pressure of the blade lessened ever so slightly. "But you have heard of it now, and you're a Prov, which means you didn't learn the word through imperial communications."

"A man kidnapped me. He claimed he'd take me to the Sharders. To my—to the friend I mentioned."

"And now we're to the heart of the matter. You claim to know Evrain."

I nodded and regretted it as the blade stung my neck. To her credit, Sirez noticed and released the dagger's pressure.

"Yes, but until a couple of months ago, I didn't even know whether he was still alive."

Finally, Sirez released me. I locked my knees to keep from slumping to the floor. When I wiped a hand across my neck, it came away with a line of wet.

The Sharder woman stepped in front of me—I had to look up sharply to make eye contact. A look of regret twisted her lips. "Sorry about that. I didn't expect you to move so suddenly."

I shrugged. I wasn't exactly in a position to withhold forgiveness.

"Why were you so interested in Stormshard that you'd agree to leave home with a stranger? You seem a clever girl, if a bit naïve."

What should I say? I needed to tell these people *something* to explain my presence here and my interest in my father. But I couldn't be sure they were my father's allies. If they knew I was his daughter, they might use that against him. Better to admit to the spiritism since they seemed to know about my abilities already.

"According to my kidnapper, if the Empire found out about my talent, they'd kill me. He said Evrain could find someone to teach me about spiritism."

"So did you go with this man willingly, or did he kidnap you? I'm confused."

I shrugged. "Both, I guess. I went with him based on his lies. And I escaped when I found out the truth."

"Which was?"

"He wanted my abilities for his own purposes."

Sirez shifted her weight onto her hip. "And now you're far from home. Evrain is an old friend. You think he can help you."

"Yes, but there's more. I really *am* interested in Stormshard. After what the protectors did to that boy—" I paused when my voice cracked. "For that alone, the Emperor should die."

My heart was thudding hard enough to pound down the gates of Steelhold. I wondered if everyone in the stable could hear it.

"The truth is," Sirez said with a sigh, "Evrain's Shard operated out of the mountains. After the quake, I went to their stronghold myself—no one else within my Shard knows the details of their location."

"Then you could take me to him!" I stilled my hands to keep from grabbing onto her sleeve like a hopeful child.

Her eyes fell. "His Shard operated out of a cavern system. The quake... the roof had fallen in. I don't know how many were inside when it happened, but the surrounding area was deserted. We've heard nothing from him since the shake."

Her words hit me one after the other, like hammer blows driving nails deeper and deeper. "But you don't know anything for sure..."

Sirez swallowed. "No. There are many reasons a message may have been delayed. Nothing is running in an ordinary fashion right now. Courier posts are deserted because there's no scrip to pay for messages. Roads have been wiped out, rivers dammed by landslides. It's not just Jaliss in chaos."

But his silence likely meant the worst had happened. I shook my head, shocked into numbness. My father, dead just days before I'd found a way to contact him? It couldn't be.

"You're from Cosmal, same as him?" Sirez asked.

I nodded.

"Listen. I want to trust you. And I believe you can earn that. But I have a whole Shard to care for. We *will* learn Evrain's fate, I promise. In the meantime, would you consider proving yourself to us? The next time we speak, I'd rather not draw blood from your neck."

I blinked. Was this what I wanted? I shouldn't grieve yet. I should learn more while I had the opportunity. But I was still reeling from what she'd said.

"Do you need me to decide now?" I said.

"Unfortunately, we've risked a lot to meet you here. I can't put my people in danger again. But with this spiritist talent of yours... We could make use of you."

In the corner of the stable, Breeze nickered again, seeming to urge me to say yes. I thought of the boy, beheaded for no reason at all. Even if I didn't find my father, I could change things. And joining Stormshard didn't mean giving up hope of locating Mother and Avill, either. Maybe I could use Sharder contacts to get word about them.

"Yes," I said, raising my chin. "I'd like to join you. Tell me how to prove myself."

Sirez nodded. "In that case, welcome to your Sharder probation."

Chapter Forty-Seven

Kostan
A smithy turned safehouse

"I need to know who stands with us," I said. "Who do we trust? The mages?"

Beside me, Vaness sat with arms crossed over her chest. Yesterday afternoon, the ferro mages had left the smithy to send word of my retrieval to the Aurum Trinity. I'd slept in a cot in the back room, oblivious for an afternoon and the following night.

Now, morning had come. The mages had left on another errand before I woke. When I had finally lifted my head from the pillow, only Vaness had greeted me. Now, I reclined on a stack of filthy canvas with my oldest friend, gnawing on old cheese and sipping water that had once been used to quench blades hot from the forge. Though we hid in the shadow of Steelhold, hunkered beneath one of the thousands of roofs visible from the Hold's walls, we could have been leagues away. The young man who'd grown up inside that fortress was a stranger to me now.

"What makes you assume I'm trustworthy?" Vaness asked.

It was a fair question. I recalled what she'd said on the wall. She'd called me the most brutal among the Scions—the most fit to rule. At the time, I'd taken it as an insult. But maybe she'd recognized a capability I hadn't realized I possessed. I'd been hard with Ilishian. Commanding. Imperial.

"I know you," I said. "I always have."

"Well, you have my loyalty. Always." She paused, staring at her hands. "We didn't know if you were alive or dead, Kostan."

I smirked. "My death would have increased your chances of becoming Empress."

She shouldered into me affectionately. "Maybe I should just kill you myself, then."

"I'd like to see you try."

A faint smile touched her lips."I'd fail, I'm sure. Aside from the... things that happened between us that time, I've always considered you a friend. My only friend, really."

"Likewise," I said.

"Anyway, when I thought about you lost in the mountains, I was worried sick. The Ministry is desperate to kill us. No doubt they sent hunters onto the trails once they figured out you'd left through the Chasm Gate."

Guilt squirmed in my gut. Before the earthquake, Evrain's band would have had no trouble dealing with a few imperial hunters. But abandoned with no mounts and Falla's broken arm...

I brushed away the thought. I'd have time to regret my actions later, maybe even to make amends. Right now, we needed to deal with the Ministry. I needed to restore the throne. Otherwise, the Sharders' lives were forfeit anyway.

"During our escape, Ilishian spoke as if the Ministry was behind the plot. Have you confirmed that?"

Vaness looked at me with puzzlement that quickly vanished. "I keep forgetting that no one has explained things yet. Yes. It was the Ministry's plan. Minister Brevt is the leader. Apparently, he used the ministers' fear of our forthcoming Ascension to pull them into his plot. None of them want to choose exile or death at such a young age. The ministers are using the Breaking as an excuse, saying that the astrologer's proclamation was in error and that the land is angry about it. The palace geognosts are with them, only because they spot the opportunity to improve their standing. Atal elite are split. No elite family wants to start over in the influence game after a mere three decades under a chosen emperor. But for all that, they respect tradition. Regardless, I don't think you can trust any elites. Not for certain."

So many people stood against me. The Ministry. Most of the mages. Without a doubt, anyone who reported directly to a minister would be loyal to the usurpers. It only made sense.

I pinched the bridge of my nose. "Then who is on our side?"

"The aurums. In secret, of course. They're our only allies inside the Hold. Well, I'm sure some of the staff might choose to follow you."

"That's it?"

She shrugged. "There's the astrologers. They've always been on the side of Ascension. That's how we contacted the aurums—the astrologers have been communicating with the Trinity via messages carried by hawks."

"What about the protectors?"

"We don't know. It's—it depends I suppose."

My brows drew together. "Depends on what?"

"The guardians taught us the protectors were bound to the Emperor's will. I always assumed they took a vow. A figurative binding, I guess."

"And? What's the real story?"

"They wear wrist cuffs similar to our ankle bands. Spirit magic, not bodily, though. The argent mages use the cuffs to steal their free will, basically. If a protector receives an order they believe comes from the Emperor, they follow no matter what."

"But how do they determine whether it's the Emperor's word?"

"Usually, the Emperor communicates through the Ministry. Decrees get passed down through the ranks. If we could convince the Prime, I think we'd have the whole Order on our side. But she's locked inside Steelhold. Ilishian thinks the Ministry will be able to hide the Emperor's death for a long time. People are used to having Tovmeil's orders filtered through the ministers."

I tapped my finger on my knee. "You just said the Aurum Trinity is inside the Hold. Could they talk to the Prime Protector?"

"It would be the Trinity's word against the ministers. For all I know, the silver cuffs allow the argent mages to influence the protectors long after the binding of their will."

Vaness didn't sound optimistic about our chances, but I couldn't let her mood affect me. A few hours ago, I'd had no one on my side. Now, I had something to focus on. I needed to figure out how to prove my Ascension to the Prime Protector. With the protectors and aurums fighting together, not even the joined forces of the argent and ferro mages could defend the Ministry.

"It's a good start," I said. "So, did you and the mages come up with a plan for using our strengths?"

"Well..." She tapped her foot on the ground, almost guiltily. "Until this morning, we were focused on discovering whether you were dead or alive. And if you still lived, we wanted to keep your heart beating."

Something in her words sparked a thought, and I laid a hand on the amulet hanging from my neck. My heart still worked, but what about the Heart of the Empire? According to Emperor Tovmeil, the diviners had never figured out its purpose, but according to the rituals of Ascension, the Emperor must wear it. Why?

I sighed. Another in the long list of things I had to figure out.

"Thanks for explaining everything, Vaness," I said as I stood.

Vaness sat up straight when I started tugging my boots over my feet. "Where are you going?" she said, a look of faint alarm on her face.

"I want to give Fishel and Savra my thanks in person. Plus, I need to understand the state of the city before making a plan to retake my throne."

A hurt look crossed her face when I mentioned my friends at the Graybranch. I wanted to reassure her, but there was nothing I could say. I wouldn't forsake the people who'd been so kind because of Vaness's jealousy.

"It's not safe," she said, eyes pleading. "We just found you, Kostan."

"Hey, shouldn't you be calling me Emperor Kostan now," I teased, hoping to turn the conversation to something light.

She cocked her head. "Actually, I meant to ask... What name will you choose for your official reign?"

I hadn't thought about it since the morning Evrain had asked what name I would take as Emperor. "Actually," I said, "as long as I'm kicking tradition in the ribs by Ascending two years early, I think I'll just keep my name."

She smiled, though a little sadly. "I like it. Emperor Kostan."

I drew myself up. "All glory in his name."

"I mean it, though. You shouldn't put yourself in danger. Especially not now."

"You said the assassins had been taken care of, right?"

"That particular trio, yes."

"Then I've got nothing to worry about."

"But there will be more."

I knew she'd just keep arguing if I remained there. "My mind's made up," I said, as gently as I could before turning for the door.

"Kostan," she said, "the girl in the Graybranch is a Prov. They hate everything about the Emperor. Please remember that. I don't want you to get hurt."

Nodding, I lifted the bar and pushed out the door.

Chapter Forty-Eight

Savra
Outside the Hall of Registry

This shouldn't be too difficult. It was hardly different from my original plan. Only now, I was working for Stormshard—or hoping to, anyway. As I followed the winding street toward the Hall of Registry, satchel tucked tight against my ribs, I kept my eyes straight ahead.

The Sharders needed information. I had a ledger assigning me a Function which would make getting that information easy. As long as I didn't attract the attention of an argent who could read my thoughts, I had nothing to worry about.

All day, the criers had been calling out orders from the Emperor. All citizens of Jaliss were supposed to return to their assigned Functions. The streets were once again full with women pushing delivery carts and couriers crisscrossing the city. Within shops, wheelwrights pounded the iron rims on wagon wheels, and farriers nailed horseshoes to mules' hooves.

But the mood was sullen. Angry. When a man carrying a sack of grain bumped my shoulder, he didn't even bother to look up, much less apologize. Within a currency exchange stall, a clerk rolled and unrolled a sheet of paper scrawled with rates for trade. No one waited in line, no doubt because no one had coin to exchange.

Uphill, the homes of the elite were shut tight, guardsmen on their sweeping marble stairs. But even those elegant manors presented shabby faces where the quake had cracked their stonework, spilling rubble onto the slate-block streets. Hardly anyone was working to clean up the mess—apparently there weren't enough masons and repair Functions to handle the damage.

In the Merchant's Quarter, a path had been cleared through the jumbled cobblestones, the rubble piled on either side. It made the going easier, but only allowed single-file passage. Over and over, I met Atal merchants coming from the other direction. Each time, they glanced at my Provincial features and kept plodding forward. My choices were to be shoved aside or to clamber off the trail before that happened. I got out of their way.

As I balanced atop a pile of stacked stones, waiting for a pair of grocers to pass with their baskets of root vegetables, my inner awareness tingled. Sometimes my aura-sight prickled this way. If I wasn't mistaken, I was being watched.

I'd belted on my small knife with the mother-of-pearl handle. Nodding at the grocers to distract from the motion, I slid my hand to the sheath.

Someone moved at the edge of my vision. Bursting into action, I scrambled away and yanked out the knife. The blade wasn't much longer than my finger; it looked pathetic held before me.

Parveld smirked as he glanced at it. "Marks for wariness in noticing my approach, but I doubt you'd do much harm with that."

I lowered the blade but didn't sheathe it. "Are people watching me through the bracelet?"

The man sighed, then gestured to a small teahouse. The doors were open, and fire flared inside where a large cauldron hung over the heat. "Will you give me a few moments?"

"I have an errand. It's too late already." That was true. I'd planned to go in the morning, but had followed Fishel's advice and waited until after midday to leave for the Hall. The lazy heat of afternoon calmed tempers if only because it made people too tired to fight. But I worried that if I didn't get to the Hall soon, I'd find the doors closed.

"Lilik was so certain she'd do a better job than me," he said with a bittersweet twist to his lips. "Seems she hasn't had tremendous success... No, no one is watching you, at least not in the way you think."

I stepped back onto the path. Once again, heat trickled from the bracelet. "I don't have time for riddles."

Parveld slid down the slope of rubble, one arm windmilling to keep his balance. Apparently, he wasn't giving up easily this time.

"I'll escort you to the Hall," he said.

"How did you know where I was heading?"

"Because I'm terrible about minding my own business when I care about someone's well being. I pulled your destination from your thoughts. I'm sorry."

"Another spiritist ability?"

"More or less," he said. He gestured for me to go first. After a moment, I sighed and strode forward. I was almost positive Parveld meant me no harm. But regardless of what he believed about me and my so-called destiny, I wouldn't change my plan to find my father—and to unseat Emperor Tovmeil.

"I suspect the Emperor is already dead," he said softly. "So at least that's accomplished."

I stopped in my tracks and whirled on him. Despite my frustration, I kept my voice low. "I appreciate what you've done for me. But I don't like you listening in on my thoughts."

He raised his hands in surrender. "I'm sorry. And I'm sorry you're so worried about your father. I don't listen on purpose, but I'll work harder to block your thoughts."

"Good."

"But there's one other thing I want to say about your plans. Be careful with Stormshard. They have noble intents, but you're too important to die for a renegade cause. I've seen that outcome. I couldn't bear to watch it come to pass."

I didn't want to die for a renegade cause either, but I was already cautious. I wasn't sure what to say, so I shrugged.

"You mentioned someone named Lilik. Who is she?"

"She's—it's complicated. I'm not sure you'd believe me." He pressed his lips together. "Listen, Savra. I wanted to thank you for the trust you've bestowed so far. All my talk of warnings and destiny surely makes you uncomfortable. And it isn't fair to you. I realize that. Knowledge is a difficult burden."

Inhaling to collect myself, I met the man's eyes. "I must be honest. I don't know whether to believe you. Even so, I have listened to your warnings. But right now, I need to focus on my visit to the registrars."

He ducked a slight bow and took a step back. "I understand. And in truth, I worry that involving myself too much right now will upset fate. But please be cautious. You must live through the coming horrors. The world will need you afterward."

With that, he stepped off the trail to let me proceed alone.

"I'll do my best," I said.

He glanced at my bracelet. "And to answer your question, Lilik is my best friend. She and her husband had their spirits imprisoned in that bracelet after their deaths."

I blinked. "But why?"

"To help you save the world," Parveld said.

The registry clerk flattened the ledger against the desk. Despite having been stowed in the scroll case, the parchment bore stains and wrinkles earned on the journey. An intricate stamp decorated the parchment's corner, the official seal of the Empire. Just four lines were written on the paper, each with a name inked upon it. I hadn't expected to be affected, but when I saw the names of the other young people from Numintown, a wave of homesickness sloshed over me.

What were they doing now? On the ledger, their Functions were listed as sluicers. If the fire in Numintown hadn't destroyed the town, they were probably working the sluices now. I wondered if they ever thought about me, wondered how my life had changed.

More likely, they'd forgotten me already.

Beside my name was the altered assignment Havialo had commissioned from the forger. I hadn't seen the work before—again I cursed myself for trusting Havialo so easily. But the lettering seemed passable. I wasn't sure how the forger had erased the other ink, and I didn't want to look suspicious by staring too closely.

The clerk examined the paper intently. I could only assume she was considering my entry. After a moment, she glanced at me.

"Wait here." She strode to a man who scanned the room with an air of authority. They spoke in low tones.

My fingertips tingled as panic threatened. Breathing deep, I struggled to calm the fear before it brought on my aura-sight. Just as the room began to fade, a chill passed from the bracelet up my arm, shocking me back to reality.

I tried not to fidget as the registrars crossed the room together. The inside of my mouth was dry. When I swallowed, my throat caught painfully.

"It's most irregular," the man said. A crest on his tunic matched the woman's, but where a single rank-star had been stitched above her insignia, three hung over the man's crest.

"Excuse me, sire?" To my ears, my voice sounded thin as the high mountain air.

"Please repeat your reason for arriving here alone," he said.

"I—The registry party I traveled with was killed. At least—I assume they were. Bandits attacked and we scattered. I rode to the nearest town and waited, but no one came."

"And which town was this?"

"Bellows in Guralan, sire."

"I see."

While the man inspected the parchment, I caught myself rubbing my thumbs over my index fingers like a nervous child. His eyes shifted from the paper to my face. I focused on my breathing. If they summoned an argent, I needed to choose my words carefully to pass an interrogation. My escorts had been killed. I could answer that truthfully.

"Well," he said, "assuming there's truth to your tale, the law demands you stand trial for abandoning your Atal escorts to their deaths. Your cowardly flight is just more proof of your Provincial inadequacy."

"But everyone fled. It's just that my horse—"

His eyes narrowed as he sliced the air with his hand to silence me. "However," he said, "we've recently received a dispatch from the Hold. It seems their previous staff members were deemed unsuitable to continue service. They've been... dismissed. Through the Chasm Gate."

I blinked as his words sank in. "Killed?" The image of the Hold's servants being pushed to their death, falling a thousand feet to the bottom of the chasm made my stomach clench.

He shrugged. "I assume there was strife within the Hold, likely leading to the current situation. No doubt the Emperor intended to rid the grounds of further agitators. In any case, Steelhold has need of a new palace scribe. You'll bathe first, and one of my assistants will find you proper attire."

I swallowed. The plan I'd worked out with Sirez assumed I would remain in the city. We'd expected I'd be given an early apprenticeship followed by a proper assignment. Every evening, I was to meet a Sharder contact at a certain location in Lowtown to convey anything I learned from the documents I penned.

"But the Hold is locked, sire," I said.

He rolled his eyes. "An exception will be made to allow the new staff entrance."

"Will we be staying there? I mean—will we be allowed to return to the city at times?"

He shrugged. "Only if you care for a stroll out the Chasm Gate."

Chapter Forty-Nine

Kostan
Common Room, Graybranch Inn

The innkeeper, Fishel, swiped his towel over the counter. "When you run an establishment like this, you see plenty of people come and go. Good folks and rotten ones both. I was sorry to see Savra leave, but not as sorry as I imagine you are to learn she's gone."

"Gone? Where?"

The man straightened and tossed his towel onto his shoulder. "Even if I knew for certain, her destination wouldn't be mine to tell. In truth, she didn't outright say she wouldn't return, but when you say goodbye to hundreds of guests a year, you learn to read their intents."

Where would she have gone? She'd talked about becoming a scribe—could that be it? If so, she'd start by apprenticing in an elite household, or perhaps for a merchant's collective. With the order for citizens to resume their Functions, it made sense she'd continue with her plans. But still... I'd let myself believe there was a reason we'd met.

Was this how things happened for ordinary people? You met someone you couldn't take your eyes off, and then they just vanished? Aside from the blind servants and Vaness, almost all the women I'd known had been protectors, staring at me with dead eyes if they forgot to avert their gazes. Or mages, who were almost worse than the soulless protectors.

Was I just a fool who'd fallen for the first woman who'd treated me kindly?

"I shouldn't be telling you this, lad," the innkeeper said, dragging me from my thoughts. "But her mount is still here. I know how it feels to be young. Hope dies slowly at your age. So take heart in that if you wish. I don't think she's left Jaliss."

But tens of thousands of people lived in Jaliss. Hundreds of streets webbed the city. Where would I even begin to look?

From outside, a crier's voice penetrated the walls. More demands that the citizens return to their Functions. It had stunned me to hear Emperor Tovmeil's name cited, but of course it made sense. Until Vaness and I were eliminated, the Ministry would have to pretend he was alive. But as long as the Ministry controlled the news coming out of Steelhold, no one in Jaliss or the greater Empire would know the   truth.

There had to be advantages in the situation. My small group of allies knew the true story. If we could just prove the Ministry's guilt to the right people, we'd unseat the Ministry in exactly the way they feared.

I needed to think about it more. But for now, the innkeeper deserved my attention.

"I came to see you, too," I said. "I wanted to thank you for taking me in. You must have known we weren't betrothed aristocrats from Ioene."

"Ale?" the man asked, turning to tap a mug for himself. "And say no more in that regard. Please. In my business, it's better that I have no confirmation regarding the truth of my guests' circumstances. Inspectors, you know."

Despite his casual stance, his voice held a nervous edge. He was worried about the argents, of course. While under a silver mage's scrutiny, no one could lie. Well, unless they had a spirit shield.

"No, thank you. You've already been more than generous."

"Kostan," he said. "I've been thinking. You have the look of an Atal elite about you, which is particularly odd given your decidedly honorable behavior—no offense to our beloved Emperor and Ministry, of course."

A flash of shame heated my cheeks. No matter how I acted, I'd always be Atal—my face proved it.

"There's been trouble in Steelhold," Fishel continued, "and you arrived here not long after."

Did he know who I really was? No. Dozens of elite Atal had business in the Hold.

"As you've already advised, I best not confirm or deny anything."

A strained smile tightened the man's lips. "Indeed. Best for all of us. I just wanted to give you a piece of advice. No matter how clever and cautious you feel you're being, Atal features stand out in the Splits like a heron in a flock of seagulls. And with the current sentiment in the city, no Atal wants to attract Prov attention."

I should have thought of that. A life confined within Steelhold's walls and instructed by an army of tutors had taught me a wide range of subjects. But it hadn't given me wisdom.

"Thank you for the warning. Perhaps we'll meet again someday," I said, sticking out my hand. "Under different circumstances."

Fishel accepted my grip. "If the stars will it."

Chapter Fifty

Savra
Corridor of Ascent, Jaliss

At the foot of the steep street called the Corridor of Ascent, at least two dozen new Hold staff had already assembled. Most were young men and women. They stood with arms crossed and heads bowed when they weren't casting fearful glances toward Steelhold. Most kept their clothing pulled tight around their bodies as if it could provide armor from the hours ahead. Surrounding the crowd, a wall of protectors stood grim-faced. Dead-eyed.

My guard, a hard-faced woman who'd forced me to scrub my face until the skin felt raw, shoved me into the crowd.

"Sorry," I muttered as I stumbled into a girl about my age. She turned, eyes wide. Her features were starkly Provincial, especially the arching brows so common among the lowlanders.

"It's okay," she whispered. As if comforted that I'd spoken to her, she edged closer. "What's your Function?"

"Scribe," I said. "I received my writ this afternoon."

"No training then. Me neither. I'm service—the registrar who came to my town said I'd have an apprenticeship to learn my Function duties. Now I'm scared that no one will tell me what to do and I'll be punished."

A few paces ahead of us, a man turned. Lines cut down his face in at the corners of his mouth, and his skin had a weathered look similar to the middle-aged sluicers in Numintown. "Find others in your Function," he said. "Ask questions. Provs help each other."

"What do you do?" the girl asked.

The man snorted. "Mason. I'm one of the few who could actually help put Jaliss back together. Instead, a Registry page pulled me away from reinforcing a wall that's ready to topple onto a Merchant Quarter street." He stuck out his hand. "Khons. Originally from Hajinal Port in Anisel."

"Savra," I said. "Cosmal Province. I just arrived."

"Oralie," the girl said. "I'm from Anisel, too. But my family lived near the border with the Wildsends."

"Hard life up there, I hear," Khons said. "You ever have to fend off free tribesmen?"

She shook her head. "My papa's Function was soldier. We only saw him a few times a year." A flicker of sadness showed on her face. "But he was brave. The tribesmen never made it past his garrison. He took an arrow last year. He was carrying a man who got hurt and fell behind during a retreat."

As she spoke the last words, Oralie raised her chin, proud of her father's sacrifice. I swallowed. What of my father's work? Would I ever get to hear what he'd done for others?

Khons nodded and clapped Oralie on the shoulder. "We can all be grateful for his courage. And it's clear you share it. I mean it about your Function and asking for help. There are plenty here who will keep you clear of the taskmaster's whip."

Oralie pressed her lips together. "Thank you."

After a short wait, movement from the back of the crowd forced us to begin trudging along the ruined cobblestone pavement of the Corridor. Above, the late evening light painted Steelhold blood red. In the city, the shadows were already deepening.

At the boundary between the Merchant's Quarter and the Heights, high walls pressed in upon the Corridor. Because the Heights encircled Steelhold's spire like a choker necklace, the mansions of the elite like gaudy gems, the only access to the ascent trail cut through the district. The elite-class Atal couldn't suffer Provs walking their streets, so the walls protected their privacy. Every few blocks, a windowless iron door opened in the wall.

Despite the devastation in the city, only a few stray cracks and fallen blocks marred the Corridor walls. Maybe the ferro mages had helped in their construction, binding black iron into the walls' structure.

I'd heard tales of the slaughterhouses for the massive herds of cattle and sheep that fed on Old Atal's grasslands. The poor animals were forced down high-walled aisles, the scent of blood strong in their noses, knives waiting at the end. Marching along the Corridor, I couldn't help feeling like one of the doomed beasts.

In a few places, I noticed peepholes in the walls, carefully mortared and deliberate. No doubt the elites watched us pass from the shadowed grounds of their mansions. Did Stormshard have eyes on the Corridor, too? Did they know what had happened to me? When I failed to make my first meeting with my Sharder contact, would they understand why?

Oralie spotted the peepholes and leaned close to whisper. "Do you think the elites pity us?"

I shrugged. "Keep your back straight and deny them the satisfaction."

Finally, the Corridor ended at the first flight of stone stairs that ascended Steelhold's spire. Here, a gate of iron bars blocked passage. It wasn't sturdy enough to keep a determined enemy off the trail, but it didn't need to be. From the walls of the Hold, archers could hit anyone trying to make the climb. Even if they missed—and buckets of hot coals poured from the walls failed too—I'd heard that the massive gates defending Steelhold itself were impregnable.

Still, a dozen protectors surround the lower gate. When our march reached earshot, their leader saluted.

"Send them up in pairs," he called. "They should have their writs ready."

A wave of rustling traveled the crowd as people dug through pockets and satchels in search of their papers. From behind, I heard shouts of protest. Standing on tiptoes, I craned my neck but couldn't spot anything. What good would protest do now? It seemed like an excellent way to get beheaded like that poor boy in the lockup.

The guards shoved us forward two by two. When it was my turn, they grabbed Oralie and pushed her with me. We clutched our writs tightly, shuffling forward under the expressionless glare of the protectors at the gate.

As we drew close, the guards extended ringmail gloves for our writs. They didn't blink as they read our Functions and compared them against a list scrawled on parchment. Then, with a wave, they parted and sent us through the gate and onto the stairs leading to Steelhold's unassailable walls.

One polished stone riser after another, we climbed. As we ascended into the layer of smoke hanging a few stories height above the city, my nose and eyes stung. The shouts from the crowd swelled until a shriek rang out.

"Oralie, look." The shouts I'd heard hadn't been the new staff protesting after all. Behind the procession of replacement palace workers, a flood of Provs filled the Corridor from wall to wall. Held back by the protectors who'd taken up the rear of our march, they yelled and raised torches. Now and again, the press of the crowd forced someone forward. Rough protectors' fists shoved them back.

A woman went down. Another scream. As I watched, mouth sagging open, a protector hefted her from the cobblestones. She fought his grip, kicking, as someone in the crowd of Provs threw a rock toward the guardsmen.

"Disperse!" the protector roared, shaking the woman in his grip.

The crowd threw back angry protests. Within the throng, scattered weapons flashed, the torchlight glinting off rusted blades.

"You must need a clearer warning," the protector yelled. He held the woman up to one of his companions. The other guard raised a fist, slammed her in the stomach. As the air left the woman's lungs, he aimed another blow for her throat. Her windpipe collapsed with a pop I could hear from the ascent trail.

She struggled for a moment, then went limp.

The protector dropped her to the ground as his companions drew swords. "Anyone else?" he yelled.

"Everyone, stop!" A voice rang out from among the Prov mob. "Pull back! This isn't the time. We can't win here."

Voices answered in anger and refusal, and the crowd surged forward. Protectors' swords flashed. Blood sprayed.

I couldn't stand it anymore. Eyes hot, I grabbed Oralie's arm, and we set off up the endless staircase, climbing toward the source of this evil. Steelhold had the power to stop this. To rebuild the city and feed the people. But the Emperor preferred to hide in his palace.

Soon, Jaliss would either turn violent or go hungry. No doubt the Hold had food and water to outlast the city. Would I survive while everyone else—Sirez, Fishel, Kostan—starved or died of exposure?

Or would I fail in my Function? Be discovered as a Stormshard apprentice? If I made a mistake, the Chasm Gate waited.

A low stone railing guarded the drop to the city, but still my head felt dizzied by the growing height. After a couple more switchbacks, vertigo nibbling at the base of my skull, I locked elbows with Oralie. She cast me a wan smile.

After about an hour's climb and so many steps I doubted I could count them if I'd wanted, we reached Steelhold's gate. Below, the city sprawled across the grassland. From this height, the devastation was clear. Stark. Whole areas of the city were unlit despite the evening hour. Uninhabited rubble heaps. Where people still lived and worked, thousands of torches lit the haze like coals smoldering in a campfire.

So many people. So much suffering.

I turned to face Steelhold's gate. Slabs of steel formed the outer shell, dark gray metal that must have incorporated black iron in the alloy. The palace ferro mages had probably enchanted them for extra defense. On either side of the gate, protectors stood in guard towers. Crossbows bristled from the wall, the wicked tips of the bolts silver in the twilight.

We waited, neither Oralie nor I speaking. Around us, the rest of the staff assembled. Aside from the huffs of rapid breathing from the climb, the only sounds were nervous shuffling and the creak of armor from the protectors guarding the walls.

The steel doors squealed when they swung outward. New recruits stumbled back as the inner gates were exposed, their iron bars the thickness of my upper arm.

A shadow appeared on the other side of the gate, the figure silhouetted by thousands of lamps burning inside the Hold. The person raised a torch high as if examining us for worthiness.

"They'll suffice," he said to the protector who'd led the way up the trail. "Provided they can satisfy their Functions."

"Yes, Minister Brevt, sire," the protector said, pressing his fist to his forehead. He turned to face us. "You are now entering the beating heart of the Empire. Your duty is absolute obedience. Anything less will mean your execution."

Within the crowd, shoulders tensed. Fists clenched. But no one spoke.

Apparently satisfied, the protector nodded up at the guard tower. Moments later, metal squealed against metal. The iron gate slid aside, wheels rolling in a track.

"Inside. No delays," the protector said.

As I passed the threshold, I felt eyes on me. A stare so malevolent it raised hairs on my neck. I glanced to the side and saw the man who'd inspected us, Minister Brevt. His gaze traveled my body. Everywhere it touched, my skin went cold.

I couldn't contain a shudder. This had happened before, but only once. A man had come through Numintown. He'd seemed affable enough, but I'd felt his black heart. We learned later that he'd been arrested for murder. Usually, I had to fall into my aura-sight to understand the color of people's souls. But apparently, some evil was so powerful it pressed right through the world and into my mind.

I felt that now from Minister Brevt. And he, apparently, saw something in me, too. His glare followed me until our procession moved out of sight.

Chapter Fifty-One

Kostan
A smithy turned safehouse turned prison

After my disappointment in finding Savra gone from the Graybranch Inn, I'd taken my time returning to the safehouse. The hinges on the smithy's door squealed when I tugged it open. Inside, a pair of lanterns cast wavering light over the faces of my allies. Vaness squeaked in relief as she hurried toward me. Ilishian appeared torn between his new vow of fealty and anger that I'd risked myself by venturing into the city. Azar's gaze flicked between her mentor and me as if she were trying to decide how to feel about my arrival.

"Gone for hours with no word... I've given you my allegiance," Ilishian said as my boots scuffed over the dirty floorboards. "But I hope you will not squander that gift by compromising your safety for a trifling matter of the heart. Especially when the object of your affection is a—" His lip curled. "—Prov."

I glared, in no mood for condescension. "Apparently you've forgotten how to speak to your Emperor."

Ilishian shook his head. "Tovmeil and I had many arguments in the years he sat upon the throne. But he was always willing to listen to my opinion."

"As am I. I'll gladly accept your advice, but I won't tolerate you casting insults at those who befriended me when I needed it. I will not stand for prejudice against Provincials in my inner circle. The notion of Atal superiority has been perpetuated for too long."

"The Atal are the foundation upon which the throne was built. Scorning your supporters will only weaken your cause."

I leaned against an anvil, arms crossed over my chest. "If the Atal can't bear to see Provs given the same opportunities Atal families have enjoyed for centuries, I don't want their support."

Ilishian sighed. "I remember the early weeks of Tovmeil's reign. His ideas were just as naïve."

"But then the Bracer of Sight showed him the consequences of gentleness. Yes, I remember. Ultimately he failed to stick to his ideals. I will not succumb to such weakness."

Vaness laid a hand on my shoulder. "Did you get to thank the innkeeper and your friend?" The hurt in her voice was well-disguised.

Relaxing my arms, I turned to her. "I found Fishel alone. Savra had already left."

A flush of shame followed the flicker of relief on her face. Her hope of being second-pickings after a Prov girl embarrassed her. But in truth, she didn't even have that hope. My meeting with Savra had shown me how pale my relationship with Vaness had been. If Vaness's feelings for me didn't fade, I'd have to tell her the truth about our chances.

"She'll be safer out of Jaliss anyway," Azar said, her voice tinged with a kindness I didn't expect. Because she was apprenticed to Ilishian, I'd assumed she shared his calculating nature.

"Maybe so, though Fishel thinks she's still in the city. She came to receive her scribe's writ."

Azar nodded politely. No one else seemed interested in Savra's story. I clenched my jaw and looked away.

High ceilings vaulted over the main room of the smithy. From the shadows that gathered in the rafters, bats squeaked as they left their roosts and squeezed out gaps along the roofline. It was late, nearly dark outside already.

"So, where are we with our plan?" I said. "I don't like the mood in the city. If possible, I want to move before the Splits and Lowtown erupt."

Ilishian was fiddling with one of his black iron trinkets, a pendant in the shape of a complicated knot. It hung from a steel chain, and he held it before his eyes as if concentrating. After a moment, he shook his head in disgust and tucked it into his pocket.

"What does that piece do?" Vaness asked.

Ilishian hesitated, a strange look on his face. "A better question would be, 'What's it supposed to do?' It's *supposed* to emit light to indicate the nearness of the person to whom it is bound. One of the less talented ferros brought it to me seeking answers on why it didn't work."

"It's bound to you?"

Ilishian cast me a glare. "I tried to assign it to Kostan while he was sleeping. I suspected we might have reason to track him. Obviously, it didn't work."

Something in Ilishian's tone didn't ring true, but I decided to leave it alone. "About the plan?"

"Well, I sent word to the Aurum Trinity," Ilishian said. "They're overjoyed to know you've been located."

"So they'll help me retake my throne?"

"Yes. Unfortunately, there's a problem. They're in full support of the Ascension, but that's just it. They support the Ascension as it was supposed to happen. In two years."

"Wait. So they plan to allow the Ministry to keep control? What about the problems in Jaliss? And the Breaking?"

"As for the Breaking, only Tovmeil connected it to the Emperor's place on the throne. Most people don't see a pattern in the quakes and rifts. Even if I were to explain Tovmeil's visions to the aurums, they are unlikely to defy custom. They do not support the Ministry's actions, but they won't act on their objections."

Two years. How could we possibly wait that long? There might not be an Empire in two years. "All right, so we can't count on the aurums. What next? Can we get the ear of the Prime Protector?"

Ilishian shrugged. "Honestly, Kostan—"

"Emperor Kostan," I said, cutting him off.

He blinked in annoyance. "Honestly, *Emperor Kostan,* I don't believe we have many options. I will continue to search for allies. Perhaps more opportunities will present themselves. But for now, I think we should consider leaving the city. It won't be safe for much longer, no matter where we hide."

I glanced toward the wall where a gap between planks showed that full dark had fallen. "No," I said. "I won't desert my subjects. I want you and Azar out at dawn. Talk to people. Find where their sympathies lie. We *will* retake my throne."

For a few days, Vaness and I stayed inside the smithy. I grew accustomed to the scents of coal and iron, the play of shadows cast by anvils and water tubs and the massive furnace and chimney. Along the walls, shelves and hooks held work abandoned by the blacksmith when the rockfall in the chasm had taken his life. On the second day, Vaness had found a bag of dice and betting chits beneath a cot the smithy had kept in the corner of his shop. To settle our nerves, we rolled the dice and talked about our childhoods. Sometimes, I could even forget about the hunger and unrest outside the smithy walls.

Over the first days, Vaness seemed to get over her jealousy about Savra. That or she'd gotten better at hiding her emotions.

Still, I felt like a coward sheltering behind the walls. Logically, I understood that it was safer for Ilishian and Azar to move about the city. The Ministry thought Ilishian dead. Most likely, the ministers wouldn't spare a thought for a low-ranked ferro like Azar. But Vaness or I could single-handedly destroy their plot to supplant the Emperor.

That's what was bothering me. If we were such a threat to the Ministry's plot, why did I feel so helpless to expose them? As best we could figure, the Ministry planned to declare themselves rulers only once Vaness and I were dead. Which meant they were terrified people would rally behind the remaining Scions and reject Ministry rule. But who would back Vaness and me? And why weren't we searching for those people now?

It was late evening on the fifth day when my frustration overflowed. Vaness was picking up the dice from our latest game when I jumped to my feet and snatched a notched short sword from a shelf. The rusted blade had been lying amongst dented helms and a stack of bent horseshoes.

Stalking to one of the wooden posts supporting the roof, I twirled the sword's hilt in my grip. The weight was off, poorly balanced for my style of striking. It didn't matter; as I approached the post, I whirled and sank a backhand blow into the wood, sending chips flying. I yelled and struck again. Danced back and slashed high to low, roaring. Finally, I delivered a kick to the post that set it shivering.

"Always an impressive sight," Vaness said. She remained where I'd left her, sitting next to the crate we used as a dicing table and looking undisturbed by my outburst.

I ran my hand through my hair. "Do you think the mages are even *trying* to find support? Or are they leaving the smithy for other reasons?"

Vaness propped her heels on a sack and yawned. "Honestly? I don't know. Ilishian is craftier than he lets on. He hides the truth. Like with that knot pendant. He was lying about it."

"I thought so, too," I said, holding the short sword to the lantern light. Aside from the notches on the blade, it wasn't in terrible shape. Glancing around the room, I laid eyes on a whetstone and a polishing rag.

"Speaking of pendants..." Vaness said, gesturing toward my chest with her chin.

I strode back to my seat with the supplies in hand. Setting the sword and whetstone on the dicing crate, I pulled the Heart of the Empire from beneath my shirt. "Emperor Tovmeil said this was attuned to him during his Ascension. But according to him, no one knows its purpose. I assume it's a Maelstrom relic."

Vaness extended her hand. Somewhat reluctantly, I pulled the pendant's chain over my head and handed it over. She cradled the stone in one hand and slid the chain through her other.

"The chain... I thought it was silver, but the metal is too hard." She worked a pair of links back and forth. "Over time, silver gets softened with use. Scratched."

"Maybe there's black iron hidden inside. Enchanted to protect the silver."

Her mouth twisted in a doubtful expression. "Do you think Tovmeil was telling the truth when he claimed he didn't know the pendant's purpose?"

I chewed my lip, surprised that I hadn't wondered the same thing. "I don't see why he would hide the truth."

"Me neither. But I can't claim to know the Emperor's heart."

I smirked. "Aren't I Emperor now? You've often claimed to know the shape of my heart," I said, thinking of our conversation on the walls where she'd called me brutal.

A look of sadness washed her face. "Of course I know yours, Kostan," she said as she returned the pendant. "In more ways than you realize."

Feeling like an idiot for what I'd said, I slipped the chain over my head. The stone dropped onto my chest, cool against my skin. It felt... right. I'd been as much a fool to remove it as I had been to make that remark to Vaness.

"Anyway," Vaness said, "I spent some time studying the diviner's art."

My eyebrows raised. "Oh? When did you have the free time?"

She rolled her eyes. "While the rest of you lazed around, a tutor came to my room. Divining is a difficult pursuit because Maelstrom relics are so varied. There are few rules to follow when determining their purpose. But I learned one thing. There's a certain... resonance to the relics. It's easier to sense if you use argent magic."

Vaness held up her hand and wiggled her middle finger with the silver band. I felt a pang of guilt when I remembered how Falla had taken mine, suggesting I wanted nothing to do with such tainted magic anyway.

"And?"

"I can't divine anything about the pendant's purpose, given what I learned about Maelstrom relics."

I cocked my head, confused. Had she really expected to figure it out when the question had remained unsolved for centuries?

The corner of her mouth twitched. "And the reason I can't divine anything is that it's not a Maelstrom relic."

I sat shocked for a moment, running through my memories of my conversation with Tovmeil. Had he claimed the pendant was a relic? Or had I simply assumed? If he'd lied, why? And more importantly, could I trust anything else he'd said?

As the questions raced through my mind, the building shook, freeing clouds of dust from the rafters and sending tools tumbling from the shelves.

Chapter Fifty-Two

Savra
Steelhold, approaching the staff dormitory

At the end of another long day in Steelhold, I shuffled with Oralie toward the staff dorm. Ink blackened my fingers and—according to Oralie—streaked my face. I'd spent the day drafting messages to be carried into Jaliss on the legs of hawks. There'd been orders for the protectors to make more examples of Prov agitators. Vague responses to the city's guilds about when the scrip payments would resume. Demands that the astrologers search the skies for auspicious signs about changes in the centuries-old custom of Ascension.

Counter to my earlier worries, the clerks who requested my services didn't really care that my handwriting was shaky or that I struggled to spell difficult words. My tendency to slip into a Provincial dialect, even in my writing, didn't seem to bother anyone. A strange tension thrummed in Steelhold's air. Occasionally, other staff members whispered about it. But no one wanted to leave through the Chasm Gate, so we largely kept quiet.

I ate one small meal when I woke and another before bed. Oralie had told me the cooks were under orders to ration. Steelhold had stores to last for a prolonged siege provided the supplies were used wisely. Of course, the Hold wasn't under attack. None of the staff knew why the gates remained locked. Anyway, I was grateful for the food I had. My stomach rumbled through the afternoon, but it was nothing compared to what people in Jaliss faced.

Three nights ago, my second in the Hold, there'd been a commotion. From the wall, a guard had spotted a line of shadow stretching along a road leaving the city. I'd been dragged from bed to pen an order to the city's protectors. Guards had been sent on horseback to stop the parade of refugees leaving the city under the cover of darkness.

I hadn't slept well that night. My hand had inked the letters that sent the Emperor's vengeance on the suffering Provs. At least the letter hadn't been explicit about punishments. I doubted I could have lived with myself if I'd written the order to execute the leaders.

"Khons came by while I was washing sheets," Oralie said. "He'd lucked into an extra helping of dried fruit. Befriended a servant in charge of the larder, it sounds like. I think he feels responsible for me after hearing what happened to my father."

I suspected she was right. Plus, surrounded by hard gray stone and harder faces, the mason probably enjoyed the company of a fellow Aniselan. As far as I knew, no one from Cosmal Province was working in Steelhold. For that matter, I doubted there were other Cosmali anywhere near Jaliss.

Unless Sirez had been wrong about my father's fate, of course. For the hundredth time since entering Steelhold, I wondered whether Stormshard knew what had happened to me. What had the Sharders thought when I missed our first meeting? Had my contact waited around for long? Had she left in disgust when I didn't show?

"What sort of fruit?" I asked, mouth watering at the thought.

"Apricots. There were almond slivers, too." Oralie grinned as she dug into her pocket. With a glance over her shoulder, she pushed a wrinkled apricot into my hand. "Taste for yourself."

I smiled. The girl's generosity reminded me of Avill. I'd never liked apricots, but I popped it into my mouth anyway.

We turned into a narrow alley, footsteps echoing off the granite walls. I left the apricot on my tongue, allowing it to soften before attempting to chew. On impulse, I locked elbows with Oralie. It was nice to have a friend.

She started humming as we approached the alley's exit. From there, we headed for the arched doorway to the staff dorm, a dour building stained by smoke from kilns outside the nearby potters' workshop.

"You, scribe." The man's voice came from behind. "You're needed in Ministry Hall.

Weariness sank through my body as I turned, squeezing Oralie's elbow before releasing it. Suppressing a grimace, I bit the apricot in half and swallowed the pieces whole.

"Now, I assume?"

The messenger, a slight man with watery eyes and thinning hair, pressed his lips together and nodded.

"Minister Brevt requests an audience."

I hadn't seen Minister Brevt since the night I'd entered the Hold. Like the Emperor, the ministers remained cloistered, confining themselves to their Hall and palace. I'd hoped I wouldn't have to encounter the man again.

Unfortunately, as I followed the messenger through the wood-paneled hallway to Minister Brevt's personal receiving chamber, I couldn't figure out a way to avoid the meeting.

The messenger tapped on the door and laid his ear against the wood. After a moment, he nodded and squeezed the latch then stepped aside for me to enter.

Minister Brevt's scrutiny pierced me the moment I stepped into his chamber. It was all I could do to keep breathing. My vision tunneled down, auras dancing behind my eyelids. I dug fingernails into my palms and focused on the details of his chamber, the velvet wall hangings, the deep wool carpet, the black iron candelabra on his desk. Everything but the man.

Still, the world faded. My aura-sight grew stronger. Before me, Minister Brevt was an oily presence. A nest of slithering eels.

Not now! The woman yelled from my bracelet. Tingles shot up my arm. The fuzzy glow surged over me, covering me head to toe.

The world snapped back into place... almost. Unlike other times, a shadow of my aura-sight remained, painted over the room but not replacing my ordinary vision.

Savra, a man said. His voice was a low tenor, like a stringed instrument. I recalled what Parveld had said. Lilik and her husband had chosen to be bound to the bracelet. *Can you hear us?*

"Yes," I said quietly.

"What was that?" Minister Brevt asked. He'd stood from his chair and peered down his nose. I felt like a mouse pinned beneath a hawk's gaze.

Don't answer aloud, Lilik said. *If you can't project your thoughts, remain quiet.*

I cleared my throat. "Yes, sire? You called for me?"

Minister Brevt stalked closer, dragging his oily aura across the room. I shivered as he stepped within a pace of me. The man smelled of scented oils that reminded me of an embalmer's work.

"I was curious about you, so I made some inquiries. My contacts among the registrars told me you arrived under suspicious circumstances."

I swallowed and fixed my gaze into a corner of the room as he circled me. "Unfortunate circumstances, I would say, sire. The bandits attacked the registrar's party without warning."

"Hmm. I'd like to think you speak true. I have need of a loyal servant, you see. A personal secretary and page. A confidante, even. Since the death of my wife-consort, I've been sorely in need of someone with whom I can speak freely. You carried yourself with a certain poise that spoke of integrity."

His hand, Savra. Watch it.

My eyes snapped to his right hand, which had slipped into his pocket. As he drew forth a small, silver blade, I stepped back, hands raised in defense.

"Sire, my Function is scribe. My writ does not allow secretarial work." As I continued back, feet sinking into the carpet, Minister Brevt advanced. Snakes of iridescent spirit whipped from his aura-form, reaching for me. I dodged at the last instant.

Minister Brevt's eyes narrowed in suspicion as his free hand reached into the inside pocket of his jacket. Paper crackled as he pulled out a folded letter.

He huffed in amusement as he used the silver blade to peel away the wax seal. "I appreciate the dangers you must have endured amongst the heathen Provs," he said as he slipped the letter opener back into his pocket. "But be assured you'll encounter no such barbarity here."

He shook the letter open and scanned it. I'd finally reached the wall, a section of bare stone between drapes. The granite was frigid against my back.

"Complaints from the astrologers over our demands," he said before crushing the paper into a ball and whipping it across the room. "Now, as I was saying... Your writ. Do you have it with you?"

Unconsciously, I patted my trouser pocket then jerked my hand away, cursing myself.

This is a distraction, Savra, Lilik said. *He knows you sensed his attack. He's attempting to compel you. You need to put up walls. Do you understand what I mean?*

I shook my head.

"You don't? It's not in your pocket there?" Minister Brevt asked, thinking the gesture had been intended for him.

"Yes—I mean, I have it. But as you'll see, my Function is very narrow. Scribing only."

Hand trembling, I pulled out the leather wrap I'd been issued to protect my writ. The paper lay inside, secured by a pair of tabs. I handed it over.

Think of it like this, Lilik said. *He wants into your mind. Not to read your thoughts like an argent mage. He wants to hollow you out from the inside. Make you his. You need to be steel. Impenetrable.*

Minister Brevt scanned the writ, running his finger along the scrawled letters and mouthing the words.

"Savra Padmi," he said. "A starkly Provincial name. When you've agreed to your new position, I'll wish to call you something else. My late wife-consort's name was Aricelli. That will do nicely, I think, and it will spare me needing to learn another name."

Pressing the tabs aside, he plucked my writ from the leather sheath and dropped the case to the floor. Pinching the top of the paper between index fingers and thumbs, he began to tear.

"Wait, please!" I begged.

As he grinned at my distress, the tendrils of spirit erupted from his aura again, whipping toward me.

Be steel! Lilik yelled. *Armor yourself.*

But I couldn't. I didn't know what she meant or how to do it. My only hope was to run. I stepped left, felt a sickening wave of cold as a rope of spirit whipped past my ear. The room began to shake. For a moment, I thought it was another effect of his nauseating aura.

When the glassware on a display shelf rattled, I realized it was another shake.

The candelabra tumbled from the table, flame and melted wax spilling across the carpet. In one quick motion, Minister Brevt tore my writ in two before leaping for the spreading fire.

As the quake strengthened, I bolted for the door, leaving Minister Brevt and my writ behind.

Chapter Fifty-Three

Parveld
The Splits, Jaliss

Parveld staggered when the tremor hit. His shoulder smacked the rough rock wall of a stable, and he shoved off, visions of toppled masonry tearing through his thoughts. Around, Jaliss citizens shouted, mothers calling for children, Provs cursing the Emperor as if the shaking in the earth was another of his decrees.

The former Emperor, Parveld corrected himself. Not that these people knew that.

A safe distance from the wall, Parveld took shelter near a wagon's wheel. He smirked in amusement at the thudding of his heart. Even after centuries of life, the rocking earth could still send him into a panic. Just the nature of being human.

With a deep breath, he sank his awareness into the aether. Around him, the sparks of Jaliss's citizens were a scintillating array of fear and rage. Ever so cautiously, Parveld extended a blanket of comfort. Aquamarine tranquility. Sea green calm. The screams grew less shrill. A man who had been roaring obscenities toward Steelhold turned away, spotted a young child sitting in a doorway beneath a heavy stone lintel, and whisked the boy to safety.

After another few breaths, the shaking eased. Wood creaked and settled. A few stray stones toppled from walls. The quake was over.

Parveld sighed in relief. Just a minor tremor, the sort experienced weekly in Cosmal Province.

But he knew others would be much, much worse. Maybe not today or even this season, but calamity was coming. And only one young woman could prevent a complete shattering of the land.

Grabbing hold of the rough wood side of the wagon bed, he scrambled upright and scanned the street. Already calmed by his touch within the aether, the Provs in this part of the Splits had recovered quickly from the shake. A few paces away, a man in a leatherworker's apron hefted a stone that had fallen into the street. He tossed it underhand, landing it in a pile of debris from the previous shake.

Good. Better they get on with their lives than curse fate or an Emperor they couldn't touch.

A block down the street, a dark alley mouth opened. Parveld set off at a trot and darted into the narrow aisle. Immediately he felt their sparks. The Sharders were furtive as they filed back through the door into the secret refuge they'd fled when the shake began.

Parveld hurried forward and snatched the hidden door before it swung shut. Instantly, a hand seized his wrist, yanking him inside.

"Who in the storm-battered coasts are you?" a woman asked.

A knife touched his throat, and Parveld raised his hands.

"Hello, Sirez," he said. "I've come with a proposal."

"How did you find us here?" The blade of the knife pressed harder, making Parveld's eyes water.

"It doesn't matter," Parveld said. "Just hear me out. There's a girl, Savra. You lost touch with her."

"And?"

"She was sent to Steelhold. It's the foothold you've been seeking. I can help you communicate with her, but only if we come to an agreement."

Chapter Fifty-Four

Kostan
A Lowtown smithy

Vaness crawled out from beneath the heavy wooden work table, looking far less disheveled than I imagined I did. We'd hidden in the shelter of the table when the quake started, hoping it would offer protection if the roof timbers gave way. But for once, the shake had been mild.

I took a deep breath, the taste of dust thick on my tongue. "Could have been worse."

She laughed, but it was a bit strained. "According to you and Tovmeil, it will be."

The words pressed thoughts of good fortune from my mind. "Indeed."

I extended a hand to help her up then noticed one of our lanterns had overturned. The flame had been snuffed, but if it had fallen in the crate of straw padding an arm's length to the side, half the smithy could have burned by now. We needed to be more cautious if we were planning to stay here long.

Which I hoped we weren't.

I gritted my teeth while I picked up the lantern. Our planning was going nowhere. It was time to do something different. I just wasn't sure what.

"My fault," Vaness said, pulling the lantern from me and striking sparks onto its wick. "I should have moved it to the ground."

"Why was it your fault? We were both sitting next to it throwing dice."

"Because I noticed it at the last minute, but you were already under the table, and I didn't want to leave you to dig my broken body free."

"A poor excuse to take the blame," I said, smirking.

She shrugged and sank back to her seat next to the dicing crate. "Another game?"

I shook my head. The thought of idly tossing dice turned my stomach. People were suffering outside the smithy walls. I shouldn't sit around playing games while Provs starved.

As if responding to my thoughts, a sharp cry lanced through the smithy walls. More shouts followed, along with the roar of flames leaping from torches soaked in pine pitch. I trotted to the wall and pressed my eye against a gap between boards. The resiny smell of the torches stung my nose and set my eyes watering. I blinked away the tears and squinted.

In the street beyond the wall, bodies were moving, liquid shadows sliding through the torches' glow. Shouts peppered the air. The stomp of feet shook the earth.

There had to be two hundred of them, marching together. A chant went up.

"Open the gates! Open the gates!"

My breath caught. An uprising. It was beginning. Though the quake had done little damage, the reminder of the last disaster had finally spurred them to action.

I ran to the smithy's front door. Should I join them? If they were marching on Steelhold, this might be my only chance to gain entrance. As I grabbed the plank barring the door, Vaness dashed to join me.

"What do you think?" I asked.

She shrugged, her eyes wide with indecision. Somehow, that was enough. Over and over she'd cautioned me to stay inside. If she thought this might be the moment, I had to take the chance.

I couldn't go out there bare handed. Sprinting across the smithy floor, I snatched the battered short sword from the shelf. Meanwhile, Vaness grabbed a bent dagger from amongst the scrap metal. When she joined me at the door, I nodded and opened it.

The sickening crack of metal against a skull reverberated across the street. My heart pounded. I knew who dealt those sorts of blows. The protectors were here.

Using my height to its best advantage, I scanned over the heads of the crowd. There. Piercing the mob at its vulnerable middle, a pair of protectors shoved into the crowd, spiked maces swinging. Where the blows landed, bodies flew. But a few paces away, the chant continued, covering the noise of the protectors' swings. The Provs marched on, oblivious.

In the dark and the torchlight, they stood no chance against the protectors' attack. Even if the full mob turned on the guards, the protectors' reinforcements would arrive before the untrained Provs organized an attack capable of taking them down.

"protectors!" I yelled as I pushed into the crowd. "Watch out!"

"Kostan!" Vaness shrieked from behind. "No!"

It was too late. The battle fury raged through me. Shoving men and women aside, I trudged for the nearer of the two protectors. He saw me coming in time to block my first slash with the handle of his mace. Steel shrieked as my blade slid down the metal and bounced off the guard near his glove. I whirled and struck again. The protector dodged handily, elbowing a wide-eyed Prov woman aside.

"Storms batter you!" Vaness yelled as she leaped into the fray. "Of all the idiot moves."

But she moved just like I remembered, like silk falling through still air. One moment, she stood outside the smithy door, and the next her dagger glinted in the light as it sank toward the protector's collar bone. The poorly crafted blade glanced off, but the distraction granted me an opening. As the protector staggered away from her blow, I whirled and aimed a slash for his gut. My sword, freshly whetted, sliced through hardened leather and into the soft flesh beneath. I shuddered at the sensation—no matter the years of practice, I'd never cut flesh. My practice swords had thumped off armor. Occasionally, I'd demolished a straw-filled training dummy.

I had little time to consider what I'd done. As blood poured over my hand, slicking my grip, Vaness leaped backward with a surprised cry. A cut yawned on her weapon hand. Deftly, she tossed her blade to her weaker arm.

The remaining protector advanced, eyes dead. He raised his mace and swung at her.

"No!" The voice came from the side. I whirled, astonished to see a Prov man barrel into the protector, knocking his blow away from Vaness. The protector cast him an expressionless glance, picked him up by the collar and threw him over the crowd. His body went limp as he struck the smithy wall.

With a roar, I sprang, steel aimed in an upward blow to the armpit. If I could disable his mace, Vaness and I could wear him down.

I needn't have attacked. Before my sword struck, the protector went down as the mob closed over him. Fists landed on his face. Rocks smashed his hand where it wrapped the mace's grip. He fought silently, throwing men and women aside, but two attackers more appeared for every Prov he repelled.

Moments later, two dead protectors lay in the street, their blood soaking into the dry earth. No more chants rose from the crowd. Instead, Provs looked on in shocked silence. What had they done? What would happen now?

One by one, shadowed figures melted away from the edges of the crowd. There would be no march on Steelhold tonight.

Some of the men and women nearest Vaness and me cast us curious glances. After a moment, I stooped and wiped the blood from my sword, leaving it on the red uniform of the protector.

"More will arrive," I said. "You should go."

"You're Atal," a man said. "Why did you help us?"

I inhaled as I considered my answer. "To start, I helped because it was the decent thing to do. But there's more. I know why the gates of Steelhold are closed. I helped you because the protectors are following the orders of usurpers. If they aren't stopped, they'll devastate the Empire and everyone in it."

A murmur of confusion traveled the dissipating crowd. A few Provs who had started to drift away stopped and returned to earshot.

Drawing myself up to my full height, I continued. "Emperor Tovmeil is dead."

Scattered exclamations rose from the gathering. I raised my hands to silence them. "Tovmeil was murdered by the Ministry. The gates are locked because they fear you'll learn the truth before their plot is complete."

"Which plot?" someone asked. "And who are you to know all this?"

I couldn't tell them everything. Not now. Not even after I'd saved their lives. If they knew I was a Scion, the mob was likely to turn on me, adding my body to the those of the protectors'.

"They wish to take power for themselves. We must stop them. You can help by spreading the word. Tovmeil is dead. The Ministry is strangling the city to protect their secrets."

A block or two away, a shout rang out. "protectors! They're coming!"

The crowd scattered, sprinting like rats exposed to the light.

I stared down at the dead men. According to Ilishian, the guards were bound to follow the Emperor's orders. Bound to me. Could I have done something different to spare their lives? Were the sparks of life behind those soulless eyes even worth sparing?

"Kostan," Vaness said, tugging at my arm. "Time to go. Now."

I nodded. She was right. The smithy was no refuge now, not after two protectors had died on its doorstep. Shoving my sword into my belt, I turned and followed Vaness into the night.

Chapter Fifty-Five

Savra
Between kilns outside the potters' hall, Steelhold

In the stillness following the quake, only the rush of the wind over Steelhold's walls broke the silence. Huddled between kilns outside the potter's hall, I strained my ears for the sounds of protectors' boots. For Minister Brevt's wheezing breath. For the guards who would march me to the Chasm Gate.

After fleeing Minister Brevt's chamber, I'd careened through the corridors of Ministry Hall. The shuddering earth had sent me sprawling twice, and the scrape on my shoulder still ached, but I'd lucked upon the exit before being caught. Out in the falling darkness, I'd stumbled away from the hall, across the bare granite courtyard and past a fountain where black sand poured endlessly from cornices and spouts.

All the while, I'd imagined Minister Brevt chasing me, his oily spirit tendrils whipping and grasping. But he hadn't caught me then, and he hadn't found me yet.

Yet.

What was I going to do? Even if I stayed hidden through the night, what would happen when the sun rose? I'd spent five days in Steelhold, most of them in stuffy chambers or the staff dorm. When I crossed the Hold, I'd been guided down well-trafficked alleys and through wide hallways. Steelhold was a stark place, absent the nooks and crannies of the city below. I had nowhere to hide. My only friend here was Oralie. She might have an idea where I could go, but asking her would mean putting her at risk.

Anyway, even if I found somewhere to hide, it couldn't last. I'd need food and water. I was no good at sneaking around and pilfering supplies, and I wouldn't ask anyone to risk the Chasm Gate to help me.

What then? Kill Minister Brevt and hope he hadn't recruited help in finding me yet?

I hugged my knees to my chest.

"Lilik?" I whispered. "Can you hear me?"

We can.

"I'm afraid."

I know. We feel what you feel.

"What do I do?"

For a few breaths, no response came from the spirits trapped within my bracelet. Then threads of confidence and hope spooled out from the bracelet, winding through my body.

"How do you do that?" I asked.

It's part of our bond. Our connection through the aether. Your ability as a channeler allows you to share our emotions as well as our thoughts.

"Channeler? What's that?"

I'm sorry. Spiritist. In our time, your kind were known as channelers and compellers. Communication between minds, and compulsion of others. You have some of both of of those abilities. Magic changes as civilizations evolve, and so do the words used to describe it.

Lilik, the man cut in. *We need to work on projecting. She can't keep talking aloud.*

A wave of agreement followed the man's words. *Raav's right,* Lilik said. *Before we continue, you must learn to speak over our bond.*

Lips pressed together, I shrugged. How was I supposed to do that?

Try this, Lilik said. *Imagine someone you care about very much.*

Immediately, images of Avill and Mother came to mind. I nodded.

Now, close your eyes and imagine telling them what they mean to you. With your spirit, not your lips. Feel the words moving from your mind to theirs.

I attempted to follow her directions, imagining Avill's face before me. *I love you,* I thought. *Please be safe. I couldn't bear to learn that Havialo hurt you.*

That's good, Lilik said. *I felt your emotions, but not the words. You must be very focused on forming your thoughts so that the aether can carry them. Try telling me how you feel about this person.*

I... I thought. *I would give anything to see Avill right now. I broke my promise to her. She was so afraid I would leave her, and I did. I have to find her. Keep her safe.*

A wave of congratulations surged from the bracelet. *Parveld said you were a bonfire of talent,* Lilik said. *I understand now.*

So... I furrowed my brow, focusing on sending my thoughts into the bracelet. *So it worked?*

An understatement, Raav said. *You're twice the channeler Paono—I mean Parveld is.*

Paono?

He changes his name through the decades, Lilik said. *We can give you the full story another time. For now, how about we focus on saving your life?*

Please, I thought, attempting to suffuse the word with gratitude.

Good! You're mixing words and emotions, already. A bonfire indeed, Raav said.

Hmm. Maybe we should back up, Lilik said. After more than an hour, nothing Lilik or Raav had tried to explain to me made sense. I couldn't understand their descriptions of magical abilities, much less use the techniques.

If you think it will help, I said.

Like I mentioned, magic evolves, Lilik said. *Sometimes, a civilization will have abilities that haven't been seen before. I've never heard of geognosty outside of Atal. And sometimes, like with channeling and spiritism, the magic changes over time. When I explain something, try searching for similarities in your experiences.*

I nodded as I scooted deeper into the niche between kilns. The smooth brick walls were still warm from the day's firing, lending a sense of comfort.

Were you a spiritist—a channeler, I mean? I asked.

A bittersweet tickle emanated from the bracelet. *I was. And though my talent was strong, it was nothing compared to what Parveld senses from you.*

I wondered if I should feel proud of my ability, but couldn't summon the emotion. Whatever spiritist abilities I possessed, I'd been born with them. I hadn't worked to achieve them, so why take pleasure in knowing how strong they were? Besides, if I couldn't figure out how to use them, my powers were worthless.

My experiences are so limited. My aura-sight flares when I'm scared. I have more nightmares than most people, but that might not be related.

That may feel limited, but the fact that you even see auras without training means you're a natural. Parveld said that most spiritists have no idea about their talent until the Empire finds and kills them.

I didn't see any point in arguing. I was glad Lilik and Raav believed in me, but their confidence alone wasn't going to help me survive Minister Brevt's attacks.

If I can figure out the armor you've tried to explain, are you sure it will work against Minister Brevt? Havialo said that spiritists were the true mages, and the metalogists were just pretending with their tainted jewelry. If they're different types of powers, what if I can't affect him?

Well, Lilik said, *I don't know for sure. But the magic is related, according to Parveld. He's spent centuries studying rifts like the one that caused the Maelstrom.*

Rifts like the canyons that open during an earthquake? What does that have to do with the Maelstrom?

A different sort of rift. The Gray Gorge and First Rift are cracks in the earth. The kinds of rifts Parveld studies are cracks between worlds.

Wait, so there's a rift leading to another world inside the Maelstrom?

Actually, the rift was sealed more than thousand years ago. It took a great communion of mages to close it, and that was after it had swallowed a continent. But it wasn't sealed properly, which is why the Maelstrom still nibbles at our world, pulling land and life into the great Hunger that underpins existence. Cosmal Peninsula is slowly being eaten by what remains of the rift, causing the continent to crack and break apart.

What's wrong with the seal? I asked.

I hope Parveld won't hate me if I get some of this wrong, Lilik said, sending a trickle of uncertainty across our bond. *Basically, the rift is closed—if it weren't, our world would have vanished centuries ago. The problem is, the seal is tainted. One of the mages in the communion had lost her family to the Hunger, and she wanted to keep a door open for their return. She twisted the spell at the last moment.*

Did it work?

Not in the way she wished. The seal leaks, throwing back bits and pieces of what the Hunger has stolen. But never without altering them.

The relics! I said. For hundreds of years, diviners had tried to understand why the objects washed up on Cosmali shores. And now I knew the answer.

And the Maelstrom-metals. It's not actually the metals which return from the other realm. It's the magic. In the case of metalogy, channeling and compulsion magic. For reasons that not even Parveld understands, the abilities bind to metals that occur naturally within the Maelstrom. But the Maelstrom magic comes with a cost. The taint. It infects those who use it.

I remembered Havialo's reaction to the currents of water and air caused by the Maelstrom. He'd feared the corruption. *What does the infection cause?*

Greed. Avarice. Madness. Those are the tools the Hunger uses to open rifts. I suspect that Minister Brevt has more ranks in metalogy than indicated by the rings he displays on his fingers.

I swallowed, hugging my knees tighter. *What about people who grew up near the Maelstrom? Are we tainted too?*

Both Raav and Lilik sent waves of affection across our bond. *Not in the least,* Raav said. *In fact, Parveld thinks spiritism arose near the Maelstrom to counter the contamination.*

From up on the wall surrounding the Hold, muffled thumps marked a patrol passing the stationary sentinels. The protectors saluted one another by pounding fists to chests. I'd heard the sounds enough times during the day to become accustomed to them, but now, it reminded me that time was short. The patrols walked the wall every hour. After another five or six series of thumps, dawn would brighten the sky.

So back to saving my life... Can you explain how Parveld sent three people to the Sandsea? That seems like my best chance for dealing with Minister Brevt.

Raav chuckled. *Parveld rarely uses his magic in visible ways, but when he does, it's usually dramatic.*

True, Lilik said. *Anyway, what Parveld did was complicated. I don't know if spiritism allows that kind of weaving—if we get you through this, we can experiment. For now, let's focus on controlling the abilities we know you possess. Has your aura-sight protected you before?*

I pressed my fingers to my temples. Yes, I'd used my aura-sight in self-defense, but I had no idea how to do it again.

On the night of the big quake, I did something to the auras of some men who planned to attack me. I forced them away.

Compulsion, Lilik said. *It can do terrible things when used by the wrong people. But in your hands, it stopped violence.*

But I have no idea how I did it, I said, coloring the thought with frustration.

Tell me everything you remember. We will crack this, Savra. You just need to believe.

I sighed, doubt settling on my shoulders like a heavy cloak. Nonetheless, I started explaining how the Atal men had surrounded me and my panicked reaction. Somewhere on the high slopes of the Icethorns, a hunting cat roared.

Chapter Fifty-Six

Kostan
The night-cloaked streets of Jaliss

Vaness and I trotted out of Lowtown and onto Tanner's Row before we slowed to a walk. With every step, I considered what I'd told the Provs. Had it been the right move? Would it help me undermine the Ministry? Or had I simply added more chaos to Jaliss's shantytowns?

I cursed our hasty departure. The discovery of the protectors' corpses would bode ill for the Prov population. If I'd been thinking clearly, I'd have demanded that Vaness help me drag the bodies inside the smithy. They'd have been discovered eventually, but I would have gained the Lowtowners some time.

Too late to go back now. The only way to blunt the protectors' vengeance was to move quickly. No more waiting for Ilishian and Azar. I needed to make a move on Steelhold within a day. Two at the most.

I needed answers. Action. The time for caution was over.

On Tanner's Row, the stench of leather tanning still flooded the street though work had finished hours ago. I took a relieved breath of fresh air when we strode into the Merchant's Quarter. Presiding over the intersection, the Hall of Registry raised a marble facade over the street. I wondered where Savra was now. Had my actions tonight made her less safe? Would I ever see her again?

I swallowed and looked away. If I'd been born into a different life, I might have the luxury of answering those questions. But whether I regained the throne or died trying, I'd never be able to search her out. Anyway, once I Ascended, she'd have no wish to see me again. I would become the thing she hated most. The man who beheaded Prov boys without cause.

Clenching my fists, I bowed my head and trudged on.

Time for action. Time for answers. Tonight.

The Ministry couldn't further their plans while Vaness and I lived. That fact kept returning to my mind. How could I use it? I'd told the mob about Tovmeil's assassination, but that wasn't enough to stop the ministers' plot. The Provs had no real reason to believe me, and even if they did, they were too hungry and exhausted to help me topple the Ministry.

I needed more allies. Powerful allies. And most importantly, I needed to get inside Steelhold. The Heart belonged on the throne. Somehow, I felt the pendant and the Breaking were related. I just wasn't sure how.

Where the street curved toward the boundary with the Splits, Vaness stalked to a stone bench outside a bakery. She sank onto the smooth granite, propped her elbows on her knees and cradled her chin in her hand.

"So," she said, "what now?"

I took a deep breath. The air smelled faintly of turned earth, escaped when buildings had shifted on their foundations during the tremor. "Did you and the mages work out a meeting point if the safehouse was compromised?"

She shook her head. "We were too focused on other things."

Pulling the sword from my belt so I could sit, I joined Vaness on the bench. I laid the flat of the blade across my thighs then grimaced at the blood still smearing the steel. I glanced around the bench for something to wipe it on. Disappointed, I set the blade out of sight.

We sat quietly for awhile. As I stared at the shuttered storefronts opposite us, an idea began to take shape in my mind. I tapped my finger on my thigh while considering the notion. It was risky, but it could work. Plus, it was better than anything the mages or Vaness had come up with.

"You need to find somewhere defensible to hide overnight," I said. "At first light, I want you to go to the Astrologers Tower. They may be worthless in a fight, but at least we can count on the star gazers' allegiance. If Ilishian is thinking clearly, he'll look for us there."

Vaness was examining the shoddy dagger she'd grabbed from the smithy. As I spoke, her fingers curled around the hilt. "What about you?" she asked, suspicion clear in her voice.

I stretched my legs out, planting heels on the slate pavement. As I draped an arm over the back of the bench, I wondered if she'd see right through my casual act. "I'll follow after. We'll attract less attention approaching the Tower one by one."

She snorted in disgust. "You are such a terrible liar. It's the girl, isn't it? You want a chance to look for her before the mages find us again."

The corner of my mouth drew up in a sad smile. If only that were my plan. But I had to forget Savra—no point in rekindling hope just to have it drowned. Still, better if Vaness thought she'd figured me out.

I shrugged. "I know there can't be anything between Savra and me. But she took a big risk to help me. I want to thank her. She'll hate me when I take the throne—all the Provs will. But at least she won't be able to accuse me of being ungrateful."

Vaness clapped a hand on my knee. "You've gotten soft, Kostan. Too much time hanging out with Provs."

Or maybe I'd found the courage to be myself. Anyway, now wasn't the time to debate with her. "So, do you agree? The Astrologers Tower at dawn?"

"The Tower at dawn," she said.

"And Vaness, if something *does* happen... If I don't show up I mean, leave the astrologers. Find another place to hide."

Her brows drew together. "Why?"

"Because I can't know where you are."

She nodded. "Argents. You don't want them reading my location from your mind."

"Right. But anyway, we won't have to worry about that. I'll see you by sunrise."

"If you say so," she said. "But Kostan... be careful. The Empire depends on you."

Chapter Fifty-Seven

Savra
Exposed by moonlight, Steelhold

The crescent moon rose late in the night, casting a bar of wan light into the niche between kilns. I pressed deeper into the recesses but couldn't escape the glow.

I need to move, I said.

Agreed, Lilik and Raav said at once. We'd been focusing on willing my aura-sight to bloom and then on dispelling it again when I need my awareness in the real world. Or, as Lilik had explained, on shifting my focus between the physical realm and the aether. But I preferred my terms. In her experience, the aether was a vast space she'd been able to sense. I felt nothing of the sort. Instead, I perceived auras more like hidden parts of our world.

At least we'd made a little progress. If I concentrated very hard, I could sense the empty auras of the protectors on the wall. They were like gashes in the world. Wounds against the sky.

I rose into a crouch and shuffled to the front edges of the kilns. Laying a hand against the warm bricks to steady myself, I focused on summoning my aura-sight. Spirits flared across my vision, the tranquil blues and silvers of sleeping people inside nearby buildings. I scanned the area, looking for patrols, but the only moving auras I saw were the shifting voids atop the wall.

Blinking, I dispelled the vision. I edged into the alley between the potters' hall and the staff dormitory. The best place I could think to go was the storehouses. The buildings pressed close together in the southeasterly region of the Hold. I'd be well hidden there until dawn. If I could just recall how I'd shoved the Atal auras away, I might be able to protect myself by the time the sun rose. Pulling my thin jacket tight over my body—without the kilns' warmth, I was already shivering—I turned south.

In the centuries since Steelhold had been carved, many buildings had been added atop the seamless architecture, turning the alleys into a maze. I turned left and right, climbed stairs and descended ramps. When I finally reached the fringe of the storehouses, I stopped and brought my aura-sight to life. As spirits awakened in my vision, a voice pressed into my thoughts.

Can you hear me?

I gasped. *Parveld?*

Warmth joined the next thought, faint but unmistakable. *At last!* he said. *Lilik got through to you.*

She did.

Thank the tides. Now listen closely. It's very hard for me to speak at this distance, and I worry the metalogists might hear our words. Consider what you say carefully. Don't give away information about who or where you are.

All right, I said, stopping short to show I'd listened to his warning.

I have a message from the group you're working with.

Do they know I didn't betray them? I asked.

I told them what happened. It's a boon for them, actually. They've long wished for a member in your current situation.

I'm a probate, not a member, I said. *What's the message?*

The leader says she has a single task for you. If you can accomplish it, you can consider your probation complete. You'll be a full-fledged member.

I leaned my shoulder against the wall. *A few days ago, you warned me about working for the group. You said you didn't want to see me die for their cause. So why convey a message for them?*

Circumstances have changed. I can't remove you from danger—my involvement would throw fate's wheel out of track. But I believe their organization has the resources to help you to safety. Right now, that's what matters.

How can they help? I asked. *The... paths are barred. Locked. I can't leave.*

Yes, but locks have different strengths. The group believes you have the key to the shadows. An hour after sunset, open the way. You'll be led to safety, and your action will aid the cause.

Unlock the shadows? Did he mean the Shadow Gate? It made sense since I'd tried to hint about the gates by calling them locked paths. But how in the wide sky was I supposed to open one of Steelhold's gates?

I don't know how—

Shh! I sense something, Parveld cut in. *We'll speak again.*

With that, he was gone from my mind.

Chapter Fifty-Eight

Kostan
An alley opposite the protectors' post, Jaliss.

I rotated the sword in my hand, adjusting the grip. Across the street, the heavy doors defending the central post for the Order of Protectors stood like wooden sentries. The chain which had secured them overnight lay in a loose heap beside the stairs. Altogether, the links must have weighed more than a horse. It had taken four men to move them.

I'd been watching the post since late evening, crouching in a narrow gap between buildings. During the first hour, pairs of protectors had passed the front of the building, unpinning insignias from their uniforms and depositing them in a slot below a window. Others had fished badges from a black-iron bin affixed to the building before setting off on patrol. I could only assume the bin was enchanted and would damage ordinary citizens who tried to steal a badge.

By midnight, I'd started to think the bodies of the men we'd slain would go unnoticed through the night. But about an hour before the crescent moon rose, two protectors, a man and a woman, had raced toward the post, boots thudding and armor jangling. The man had swatted away a black-iron hatch on the front of the building and reached inside. He'd yanked on something that set an alarm bell tolling in the depths of the building.

Half the city's protectors had converged on the post after that. Patrollers had been trotting through the streets since, a double shift of empty-eyed men and women seeking vengeance for their soulless brethren.

But they hadn't searched the alley across from their post. After sunrise, a high-ranking officer had arrived with three strong helpers to remove the chains and open the post for daily business.

And now that Functions had resumed in the rest of the city including—I assumed—the hawk keepers who could send messages into the Hold, I had no more excuses.

Time for action.

I glanced down at my sword. I hated to leave it, but I had no choice. No one walked into a protector post armed, not even an elite-class Atal. I gave the grip a last spin in my palm and laid the blade on the broken cobbles of the alley. Dunking my hand in a rain barrel to rinse off the remaining blood, I wiped it dry on my trousers and strode across the street.

There were two ways this could go. I'd try the easy path first. And if that failed, I'd have to hope fortune would favor me.

"I need to speak with the highest ranking officer in the post," I said as I strode through the door.

A few protectors were working in the post's front room. Writs and weaponry lined the walls of the mid-sized chamber. Unlike most official buildings in Jaliss and the Hold, there were no desks or tables, no quills or parchment. The protectors did not spare time for documents or written requests. Their business was death and intimidation, and they pursued it without distraction.

Standing at a waist-high workbench, a woman looked up from the leather sheath she was oiling. She scanned my clothing, her face set in the same flat expression as every protector in the Empire. But I imagined what she was thinking. Judging by my garb, I didn't have the status required to make such a demand. But when her eyes reached my face, she paused, confused. My Atal features didn't match my attire or apparent circumstances.

She set aside her rag and capped the flask of oil. "Under whose authority?"

"Under the authority of the Emperor and his Scions."

The protector blinked. Given her Function, it was the closest she'd come to looking surprised. "The Emperor speaks through the Ministry and Prime Protector. And the Scions have no authority. Not yet."

"Emperor Tovmeil is dead, as are eleven of the thirteen Scions. The old hierarchy no longer stands."

At my words, a pair of guards moved toward the weapon racks on the walls. The woman I was speaking with set down the leather sheath and edged her hand toward the dagger it usually held.

"Who are you to carry such news?" she asked.

I inclined my head, grateful to have steered the conversation correctly. "I am one of the two surviving Scions. Kostan was my birth name. I've chosen to keep it as Emperor."

The woman swallowed. Her fingers crept to the dagger's hilt.

I'd carried a faint hope that the protectors would immediately recognize my authority as Emperor. If so, they would have been bound to obey my words. But apparently, it wouldn't be that easy. On to the next plan.

I held my palms forward to show I meant no threat. "It would be a monstrous claim if it weren't true. I'm not asking you to believe me. I only wish to speak with your duty officer. Let my honesty be judged by someone with a rank matching the seriousness of my assertion. That may mean sending a hawk to the Prime."

This, at least, made sense to her. With a nod, she headed for the back room. "Wait here," she said.

After a few moments, a man with three stars embroidered above his protector's crest emerged. A mid-level rank, no more. He gave me the same inspection the woman had, ending on my face.

"If you weren't Atal, I would execute you for spreading such rumors about our glorious Emperor."

"I realize that," I said. "As I said to your fellow soldier, I am not asking you to believe me. In fact, I'd rather you send a hawk to the Hold. Address the message to your Prime and the Ministry and let them know that I claim to be one of two living Scions. And please tell them I can help find the other Scion. Her name is Vaness, and she's fled the city for a distant refuge to await Ascension—we feared for our lives after the problems in the Hold. But I'm sure the Ministry will be relieved to know we've survived, and they'll be eager to gather us under their protection once more."

Chapter Fifty-Nine

Savra
Storehouses, Steelhold

Tucked between barrels of flour outside a storage shed, I closed my eyes and focused yet again. My control of my aura-sight was improving, and I could now sense spirits halfway across the Hold. But I still couldn't *do* anything with them. As I slipped my awareness across the top of the wall, looking for a gap between sentries—at this point, I was considering an attempt to climb out of Steelhold and down the sheer cliff—footsteps thumped against the stone alley near my hiding place.

I shrank back into the gap between barrels, flinching when the motion rattled a loose lid.

The footsteps halted. Turned. Heart thudding, I fell into my aura-sight as the guard approached. As his empty gaze arrowed into my hiding place, I made a desperate *push* against his spirit. At once, I felt his attention split and wash over me like water around a rock in a streambed. He gave a grunt of confusion, scanned the wall behind me. Finally, he turned and left the alley.

I sagged against the wall in relief.

Congratulations, Lilik said. *Can you repeat it?*

Swallowing, I focused on the memory of that deflection. *Yes,* I said. *I think I can.*

Good. Then now would be a good time to move. The guard was confused enough that he might return.

I glanced at the sky. The pink of dawn had faded into the clear blue of morning. If I made it through the day, I'd need to figure out the Shadow Gate. Best to start early. Nodding, I stood and slipped out of the alley.

As I slid along the outer walls of buildings, I tracked the auras surrounding me. Staff members moved with gray resignation veined with tendrils of fear, especially when passing the Chasm Gate. Ministers and high-level aides armored their olive-green unease with expressions of assuredness. Mages wore concentration thick about themselves while families of the leadership lounged in their chambers, their auras drab with boredom.

I walked slowly and steadily, focusing on nudging auras and attention away from me. If my footsteps grew too fast, I lost my concentration and my aura-sight faded. Too slow, and I worried my deflection wouldn't keep attention off of me.

As I moved, I grew more comfortable with my new trick. The Hold was a stream of auras, and I slipped unnoticed through the currents of attention. Gazes washed over me as if I weren't there. Alley by alley, wall by wall, I made my way toward the Shadow Gate.

Near the entrance to the central courtyard, I paused and peered at the Emperor's palace. Parveld had said he believed the Emperor was dead. If so, would the palace chambers be empty of auras? If I managed to reconnect with Stormshard, they'd want information about Tovmeil's status.

A handful of auras moved within the palace walls. Their colors were a mix of the emotions filling the Hold. With no way to know whether one of those glowing spirits belonged to Emperor Tovmeil, I shrugged and moved on.

Ahead, a hawk glided down and alighted on the glove of a handler who stood atop a two-story watch post. The woman held up a strip of meat. The red flesh disappeared into the bird's wickedly curved beak. Cocking an eye at the nearby perch, the hawk flapped over and settled onto the wooden rod.

As the handler murmured to the bird, her aura pulsed with contentment and affection. Here, at least, was one person who took pleasure in their Function. I wondered whether she was new to the Hold, or if she'd survived the purge through the Chasm Gate. Until arriving in Steelhold, I hadn't even known that hawk keepers existed. If I were to guess, she was one of the lucky few staff members who would have been too hard to replace.

Still cooing to her bird, the woman untied a burgundy-colored leather string from around the hawk's leg, freeing a rolled strip of paper. Many of my messages had flown from the Hold in this way, but I'd never seen the hawk keeper work. I pressed myself against the wall to watch.

The hawk keeper dangled the leather tie over the rail of her post. She scanned the street below until catching the attention of the messenger on duty.

"Get word to the ministers and the Prime Protector. Jaliss's protector post has an urgent message."

The messenger nodded and raised his hand for her to drop the fluttering note, but the hawk keeper shook her head. "I'll carry this one by hand. First time I've seen them use the burgundy tie. Oh, and fetch the scribe. The protectors will want an immediate response."

Storms, I thought. *Not now.* I swallowed and hurried forward. The Shadow Gate was my last hope. Maybe I'd spot something quickly. A weakness. Stormshard believed I could open the gate, and if ever I needed an escape, it was now.

Across twenty paces of bare stone, the gate stood closed. Unlike the Sun Gate where we'd entered, there were no bars here. Just a steel plate that was probably as thick as the width of my hand.

Around me, auras swirled. My heart hammered against my ribs. The conversations of servants were a dull hiss. The wind rushing overhead was like the pulse roaring through my ears.

With care, I could divert the attention of people who weren't actively looking for me. But once the messenger failed to summon me to an audience with the entire Ministry and the Prime Protector? The guards would march through the Hold shoulder to shoulder until someone walked right over me.

Care for some advice? Lilik asked.

My knees wobbled at the sudden words. At this point, I would take any help I could get. I nodded.

Do the unexpected. Answer the summons. Minister Brevt hasn't raised an alarm. I don't believe he intends to. Either he enjoys knowing

315

you're out here, scared with no hope of escape, or he wants something else.

So I should just deliver myself to him?

Unless you can think of a better idea. Your deflection is good, but it's just a trick. It won't defeat careful scrutiny. You need more time to learn your abilities.

My palms were clammy. I wiped them on my pants before nodding. Giving a last look at the gate—a protector stood on either side, with one more standing near a lever that was secured by a heavy chain—I turned and headed for the staff dormitory.

The messenger, hair tousled above his forehead, cast me such a look of frustration that I blushed in shame. He'd been pacing the entryway to the dormitory when I pushed through the door. I didn't blame him for hesitating to report me missing to the Ministry—the slightest failure on a servant's part could mean a plunge into the chasm. I should have thought of that when I'd fled toward the Shadow Gate. My actions affected more than just me.

"Ministry Hall. Hurry," he said.

I followed on his heels as we trotted back the way I'd come. Within minutes, we crossed into the cool entrance foyer of the Hall. A page was waiting outside a pair of heavy doors. Even with the thick wood blocking sound from the chamber, the raised voices within were enough to make me wince.

The page cast me a pitying glance before tapping on the door. Within a breath, the door flew open, exposing Minister Brevt. The man's face was stark white, just two spots of purple centered in his cheeks. Immediately, I attempted to throw walls around my mind.

I couldn't tell if the defense worked. If Minister Brevt tried and failed to assault my thoughts, the attempt didn't show on his face. Skin tight across cheekbones and chin, he motioned me inside with a gesture as sharp as a sword strike.

My feet clicked against the polished tiles in the Ministry's audience chamber. Twelve people sat at a long table, eleven ministers and a chainmail-clad woman who had to be the Prime Protector. Minister Brevt stepped to the head of the table.

Unsure what to do, I bowed to the gathering.

"We're agreed, then?" Minister Brevt asked the collected leaders. "We'll let the argents have a chance with his mind? We must locate the girl, too, and he is our best lead."

Another minister shook her head. "I don't understand why he came to us. Is he really that stupid?"

Minister Brevt scoffed. "Obviously he is. Anyone else care to comment?" he asked, lip twitching. Around the table, gazes dropped. "Good then. Prime, please instruct our scribe in the wording."

"You'll pen a missive to the protectors' post in Jaliss," the Prime Protector said, turning to address me. Unlike the other guards, her eyes were clear and calculating, not soulless and empty. "It shall read exactly like this: Within two hours, the man posing as a Scion to our glorious Emperor will be presented at the Sun Gate for punishment. Twelve protectors will escort him. None shall speak with him. No harm will come to the impostor. That honor is reserved for Emperor Tovmeil alone."

Careful to keep all emotion from my face, I nodded. Whoever this impostor was, I felt awful for him. He must be a touch mad to try to pose as a Scion in the first place, and now the ministers had an outlet for their cruelty. Or maybe they'd give the impostor over to the Scions to torment.

And I would write the letter that would seal his fate. I pressed my fingernails into my palms. There was little I could do about it—if I refused to write the letter, one of the ministers would do it. Distaste for ink stains on their fingers didn't mean they couldn't read or write.

"Where shall I write, madam?" I asked.

The Prime looked to Minister Brevt who gestured at a small desk in the room's corner. "And be quick," he said.

Chapter Sixty

Kostan
Ascent trail, Steelhold Spire

Cuffs and a chain of mundane iron bound my wrists. The steps climbing Steelhold's spire were too steep for leg irons, so the protectors had left my ankles free. As we marched along the Corridor of Ascent, my guards kept a square formation around me, weapons drawn. From the peepholes in the walls bracketing the street, I heard gasps of surprise.

An Atal taken prisoner and escorted to the Hold. The elites would spread the tale as quickly as the protectors' blood had spilled in the street. Good.

At the lower gate which closed off the ascent trail, the protector in charge ordered a halt and stalked forward to speak with the gate guards.

"I will not judge you for this," I said to my escorts while the discussion at the gate continued. "Ignorance is a suitable defense. But if I may say one thing: the coming events will try your loyalty. You must trust your bond with your Emperor. When nothing else makes sense, rely on that simple truth."

The gate swung open with a squeal, and the head protector nodded to my guards. I'd overheard the message from Steelhold. The protectors were to deliver me to the Sun Gate unharmed. Nonetheless, the guards shoved more roughly than necessary to urge me forward.

As I crossed the final paces before the gate, I scanned the walls of the Corridor. I hoped this wasn't a mistake. I had to believe I was making the right decision. Because otherwise, my arrogant refusal to listen to Ilishian and the others might doom the Empire.

At the gate, the protectors narrowed their march to single file, six ahead of me and six behind. It had been over a year since I'd made the climb from Jaliss to the Hold during a guardian-chaperoned trip into the city. Last time, my thighs had been useless afterward. Today I need all my strength to compensate for my difficult journey through the mountains and the sparse meals afterward.

The ministers would use all their tricks against me. Argent mages would batter my mind. Ferros would do... whatever dark things they felt would be useful. But the Ministry wouldn't kill me. They needed Vaness first. And because I'd told her to run, I wouldn't be able to give her to them. The impasse would buy me time to arrange an audience with the Prime Protector. Once I convinced her, the rogue mages would fall in line rather than face the protectors. I might even retake the throne without violence.

Setting my foot on the first step, I began the climb to the Hold. To my left, the solid granite of the spire radiated the sun's warmth as if in welcome. It was the flesh from which Steelhold was carved. My home. The seat of my throne.

As we climbed above the rooftops, I paused and looked out over the city. Despite the Ministry's obstruction, some repairs had been happening. The Provs must have been working at night after their official Functions were satisfied. I surge of pride warmed my chest. Citizens of Jaliss were resilient. Certainly more resilient than the ministers who were so paralyzed by a failure in their plot that they'd needed to lock down the Hold.

I vowed to myself that I would be a ruler worthy of Jaliss and every other settlement on the continent. But first I had to win through the coming hours.

As I started moving again, a flicker of motion from the grounds of an elite mansion caught my attention. Many people moved about the Heights this time of day. I wouldn't have noticed if the fall of coal-black hair had been less recognizable. When I shaded my eyes for a better look, the figure waved to someone out of sight. Two more people stepped from beneath a stone balcony and looked up.

My heart sank. Despite what I'd specifically asked her to do, Vaness had tracked me. She probably thought I'd been captured—on accident, that is—and hoped to rescue me with the mages' help.

I shook my head, a hopeless gesture at this distance. I could only hope Vaness would reconsider. Run. But somehow, I doubted she'd abandon me so easily.

Minister Brevt waited at the Sun Gate. When his eyes met mine, I saw triumph in his gaze. I stared back, challenging him. If I could break his composure now, I could plant more doubt in my escorts' minds. After all, why would a simple impostor merit a greeting by an actual minister? More, why would a minister allow a simple criminal to bait him?

Unfortunately, his imperious expression didn't waver. With a nod, he gestured to someone inside the wall. After a moment, the inner gates rolled aside, parting just wide enough to accommodate my shoulders.

"Minister," I said in greeting. "It's been a few days since we saw one another. How do you fare?"

His cheek twitched, but he said nothing. As I stepped across the threshold and into my former home, men stepped in from either side and took hold of my upper arms. I made a point of meeting their eyes. The protectors who had escorted me up the spire didn't know me, but the palace guards would. Years of training should force them to drop their gazes out of habit.

When neither seemed to notice my glance, faint worry stirred beneath my breastbone. The ministers and mages had made the choice to turn away from the Emperor and Scions. But the protectors were bound to us by vows and argent magic. Did the lack of deference mean the bond had been severed?

Behind me, the inner gates rolled into place with a squeal as the outer steel slabs clanged shut. Minister Brevt sneered.

"Are you surprised that the protectors don't afford you the customary respect, Scion Kostan? Well, perhaps you should have considered your actions more carefully. You believed you'd eliminate competition for the throne by murdering your fellow Scions along with the Emperor. But all you've done is signed your execution writ. The Prime Protector is demanding the right to kill you herself."

I held his stare. I'd known the Ministry wouldn't let me walk straight to the throne room and take over. But his words sent a tremor of insecurity through me. Had I acted too rashly and thrown away my chance to win this?

With a nod, Minister Brevt instructed my guards to follow him. He turned for the center of the Hold, and the grips on my arms tightened as the men shoved me forward. I yearned for the short sword I'd abandoned in the alley. Not that I could fight my way out of a Hold full of elite fighters and mages. But I felt more confident with a blade near.

We marched up a corridor between the storehouses and the clerks' hall. I kept my eyes alert for observers, anyone who I might make into an ally. But the only people moving about the grounds seemed to be servants. A couple curious glances passed over me, but the Provs quickly ducked their heads and moved on. Not a surprise; Steelhold's staff was accustomed to swift punishment for unsuitable interest in the palace doings.

When we stepped out of the alley, the Hall of Mages came into view. Within, I had genuine support, even if the Aurum Trinity and their followers believed I must wait until my twenty-first birthday to Ascend. I stared up at the Aurum Tower, dark granite capped with a peaked roof plated in gold. From a high window, I glimpsed motion. The aurums knew I was here. That was something, at least.

In the central square, the sand fountain still hissed as grains of black iron spilled from the upper tiers. It was as if nothing had changed. But everything had.

Minister Brevt stalked to the palace entrance, my guards dragging me along behind. When we entered the foyer, the minister turned for the Scions' wing. I calmed my face to hide my reaction. I'd expected to be tossed in the stocks or locked in a storeroom, not taken into my former rooms.

We threaded the hallways to my old chambers. Two stone-faced guardians stood outside the door. I didn't recognize them—either they'd previously been assigned to another Scion, or they were newly trained. As passed into the room, I noticed the glint of silver and gold studs stuck through a guardian's earlobe. Like the protectors with their silver wrist cuffs and we Scions with gold anklets, I doubted the guardians wore Maelstrom-metals by choice. Most likely, the jewelry meant their minds and bodies were being controlled by others. Mages and those to whom those mages owed their allegiance.

A girl clad in loose silks knelt inside my sitting chamber. A mask covered the upper half of her face, hiding the scars that had replaced her eyes. I clenched my jaw so hard I thought my molars might crack, but I forced a Scion's emotionless expression onto my face.

"I'm sure you've missed having your brand cared for," Minister Brevt said. "I'm surprised you and Vaness have survived without the cleansings, to be honest. Either you have allies in the Hold—I'm guessing the aurums—or you've done something to eliminate your need for fresh dressings."

As he glanced at my feet, I kept my eyes straight ahead. "I do not need my dressing changed," I said. "She may leave."

"I think she'll stay. As you recall, I grew up with Tovmeil. I remember his weakness for the servant girls—did you know he tried to help one escape and ended up getting her killed? There is much about you that reminds me of Tovmeil as a young man."

"You see what you wish to see. Perhaps when I sit on the throne you'll have the chance to test your observations. Will I be a gentle ruler? Allow you the choice of exile or execution that was your right before you murdered your Emperor? Or will I have your belly slashed open and your entrails tied to the Chasm Gate before you're shoved over the cliff?"

The minister's lower eyelid twitched. "As soon as we pry Scion Vaness's location from your mind, you will be hung by your wrists from the walls. The city will watch the crows eat you alive."

"Your confidence is perplexing given your suggestion that I have allies inside Steelhold. You are not as powerful as you think. I am the rightful Emperor of Atal, and the sooner you recognize that, the more merciful your death will be."

Minister Brevt sneered and shifted his gaze to the girl. "Why don't you take some time to speak with Lyrille here. Most of the Hold's staff members were recently dismissed. Perhaps by cooperating, you can spare her their fate."

Chapter Sixty-One

Savra
Shadow Gate, Steelhold

Shadow Gate's steel slab must have weighed as much as my two-room house in Numintown. As I leaned against the stone-carved wall opposite, I stared and shook my head. Most of the time, the guards on the towers above the gate kept watch over the approach trail, but occasionally one turned to survey the Hold. It was getting easier and easier to deflect their attention, almost second-nature. Plus, Minister Brevt was distracted by the issue of the Scion impostor—after I'd finished scribing the message, the minister had snatched the paper from my hand and stormed out. Not long ago, I heard some carpenters mentioning that the man had been brought to the Hold. A lucky event for me if not the impersonator.

Unfortunately, I still had no idea how to open the gate. The guard who stood watch beside the lever never moved. She stared at a point about three paces in front of her feet, hand on the pommel of her sword. Before noon, a man had guarded the lever. He hadn't budged during his shift either.

As for the lever itself—I assumed this was how the gate was opened—the chain links securing it were as thick as my thumb and closed with a heavy padlock.

A woman pushing a cart passed between me and the gate. When I noticed the pile of bedsheets in the cart, I looked expectantly toward her face, hoping it was Oralie. No luck. I didn't recognize the woman, and her gaze slid over me. One of the watchtower guards turned when a wheel on the cart creaked. As he did, I noticed the glint of a silver cuff around his wrist.

Maelstrom-silver, no doubt, likely enchanted by an argent mage. What effect did it have on the man's spirit? Focusing on my aura-sight, I recoiled at the vacant hole where the man's life force ought to have shimmered. The emptiness had to be related to the cuff.

A footstep crunched behind me, and with hardly a thought, I shoved away the newcomer's attention, directing it around and over me as easily as batting away a fly.

"You show a lot of interest in this gate. Thinking of escape?"

I stiffened at Minister Brevt's voice. My deflection had failed—no point in ignoring him. I stood and turned to face the man, once again trying to raise my mental armor.

"If you were in my place, wouldn't you?" I asked.

His lips twitched, almost a smile. "I'm elite-born Atal, and a minister besides. I'd never be in your place."

"What do you want with me?" I said.

The minister leaned against the wall. "If the Emperor knew about your ability, he'd have you executed. Did you know that?"

I shook my head. "I don't know what ability you're talking about."

"Yet you dodged my rather powerful argent compulsion." As he spoke, he pulled up a sleeve to reveal a bracer of solid Maelstrom-silver. "You wear no metals, but I sensed your power the moment you entered the Hold. I know what you are, Savra."

"If you say so," I said, shrugging.

"And I'll keep your secret," he continued. "Provided you agree to my terms. Otherwise, Tovmeil will hear of your talent."

Should I play along? Act meek and hope he'd leave me alone long enough that I could figure out the Shadow Gate? No. Weakness would only embolden him. Minister Brevt had spent years being obeyed, and he thrived on it. Better to stand up to him and put him off balance.

"I heard Emperor Tovmeil is dead," I said.

His eyes narrowed. The moment stretched before he spoke. Was he trying to come up with an explanation? "A rumor begun by Provs who will do anything to undermine the Emperor." He shook his head. "If you speak such things again, I'll kill you myself. Your spiritist abilities would be tremendously useful to the Empire, but treason cannot stand."

"I've been here six days and haven't caught a single glimpse of Emperor Tovmeil. If he's concerned about rumors, why not show himself? Why not stand atop the wall and restore the Provs' faith—maybe he could do something about the earthquake damage and lack of food, too."

"The ruler of Atal need not coddle his subjects."

"Then he shouldn't be surprised when those subjects begin to doubt him."

Purple splotches darkened the minister's cheeks. "As I said, I won't hesitate to execute you for treason. Or disobedience. You're no good to me with this kind of attitude. And I likely won't stop there. Your impudence suggests neglect on the part of your elders. No one taught you respect. I'll have to look into the situation in Cosmal, see that a few examples are made." As he spoke, he glanced over my shoulder at the Shadow Gate. "In the meantime, I quite dislike your interest in the gate. The guard will be doubled."

I crossed my arms over my chest. "I won't help you hurt Provs."

His eyebrows raised in offense. "Do you think that's what I want? How disappointing. No, I only wish to strengthen the Empire. The situation in the city never had to happen—all we need is better leadership. You could help me achieve that. Or you and those you love can die. I need your answer by sundown. Now, I have a traitor to deal with."

How did Parveld cut me off from my aura-sight? I asked Lilik as I hustled along behind a messenger. After the talk with Minister Brevt, I decided I wouldn't learn anything more by studying the Shadow Gate. Plus, the more interest I showed, the greater his suspicion would become. Just a few minutes after I'd returned to the staff dorm, a messenger had dragged me back out onto the grounds, heading for the Hall of Mages.

What do you mean?

When Havialo's friends tried to kill me, I panicked and started to lose contact with my other senses. Parveld did something to shove me back into the physical world.

I'm not sure, Lilik said. *Let me think about it.*

The entrance to the Hall of Mages was an archway of carved onyx with small, black-iron faces set into niches. As we approached, hundreds of little iron eyes turned to look at me while lips pulled back from pointy black teeth. I shuddered.

When I passed beneath the arch, cool air raised goosebumps on my arms. The entrance hall was massive, tiled in black marble with thick green veins. Three large corridor mouths yawned, each rimmed with one of the Maelstrom-metals. Tucked off to the side, a fourth hallway seemed like an afterthought. Natural granite blocks lined the doorway. Recalling what Havialo said about the lack of respect given to the earth mages, I decided this last door must be the entrance to the geognosts' portion of the Hall.

Feet whispering over the polished floor, the messenger led me through the gold-rimmed door and into the aurum mages' wing. Along the corridor, light glinted off gold finishings and deep carpets absorbed all sounds. Archways opened into side chambers, some with training dummies and martial weapons and some that looked like healers' chambers with pots of salves and unguents and a frightening array of surgical tools.

It made sense. Aurum magic was the magic of the body. Mages might specialize in unnatural speed or strength. Or in healing. Or in curses afflicting others' bodies.

My belly tightened at thoughts of being unnaturally sickened. Thank the clear skies I was only here to scribe a message.

At the end of the corridor, the messenger stopped beside an open door. Through it, a spiral staircase climbed up and out of sight. "Ascend to the highest chamber in the tower," he said. "The Trinity wishes a message sent. After you've written it, bring it to me and I'll see it delivered to the hawks."

"Trinity?" I asked.

"The three leaders of the Order of Aurums."

I glanced at the stairs. "I see."

"Be respectful and quick," the messenger said. "You'll be fine."

With a nod, I started climbing the stairs. The steps went on and on, around and around past closed doors and an occasional gold statue. When a window finally broke the tower's wall, the height set my head spinning.

Finally, after what felt like a thousand stairs, I reached the last doorway. Swallowing, I tapped lightly on the warm brown wood. The door flew open, exposing a kind-faced woman. Behind her sat two others, a woman and a man dressed in matching robes that seemed cut for freedom of movement. Crow's feet wrinkled the corners of the first woman's eyes, a grim smile flashing she beckoned me in.

"I've come to scribe for you, madam," I said quietly.

"No need for honorifics," she responded. "Nor should you address us individually. If you wish, you may call us Trinity. Or nothing."

"Yes... Trinity."

She nodded then waved her hand toward a desk. An inkpot, quill, and a strip of parchment already rested upon it. I sat in the simple chair then picked up the quill, checked the point, and dipped it into the ink.

"Write this, please. 'We can do nothing for him. The act was ill-considered. Keep the remaining girl safe at all costs.'"

I finished quickly. "That's it?"

"Were you taught to question the messages?" she asked.

I bowed my head. "Sorry, Trinity."

"It's a common mistake. Now. Please see that it's delivered quickly. The destination is the Astrologers Guild."

"Yes, Trinity," I said.

With the briefest nod, she opened the door and ushered me out.

Chapter Sixty-Two

Kostan
Scion's bedchamber

"Your binding, sire. I'll change the dressing." Lyrille knelt before my chair and pulled a gold key from the folds of her robes. She groped for my ankle. I thought I might be sick.

"It's not necessary, Lyrille," I said. "I removed my cuff."

"But perhaps sire would allow me to clean the wound. If you don't receive the proper care, you might fall ill."

"I don't need it!" I growled, gripping the arms of my chair. The girl flinched, and I instantly regretted my temper. I sighed. "I'm sorry. I'm not angry at you. If anything, I'm furious about how you've been treated."

Her lower lip trembled. "It is my honor to serve the Empire's Scions."

"Honor? They took your eyes! Aren't you angry?"

She was trembling. Her lips parted as if she wished to say something but couldn't put voice to her words.

"It is not my place to be angry," she said after a moment.

I sighed. "No, I suppose not. You aren't allowed emotions if you wish to live."

She clutched her hands tight in her lap. "The other girls..."

"They're dead?" I asked.

Lyrille nodded. "Minister Brevt came to our chambers. He beat them. He said it must have been one of us that warned you to flee. The girls that didn't die from their injuries were thrown from the Chasm Gate."

I swallowed another surge of nausea. With a deep breath, I clenched my fists then began an exercise I'd learned to settle into a Scion's emotionless calm. Exhaling, I uncurled my fingers and relaxed my shoulders. Counted three breaths and imagined my face as still as Steelhold's granite.

"Why are you still alive?" I asked. I was afraid of her reaction if I touched her in reassurance, but I realized what a coward that made me. Swallowing, I leaned forward and cupped her elbow. She started but didn't pull away. "Please, take my chair," I said as I helped her up.

She shook her head. "I'd rather not. Minister Brevt has given me specific instructions."

"Minister Brevt will not live out the day. Now please. I can't have you kneeling on the floor, not after everything you've been through."

With a sigh, the girl nodded. She patted the air until she found my chair then turned and sat. "Can the guardians hear through the door?" she whispered.

"Not as long as you keep your voice low."

"Then to answer your question as to why I'm alive, it's luck. Nothing more. Minister Brevt worked his way through our chamber girl by girl. Those who tried to run were beaten the worst, so most of us stayed in our beds. By the time he reached my bunk, he'd worked out most of his rage. I could sense his need to feel powerful, so I begged for my life. Groveled, really. I called him a great man. A powerful man. The rest of his fury left him, and he asked me to join his personal staff. He said he intends to take the throne and will need many loyal servants."

"He doesn't hide his plans from you?"

She shook her head. "The more I flatter him, the more he talks. He's very fragile on the inside."

I smirked even though she couldn't see my expression. "It sounds to me as if your cleverness did more to spare you than your luck. And to think when I walked in here, I imagined you as the one needing protection."

"I'm blind, not weak or witless."

"Indeed. So—"

I bit off my words when the door flew open. As Lyrille jumped to her feet, I stepped to shield her from the door.

The newcomer wore ten silver rings. No doubt he hid more silver under his robes. In a strange echo of Ferromaster Ilishian's arrival in my chambers just a few weeks ago, I recognized the man. Argentmaster Yevinish, leader of the Order of Argents.

My heart thudded as I emptied my mind of speculation about Vaness's movements. I had no doubt he'd pry her last known location from my memories eventually, but I hoped to resist for a while. In truth, my arrival hadn't gone as well as I'd hoped. I'd imagined the aurums would rise to my defense sooner, or that I'd have swayed the Prime Protector by now. But I'd have to work with the situation.

The man's lips twitched in a humorless smile. "Scion Kostan... have you ever seen a kitten try to fight? Your pathetic attempt to hide your thoughts would be humorous if the argents hadn't been tasked with training you. Surely they taught you better."

"I don't know where Vaness is," I said.

No, you don't, the argentmaster said directly into my mind. *But neither do I know for certain whether the world still exists outside your chamber door. I believe there is a corridor beyond the door because of my previous experiences. You might even call it a guess. Your history with Vaness will allow you to make similar guesses. And as I pluck them from your mind, the Ministry will send trusted men and women to search for her. Now, shall we begin?*

"Let's talk first," I said. "I prefer to get to know someone before I let them inside my head. So, do you feel guilty for betraying your Emperor?"

The argent's gaze bored into me. "I do not. Now, where do you believe Vaness to be hiding?"

I formed a picture of the high mountain valley I'd stumbled through after fleeing the Hold and shoved it to the front of my mind.

"Amusing," he said. "But if tricks like that worked, the Empire would have little use for argent truthseekers. I'll ask again, where is Vaness?"

I couldn't allow myself to wonder that. Instead, I imagined walking with Vaness along Steelhold's wall. In profile, her features were so finely sculpted. I'd genuinely enjoyed our friendship.

A relationship between Scions is strictly forbidden, the argent said.

"It was nothing," I said. "A fling."

The man's eyes widened. "But there were others who interested you recently."

Others. Kei. Savra. I couldn't help it when their faces sprang into my mind, a flood of images and memories. I remembered Kei's ponytail in the moments before she died. Her bright voice suggesting I join Stormshard. And Savra. The blush in her cheeks after she called me her betrothed in front of Fishel. My bone-deep disappointment at finding out she'd left the inn before I returned.

Frantic, I tried to shut down the memories, but they wouldn't stop. I thought of Savra's sorrow for the beheaded boy. Her courage in coming to Jaliss alone.

Argentmaster Yevinish curled his lip in disdain. "Too easy. A basic misdirection, and I know more than I need to get started. It's the easiest of the argent techniques. Anyway, an interesting journey you've had... the Ministry will be grateful for the tip on Stormshard's whereabouts."

"They're gone. The earthquake destroyed their mountain refuge," I said, knowing he'd sense the truth of my statement. I just had to hope it was enough to divert attention from Evrain and his friends.

"No matter. It's a trifling detail compared to finding Scion Vaness. We'll start at this Graybranch Inn. Perhaps burn it to convince your friend Fishel how serious we are about finding Vaness. If he can't help us locate her, I'm sure we'll learn something from Savra. From what you recall, it seems she intended to visit the registrar and become a scribe. It won't be difficult to follow her trail from there."

"Fishel and Savra have nothing to do with this. They didn't even know I'm a Scion."

"I gathered that. Won't they be surprised when we capture them and bring them here for questioning? I think you'll be quite willing to help us locate Vaness once you realize the... consequences of continued resistance. As you said, they have nothing to do with this. Would be a shame if they were harmed due to events beyond their control."

My pulse roared in my ears as fury took hold. I couldn't let the Ministry hurt my friends. Especially not Savra. I unfocused my eyes, allowing objects at the edge of my vision to enter my awareness while my gaze stayed on the argentmaster. There, on the wall two paces behind him. My practice scimitar.

"Lyrille?" I asked.

"Y—yes sire?" she said from behind me.

"You are a loyal servant to Brevt. I respect that, and I don't wish you to face punishment for betraying your master." While I spoke, I watched Argentmaster Yevinish's eyes. The instant they flicked to Lyrille, I sprang. I aimed a kick for the mage's knee while landing a fist in his gut. Neither blow did much harm, but they sent him reeling. As I leaped for the scimitar, he backpedaled, eyes wide.

Lyrille was silent as she rushed forward, hands clawing at the mage's face. Storms. I hadn't wanted to involve her, only to create a distraction. She missed his face but managed to land a blow on his chest, sending him spinning into the first slash of my dull-edged blade. Steel bit into his cheek, tearing flesh.

The next instant, I felt an icicle ram through my forehead into my mind. Agony exploded behind my eyes. My knees buckled under the full force of the argent assault. As I collapsed, I aimed a desperate blow at the mage's hand, hoping to sever fingers and the rings that encircled them. My scimitar glanced off, useless.

Chapter Sixty-Three

Savra
An alley mouth, Steelhold

Nearing the dormitory, I heard a cry from a narrow alley. I darted to the corner, just out of view, and focused my aura-sight into the recesses. My stomach turned. Minister Brevt's oily spirit squirmed in the darkness, like a many-headed snake striking at another soul. The aura of the woman who'd screamed was bright with anger and fear.

I didn't know what to do. I didn't want any more attention from the minister. My task of unlocking the Shadow Gate was hard enough. But he was hurting whoever he had trapped in that alley. I couldn't just walk away.

Pressing my fingernails into my palms, I stepped into the alley.

Oralie's terrified eyes met mine. Minister Brevt had her pinned against the wall, using both his physical form and his spirit tentacles to hold her. Anger roared through me like a Maelstrom-spawned storm. I couldn't let him do this. I sprinted for the man, fumbling for my belt where I kept my fishing knife hidden.

The minister whirled and grinned, exposing glistening teeth. A tendril of spirit whipped toward me and slapped my arm before I could raise a defense. My hand went numb, and the blade clattered to the stone.

"Savra," he said. "I heard that you and Oralie are close. I thought she might have insight on how I could win your allegiance."

Behind him, my friend shook her head, eyes wide. As if in response, a snarl of spirit tentacles erupted from Minister Brevt's aura and struck her from all sides. Oralie's shriek died as a thick rope of oily darkness wrapped her throat. Her face began to purple.

"Stop!" I screamed. I groped for my protections as another tendril lashed toward me.

Enclose him! Lilik shouted into my mind. *I think that's how Parveld cut off your abilities.*

Heartbeats passed while the tendril descended and I tried to understand her words. Enclose him. Did she mean surround him?

My gorge rose as I flung my aura-sense around Minister Brevt. The touch of his roiling hatred was like plunging my soul into estuary muck. Eels squirmed beneath my embrace. With a final swallow to keep my lunch in my stomach, I cinched my spirit over his, containing him.

"Oralie, run."

Her mouth worked for a moment, but the protest died on her lips. Staggering with arms wrapped over her belly, she hurried for the alley mouth and out of sight.

I'd cut off Minister Brevt's power, but I couldn't control his body. His face a mask of rage, he paced forward, arm cocked. I wasn't fast enough to deflect the blow. The slap stung my cheek, knocked my head sideways. I spun and collided with the stone floor of the alley, stars dancing in my vision. The minister aimed a kick for my gut, knocking the wind from my body.

My aura-sense vanished. I couldn't bring it back. Somehow, I clung to the walls surrounding my mind, though I felt his power battering against them. The armor worked. Deep in my heart, I felt a surge of accomplishment as pain flooded my body.

"Protectors!" he yelled.

I curled, groaning, as booted feet approached. My breath came in small gasps as armored hands grabbed my arms. Two guards yanked me upright to stand face to face with the minister. His breath stank of eggs as he leaned close and narrowed his eyes.

"Clearly, you are unwilling to make yourself useful to me. Worse, you're beginning to learn about your powers." He glanced at the protectors. "Lock her in my chambers. We'll make an example of her after my other business is concluded."

Chapter Sixty-Four

Kostan
A bedchamber doorway, palace, Steelhold

My scimitar thudded onto the carpet as the agony in my mind drove out all sense. I fell to the floor beside my weapon as Argentmaster Yevinish stood over me. His cheek streamed blood. Teeth and gums showed through the open flap. He smiled anyway.

Images flashed through my mind, forced there by his argent magic. I saw Fishel's inn burned to the ground. Savra's green eyes filled with terror as the ministers dragged her up the ascent trail. They'd force me to watch her execution.

I cried out, my voice hoarse and booming as he dug through my memories of Vaness.

"She loves you," the argent said, laughing. "Poor Vaness. The story about her fleeing to a distant sanctuary never would have held up. She'd never leave Jaliss while you were in danger. And meanwhile, you're betraying her."

As he spoke, claws pierced deeper into my mind. Twisting and rending. My back arched as another scream escaped my throat. In the corner of the room, Lyrille covered her sightless eyes with her hands and cried.

"The Ministry has awarded the honor of your execution to the Prime Protector," the mage said. "But given your work on my cheek, perhaps they'll reconsid—"

The door flew open, cutting off his words. As the pressure on my mind eased, I gagged and rolled to get a glimpse of the hallway.

Minister Brevt stalked toward me as I made a feeble attempt to reach my sword. He stomped on my hand, mashing the bones together. "I'm no longer in the mood for patience," he said. "Do we have enough information, Yevinish?"

"*Master* Yevinish. And yes. I've gathered what I can about the remaining Scion. Furthermore, there are two others he cares for. An innkeeper and a scribe. Fishel and Savra. Damaging them will provide much-needed vengeance, I believe."

A look of shock landed on the minister's face. He seemed to fumble for words for a moment. Was it really that surprising that I—a Scion—could find others to care for? "Savra. A Provincial name. How interesting. I shall see to their capture. Now—" The minister looked over his shoulder and summoned a group of four protectors. "—bring the traitor to the central courtyard. We'll let the Prime Protector soften him up for his execution."

I groaned as the protectors dragged me upright. The inside of my skull felt pierced by a thousand nails. My throat was raw from screaming. I kept my eyes off Lyrille in hopes Brevt wouldn't notice her. But as the guards muscled me forward, the minister turned to the girl.

"Master Yevinish, please throw her out the gate. If you don't wish to dirty your hands with Prov blood, feel free to command a protector in my name."

"Do you believe me a servant ready to do your bidding?" the mage said in a mild tone that belied the ice in his eyes.

Minister Brevt's face hardened. "Consider it a favor, then."

After a moment, the mage nodded. "The ferros will appreciate another available spirit, I suppose."

The first lashes struck my back and shoulders, raising lines of fire on my flesh. I clenched my teeth, but the moans still escaped my lips. My wrists were lashed high up the whipping post. Iron cuffs clamped my ankles, joined by heavy chains to stone pillars.

The sun beat down, setting my head spinning. As I sagged against the post, the Prime Protector snarled and struck again.

"Emperor Tovmeil is dead," I grunted. "The Ministry wishes to usurp him."

"And you are his murderer," she said. "For killing my liege, I will make your death last for days."

"Not by me," I said. "Brevt. A conspiracy."

"Lies."

The whip struck again, lashing across an earlier welt. Darkness fluttered at the edges of my vision. My knees buckled.

"Where are the aurums?" the Prime called across the courtyard. "He's going to die before we get our proper revenge. He needs healing."

In the depths of my mind, hope flared. The aurums were on my side. With the excuse to lay hands on me, they might find a way to free me.

Another of the ministers, Thani, stepped into view. "Unfortunately, the Ministry has reason to doubt the Trinity's loyalty. Until their allegiance can be proved, they've been sealed in their tower."

My head dropped forward. So much for that. I'd thought boldness would win me the throne. I'd thought my allies would come to my aid. Unfortunately, I'd misjudged.

I'd failed the Empire. Worse, I'd condemned my friends. How long before Fishel's inn burned? When would the Ministry's agents track Savra to her new job as a scribe. Would she learn that I'd betrayed her? Or would she go to her death never knowing that her sin lay in befriending me?

Another lash of the whip stole the breath from my lungs. I fell into the post, splinters piercing my cheek.

"Stop," Minister Brevt said quietly. "I wish him to witness something before he loses consciousness."

I rolled my head to see Brevt nod at a messenger who ran off toward Ministry Hall. With a sneer, Brevt turned his gaze to me. Something in his face sent a chill up my spine.

Chapter Sixty-Five

At the door to Minister Brevt's chamber, one of my guards stepped forward and exchanged words with a sentry. As the sentry fished a key from his pocket, a messenger came sprinting down the hall.

"The plan has been moved up. Minister Brevt requests that you bring the captive to the courtyard now."

The guards turned dull eyes on the messenger. "Anything else?"

"Only to watch her carefully," the messenger said. "She's dangerous."

I recognized the messenger now; he'd been one of the new staff brought into the Hold at the same time as me. I tried to put my question into my eyes. What was this about?

A tiny shake of his head was my only answer. The messenger stared at the floor. Not good then. I swallowed.

Rough hands shoved me forward. Ahead, the corridor opened into the entrance hall. From there, just a few paces would lie between me and the central courtyard. All at once, reality struck me. Minister Brevt was going to execute me now. I'd pushed him too far.

Maybe I should have agreed to ally with him until I figured out the Shadow Gate. Maybe I should have left him alone with Oralie. I doubted he would have killed her when she might have been of use to him.

Or maybe my mistakes began earlier. The plan to present myself at the Hall of Registry with a forged ledger had been Havialo's. Why had I followed it? Why hadn't I returned to Cosmal Province after

Parveld rescued me? For that matter, why had I trusted Havialo in the first place? I should have listened to Avill and gone fugitive.

All along, I'd made the wrong choices. But I wasn't going to go meekly to my death. As we neared the end of the hallway, I planted my feet, forcing the guards to drag me forward. My toes bumped over ridges on the floor. The guards snarled and tightened their grips on my arms.

Sunlight fell into the entrance hall, gleaming off polished stone and stabbing my eyes. I couldn't see beyond the glare of the outer doorway.

Savra, Lilik said, low and commanding. *It doesn't end like this. Do something.*

Like what? I glanced at the protectors, their vacant auras filling bodies bulging with muscle, armor, and weapons. With every step they dragged me forward, the void in their souls kept pace. I'd beaten Minister Brevt by suffocating his magic with my aura, but he'd still knocked me flat with a slap. I couldn't use the same technique here.

If I knew, I'd tell you.

With a deep breath, I focused on their auras and attempted to dispel their attention. No use. Very little of their attention was focused on me anyway. Another force held their focus. It compelled them to keep a grip on my arms, but they gave little thought to me beyond that.

The brilliant rectangle of light at the Hall's exit grew closer. I kicked at the backs of their knees and earned nothing but a few rough grunts and a tighter clamp on my arms.

Useless, Lilik said. *You already know you can't fight them outright. Even if you were trained. Which you clearly are not.*

I don't know what to do! I yelled into my own head.

A faint thread of calming energy tunneled into my mind. Parveld's voice was faint. *The night of the quake. You did more than force those men away. You frightened them.*

That was true. My first night in Jaliss, I'd sent a group of Atal men fleeing. The trick with redirecting attention was similar, but not quite what I'd done. The problem was I couldn't remember what I'd done. I'd grabbed their auras... yanked and twisted. But how?

I focused on the guard to my right, closed my eyes so that only his aura showed. Imagining spectral hands, I reached for his spirit. When a portion of my consciousness contacted his aura, I screamed and recoiled as his frigid spirit flooded me.

Part of my mind went numb as if punched in a nerve. Only a faint tingle gave me hope it would recover.

From outside the entrance hall, I heard a shout. More people took up the cry.

The guards dragged me closer to the exit.

"Ministers," someone called from the courtyard. "Word from the protectors' post. Full riots have broken out in the city."

My guards slowed to listen. It wasn't that they lacked the ability to make decisions. More that whatever had been done to their auras stole their willpower.

I yanked at their grips, trying to take advantage of the distraction. It made no more difference than if I'd tried to break through iron cuffs.

The cuffs. I remembered the glimpse of Maelstrom-silver I'd noticed on the gate guards. If silver altered the spirit, did that mean the cuffs forced the guards to obey? Could I break the magic's hold by severing the link to the bracelets?

Minister Brevt's nasal voice rose above the din in the courtyard. "Send a response immediately. The Emperor demands an immediate and savage response. Any Prov caught with a weapon or in Atal districts will be severely punished. Any Prov caught engaging in violence will be killed on sight."

I couldn't hear the response, only muffled words of confusion.

"The scribe is not available," the minister responded. "Pen it yourself, or if you're too illiterate, find someone who knows their cursed letters."

The guard on my left shook his head and yanked me forward. "Not our concern," he said to his partner.

As we neared the door, my eyes began to adjust. At least a score of people had gathered in the courtyard. A tall post had been propped upright, and if I wasn't mistaken, a man had been lashed to it by the wrists. His back was turned, but the lines laid down by a whip were dark stains on his shirt. The impostor?

Was this how they intended to kill me, too?

I threw my awareness into my aura-sight, desperate for some sense of the Maelstrom-silver that bound the guards. Back in Numintown, I'd had an uncanny knack for sensing the nuggets in the sluice box. I'd always figured I just paid closer attention than most people. Now, I hoped that was wrong.

There. I sensed coldness flowing from the guards' left wrists. As I had with Minister Brevt, I allowed my aura to expand. But rather than enveloping the protectors' souls—I didn't dare contact their auras again—I wrapped my aura-sense around their wrists.

Instantly, the grips on my arms loosened while the guards grunted in confusion. I didn't stop to think. I yanked my arms free, sprinted into the courtyard and cut hard to the right. My feet pounded the stone, sending knives into my knees. Sucking hot air that tasted of baked granite, I careened for the alley at the far side of Ministry Hall. All the while, I expected a crossbow bolt to pierce my spine. I waited for the thump of boots and the guards' long strides to run me down.

As I veered into the alley, I felt a strange tugging at my mind like a rope pulled tighter and tighter. I'd forgotten to release my aura's grasp on the guards' cuffs. Shuddering as the link stretched taut, I visualized the Maelstrom-silver bands and imagined slipping away from them.

The tendrils of my mind snapped home, a lightning strike within my head. I coughed and staggered but kept my balance. Behind, I heard the shouts of the protectors as they regained their senses.

Another voice boomed across the square.

"Ministers! You are commanded to halt your proceedings and to gather at the Sun Gate."

"What?" Minister Brevt shouted. "A gate guard thinks to command the Ministry? You are in direct violation of your Emperor's orders!"

The shrill edge to the minister's voice was so unexpected I slowed to hear the gate guard's response.

"I would never break my vow of obedience, sire. I was sent by Emperor Tovmeil himself."

An immediate silence descended over the courtyard. I stopped and pressed myself against a wall to listen. Something unexpected was happening. My roaring pulse told me to keep running, but I'd already learned there were few hiding places within the Hold. Better to get information first.

"Emperor Tovmeil is confined to his chambers," Minister Brevt said into the quietness. "He remains in deep meditation regarding the difficulties brought by the latest quake."

"I must correct you, sire," the protector responded. "Emperor Tovmeil is standing outside the Sun Gate. And he appears rather angry."

Chapter Sixty-Six

Kostan
Lashed to a whipping post, Steelhold courtyard

Tovmeil?

My head was full of wet gravel, rolling on my neck. The rough wood of my whipping post rasped against my face. Knees wobbling, I groaned as I pushed myself upright to take the weight off my shoulders. As I stood, the Heart of the Empire settled against my breastbone. In response to the touch of the pendant, my heart beat stronger, sending life surging through my body.

Sounds flooded my ears, a confused babble that filled the courtyard.

"Explain yourself," the Prime Protector said as she stalked toward the gate guard.

"It's as I say, Prime. He claims treachery from within the Hold. According to his eminence, everyone here has been misled."

Whatever this was, it might be my only chance to escape. As I craned my neck to watch the conversation, I plucked at the knots binding my wrists. No use—the knots were so tight they might as well have been forged of iron. A tug of my ankle set the chain clinking on the granite of the courtyard. I cringed, but the Prime Protector paid me no mind. Her keen eyes bored into the guard.

I looked toward the Hall of Mages, hoping the chaos would finally move the aurums to help me. But the shades were drawn over the windows in the gold-capped tower.

"The Emperor is dead, Protector," the Prime said to her subordinate. "Killed by this man." She stabbed the air with the handle of her whip as she gestured toward me. "I command you to cease this nonsense."

As I glanced back at the pair, the gate guard shook his head, dead eyes meeting the Prime's gaze. "I cannot disobey my Emperor's order. Even for you."

The Prime's face hardened. I expected her to strike the man, but after a moment, she blinked and turned to the ministers. She grabbed the guard's arm and exposed the silver cuff encircling his wrist. "He is speaking the truth. You know as well as I that the Emperor's command is the final word for a protector."

As I contorted my fingers again, straining to get better purchase on the knots, the words sank in. Could this be true? For a protector, the only person who could override the Prime was the Emperor himself. I'd hoped to use that very fact to bring the Order of Protectors to my side.

Ilishian claimed he'd seen Tovmeil's body. Could he have been fooled? Worse, could he have been lying? Storms. If Emperor Tovmeil was still alive, I hoped he'd forgive me for attempting to claim his throne.

Minister Brevt's face had blanched to a pale cream, purple spots high on his cheeks. He stomped toward the Prime, drawing himself up.

"This is outrageous. The Scion murdered our Emperor and must be punished. Your guard is confused."

Winding the whip around the handle, the Prime Protector shook her head. "Perhaps. But I believe we owe it to the Empire to investigate the matter. I believe you were summoned to the Sun Gate. Shall we proceed there together?"

"Absolutely not," the minister said, crossing his arms.

"Protectors," the Prime said, "attend me."

Across the square, fists pounded chests.

"Please escort the ministers to the Sun Gate. Harm only those who resist."

"What about the prisoner, Prime?" a protector asked. I relaxed my fingers and hoped no one had noticed me working at the knots.

The Prime Protector stalked closer to me and peered. Her gaze seemed to pierce my mind as easily as an argent's, though I knew she had no such powers.

"Bring him some water," she said. "I can't have him dying until we figure out what's happening here."

I drank greedily, lukewarm water pouring over my chin and cheeks. The protector holding the water skin remained expressionless save for a squint to keep out the glare of the afternoon sun. Around the perimeter of the courtyard, servants shifted.

As I scanned their faces, my thoughts circled back to Lyrille. Had the argentmaster thrown her into the chasm yet? Had she screamed when she died, or had she kept that unbreakable pride? I shuddered at the thought of her fall, no vision to warn her when the jumbled rocks at the bottom of the chasm approached.

My face went hot, eyes stinging. She'd been doomed because of me. What a fool I'd been to come here. Savra. Fishel. Lyrille. Evrain. No doubt I'd have added more to that list if I'd remained free. Maybe my death at the whipping post would be a mercy if this commotion with Tovmeil proved nothing but a ruse.

I choked when the water spilled into my mouth too quickly for me to swallow. With a grunt that might have been disdain, the protector withdrew the water skin and capped it. He walked away without a word, leaving me alone in the center of the granite courtyard. Dozens of pairs of eyes watched me sag helplessly against the post.

"Go ahead and look!" I tried to yell, but my voice was weak. Still, feet shuffled as a few people moved closer to hear. "This is what the Ministry will do to hold power," I continued. "I did not kill Emperor Tovmeil. More, I bear the Emperor's Mark. They're killing me for it."

Near the entrance to the Hall of Mages, a robed woman snorted. Her silken garb marked her as a ferro. No doubt she'd been promised rich rewards to support the coup.

"Anyone brave enough to remove my boot will see the Mark. Ascension is my right," I said. I caught the eye of the hawk keeper. Unlike many of the Hold's staff, I recognized her from my time as a Scion. She had access to the Ministry's communications and had possibly seen enough to doubt their story. Aside from the palace scribe, an elderly man I didn't spot amongst the onlookers, she was most likely to believe me. Doubt flickered in the hawk keeper's eyes.

She knew something wasn't right. But she didn't move from the edge of the square.

I licked my parched lips, preparing to speak again, when a command echoed across the courtyard.

"All hail Emperor Tovmeil! Avert your eyes and keep your distance."

I whipped my head around and looked into the eyes of my Emperor. The man nodded a greeting.

Emperor Tovmeil wore the official garments he'd always donned for audiences in the palace hall. Bejeweled rings—Maelstrom-relics most likely—crusted his fingers. The forearms of his ornate tunic were thick enough to disguise the rigidity of the Bracer of Sight. Yet as he approached me, I recognized the man who'd worn simple clothing and spoken to me as an equal.

"Your eminence," I said, bowing my head.

"Scion Kostan." He stopped a few paces away, feet set in a wide stance. "As I approached the courtyard, I heard whispers that you claim to bear the Emperor's Mark. Apparently, you seek to break custom by Ascending before the ordained date."

"I believed you were dead, your eminence, and only wished to uphold your wishes," I said, meeting his gaze despite the effort it took to stand upright. "I would never seek to usurp you."

The Prime Protector stepped to the Emperor's side. "I was not informed of the Scion's claim, your eminence. This punishment was due to the allegation by Minister Brevt that Scion Kostan was responsible for your murder."

"And what investigations did you conduct to validate the minister's claim?" Emperor Tovmeil turned his glare on the woman, who blanched at the expression.

"I—The evidence was compelling. The ministers claimed to have your body. You were nowhere in evidence. Scion Kostan fled across the Chasm Span shortly after your murder."

After a moment, the Emperor gave a curt nod. "Release the Scion. I will consider your actions and my response this evening." He turned to the gathered servants. "Whomever among you is a messenger, summon the Aurum Trinity to the Scion's chambers with healing supplies. And as for the Ministry..."

The twelve ministers had clustered together to whisper at the edge of the square. As the Emperor's gaze fell on them, the group seemed to wilt. Those at the rear glanced toward the alleys as if contemplating escape. A gesture from the Emperor brought a line of protectors up behind them.

As the men and women cowered and shuffled closer together, a guard released the rope binding my wrists and unlocked the shackles around my ankles. I rolled my shoulders and bent my knees slightly to keep from swaying. Still unsure of my situation, I scanned the surroundings for a weapon. I wouldn't be captured again without a struggle. Unfortunately, every blade in the courtyard was in a protector's belt or hand.

"The ministers shall be confined to their chambers until further notice," Emperor Tovmeil stated. "See that they relinquish any metalogy bands first."

The ministers shouted protests as the protectors closed in.

"Your eminence," I said. "There's a servant who cleaned the Scions' wounds. Her name is Lyrille. Minister Brevt instructed the argentmaster to throw her from the Chasm Gate, but there may still be time."

The Emperor's cheek twitched as he turned to the Prime Protector. "Send guards to search out Master Yevinish. If the girl still lives, I will not have her services wasted so thoughtlessly."

I clenched my jaw to avoid commenting. The Emperor couldn't afford to look weak, especially now. But to hear him speak of Lyrille's value simply in terms of her services turned my stomach.

As the protectors began separating the ministers and stripping them of their rings, Minister Brevt shouted, a bestial roar. He threw his arms wide, gold and silver rings gleaming, and the protectors attempting to control him staggered backward and fell.

Darkness swelled in the air around the minister as he marched toward the Emperor. Tovmeil crossed his arms over his chest, smirked, and stepped behind the wall of protectors who immediately rushed to defend him. He reached into his collar as if fishing for a pendant. My hand fell on the Heart of the Empire where it lay beneath my tunic. Did Tovmeil need it to defend himself? I got ready to pass it to the Emperor when he pulled an amulet free.

I recognized the piece. In our smithy turned safehouse, Ilishian had examined the black-iron pendant, strands of metal twisted in intricate knotwork. I had no doubt the necklace Emperor Tovmeil wore was the same. Did that mean... was the Emperor's arrival an illusion? Did Ilishian wear Tovmeil's likeness as a disguise?

As the Emperor wrapped his hand around the pendant, light shot from between his fingers. His eyes changed, ever so slightly. If I wasn't mistaken, Ilishian's gray gaze peered from Tovmeil's face.

The minister halted his advance, muscles locked in place. A breath later, I realized he wasn't the only one frozen. The entire courtyard had stilled. Yet the Emperor—or rather, Ilishian—and I remained free to move.

"Kill him," Ilishian said with Tovmeil's voice. "Now."

I didn't hesitate. Despite the lines of pain on my back and my weakness from loss of blood, I sprang for the nearest protector and yanked her scimitar from her belt. The blade flashed as I advanced on Minister Brevt. An instant before I opened the minister's throat with a broad slash, Ilishian released his spell. The minister gasped as his eyes met mine.

Blood sprayed and he fell at my feet.

"Anyone else?" I yelled. "Or will you now kneel before your Emperor." As I spoke, I faced Ilishian and dropped to a knee. Behind me, clothing rustled as the ministers submitted.

Ilishian met my eyes before he faded from the Emperor's face, once again replaced by Tovmeil's implacable gaze.

"Proceed to your chambers, Scion Kostan. We will speak once your lashes have been healed."

Chapter Sixty-Seven

Savra
Hiding near the Shadow Gate

The fading glow of day colored the crest of the Icethorns a deep rose. On the grounds of Steelhold, shadows pooled. It had been a couple hours since the Emperor's return to the Hold, and the alleys buzzed with speculation and anger from the servants. Where had he been all this time? Why was he hiding away inside the palace while the city rioted? During the afternoon, a member of the cleaning staff had caught a glimpse over the walls from high in the Argent Tower of the Hall of Mages.

Lowtown was burning. Now, the plume of smoke was blood-red in the last kiss of the sun.

At the thought, anger surged in my chest. I stared at the Shadow Gate and glanced again at the sky. Soon, I'd have to put my plan into action. I'd just have to hope it would work.

About an hour ago, the extra guards on the gate had been recalled. The protector who'd delivered the summons had explained that Minister Brevt's orders no longer stood. Only three guards remained.

I'd been practicing, lurking in the alley across from the gate while I focused on the guards' silver bands. I knew I could sever the protectors' spirits from the Maelstrom-silver at their wrists. I'd tested twice, surrounding the cuffs and watching the stunned reaction of the guards as their free will returned. In those precious breaths before I released my grasp, their auras regained life and color, confusing swirling in their spirits.

But that was only the first step toward getting the gate open. I had no idea whether the rest of my plan would work and no way to test it beforehand.

When the last alpenglow faded from the mountaintops, I stood. Cold evening air rushed over me, sinking through my trousers where my calves had been pressed against the backs of my thighs while crouched. A waft of smoke from the blazes in the city stung my nose.

This was it. I allowed the shield that repelled attention to dissipate and strode toward the guards.

"State your business," the closest of the protectors said, dull eyes passing over me without interest.

"Apologies, Protector," I said as I advanced—the closer I stood to the men, the easier it was to sever their bonds to the Maelstrom-silver. "I'm looking for the Sun Gate. An aide to the Emperor who has been posted there needs a scribe."

The guard laid a hand on the hilt of a long dagger sheathed at his ribs. "Follow the wall to the left. Now move along. Servants are not permitted near the gate."

I risked a single step closer. With a hiss, the guard drew his steel. I sucked in breath, my aura whipping forth and slapping a blanket of insulation over his Maelstrom-silver.

"Huh?" the guard said, shaking his head.

The men watching from the gate towers snapped their hands toward weapons, but not fast enough. Striking out with my spirit, I severed their links.

"Please listen to me," I said. "I know you're confused."

"What's going on?" the first guard asked. His voice sounded strangely young. Lost, as if he remembered nothing since the cuff had been clamped to his wrist. Good. I'd hoped as much.

"Enemies of Atal have had control of your mind. I've just freed you from their grasp. Do you remember anything of it?"

He shook his head, confusion roiling in his aura. As he peered at me, a thread of violet suspicion swirled into his spirit. "I took a vow to follow the Emperor's orders. It is my duty. That is what I remember."

"And you have, sire. You served admirably until the recent subterfuge."

"What is the girl talking about?" the guard in the nearest watchtower called down.

"Do none of you recall the Emperor's murder?" I asked, looking at them in turn.

A sword sang as it was pulled free from the sheath. I tensed, expecting one of the tower guards to rush down the ladder and attack. But no footsteps sounded. The protector in the watchtower stared at his sword, his perplexed expression reflected in his aura.

"How?" the first guard asked. "How has my liege fallen?"

"Treachery," I said quietly. Now came the part I was dreading. I wasn't good at lying, even to a protector. I wished I knew more about the Emperor's disappearance and apparent return. It would have been easier than concocting a tale. "The geognosts worked with the Free Tribesmen to abduct and murder him."

Boots clicked against the polished stone stairs as a tower guard began descending. The man's face held a mix of shock and incredulity, the emotions reflected in his aura. I gritted my teeth. This part of the plan wasn't going as well as I'd hoped.

"Why would the earth mages betray their ruler?" the guard nearest me asked. He rolled the hilt of his dagger in his palm.

"I'm just a messenger," I said. "Sent by those loyal to the throne. I know little more than I've told you. The Empire can be saved if we root out the traitors and protect the Scions. We need to open the gate quietly to let in defenders of the throne."

The guard blinked as his brows drew together. He glanced at the steel slab behind him. "I remember... my duty is to guard the gate. I was given my orders by the Prime, in the name of the Emperor."

Like a slow summer dawn, hardness replaced the confused look on his face. "I was instructed to allow no one passage. Steelhold is threatened. None can be trusted." He narrowed his eyes at me.

A hard stone filled my throat as I backstepped. The guard advanced to fill the space I'd put between us, hands up in a fighting stance. My memory flashed to the pain when the protector at Dukket Waystation had punched me in the jaw, and I winced.

The guard descending from his watch post stepped onto the granite street, blade raised. Atop the other tower, the remaining guard withdrew a bolt from his quiver. Confusion still dominated their auras, but the violet threads of suspicion were spreading from the first guard to his brethren. It mattered little. One protector's dagger was more than enough to finish me.

Desperate, I clamped harder on the aura-holds I maintained over their cuffs in hopes their confusion would resurge. As I squeezed my aura over the Maelstrom-silver, I sensed a probing thread of magic infected with a greasy taint. The spell that bound the men pulsed against my grip, reaching for their spirits.

My only warning before the guard's mail-armored fist struck my gut was a whoosh of moving air. My breath gusted from my body while agony jolted my belly. I stumbled and fell, coughing out the last of the air from my lungs. I couldn't inhale. My throat produced a silent scream and the world faded to nothing but the red throbbing in my gut.

Distantly, I heard a grunt of approval and the creak of leather as the guard prepared another blow.

I grasped again for the feeling I'd encountered from the cuff. An argent mage had impressed their command into the silver, allowing the cuff to control the protector as long as it was worn. The command worked by dominating the guard's aura. A prison of the mind. If I could just figure out how to mimic the effect...

I looked into the guard's eyes, no longer vacant, but rather filled with hate. He'd been born Atal, and no matter how the throne had treated him, he would never have accepted my word without another Atal to vouch for it. It had been stupid of me to think I could manipulate him into opening the gate for me.

A prison of the mind. I needed to overpower his soul from within.

As the dagger rotated in the air above me, the guard toying with me while deciding the angle the blade would enter my body, I aimed a spear of my aura into his spirit. He gasped and the dagger fell from his hand, clattering beside my ear. I smelled the oiled metal of the blade and imagined it piercing my heart.

With a burst of power, I splayed my aura-lance wide and shattered the man's willpower.

"Back. Away."

The guard's eyes widened in terror as he scuttled back. Behind him, the other men stared in disbelief. As I climbed to my feet, I sent bolts of aura into their spirits, exploding the missiles to grab hold of their souls. Their arms went limp, weapons dropping to the ground.

Breathing evenly to keep my concentration, I glanced at the Icethorns as I advanced toward the gate. The distant summits were ghostly against the purple sky. A smattering of stars twinkled in the dusklight.

It was time.

"Open the gate," I said to the men.

As one, they moved to the lever. Panic threatened when I remembered the lock and chain. I hadn't considered what I'd do if the protectors couldn't unlock it. Relief swept through me when a guard pulled a key from a pouch on his belt.

"Open it far enough for a person to slip inside," I said once the chain had been freed. "No farther."

The guard pulled the lever, metal sliding with a squeal loud enough to raise the dead. Groaning on its hinges, the Shadow Gate swung aside.

Sirez greeted me with a nod as five Stormsharders slipped into Steelhold. "It's time to end the Empire," she said.

Chapter Sixty-Eight

Kostan
Scion's bedchamber, recovering from lashes

"I have little time," Ilishian said as he stalked into my chamber wearing Tovmeil's likeness.

"It's an impressive illusion," I said once the door was shut behind him. "Not to mention freezing everyone in the courtyard. All from your pendant?"

The man sighed. "You noticed Ilishian intruding for a moment, I guess."

After the Aurum Trinity had finished healing my lashes, all without speaking a word, I'd moved from my bed to an upholstered chair. I looked up at the man, confused by his words.

"I'm not sure I understand you. You *are* Ilishian, right?"

He shrugged. "I'm no one, really. And as for Ilishian..."

The melancholy in the man's voice struck me like notes pulled from a lamenter's harp. I pushed off the arms of my chair and stood. "Please explain."

"You noticed the pendant." The man reached into the neck of his garment and produced the necklace. "I understand that Ilishian misled you about its purpose. He was struggling with the situation, I suppose."

Earlier, the Trinity had removed my boots. As I stepped to the window, I noticed the softness of carpet against the sensitive skin where my brand had healed. In all the years I'd spent in this room, I'd never experienced the feeling on my branded foot.

"What situation?" I asked as I peered out the window at the courtyard. The whipping post had been removed, leaving the black-sand fountain alone in the square's center. "And how should I address you?"

"I am Tovmeil," he said, hands spread. "Or at least, I was. But please don't go back to 'your eminence.' That time has passed. I died the night you escaped."

The black iron in the pendant. From what I understood, the metal held strange powers over the spirits of the dead. I never imagined it could be so powerful as to return a man to life, however. "So Ilishian has—he's summoned your ghost?"

"In the days after I spoke to you of my visions, the premonitions got worse. Ilishian came to me with an offer to bind my soul to the pendant. If the worst happened, the black iron would grant me a chance to appear again."

"By taking Ilishian's body?"

A cloud passed over the Emperor's face. "That was what he offered me. I didn't know that Ilishian had performed the same binding on himself. When he fell from the Chasm Span, we found ourselves tied to the pendant together. Both able to appear, but not at once. And... without a live body to give us structure."

"Wait... Ilishian's dead?" My thoughts reeled back to his appearance in the Graybranch Inn. I'd assumed some Maelstrom-relic had spared him during the fall. "He's been a ghost this whole time?"

The Emperor smirked. "He was rather pleased with himself for the ruse." As the man spoke, he advanced across the room. When he came to my empty chair, he paused, glanced at me, then walked through it. My mind recoiled at the sight.

"But he..." I tried to think of actions Ilishian had taken. Had he lit a lantern? Touched any of us? Azar had carried the coin purse. Over and over, she'd scurried ahead to spare the ferromaster the effort of opening a door or preparing a meal. I'd never seen the mage eat.

"Ilishian made a tremendous sacrifice for you and the Atal Empire today," Tovmeil said. "Which is why I'm here speaking to you in his place. You asked whether the pendant froze the others in the courtyard, and the answer is 'no.' The pendant serves only to anchor a spirit to the world—it provided a conduit for Ilishian's act, nothing more. The spell that stopped Minister Brevt from killing you and exposing me was born solely from the vitality of Ilishian's soul."

"So he... used his own spirit?"

The Emperor nodded. "And in doing so, erased his pattern from existence. When we die, our spirit lives on. It's not so bad, really. But Ilishian... he no longer exists."

"With no hope of return?"

"None."

I swallowed, feeling sick. I'd never been fond of the mage, but sorrow over his loss flooded me, far more profound than my earlier regret for his fall into the chasm.

"I wish I could thank him," I said.

"As do I. But that will never be. And as I said, there is little time. Ilishian's ferro affinity allowed us to maintain our connection to the mortal realm, but now that he's gone, I feel my hold slipping. We must see to your Ascension. Tonight."

The seesawing emotions were finally too much for me. I heaved a sigh and shuffled to the chair. Pressing my fingers against my forehead, I shook my head. "I'm not the right man for this, your eminence."

"Please. It's Tovmeil. Or if you'd be so kind, Caddill. That's the name my parents gave me before relinquishing me to the guardians." As he spoke, I saw someone else inside the Emperor's body. Before me stood a man who'd once had a mother. A father. Like me, he'd had no choice in the stars of his birth. But he'd had desires once. A childhood. A name not associated with the throne.

I nodded. "Caddill. It suits you."

The corner of his mouth quirked. "When we were Scions together Brevt called me 'cattle.' It was quite a surprise to my fellow Scions when a lowly cow Ascended the throne."

It was so hard to think of the ministers as Scions. As for Brevt, it was hard to think of him as anything but the monstrous man he'd been when he died. But enough of the small talk and memories. Far more serious matters gathered in the room like specters.

"I still don't see myself on the throne," I said. "Not after the way I fouled everything up."

"I've spoken to the Prime Protector," Tovmeil—Caddill said.

"And?"

"I explained my intent to abdicate and name you my heir. Her vows leave her no choice but to support your Ascension. You will do well, Kostan. I know you better than you might think. You were always meant to succeed me."

"I'm not strong enough. I can't make the sorts of decisions you did."

"For the most part, the dead don't concern themselves with the living. But with the proper motivation—and in my case, with the pendant as an aid—we can peer through the veil. I've witnessed you making difficult choices already. Mistakes, too, of course. But I have no doubt in your abilities."

I scratched the back of my head, self-conscious at the idea that he'd seen my journey through the mountains. My choices in the city. Despite my errors, though, he still believed in me. That or I'd edged out Vaness. In any case, I thought back to the message sent from Jaliss earlier in the day. The Provs were rioting. The city remained in shambles. Someone had to take charge.

With a heavy sigh, I looked up at my former emperor. "All right, so the protectors will support me. What about the argents and ferros? They sided with the Ministry."

Caddill cocked his head, considering. "They may be traitors, but they're pragmatic. Once the protectors execute the ministers, the mages will fall in line. For a time, anyway. It will be up to you to keep them there."

"Is execution the only answer?" No matter the treachery, I felt sick at the thought of killing powerless men and women.

"You're the Emperor now," Caddill said. "So I suppose it will be up to you. You know the stakes, and I won't demand you follow anyone's heart but your own."

"Speaking of..." I pulled the Heart of the Empire from my shirt. "Why did Ilishian give me this if no one knows its purpose? Why not send me off with the Bracer of Sight if he only had time to choose one relic?"

Caddill's smile was wistful. "It was one of my instructions to him. True, no one knows the Heart's purpose. But in all my visions, the stone hung from your neck. And I wanted the chance to give you one thing that isn't a burden. I hope you'll think of me when you wear it. Remember the man I wanted to be, not the Emperor I was forced to become."

I met the man's gaze. "I will never forget it, Caddill. When a Scion replaces me, they'll hear the tale of your attempt to save the servant girl. Among other things."

Light entered his eyes. "Lyrille... She's alive. No matter his treason, Argentmaster Yevinish had no desire to murder an innocent young woman. He was still delaying her punishment when the protectors entered his chamber."

Relief spread through my chest. "Thank the clear skies."

"Now," Caddill said, "shall we proceed to the courtyard? I've left instructions to prepare for your Ascension. The arrangements should now be complete."

Chapter Sixty-Nine

Savra
Approaching Steelhold's central courtyard

"Which way to the palace?" Sirez hissed.

We crouched in the shadows cast by the palace kitchens. Distantly, I felt my link to the three protectors under my control. They continued to stand guard over the Shadow Gate. The men struggled against the compulsion, but so far I managed to keep a firm grip on their wills. A Sharder had suggested I command them to throw themselves off the ascent trail. She'd grinned as she'd said it, leaving me uncertain whether she was serious. In any case, I wasn't going to murder the men while I had another choice. Besides, leaving the Shadow Gate undefended would draw unwanted attention.

I hesitated before pointing the way to the Hold's central courtyard. I couldn't ignore the line of throwing daggers sheathed along one of the Sharder's legs. By the way the man spoke to Sirez, I knew his expertise. Assassination. Stormshard had come to strike a killing blow to the Empire.

I wasn't sure whether I'd regret helping them or not. I'd seen how the Ministry and Emperor treated the Provs in Jaliss. Countless lives would be improved if the Empire fell—after the chaos settled, anyway. But I had never expected to hold responsibility for the killing of the leadership.

I forced myself to remember Minister Brevt's evil aura. A taint infested metalogy and all who used the power. The heart of the Empire was rotten. Better to cut it out than allow the sickness to spread.

With a nod, the Sharders set off, slipping from building to building. As we neared the courtyard, I focused on their auras and extended my repelling shield over them.

Approaching the square, the Sharder assassin stepped into the lead. He crept forward, snatched the single torch that lit the alley, and doused it in a rain barrel. Concealed by the new darkness, the rest of the Sharder band slipped toward the alley mouth.

I stopped short at the sight of the courtyard.

"Wait," I said. "Something's not right."

After the commotion with the Emperor's arrival—or that of his impostor—I hadn't ventured near the Hold's central square. In the meantime, the courtyard had been transformed. A wide dais had replaced the whipping post. Torches blazed around the platform, sparks swirling into the mountain air. Ranks and ranks of protectors surrounded the dais, facing outward in rigid attention. A single drummer stood beside a massive gong.

Was this some sort of ceremony? Another execution?

As if in answer, the drummer swung a massive, leather-wrapped mallet at the gong. The sound vibrated my bone marrow. I clapped my hands over my ears before he smacked the metal disk again.

After the gong had been struck thirteen times, the palace doors swung open. A herald stepped from the door and raised his speaking horn.

"Emperor Tovmeil, first of his name."

I sucked in a breath. So he wasn't dead after all. Beside me, the assassin stiffened as the Emperor stepped from the palace. The killer's hand went to the knives at his thigh. I stared in horror. Was he insane? More than one hundred protectors guarded the square. We were as good as dead if he attacked now. As if hearing my thoughts, Sirez laid a hand on the man's shoulder and shook her head.

"Wait until it's certain," she whispered.

The Emperor stepped onto the dais. He looked different than I'd expected. I wasn't sure what I'd imagined I'd see. Pointed teeth and blazing eyes? But Tovmeil was just a man wearing ornate clothing and the demeanor of someone used to authority.

From atop the platform, he scanned the gathered protectors. After a nod, he regarded a group of metalogists arrayed before the

Hall of Mages. Their robes were cut in the same style, loose-fitting but without spare fabric. At this distance, I couldn't make out the jewelry on their fingers, but I guessed they were from the same Order. In front of the larger group, three people stepped forward and bowed, precise and synchronized.

Emperor Tovmeil stared at the mages. "Where are the ferros and argents? I requested full attendance."

A woman in protector's armor stepped from the ranks of soldiers. She pressed her fist to her chest in salute. "They claim to be busy investigating solutions to the riots, your eminence."

"Cowards," Emperor Tovmeil said with a snort. "Trinity, have your aurums bring me the argentmaster and the highest ranking ferro after Ilishian. The lower ranks can hide in their towers for all I care. They'll follow where their masters lead."

Nodding as one, the three apparent leaders of the gathered mages whirled. Every motion was calculated and indistinguishable. Speaking in unison, they addressed their followers. "Do as the Emperor says. The masters of the ferro and argent orders are summoned to the courtyard."

A sudden whirlwind, the aurums burst into motion. They entered the tower like a swift breeze, none interfering with another, and vanished before I could finish a breath.

"Mages at odds with the palace," Sirez whispered. "It's an opportunity."

The assassin nodded. "Look there," he said, pointing to the right-hand side of the courtyard where Ministry Hall loomed over the square. A massive colonnade jutted into the courtyard, the columns set close and casting complicated shadows in the torchlight. "Good cover. I can get near without being seen."

Sirez nodded. "And you won't call attention to the group by acting. Go. But remember, only strike if it's certain. There will be other chances."

As Sirez spoke, she glanced at me. My breath stuttered. Other chances... Was she considering leaving me here if the assassination attempt failed? It would be difficult to insert another Sharder into the Hold. I swallowed. I'd explained my difficulties with Minister Brevt. Plus, I couldn't keep control of the three protectors forever. Once I released them, my secret ability would be exposed. I hoped the Shard leader didn't intend to go back on her promise to help me escape.

The assassin nodded and melted into the alley behind us. No doubt he intended to circle around to Ministry Hall. I chewed my lip and hoped he knew what he was doing.

A tense silence filled the courtyard while the aurum mages were inside the Hall, broken only by the crackle and spit of the torches and a stray cough. It felt as if Steelhold's peace teetered on the brink. If the ferros and argents decided to openly oppose the Emperor, what would happen? Could they win against the aurums and protectors? And what would befall those of us trapped between them?

Finally, the doors to the Hall of Mages opened. The aurums emerged, surrounding a pair of mages wearing deep scowls.

"You've summoned us from important work, Emperor," one said.

"You're fortunate I'm giving you the chance to attend, Yevinish," the Emperor responded.

"Master Yevinish," the mage replied. "Or do you forget my position?"

"Does the master of an order betray his sovereign? Or is that act reserved for first-rank children who can't contemplate the consequences of their actions? I am granting you the chance to repent your treason. You as well, ferro," Emperor Tovmeil said to the other mage.

Unlike the man who'd corrected the Emperor in the use of his title, the ferro mage dry-washed his hands and nodded. "I was misled, your eminence. And without Ilishian's guidance, I took the Ministry at their word."

Emperor Tovmeil narrowed his eyes. "A lie. But a forgivable one, as long as you kneel. I am not a vengeful man. I care only that the Empire remains strong."

So quickly it looked like he tripped, the ferro mage fell to his knees. The other, Master Yevinish, held the Emperor's eyes for a long time.

"Your power depends on the argents," Master Yevinish said.

"And your continued right to life depends on my forgiveness," Emperor Tovmeil said. "Now, kneel!"

The argentmaster clenched his jaw. Finally, one leg at a time, he lowered his knees to the floor of the courtyard.

Emperor Tovmeil faced the crowd. "I've been away. My departure was both hasty and necessary, an escape under threat of my life. Eleven of the Scions were not so fortunate and were murdered in their sleep."

Around me, the Stormsharders stiffened in shock. That alone suggested they weren't responsible. When I caught Sirez's eye, she shook her head, denying Sharder involvement.

At the Emperor's words, the gathered protectors remained still, no doubt due to their deadened spirits. The mages offered no overt reaction, but I got the sense that the aurums were like taut bowstrings, ready to strike in revenge for the attack on the throne. From a few of the alleys leading into the courtyard, movement hinted at servants watching the proceedings. I glanced over my shoulder; though I kept a shield over our group in hopes of avoiding attention, we'd be in a bad position if a palace staff member happened upon us.

"The circumstances are shocking enough," Emperor Tovmeil went on. "But more shocking is the source. The Atal Empire has been betrayed by its own Ministry. The men and women I've known since birth attempted to have me murdered. Minister Brevt confirmed their guilt just this afternoon by trying to personally assault me in this very square."

"Sirez," one of the other Sharders, a man with an old scar across his forehead said, "we haven't planned for this. The idea was to slip an assassin into the palace. If Tovmeil were alone, he could be taken down easily. But now?"

The Stormshard leader pressed her lips together as she squinted toward the Ministry Hall colonnade. "I shouldn't have let Grawsen leave us. Makes a retreat difficult unless we abandon him. Let's wait it out a little longer. I trust his judgment."

Though the scarred man looked doubtful, he nodded. Sirez had more authority than she'd admitted during our negotiations. I hoped she would use that wisely when it came to freeing me from this place.

"I have returned to Steelhold," Emperor Tovmeil called out, "but the time of my reign is over."

At this, even the protectors stiffened. The aurums whispered to one another, movements fluid as they shifted position.

"What in the wide sky?" Sirez muttered.

The Emperor nodded at the drummer who smacked the gong. As the tone reverberated in the square, servants emerged from alleys, curiosity overriding the Provs' fear of the Emperor. Motion near the colonnade caught my eye. Like ink flowing through a dark sea, the assassin wove between columns, his movements covered by the general disarray in the square.

After another ring of the gong, the Emperor raised his hands for quiet. "I am invoking an ancient code, set down so long ago that few but the stones remember. Among the canon of the Atal is a provision for the Emperor to name his successor should Ascension be disrupted. I claim that right tonight."

At that, the Emperor turned and gestured toward the palace. The entrance stood on the opposite side of the courtyard from our hiding place in the alley. Over the heads of the protectors, I could see the top edge of the doors as they opened wide, but I couldn't see who emerged.

"A new Emperor?" one of the Sharders whispered. "If Grawsen is quick enough, he can eliminate both of them. End the storms-cursed dynasty for good."

As the newcomer crossed the square, protectors turned to face the procession. First, the top of a head appeared above the crowd. Short hair, tousled. Judging by the person's height—taller than almost everyone in the square—I guessed it was probably a man.

A boot clicked against a wooden stair that ascended the dais.

When the new Emperor's face rose above the crowd, my heart stopped.

Kostan?

Chapter Seventy

Kostan
Ascension Dais, Steelhold

Prov servants began to trickle from the alleys surrounding the square. I ran my eyes over them, nodding in acknowledgment whenever I managed to make eye contact. More than the metalogists or the protectors, I wanted the Provs to accept me. I needed them to know that I saw them as equal to the Atal.

Unfortunately, most everyone who met my eyes instantly dropped their gaze, a mix of fear and hatred obvious on their faces.

I clenched my fists. I'd known this wouldn't be easy, but I'd still allowed myself to hope.

After allowing the moment to linger, Caddill nodded to the Aurum Trinity. As one, the mages approached the dais and climbed the stairs on its flank. Carried on a cushion was the Bracer of Sight. Though Caddill and all the emperors before him had hidden their use of the bracer, I was determined to be honest with my subjects. They would know why I made the decisions I did. I would be clear when describing the threats we faced.

Eventually, the Provs would trust me. I had to believe that.

A slight tremor shook the Hold as I pulled back my sleeve and extended my forearm. Fringing the square, Prov eyes widened at the reminder of the quake that had leveled so many of their homes.

I straightened my shoulders, projecting strength. After the ceremony, I would speak to them, laying out my plan to rebuild the city and raise up the Provs. With luck, these servants would be among the first to carry the news of my changes back to their homes.

One of the women in the Trinity fastened the bracer around my forearm. Before my difficult journey through the mountains and my sparse meals in Jaliss, the buckles might not have fastened—they were still fitted for Caddill's slighter build. But now the relic clamped snuggly around my arm without pinching.

I took a deep breath as the truth sank in. After everything, the worries and struggles and mistakes, I was truly Ascending. Though Ilishian had recognized me before, I'd considered his oath to be something of a sham. I hadn't thought of myself as Emperor. Would I after this? After the Trinity vested me with the relics of the throne and the protectors swore vows to defend me? Or would I always feel like an impostor?

I lowered my arm, glad that the bracer wouldn't be attuned to me until later. A diviner would bring the Tempest Goblet, and I would drink Maelstrom water to join the relic to my soul. Until then, I'd remain free of the burden of its visions.

The Trinity turned to face the crowd. They spoke as one. "Emperor Tovmeil, first of his name, hereby cedes the throne to Emperor Kostan. On the occasion of Kostan's second birthday, we branded his foot with the Gilded Iron. We have looked upon the scar. We verify the Emperor's Mark."

Not, of course, without making their displeasure over my actions known. If not for Caddill's command, the aurums would have rejected this Ascension outright. While they'd examined my foot, I'd searched their faces for guilt over adorning me with a cuff that caused permanent infection. No remorse had shown in their eyes.

Next, the Prime Protector climbed onto the dais. She faced her soldiers and guards. "Repeat after me. Emperor Kostan, first of his name, my sword is yours forever."

As the guards began to recite, the ground trembled once again. Among the Provs, whispers rose. They looked at me with accusing eyes, as if these shakes were ill omens. I wanted to cut the ceremony short, explain that only my Ascension could protect them from worse things to come. They needed to know about the Breaking, that a strong Empire was our only chance of avoiding it.

As the protectors finished their oath, a rumble rose from the Icethorns at our backs. Moments later, the Hold jolted to the left.

Servants yelped. The aurum mages dropped into lithe crouches to keep their balance.

"No!" From an alley mouth ahead and to my left, a woman's shout pierced the air. "Kostan! Watch out!"

What was this? I rose on my toes and caught a flash of auburn hair. A shock traveled my body. The color was so rare I thought it must have been my imagination. Savra couldn't be here.

As the ground rolled under the Hold, I whipped my head left and right, looking for the woman and the apparent threat. Upset by the shaking earth, the ranks of protectors fell into disarray as the soldiers stumbled.

And suddenly, I saw her. Savra planted a foot on the back of a protector who'd fallen to his knees and vaulted over the man. She sprinted across the courtyard, not toward me, but straight for the side of the dais.

"Savra, no!" someone else yelled from the alley.

Too late. Savra slammed into a black-garbed stranger who'd just set foot on the stairs leading onto the dais. She and the man tumbled beneath the mob of protectors. A blade went flying, scoring the cheek of an unwary protector. The guard slapped a hand to the cut, a perplexed expression on her otherwise stony face. Moments later, she began to shudder. Convulsing, she fell to the ground.

"Protectors!" called the Prime from beside me. "Defend your ruler! A poisoner is amongst us!"

I shook my head, bewildered. How had Savra come here? And the man... had he intended to assassinate me?

Bodies closed over the convulsing woman as the guards closed ranks and encircled the dais. As the protectors trudged forward, knees bent to accommodate the rocking ground, the black-clad man scrambled to his feet and ran through the panicked crowd at the edge of the square.

I craned my neck and shoved aside a guard who'd come between me and the scene. Had I only imagined what had happened? Had Savra been a vision, come to me like Vaness had in the mountains?

And then I saw her. Savra stood, chest heaving, on the bare granite a dozen paces from the dais. Our eyes locked. Questions roared through my mind. Why was she here? What did she think of me, now that she knew my secrets?

All sound faded, save for the thud of my heartbeat. Torchlight flickered on her face. I couldn't see the green of her eyes, but I remembered it. She wore a scribe's tunic. It suited her. I blinked in surprise when I noticed the palace insignia embroidered above her scribe's crest. Savra worked here? In Steelhold?

The slap of running feet jarred me from my spell. Protectors were breaking off from the group, chasing after the man who'd tried to skewer me with a poisoned dagger. Or had Caddill been his target? I glanced around, looking for the former Emperor, but he had gone. Slipped out in the chaos, or vanished when his connection with the mortal world finally snapped. I might never know.

I turned back to Savra. Dressed as a palace servant and responsible for saving me, no one was paying her any mind. As she looked up at me, her brow creased. Concern? An apology?

Something caught her attention. She stiffened as her eyes shot to the edge of the courtyard. More footfalls sounded, but not the heavy tread of protectors. Shadows arrowed from the alley, their gliding shapes clad in black and wrapped in light cloaks. The arrivals were there, yet somehow, not. I felt as if my attention slid off them as they ran through the chaos.

"I—" Savra cried out as two of the dark figures swept her up. As fast as they'd abandoned the alley, they carried her to the nearest aisle between buildings.

"Wait!" I slapped a hand on the Prime Protector, who turned to me in shock. "The girl. The one who saved me. They took her!"

"Which girl?" she asked.

"There." I pointed. "She was standing there, and then a group of the assassin's friends ran from an alley and grabbed her."

The Prime furrowed her brow. "I don't know what you're talking about. I've had eyes on the square the whole time. I saw no one."

"You didn't see her attack the assassin?"

"The earthquake unsteadied him. A lucky tremor. Are you all right, your eminence?"

"I'm fine. And you're mistaken. I just saw her. Send guards down that alley," I said, pointing. When she balked, I added, "Now."

"As you say, your eminence."

Failing to disguise her skeptical glance, she summoned a handful or protectors and sent them off. Meanwhile, I stared at the place

Savra had been. Had I been mistaken? I couldn't see how the Prime could have failed to notice a scribe standing alone in the middle of the courtyard.

"Come, your eminence," the Prime said. "It's not safe out here. These men will escort you to your chambers, and I'll have a double guard shift standing watch until we've secured the Hold. With the gates sealed, the assassin has no way out. We'll find him and put this matter behind us so that we can begin organizing your rule."

Chapter Seventy-One

"Make them open the gate," Sirez growled. The woman kept a firm grip on my arm, her fingers like talons.

Swallowing, I nodded. As I focused on my links to the protectors, I remembered my attention-repelling shield. It had become so second-nature that I hadn't realized I'd kept it active. It made sense why the guards hadn't chased us from the courtyard. They hadn't noticed us.

But Kostan had. He'd seen me. I was sure of it.

I pressed my will on the protectors, commanding two to stand sentry on the open street in front of the gate. The other I forced to take hold of the lever. But then I hesitated. I'd betrayed Stormshard. As soon as I helped them escape the Hold, they'd probably kill me. Tentatively, I expanded my awareness to their auras. Could I force my will on them as I had the protectors?

And could I live with myself afterward? I'd betrayed them once already.

Sirez's dagger touched my neck. "I may not be a spiritist, but I can sense your thoughts. With the power you've demonstrated tonight, none of us would stand a chance against you. Not without magic to counter yours."

"Why threaten me with your dagger then?"

"Because a Sharder never gives up without a fight. And because I wanted your attention. There's something I haven't shared with you. Evrain is alive. Betray me again, and you'll lose your only chance to find him."

Despite the situation, my heart soared. My father wasn't dead—assuming Sirez was telling the truth, anyway. Immediately, I withdrew my aura-sense from the Sharders. If there was still a chance they'd take me to my father, I needed to do everything I could to persuade them I'd meant well.

"I'm sorry for what I did," I said. "The new Emperor. I know him. He's different."

But was he? I'd spent a few hours in his company, and he'd lied to me the whole time. Well, that wasn't exactly true. He'd chosen his words carefully. A home he couldn't return to. Jaliss-born. Both those things were accurate, if misleading. And hadn't I done the same thing, hiding the truth about my journey with Havialo?

"Forgive me if I hesitate to trust you."

"I couldn't let you kill a good man. He's innocent. He cares for the Provs."

"As innocent as the people starving in the Splits? As the Lowtown families who lost their homes and have nowhere to go?"

A scuffling sound from behind caused Sirez to dig her fingers into the back of my arm.

"Grawsen," she said when the assassin stepped into the torchlight. "Thank the skies. I worried we might have to abandon you."

"The protectors are determined but not very clever. Not too difficult to evade for a short while." The assassin turned a hate-filled glare on me. "Faithless wretch. What are we going to do with her?"

Sirez flared her nostrils as she stared at me. "She's supposed to be getting the gate open," she said, pressing the dagger harder against my throat. "I'd like to throw her from the spire afterward, but she claims to know the new Emperor. It's information we could use."

"One more step and the Atal Dynasty would have been finished," Grawsen said.

"I realize that, and the conclave will decide a fitting punishment for her betrayal."

"I hope you intend to collar her," the assassin said.

"I'm not an idiot. But she'd comply without it, I believe. We know the whereabouts of someone she cares for."

"Do as you wish, I suppose," Grawsen said, still pinning me with his glare, "but please convey a request to the conclave. I'd like to exact her punishment myself."

From behind, the march of booted feet marked the searchers' approach.

"Done. And now, Savra," Sirez said. She pushed her dagger harder against my throat. "Open. The. Gate."

Chapter Seventy-Two

Kostan
Emperor's bedchamber

The sun rose on my first day as Emperor of Atal. I felt no different. Well, that wasn't entirely true. I was cleaner. I'd had my first bath in days, alone in the chambers where Caddill had so recently been murdered. A new rug covered the marble tiles in the receiving chamber. I assumed bloodstains had made the other unsalvageable. The bedding was freshly laundered and aired. Clothing from my Scion's chamber had been moved into the wardrobe.

Breakfast arrived on a wooden tray. I'd refused to eat off anything crafted from Maelstrom-metals until I could be sure of the mages' loyalty. As I scraped the last of the scrambled eggs from my plate, a tapping came at the door.

"Come ahead," I called.

An expressionless protector opened the door and stepped inside. "Scion Vaness requests an audience, your eminence."

Warmth suffused my body. "Yes, of course! Bring her in."

My friend entered the room, bedraggled and smelling of smoke. "Your eminence," she said, sketching a bow as the protector retreated and closed the door.

"Thank the skies," I said, dragging her into an embrace. "The fires in Lowtown. Were they bad? And please call me Kostan. No one else will. I need at least one friend."

Her face grew somber as she nodded. "The city is a disaster. I don't know how you'll restore order. I hear Ilishian is nowhere to be found... he picked a fine time to abandon us."

I sighed. "Ilishian is dead, Vaness. He died the night I fled the Hold."

"But then..." She shook her head, her eyes far away while she considered the revelation.

"I'll explain everything. But for now, as you said, the city is a disaster. Collapsing. The Empire will follow if I don't do something. Tovmeil is gone. Ilishian and the other Scions are dead. It's just us now. Will you help me?"

I looked aside at the sudden hope in her eyes. Vaness still wanted something I could never give. As if sensing my thoughts, she dropped her gaze. "Of course, Kostan. Alone, I won't fulfill the responsibilities of a complete Ministry, but I'm yours for whatever help I can give."

Her mention of the Ministry brought thoughts of the traitors roaring back. Caddill's remaining ministers were still confined to their chambers. I had to deal with them today. I'd lain awake most of the night thinking about it.

Exile or execution. It was the historical choice offered to the ministers of an abdicating emperor. I could allow Tovmeil's ministers the option, but to many it would look like undeserved mercy. If I wanted to keep control of the ferro and argent mages, I needed to be stronger than they expected.

To keep my Empire, I would have to send eleven people to their deaths. The choice was clear. And it was only the first of the awful decisions I'd have to make. The previous night, I'd managed to avoid having the Bracer of Sight attuned by claiming to be too fatigued. But I couldn't dodge the responsibility much longer. Soon, I would know the burden Caddill had borne.

I took Vaness's hand. "There was a time when I thought we might defy custom and have a relationship," I said. "Vaness, you are an amazing woman. My very best friend. But I will never be free to share my life in that way. With anyone." As I spoke, I saw Savra standing in the courtyard, the moments we'd held each others' eyes before the strangers spirited her away. It had been real. Regardless of what the Prime Protector claimed, Savra had saved me. But now she was gone. I hoped she was safe. In the coming weeks, I hoped she would hear of my actions and come to believe she'd done the right thing. We could never be together, but I'd like to think that I would make her proud.

"Don't," Vaness said. "I can't bear the condescension. I am your loyal servant, Kostan. Accept it for what it is."

Squeezing her fingers, I released them. "Fair enough. And as for your position, I've been thinking. I need someone trustworthy to lead my efforts in bettering life for the Provs. I plan to start by dismantling the Decree of Functions."

She blinked in surprise. "Me? But I'm Atal-born."

"And I've watched and heard you echo the typical Atal prejudices. But I know you, Vaness. Peel away the armor you were forced to layer around your heart, and you care. You know it's wrong how they're treated."

After a moment, she nodded, a quick motion. "If my Emperor commands it."

I let the formality go. She needed time to come to terms with the assignment, but she would be faithful to the task. And once we gained a small measure of trust among the Provs, I'd bring some of them in to advise her. The Empire would no longer be governed exclusively by Atal. No matter what Evrain and his Stormshard friends claimed, I would bring Old Atal and the Provinces together. I vowed it.

"Did you speak to anyone else inside the Hold?" I asked. My only visitor this morning had been the servant who'd delivered breakfast.

"The Prime Protector and the Trinity," she said.

"Do you think I can trust them?

"I don't know if you can trust anyone. But for now, the Prime seems to have your interests in mind. She's rather agitated that the assassin wasn't caught. Right now, she's interrogating three guards who were stationed at the Shadow Gate. They claim a young woman with flame-colored hair took control of their minds and forced them to open the gate."

Savra. At the confirmation that she'd been here, my chest tightened. It hadn't been an illusion spawned by my regret over losing her. I could hold on to that, at least. And if she'd held that power over the guards, perhaps she had the ability to survive the assassin's friends. I swallowed back the lump in my throat and nodded.

"Thank you, Vaness," I said, my voice hoarse. "For everything."

Her smile was bittersweet as she knuckled me in the shoulder. "Thank me if you manage to save this storms-cursed Empire. Now, shall we get to work?"

Chapter Seventy-Three

Savra
Somewhere in the Atalan grasslands

I knew the sun had risen when warmth touched my cheeks. Beneath me, the horse continued its rolling walk, the saddle swaying with each step. We'd been riding since escaping the Hold. I'd been blindfolded the whole time. A collar of black iron had been clamped around my neck shortly after we finished the descent from the spire. The metal's touch made me shudder whenever I allowed my awareness to brush it. More, it confined my aura-sight to my body alone. I sensed the spirits inhabiting my bracelet, but nothing beyond the bounds of my flesh and those touching it.

As the hours had passed, I'd spoken with Lilik and Raav. I'd expected them to be disappointed in what I'd done, but they had understood. Lilik had claimed that I had a long way to go to be considered impulsive. This had made Raav laugh and comment on Lilik's character. I sensed a long history of rash decisions hiding beneath the reactions, but I didn't pry.

Mostly, I wanted to know whether they still considered me worthy of centuries of imprisonment inside a trinket. But I couldn't bring myself to ask. Instead, we spoke of spiritism and the similar magic Lilik had wielded.

And we spoke of relationships. I couldn't hide my feelings from them. I hardly knew Kostan, yet I'd risked everything to save him. Lilik said it meant we were destined for each other. Raav was more realistic. When Kostan and I had met, neither of us had known the other's true circumstances. It was a fantasy to think a common rebel and an Emperor could be together. Besides, Raav said, we'd soon see how Kostan reigned. Everything I'd thought about him might be exposed as false.

After that, Lilik and Raav had fallen into an argument about it. I'd shut my mind off from them and turned my face to the new-risen sun. Not long after, the horses stopped moving.

"I'll take her alone from here," Sirez said.

I turned my head to orient on her voice while the horses blew and snatched bites of grass. It made me think of Breeze. I hoped Fishel would care for him.

A hand fell on my forearm. "Dismount, please," the Shard leader said.

My legs were stiff as I climbed from the saddle, bound hands clutching at straps to keep my balance. Stalks of grass pricked me through my trousers when I landed on the ground. We must still be on the Atalan Plateau. The light breeze smelled fresh enough that I sensed the Icethorns near.

Sirez grabbed the end of the rope that bound my wrists. "Follow."

Legs wooden, I stumbled after her. We walked for maybe half an hour, the scents of pines joining the warm heat from the grassland before Sirez nudged me to stop. Metal squeaked as a door was opened. Sirez dragged me behind her, into some sort of building that smelled of old wood and had flexing floorboards underfoot. Laying a hand on my back, she pushed me ten paces across the room until my knees hit something.

Fiddling at the back of my head, she untied the knot securing my blindfold. I blinked when the cloth fell away then looked around. The building appeared to be some sort of wilderness refuge. Storage barrels stood against one wall, a massive stack of fire lining another. A narrow cot lay before me. The only other furniture was a large table with a handful of chairs surrounding it.

"Sleep," the Shard leader commanded, dropping a water skin on the floor beside my feet.

"What are you going to do with me?" I asked.

Sirez's face held no expression as she untied my wrists. "I don't know yet. But if it gives you solace, we're unlikely to kill you immediately. I hope you'll be able to rest with that in mind."

My lip trembled at the unexpected kindness. During the ride, I'd doubted my earlier hesitation to use my compulsion on the Sharders. I could have forced them to release me before they'd fastened the collar on me. But I'd already betrayed them once. My father had chosen this group. I'd made the choice not to hurt them again, and I would hold to it.

After slurping a few big swallows from the water skin, I clambered onto the bunk. Moments after I pillowed my head on my arm, blackness descended.

"I must admit, this wasn't the reunion I'd imagined."

My eyes flew open. I knew the voice that had dragged me from sleep. Craning my neck, I searched for him.

"Papa?"

"Oh, Savra, what have you done?"

Tears spilled from my eyes when my father stepped into view. He looked harder than the man I remembered. The wrinkles in the corners of his eyes had deepened, and new scars slashed across his arms. But I could have picked him from a crowd of a hundred. "I—Papa, he's not a bad man. I never meant—I wanted to find you, so I asked Sirez when I heard she was Stormshard. They gave me a mission."

He laid a hand on my arm as I sat up, firm but not unkind. "Shh. I know. You should have said you were my daughter."

"But I didn't know if I could trust them. What if someone used me against you?"

A considering look entered his eyes as he pulled over a chair. "I suppose it was good thinking. Unlike your decision in Steelhold."

I looked at my lap. "I met Kostan in Jaliss. He was a refugee like me. Or at least he pretended to be. But he's not like the other Emperor. Things will be better."

Immediately, my father's eyes hardened. "Sirez said the man's name might be Kostan. I just didn't believe her." He sighed. "Well, I understand why you were fooled."

I shook my head. "I don't understand. You know him?"

"It's a long story, Sandpiper. But yes. And I know how easily he gains someone's trust. As sorry as I am that he misled you, at least the others will accept your actions once I explain that he tricked me too. Even Falla believed him, and she has abilities like yours."

My emotions felt torn like a raft in the Maelstrom. First, sweet joy at hearing my old nickname. Then disbelief. Despair. It couldn't be true, could it? I couldn't imagine I'd had the wrong idea about Kostan. But I'd always trusted my father. I didn't know what to think.

I looked away to hide the anguish that I knew showed plainly on my face. After a moment, I swallowed.

"Mother and Avill. A man took me—"

"I know," he said, cutting me off. "Sirez told me about what happened to you. And I swear that I'll make Havialo pay. We've already sent a dozen Sharders to Numintown. We'll find your mother and sister. I promise."

I found his words difficult to believe. Havialo's men wouldn't make it easy, I was sure of that.

"Savra," my father said, pressing a finger under my chin to bring my eyes to his. "I swear it. The geognost is not as clever as he pretends. If the people we sent aren't back with the rest of our family before Chilltide, you and I will go to Cosmal Province together. We won't give up until we save them. Do you believe me?"

I took a deep breath and nodded. "Maybe we should just go now."

My father shook his head. "I will put nothing before our family, but I believe in the people we sent to rescue them. And we have important work to do here. Stormshard nearly succeeded in freeing the Provs yesterday."

At the mention, I looked away, shame coloring my cheeks. I hated that I'd failed his cause. More, I hated the knowledge that I'd probably do it again if given the same opportunity. I just couldn't believe Kostan to be the person my father seemed to consider him.

"Move past it, Savra," he said. "You acted for what you believed to be right, despite the risk. That's the sort of thing heroes are made of. So take that honor—and the spiritism talent I've been hearing about—and use it for the good of Provs across the Empire. You are exactly what Stormshard needs to finally achieve our dreams."

A wave of dizziness crashed over me, and I dropped my face to my hands.

Savra, Lilik said gently. Sometimes choices seem too big. Sometimes it feels like events are more than you can handle. But remember, Parveld saw you in the days and years ahead. You will get through this. You will make the right decisions. You just need to trust your heart and your wits.

You don't need to solve everything now, Raav added. You're safe. You're with your father. Rest a day or two before you get back to saving the Empire.

I sent pulses of gratitude across our bond. *Thank you,* I said.

No need to thank us, Lilik said. We're here because we believe in you. Now enjoy your reunion.

Inhaling, I looked up into my father's eyes. "The Sharders thought you were dead. If I didn't say before, it's good to see you, Papa."

My father grinned. "I'm harder to kill than most. And it's good to see you too, my little Sandpiper."

Chapter Seventy-Four

Havialo
On the border of the Sandsea

A horse made of sand carried Havialo out of the dunes. Given life by stealing energy from the sun, the steed's continued gallop cast a veil over the landscape, a subtle darkening that slid over trees and hills. When the leading edge of shadow touched Relim Post, a far-flung settlement at the edge of Guralan Province, villagers shaded their eyes and stared at the sky, perplexed. No clouds marred the blue dome overhead, yet the chill and darkness were unmistakable.

An hour's ride away, Havialo drew a halt. Relaxing his command of the sun, he allowed the horse to disintegrate beneath him. Sand grains hissed as they spilled away, finally leaving the earth mage standing on a low dune. The sky once again brightened as he stepped away from the remains of his mount, sun glinting off the blond grains of sand.

The earth mage threw his arms wide and opened his senses to the vibrations of power surrounding him. Not far away, the Guralan winds howled over the forests, so potent but so tainted. If necessary, he could harness the wind and accept the consequences.

But that wouldn't be necessary. Things had changed since he'd been whisked away from the Atalan Plateau, dropped in the middle of the Sandsea with those incompetent servants of the Ministry. The threat of earthquakes had always been present, a tension that promised great, if unpredictable power.

Now, the continent was brimming with pent energy. Nudged in just the right way, he could shatter the land from sea to spine.

Cosmal Province would sink. Chasms would slice Old Atal to pieces. Soon, the Empire would pay for what had happened to his daughter. Soon, the throne would suffer for rejecting geognosty.

He had work to do, the very actions he'd resisted when some amongst the Ministry's allies wished to take severe action. Manipulating the Breaking in the proper way would take all of his ability. To fill his weaknesses, he'd need the cabal of young spiritists he'd saved from the Provinces, those recruits who the Ministry had never properly appreciated. The cabal hid in a mountain stronghold, a difficult but necessary journey from Guralan. After, he'd strike out for Jaliss.

The Empire would fall, and Havialo would stand in its beating heart when it did.

Dear Reader,

Thank you so much for joining me for Savra and Kostan's journeys! This book would mean nothing without readers to share it.

Next up, the series continues with *Rise of the Storm*, coming Fall 2017.

If you would like to receive early access to review copies of my books, bonus materials, and notice of new releases and sales, please go to www.CarrieSummers.com and sign up for my reader group. I'd love to have you!

Last, if you enjoyed this book, I encourage you to leave a review. As an author, I depend on them to gather new readers so I can keep writing books. Thank you so much!

All best,
—Carrie

carrie@carriesummers.com

6083

67274941R00241

Made in the USA
Lexington, KY
06 September 2017